# Burning Embers

Last Flame of Alba, Book 3

## Mary Lancaster

© Copyright 2023 by Mary Lancaster
Text by Mary Lancaster
Cover by Dar Albert

Dragonblade Publishing, Inc. is an imprint of Kathryn Le Veque Novels, Inc.
P.O. Box 23
Moreno Valley, CA 92556
ceo@dragonbladepublishing.com

Produced in the United States of America

First Edition February 2023
Print Edition

Reproduction of any kind except where it pertains to short quotes in relation to advertising or promotion is strictly prohibited.

All Rights Reserved.

The characters and events portrayed in this book are fictitious. Any similarity to real persons, living or dead, is purely coincidental and not intended by the author.

## ARE YOU SIGNED UP FOR DRAGONBLADE'S BLOG?

You'll get the latest news and information on exclusive giveaways, exclusive excerpts, coming releases, sales, free books, cover reveals and more.

Check out our complete list of authors, too!

No spam, no junk. That's a promise!

### Sign Up Here

www.dragonbladepublishing.com

*Dearest Reader;*

*Thank you for your support of a small press. At Dragonblade Publishing, we strive to bring you the highest quality Historical Romance from some of the best authors in the business. Without your support, there is no 'us', so we sincerely hope you adore these stories and find some new favorite authors along the way.*

*Happy Reading!*

*CEO, Dragonblade Publishing*

## Additional Dragonblade books by Author Mary Lancaster

### Last Flame of Alba
Rebellion's Fire (Book 1)
A Constant Blaze (Book 2)
Burning Embers (Book 3)

### Gentlemen of Pleasure
The Devil and the Viscount (Book 1)
Temptation and the Artist (Book 2)
Sin and the Soldier (Book 3)
Debauchery and the Earl (Book 4)
Blue Skies (Novella)

### Pleasure Garden Series
Unmasking the Hero (Book 1)
Unmasking Deception (Book 2)
Unmasking Sin (Book 3)
Unmasking the Duke (Book 4)
Unmasking the Thief (Book 5)

### Crime & Passion Series
Mysterious Lover (Book 1)
Letters to a Lover (Book 2)
Dangerous Lover (Book 3)
Merry Lover (Novella)

### The Husband Dilemma Series
How to Fool a Duke

### Season of Scandal Series
Pursued by the Rake

Abandoned to the Prodigal
Married to the Rogue
Unmasked by her Lover
Her Star from the East (Novella)

**Imperial Season Series**
Vienna Waltz
Vienna Woods
Vienna Dawn

**Blackhaven Brides Series**
The Wicked Baron
The Wicked Lady
The Wicked Rebel
The Wicked Husband
The Wicked Marquis
The Wicked Governess
The Wicked Spy
The Wicked Gypsy
The Wicked Wife
Wicked Christmas (A Novella)
The Wicked Waif
The Wicked Heir
The Wicked Captain
The Wicked Sister

**Unmarriageable Series**
The Deserted Heart
The Sinister Heart
The Vulgar Heart
The Broken Heart
The Weary Heart
The Secret Heart
Christmas Heart

**The Lyon's Den Series**
Fed to the Lyon

**De Wolfe Pack: The Series**
The Wicked Wolfe
Vienna Wolfe

**Also from Mary Lancaster**
Madeleine
The Others of Ochil

# Twelfth Century Scotland

## ROYAL KINDREDS OF SCOTLAND:
## CENÉL LOAIRN

Macbeth, King of Scots (2)m. Gruoch m (1) Gillacomgain

Lulach, King of Scots (died 1058)

- Maelsnechtai, Earl of Moray
- Daughter m. Aed, Earl of Ross
  - Angus, Earl of Moray (died 1130)
  - **Malcolm (MacHeth), Earl of Ross** m. **Halla of the Isles**
    - **Donald**
      - **Adam**
    - **Adam**
    - **Gormflaith**

## CENÉL GABRAIN

Duncan I, King of Scots

Malcolm III(Canmore), King of Scots m.(2) Margaret

- Edgar, King of Scots
- Alexander I, King of Scots
- David I, King of Scots (died 1153)
  - Henry, Earl of Huntingdon
    - **Malcolm IV, King of Scots**
    - William

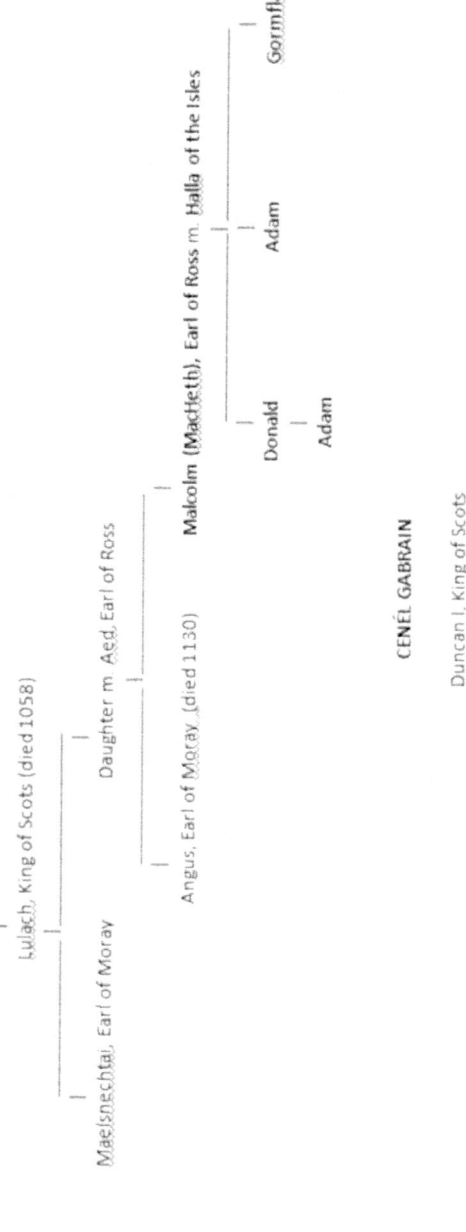

# A Brief Note on Names

Because Gaelic, Norse, English, and French were all spoken in twelfth-century Scotland, my heroine is known in this story variously as Christian (English), Christina (French), and Cairistiona (Gaelic). But mostly, where there is a common modern equivalent of Gaelic names, such as Malcolm and Donald, this is the version I have used.

Scotland itself had many names at the time: Scotland in English, Alba in Gaelic, Scotia in Latin.

Though the matter is beyond my control, I have to acknowledge there are too many Malcolms in this book! Unfortunately, they are all historical characters and their appearance or reference necessary to the story. For clarity, they are:

Malcolm MacHeth, one time Earl of Ross, father to Donald and Adam.

Malcolm IV, current King of Scots.

Malcolm III, also known as Malcolm Canmore, late King of Scots, great-grandfather of the current King Malcolm.

And finally, the "mac" issue. Surnames/family names were still rare in twelfth-century Scotland. It was normal to be known as the son or daughter of one's father, e.g., Adam, son of Malcolm, or Adam mac Malcolm. On the other hand, Adam's family *is* also known by the surname MacHeth, probably a corruption of MacAed, because of their ancestor Aed, who linked them to the throne of Scotland. So I have given "mac" as a patronymic, i.e. "son of," a small "m," and MacHeth as a surname a capital M.

# PROLOGUE

*Ross, winter 1203*

THE OLD MAN dreamed of fire, as he often did, and of a boy who was not him or his brothers or sons. At first, he thought they were different visions. One showed him the burning hall that looked very like his old home of Brecka, where Donald's son still lived. The other focused on the boy who raised the crown so high that it soared above all the fires blazing across Ross and the whole of Scotland and seemed, gradually, to extinguish them.

But then the dreams blended. Brecka still burned, and the boy, torch in one hand, strode through the flames, pulling with him a little girl that the old man knew only too well. His granddaughter. She skipped, smiling, from the flames. From their joined hands, a tree sprouted, and when the old man peered again at the boy, he was gone. So was his granddaughter.

In their place was an old man, striding from the flames. *Him.* But with more energy than he had felt in years. Somewhere, he knew he had lit the flames that consumed Brecka, whether as the symbol of MacHeth power or as the physical building. But there were fires all over the moors and hills of Ross, now, carnage and misery stretching from coast to coast, and it was his sword, so long unused, that was striving to put out the flames.

It had happened before. But this dream was new. He tried to delve deeper, searching for meaning, but the vision was already fading, and the child before him, offering the bowl, was real. Solid, earthly, and dear to him.

Nowadays, he cared little for dreams of the future. His heart dwelled in the past with his wife, and in the present blessings of his children who alone anchored him here. But this dream had told him something important. That perhaps he still had a part to play. And that whatever happened to his family, it would endure. The affectionate smile of his granddaughter told him that as he took the bowl from her.

"Eat, Grandfather," she commanded, and he did. As he ate, he realized he was waiting for the boy who had led her from the burning hall, from the end of the MacHeths.

# Chapter One

*Ross, summer 1204*

THE SON OF the priest scrambled over St. Duthac's Church roof. A bow and quiver bounced against his back, and he was grinning in a manner that *hurt* Affrica MacHeth.

On the beach below the little church, she wrapped her arms around her stomach and halted, staring at the boy now straddling the ridge of the roof. Whether taken by surprise or urging her to play, Wolf, her large hound of indeterminate parentage, thudded into her back and knocked her onto her face in the sand.

By the time she'd wrestled the dog off and shielded her face from his licking tongue, the boy on the church roof had company and was hauling others up beside him. His back was to her now. The excited whispering of the boys with him—mostly younger, though at least one was about the same age—told her they were involved in some wild game. The sort of game her brothers and cousins would never let Affrica join.

There was no longer even resentment in that. She was happy playing by herself with Wolf on this beach, which was one of the reasons she liked coming to Tain. The other was that Ferchar, the son of the priest, had begun to intrigue her. She didn't know why—he was neither handsome nor graceful. And though he had never been rude to her, she doubted he actually noticed her. None of that mattered at this moment, because something was *wrong*.

She sprang to her feet. "Come, Wolf." She struggled over the soft sand toward the path that led to the church and the village beyond. For once, she was blind to the pleasing picture presented by the low hills behind the town, deaf to the wailing cries of the circling seagulls, which usually inspired so many stories in her head. She was barely even aware of Wolf's reluctance to leave the beach, though somewhere, distractedly, she was glad when he followed her at last.

Her anxiety was focused on the boys on the roof. And on the jeering sounds coming from the far side of the church, which she recognized only too well.

"They're on the roof!" exclaimed her brother Nechtan. "Hiding!"

"In plain sight," came a retort from the roof as Affrica ran along the lane at the side. "Though it took you long enough to notice."

"You can't change the game," sneered Affrica's cousin, Kenneth MacHeth, heir to the earldom of Ross. "You asked us to teach you to fight. You can't cry and run away because your knee got skint. It's nothing to *real* battle."

Affrica all but fell into the church yard with Wolf at her heels. No one paid her any attention. A crowd of her grinning, laughing brothers and cousins and assorted acolytes had halted on the ground, armed to the teeth with swords and daggers as if facing an invasion. Kenneth was no longer a boy with a toy sword. He was sixteen years old, well-trained, and his weapons were real.

Behind the MacHeth boys, a gate and a green shrubbery separated the church yard from Father Ruadri's garden. Several laden branches of an apple tree stretched out over the hedge as though to God or the sun.

And several yards away, straddling the roof, sat two boys of about fourteen, and several rather younger who were clearly trying not to be frightened. They all looked torn and ragged and slightly though ominously bloody. And yet, apart from Ferchar's bow, they did not seem to be armed at all.

"But you didn't teach, did you?" shouted the older boy who'd spoken before. Affrica knew him, too. Lulach, whose father had land to the south of Ross. "You broke your word."

Kenneth stepped forward. "Come here and say that if you dare!" he cried furiously. "Easy to hurl insults at your betters when you're out of reach. Come down. Or we'll come up and get you."

"And let you slice up our clothes again?" Lulach shouted. "Trip us and cut us as if we're meat? Some lord you will be!"

Kenneth laughed savagely. "And you had best remember it! Up we go, lads!"

"I wouldn't," said the son of the priest, his bizarrely cheerful voice cutting through the forward surge like a dagger thrust in Affrica's stomach.

*Wrong. Still wrong...*

Ferchar, a loose-limbed, gangly youth of about fourteen, who seemed to have been flung haphazardly together rather than created with any elegant purpose, now stood on the sloping roof beneath the ridge, his bow stretched, and an arrow threaded and aimed. Straight at Kenneth's heart.

*He can't! He can't kill the Earl of Ross's son! He daren't even injure him!*

And Kenneth knew it. He laughed himself silly. So did Affrica's brothers.

"Is that supposed to frighten us?" Kenneth gasped. "Dear God, you couldn't shoot if your life depended on it. Which," he added ferociously, "it just might."

Ferchar smiled. It lit up his bony, almost-ugly face, curving his long, full lips in what must have been genuine pleasure, for this time, it didn't hurt her. Affrica's arms fell away from her stomach in wonder, tension falling away, even though his hands were steady, his aim true. And just for an instant, Kenneth's face froze.

The bow shifted minutely in Ferchar's grip, the arrow loosed, and a gasp of horror echoed below. Kenneth dived to the side, but the arrow thudded into the thick tree branch above him, vibrating with the force of it. An apple shook itself onto his head, jolting him, just as another dropped onto his shoulder and on his boot. Others thumped like pebbles onto his brother Ranald, and onto Affrica's brothers, Nechtan and Colin, and smashed to varying stages of pulp on the ground around them.

"Now!" said Ferchar happily, and, with Lulach and the smaller boys, launched a lightning attack of tiny, rotten, windfall apples, hurling them with varied accuracy at their tormentors. With roars of rage, the MacHeth boys were forced to raise their arms for protection as they tried to stride through the hail of missiles. But of course, the fallen apples had made the ground slippery, and they staggered and fell, while Lulach shouted with glee amidst the joyful laughter of the younger boys.

Ferchar's lips parted in command. "Take them down and into the church. Bar the door." As he spoke, he leapt back up onto the ridge, beginning to scramble in the opposite direction, toward his father's nearby house. His movements were disjointed, almost clumsy, yet undoubtedly effective.

Affrica was already running below him on the ground but in the same direction. Her brothers and her cousins would simply shove her out of the way or jump over her to take out their rage and humiliation on the despised son of the priest who had bloodlessly bested them. She needed her father. She needed the earl. At the very least, she needed Ruadri, the priest.

Though it seemed now that Ferchar would reach the cottage first. Either way, all would now be well.

Except he had reckoned without the excitement of the younger boys, and so had she. One of them let out a cry amidst an ominous thump. Affrica spun around in time to see the smallest boy sliding helplessly down the slope of the roof toward the charging MacHeths.

Before she could even think, Ferchar catapulted diagonally past on his rear, preventing the child's fall with his body, although the force of his dive drove him over the side of the roof. He hung on to the edge with one hand, thrusting the boy upward toward Lulach's reaching arms with the other.

By then, of course, Kenneth had Ferchar's boot in his grip and tugged him viciously to the ground.

"Wolf, guard!" Affrica yelled desperately, and flew through the gate to the priest's cottage, where she flung open the door without ceremony or even manners. "Come! You must come!" It was only later as she pelted back the way she had come, with all the men behind her, that she realized she had commanded not only her father, the earl, and Father Ruadri, but the Bishop of Ross, too.

And Wolf was walking excitedly up and down, guarding not the priest's son whom he'd never met, but the boys of his household who were beating the other to a pulp.

"What's the meaning of this!" roared Angus, Affrica's father. Colin and Nechtan leapt to their feet as though fired from a bow. So did Ranald. Even Kenneth staggered back on his haunches, although this may have been due more to the violence of Ferchar than the voice of authority.

Ferchar sat up, which was a further relief to Affrica, even though there was blood. A lot of blood. Wolf, jumping and shoving his face into hers as though looking for praise, provided the excuse not to see the injuries. And then, like the adults, she gazed around the carnage.

On the church roof, white faced and hoarse with shouting out his helpless rage, sat Lulach with the younger boys, clutching Ferchar's bow. Clearly, they had not sheltered in the church. There looked to be a hole in the thatch of the roof. There was certainly blood in the yard, and, farther back, a mess of apple pulp and skin and mud.

"On your feet," commanded the Earl of Ross dangerously. Kenneth and Ferchar rose. Blood streamed between the latter's fingers and down his face There were abrasions on Kenneth's cheek and knuckles, and bruises scattered evenly among Ranald, Nechtan, and Colin. The others had backed off before the earl's arrival, but not quickly enough to vanish. They stood under the now bare branch of the apple tree, slipping slightly in the mush.

The furious eyes of Gilchrist mac Donald MacHeth, Earl of Ross, encompassed all of them.

"You disgust me," he uttered. "Between you, you have broken all the rules of hospitality, of guests and host. You have disgraced your families and defiled the sanctity of St. Duthac's shrine. Dear God, this is a holy *sanctuary*, and you treat it like a boar's den! To you MacHeths, this will not be the last punishment you receive for this day's work, but before you leave here, you will clean up the mess you have made. You will repair the church to the satisfaction of Father Ruadri, and you will walk home. When you get there, Angus and I will decide if you are fit to be received. Apologize to Father Ruadri and to the bishop."

There was a rumble of shame-faced muttering from all the boys.

"And, I think," said Affrica's father serenely, *"pray."*

"On your knees," uttered Reinald, Bishop of Ross. Skinny to the point of emaciation, his deep, booming voice always took Affrica by surprise, as though it spoke for God Himself.

Kenneth glared indignantly at his father, probably disbelieving that such behavior was expected of *him*. The earl glared back and Kenneth, with further if suppressed fury, dropped slowly to his knees with the others.

Only Ferchar knelt with any alacrity—or it may have been simply that his knees would no longer hold him upright. At any rate, he knelt among his own blood, in his stained, tattered clothing, and the injustice almost swallowed Affrica.

*Not him!* she wanted to scream. *He is not to blame!*

For she could guess fairly exactly what had happened. They had all known each other since going to the song school in Rosemarkie, and the older ones from grammar school, too. The MacHeths would have been glad to meet up with the local boys again, for they had all been running wild together, probably in a friendship that took no account of rank or wealth. And then, it had got more serious.

Ferchar, the son of the priest, as host, had probably tried to diffuse it, but it had become most people's habit to calm and placate Kenneth MacHeth. From Lulach's earlier words, he and Ferchar must have asked the sons of the great noblemen to teach the others to fight properly. And inevitably, Kenneth, with his own brand of malicious humor, had done the opposite. As always, Kenneth had gone too far, dragging his followers with him, hurting, damaging as Lulach had accused him. And so Ferchar had indeed changed the game, swapping apples for lethal weapons, preventing bloodshed.

Well, preventing any *worse* bloodshed, as it turned out.

And yet he was receiving as much blame as her spoiled cousins and stupid brothers.

Affrica marched up to Ferchar and dropped on her knees beside him. Ferchar did not appear to notice. He swayed slightly, and she wondered if he would fall. At least then, his wounds could be tended.

The boys all cast down their eyes as Bishop Reinald harangued them in the form of prayer for all the crimes the earl had already enumerated, although Reinald was considerably more forceful and a lot wordier.

Wolf licked the tear trickling down Affrica's face.

Ferchar barely moved his head, but she felt his gaze swivel to her. She didn't look back.

"What forgiveness are *you* praying for?" he murmured. He sounded, if anything, amused. She didn't mind, for she liked his voice, low and deep enough to vibrate under her skin like music.

"The same as you," she said to the son of the priest. "I'm not."

SOMEHOW, THE GIRL'S words broke through Ferchar's sick dizziness and the drone of the bishop's voice. His head pounded, everything hurt, and he could barely speak for the swelling of his lips. She was the beloved MacHeth child, pretty, sunny and contented. Her grandfather and Kenneth's had been brothers. Her father, Angus mac Adam, was a great lord in his own right. And yet she not only knelt beside him, Ferchar, when she had no cause to kneel at all; she wept.

"What forgiveness are you praying for?" he had asked.

"The same as you. I'm not."

Perceptive, too, but then children often were. His lips stretched painfully, and her gaze flickered to his in surprise. In childish terms, she had betrayed her brothers, her cousins, to stop the beating. But her big, dark brown eyes looked not childlike but…ageless.

He looked away, back at his clasped, bloody hands. "Perhaps it is you who should be the next Earl of Ross."

Her dog, apparently of its own volition, began to lick his knuckles and clean him up. He swallowed, hard, for he would not break down because of a dog or a confused little girl's compassion.

When the interminable prayer ended, he got to his feet, the dog's head steady under his hand. Then he released the beast's fur and walked over to his father.

"The spoiled fruit," his father ordered without looking at him. "Lulach, you and the boys may wash away the blood spilled beside St. Duthac's Church. My young lords—the church roof."

By the time Ferchar had finished, his vision was fuzzy, and he wanted nothing more than to fall on his bed. But there was more to come. The talk with the bishop and the earl about his future. It would not be the talk he and his father had hoped for, and as for his future—well, he'd pretty much dealt with that. One mistake. Letting Thomas fall…

He managed to haul himself back to the cottage and up the outside staircase to his own chamber, where he eased himself out of his spoiled, tattered clothes, washed, and put on his remaining shirt and tunic. Today, he had merely to concentrate on not disgracing his father further. Tomorrow, he would think of other plans, a different future to establish before Kenneth MacHeth became earl.

He left his room, walked downstairs, and let himself into the living area of the cottage. Movement from the kitchen caught his eye, and he glanced in to see Bethoc, their housekeeper, setting a cup and a plate beside someone who sat by the fire, gazing into the flames. The MacHeth child again, curiously alone without even her dog.

He tore his gaze free and walked on to the main room. For the first time that day, he felt ashamed because somehow, he had wiped the sun from her face. And then he felt annoyed and had to pause for a moment before going in to his father and the great men who could and would decide his fate.

They were gathered around the table, so he bowed in their general direction.

"Pour yourself some ale," the earl said unexpectedly. "You look as if you need it."

The earl's cousin, Angus mac Adam, pushed the jug toward Ferchar as he sat down. "My daughter told me what happened. I'm sorry for my ruffians."

"Who are inclined to follow mine," the earl said with a kind of rueful pride. "We are not here to apportion blame but to decide on your future."

"As you know," the bishop said, "the church will no longer tolerate married clergy or inherited offices, and you cannot follow your father in his post as priest and coarb of the sanctuary of St. Duthac without holy orders. In which case, you will never be able to marry. You wish to enter the priesthood?"

Ferchar drank, giving himself time. It seemed his plan was, miraculously, not yet in tatters. "I don't know," he said candidly, avoiding his father's gaze. "I would like to learn and at least discover if the priesthood and I would suit."

"You want to go to the university in Paris," the bishop said. "And study theology? Canon law?"

"And the arts," he said, trying not to sound defiant. "It is my greatest wish."

"A rounded education is good in a churchman," Bishop Reinald allowed.

"And in all walks of life," Angus mac Adam said. "Forgive me, but there seems little of the clergyman in you, Ferchar."

"I am fourteen years old. I have time. But if I do not serve the church, I can serve the earldom or the state as required."

"Then you have ambitions beyond Tain?" Reinald pounced.

*God, yes.* His father, a good man, had inherited his post as priest of St. Duthac's church and coarb—or supervisor—of the attached place of sanctuary. His greatest wish was for Ferchar to succeed him, which was no longer merely a matter of following in his footsteps. The old ways of the Church were falling to the new rules imposed by Rome, which suited Ferchar well enough. "I want to learn," he repeated.

Reinald sat back. "I was appalled by your violence this morning," he said bluntly. "But according to the child, Angus mac Adam's daughter, you are not dead to all responsibility. You were on your way to summon us when the boy fell. Had it not been for that, I would not have recommended funding your studies in Paris."

Clearly it behooved him to keep his mouth shut.

"I have to say your studies here are surprisingly advanced," the bishop continued. "Your teachers speak well of you. Ross—indeed Scotland—could use men of your intellect. I am inclined to send you to Paris."

"Thank you, my lord," Ferchar said. Was it really to be this easy, after all?

"Or," the earl said delicately, "there is an alternative. That you join my household and train as a soldier."

"Or mine," Angus mac Adam said. "In the circumstances, mine might be better. You can influence my sons while you learn."

Stunned, Ferchar blinked from one to the other. "I don't understand."

The MacHeths exchanged glances.

"One thing we learned from our fathers and our grandfather," the earl said carefully, "is that successful warfare involves the mind. Intelligence. Strategy. Logistics. Planning and replanning and adapting. I think you have…potential."

"Why?"

Angus mac Adam let out a breath of laughter. "My father would like you. I hope you will meet him one day. As to the why… We too have our own intelligence."

Ferchar met his gaze. "Your daughter."

"A precocious infant," the earl said, "who never lies and who sees with remarkable clarity." He stood. "You need not make your decision now. If you would go to Paris, the earldom and the diocese will fund it with no conditions. If you would be a soldier instead, we would welcome you. Our sons need not trouble your thinking. They are not, at heart, ill-natured."

Ferchar, dazed, stumbled to his feet.

"Come to Tirebeck in a fortnight," Angus mac Adam said. "And tell us then."

"You are very good," Ferchar managed. "Thank you."

On the way out, he met the gaze of his father, who was grinning with the same dazed pleasure that filled Ferchar's heart. Not in his wildest hopes had he imagined this outcome, this embarrassment of choices, could possibly issue from the morning's disasters.

Somehow, he was out of the room and staring in at the kitchen door.

From the fireplace, the MacHeth girl turned to face him. Both immeasurably above him and, at nine or ten years old, beneath his notice. And yet she smiled at him as she always did, friendly, uncomplicated. Something he didn't quite understand impelled him into the kitchen.

Bethoc, the cook, was not there, only the girl.

He dropped onto the hearth beside her. "You spoke for me."

"I spoke the truth."

"Even though it meant betraying your brothers and cousins?"

She shrugged. "Their punishment is less than yours. And the bishop is here."

Ferchar held his gaze. "He holds the final say as to whether or not I can study in Paris."

Her eyes widened. "Paris! I wish I could study in Paris... Will he let you?"

"Surprisingly, yes. Thanks to you. Why did you say I was going to them for help when Thomas fell?"

"Weren't you?" she asked, frowning.

He shook his head. "I was going to lead your cousin on a chase over the dunes while Lulach got the children into the church."

"Then Kenneth would have caught you just the same..." She broke off, her brow twitching with sudden understanding. "But not, perhaps, until it was a game again?"

"Perhaps." He stirred. "Thank you for what you said. And did." Unable to be still, he sprang to his feet, and heard his breath hiss with the inevitable pain. As he strode from the kitchen, falling on his bed was the furthest thing from his mind.

# CHAPTER TWO

*Ross, summer 1204*

TWO WEEKS AFTER the incident at Tain, Kenneth MacHeth rode with his following from his father's favorite hall at Brecka to his cousin's at Tirebeck. He told himself he was merely *en route* to Dingwall to meet friends and discuss castle building. But the discomfort in the pit of his stomach would only be dispelled by some kind of resolution with Ferchar "Maccintsacairt," the "son of the priest."

Kenneth did not care to be in the wrong. In particular, he did not care to be in the wrong to *him*. He could tell himself that was because Ferchar was so far beneath him, being merely the son of a kinless priest who mattered not one jot. He, Kenneth, was a MacHeth to his toes, the son and designated successor of the Earl of Ross. He was allowed to lose his temper occasionally, and if Ferchar couldn't take a joke, well, that was not Kenneth's fault.

Except, he knew in his heart that the Tain incident *was* his fault. This self-awareness had little to do with the lectures or punishments of his father. It was just something that nagged at him. At any rate, he was not sorry to come upon Ferchar on the coast road along the Cromarty Firth.

The younger lad rode a mere pony, though, at least, it wasn't a donkey. His face had mostly healed, save for the faint discoloration under his eye.

"Stand and give me all you possess!" Kenneth said jovially as they caught up with him in a whirl of mud and snorting horses.

If Ferchar was surprised, he didn't show it, merely flipped a tiny silver penny across the distance between them.

Kenneth caught it, grinned, and tossed it back. "Going to Tirebeck?"

"As bidden."

Kenneth spurred on a little faster to gain some privacy from his men and was almost surprised when Ferchar troubled to keep up. "My father tells me he offered you a place. I don't mind. Would you?"

He couldn't resist the challenge at the end and was glad to see Ferchar's lips twitch in amusement. But the priest's son said, "I don't know."

"Will you take it? Or become a priest in Paris?"

"I will go to Paris."

Disappointment made Kenneth's response unnecessarily savage. "And study what?"

Ferchar turned his head and smiled. "Everything."

It made Affrica smile to see Kenneth ride through the gates with Ferchar. They seemed on perfectly friendly terms—perhaps Ferchar had been right that he could have won Kenneth over without blood in some mad chase over the dunes. But curiously, as she watched them talk and dismount, she had the impression that today it was not Ferchar but Kenneth who was striving for the friendship of the other.

"They're here," she told her father, who was busy at the table with his clerk and the administration of justice.

Angus stood and came to join her in the doorway. "He hasn't brought much. I suspect he won't stay."

Affrica knew he wouldn't, though it hadn't stopped her hoping. If he joined the household, she knew he would pay her no more attention than her brothers did, and yet it would have been good to have even an *occasional* friend.

Kenneth strode over to them, leaving servants to care for the horses. Reluctantly, it seemed, Ferchar followed behind.

"Greetings, Cousin Angus!" Kenneth shook hands with her father and ruffled Affrica's hair, which was annoying when she had only just brushed it.

"Kenneth. Ferchar, welcome to Tirebeck."

Kenneth stood back in a rare moment of grace.

Ferchar said, "I should tell you at the outset. Despite my gratitude and a definite temptation, I have decided it's best to go to Paris."

"You're probably right. Come into the hall, and I'll give you a letter of introduction to my brother Peter, who is prior of a Cistercian house not far from Paris…"

Affrica stopped listening. Ferchar's gaze found hers. An upward twitch of the lips surprised her more than the civil inclination of his head. She returned it before she slipped from under her father's arm and ran out into the yard calling to Wolf.

Unexpectedly, it was Ferchar who searched her out an hour later in the stables where she had just supervised the birth of a litter of tiny kittens to the fat old tabby who had lived there as long as Affrica could remember.

"Are you leaving already?" she asked in surprise as he sauntered in alone, all gangly limbs and defiant shabbiness.

"No. Your father wants you to take me to your grandfather."

She set down the tiny, blind kitten among its siblings, but to her surprise, he came right into the stall and sat down on the pile of straw beside her.

"I wanted to ask you something first." His attention appeared to be on the kittens.

"About my grandfather?"

He shook his head. After a moment, his gaze lifted to hers. His eyes were a strangely deep, compelling shade of hazel to be matched with such pale hair. "At Tain, when I climbed onto the church roof, I saw you playing on the beach with your dog. Yet within moments, before Kenneth even saw us, you were at the other side of the church."

"No one told me to stay on the beach all day."

"Then you didn't come to the church for any reason in particular?"

"Like what?"

His face didn't change. He hid his expressions like an adult. And yet she felt his reluctance as if it were her own. He didn't want to ask, and yet for some reason, he had to know. "Did you know something was happening? Did Kenneth plan that fight?"

She jumped to her feet, relief rolling off her in waves, although she supposed, guiltily, she should be angry on Kenneth's behalf. "Kenneth never plans anything. He just reacts. Come, I'll take you to my grandfather."

He could have made it difficult for her by asking more questions or even just remaining where he was until she chose to say more. But after the barest instant, he rose without a word and walked with her out of the stable.

With relief, she led him across the yard toward the little house in which her grandfather had chosen to stay.

"You'll know of Adam mac Malcolm?" she said brightly. "In his youth, he was a great warrior and seer. Now, he sees things all the time, so you will probably find him strange. You can ask him anything you like, of course, but he may not answer at all. Or he may answer a different question entirely."

One did not need to be fey to sense the skepticism radiating from the priest's son, though he waited politely for her to knock and enter in front of him.

To her surprise, her grandfather was not in his usual chair beside the fire, but by the shelves built into the far wall. Tall and lean and only slightly stooped about the shoulders, he was a living legend in Ross. One of those sons of that other legend, Malcolm MacHeth, who had taken on the King of Scots and won in many ways, Adam mac Malcolm still bore the respect due a great military leader, even though he had done little fighting in many years.

He had not heard her enter, so she skipped up to him, taking his arm. "Grandfather, it's Affrica. I've brought someone to meet you."

The old man blinked at her in surprise. His hair was still thick but pure white, framing a face of elegant bone structure, strong features, and wrinkled, papery skin. His eyes, once brown, grew increasingly filmy, though she doubted he missed his sight. Most of the time, it was other worlds he saw. If she hadn't loved him, this might have repelled as much as it bound her to him.

"This is Ferchar," she said. "Ferchar, my grandfather, Adam mac Malcolm MacHeth."

Ferchar bowed. "I'm honored to meet you, my lord."

The glazed old eyes swiveled. Almost as though he couldn't help it, her grandfather raised one thin, veined hand and Ferchar took it in his.

At once the old man's eyes widened. He stumbled backward, and Affrica caught his arm, guiding him back to his usual chair.

"Ferchar Maccintsacairt," Adam muttered.

*Son of the priest.* It was the nickname Kenneth had given him. Either Adam knew that, or...

Ferchar said evenly, "My father's name is Ruadri."

The old lips curved upward. "Wear the surname with pride, too, my lad. We always did. And there was a time no one said it as a compliment." With rare wariness, he raised his eyes to look into Ferchar's. The boy's breath caught, but he said nothing. "Have you come to ask me if you'll be a great man?"

"Why would I do that, lord?"

"It's why most people come to see me." He frowned. "I think."

"*I* never ask you that," Affrica pointed out.

Her grandfather smiled and tugged gently at a lock of her wild hair. "You are different. We all know you will be great. Sit, lad, and Affrica will bring us some refreshment. You are the coarb's son at Tain? What brings you to my hall?"

Tirebeck *was* Adam's, though Affrica often forgot the fact since her father ruled here now. While Affrica poured water from the big jug on the table and found the warm honey cakes newly brought from the kitchen, Ferchar lowered himself to the stool at her grandfather's feet and replied, "The earl and the Lord Angus offered me a place with them."

"To become the soldier. So, you are going to join us?"

"No. With some regret, I have declined. I will go to Paris to study. I have surprised you, sir?"

"Perhaps it would have been too easy," Adam said vaguely, and took the cup of water from Affrica. "And too difficult. You have surprised me."

"I understood that was impossible."

"But then you are fourteen years old and understand very little."

Ferchar's skin flushed. He knew he had been caught out in insolence and reprimanded, but Affrica doubted her grandfather noticed. To him, keeping children in order was like eating or drinking or even parrying a blade: he did it by instinct while his mind was elsewhere.

"How has he surprised you?" Affrica asked, helping herself to a cake.

Her grandfather's head was already turning toward the fire, but at her question, he moved back and gazed at Ferchar, though how much he could actually see of him was debatable.

"I suppose I will be dead," the old man said hoarsely, "but I would not have it end..." He broke off, turning back to the flames without hurry or desperation, and yet, appalled, Affrica saw that his eyes were wet. "There is kindness in you, too. I hope you will keep that."

Unnoticed, the unshed tears dried, leaving her grandfather's filmy eyes unfocused and rapt. Ferchar shifted uneasily, a frown tugging at his brow.

There was nothing Affrica could do for Adam MacHeth. She rose and took Ferchar's hand, tugging him to his feet.

"What's wrong with him?" he asked abruptly as she dropped his hand and closed the door on her grandfather's house.

"Nothing. He is always like that. But he saw something when he touched you."

"You don't believe that nonsense, do you?"

"My family has acted on that nonsense for more than half a century."

"And turned Scotland into a battlefield more than once."

"And then brought peace and pride back to Ross," she disputed. "Besides, wouldn't you do the same? For *your* father?" Their imprisoned parent, Malcolm MacHeth, had always been Adam and his brother Donald's cause, until he was freed and came back to rule.

Ferchar drew in a breath. "My father would neither expect nor allow it, even supposing I wished to. And don't tell me my father is not one of the great MacHeths."

She frowned. "Why are you so angry? Because he said you were kind?"

He stared down at her, his eyes turbulent before, slowly, they lightened and a breath of laughter escaped him. "You have too many brothers."

"That's what I tell them."

His grin was encouraging, so, her heart beating faster, she said in a rush, "I had to tie Wolf up so he would leave the new kittens alone. We can take him to the beach, if you like."

Ferchar had no objections to the girl's company. She was unexpectedly sharp and funny, and she made him think of sunshine. Of which he stood in need after the bewildering encounter with Adam MacHeth.

All the same, he had been offered the honor of a fighting place with her lordly father and with her uncle, the earl. As the son of a lowly priest among the powerful, he had to be on constant guard of his dignity. Choosing a girl child as his companion would hardly enhance his standing. He should, he knew, return to the hall, to her brothers and to Kenneth who still lurked somewhere in the vicinity.

As he hesitated, she smiled, and bent to untie the delighted dog. "It's better if I take him on my own."

With a jolt of understanding, he saw it wasn't better for her. She was surrounded by brothers and cousins and yet she'd played alone on the beach at Tain. Was that why she had run to the church so fast? Because she was adventurous and had no one to climb trees and rooves with? Hemmed in by her own birth and sex and her carelessly noble guardians, she was too used to loneliness for so bright and happy a child.

"Better for you, probably," Ferchar said. "But I've never had a dog."

Her smile brightened impossibly, almost dazzling him. "You can share Wolf," she said and skipped off, the dog bounding at her heels. Ferchar gave in and ran with them.

The next hour was unexpectedly fun. They ran barefoot along the sand and threw stones and sticks into the sea, laughing at Wolf galumphing through the waves to retrieve them. She didn't mind when the dog shook his wet fur all over her. Instead, she chattered away, amusing and confiding, about her days and her lessons, her family and servants and neighbors.

Sometimes, she stopped to greet the fishermen mending their nets on the shore, and they all smiled as they answered her—not because she was a MacHeth, Ferchar suspected, but because she brightened their lives. They liked her.

She asked innocent questions about Ferchar's life, too, questions that were strangely easy to answer, even for one careful of his dignity. She was too young for judgment or superiority. She was merely insatiably curious and friendly.

When her brothers turned up to take him away, he invented a game to keep them there. As a result, they were all playing together, shouting and laughing, when Kenneth strode along the beach. There was an instant when Nechtan and Colin paused, as though waiting for mockery or permission. But when Ferchar threw the big, rounded pebble to Kenneth and yelled, "Run," the earl's heir merely caught it from instinct and obeyed Affrica's laughing instructions.

By the time, they returned to the hall, the light was fading, and so Ferchar stayed the night after all. As he lay on the bed roll provided, surrounded by MacHeth boys, tumbling into sleep, he knew he was glad to have given Affrica the happiness of this day. And to have taken it for himself.

# Chapter Three

*Paris, summer 1207*

Angus MacHeth, walking through Paris with only one man-at-arms—Finlay, whom he'd known all his life—was conscious of a surge of excitement. Although not quite incognito, he was definitely unknown in these streets. A private gentleman of little account in France, where he hoped to reunite with Peter, his respected brother the prior, though not today. Today, he let the sights and sounds of the city wash over him with pleasure, for while the smells might be noxious, the streets too cramped, and the natives too eager to relieve you of your coin, Paris was blessedly *different*.

In fact, it was an unexpected joy to be away from home and the usual responsibilities. He wondered if his father had felt like this when he went off raiding in his youth—a sense of freedom and adventure that was almost relief. Well, Angus's adventure was a little tamer. There would be no theft or bloodshed, but he was, he hoped, beginning something of worth and importance for his family, his people, and his country. An end to an old, pointless feud, to vengeance and enmity.

Mocking himself for such a grandiose view of a private meeting, he turned the corner and came in sight of the River Seine, which he had been smelling for some time. Opposite him now, on the Isle de la Cité, was the magnificent palace of the King of France. Angus, who had met the kings of Scotland and England in their own castles, was impressed. But he was not here for kings.

The inn, called *Le Soleil*, at least gave the appearance of respectability. Entering, he was approached at once from three different angles by the innkeeper himself and two different menservants. Finlay, his bodyguard, stepped forward at once, his hand on his sword hilt, and the innkeeper and the servants both stopped and bowed.

The nearest servant spoke quietly in respectful Gaelic. "Angus mac Adam, welcome. Allow me to take you to my master." And he made no demur when Finlay came, too.

The final arrangement had been for Angus to come here alone to meet Guthred MacWilliam face to face. Guthred, the son of Donald MacWilliam, who had done his best to wrest Ross from Earl Adam, Gilchrist's older brother, as a prelude to making himself King of Scots. As the servant threw open the door of the next room, three men, not one, sat around the table with as many armed servants in attendance.

All three gentlemen stood up. Angus gazed from one to the other. Clearly, they were not going to make it easy for him. After all, in days gone by, the MacHeths had been their rivals for the throne as well as fellow rebels. They had been bitter enemies. And were still family.

Angus had never met Guthred MacWilliam, who had some claim to being the true King of Scots, and none of these men resembled the angry, determined Donald MacWilliam. The smiling black-haired man, armed to the teeth, was too young. Of the two older, fairer men, there was little to choose between them, except that the one with lighter hair bore ink stains on his right hand, which rested on a piece of parchment.

Angus picked the one with clean hands and inclined his head. "Do I address Guthred, son of Donald MacWilliam?"

"You do indeed." A little stout, the fair-bearded man stepped forward, extending his hand, almost as if he expected Angus to kneel. He was probably younger than Angus by five or six years, though exile or undisciplined living made him look older. Still, his eyes were sharp enough.

Angus took the outstretched hand. "I am Angus son of Adam, surnamed MacHeth. My father and my cousin the earl send greetings to you and your kin."

"We are sorry the great earl could not spare the time."

Angus pretended not to hear the polite mockery, though it irritated him. Did the MacWilliam take him for a dolt? "Your messenger mentioned privacy," he said pleasantly, "which is something the earl cannot command."

"Believe me, even we exiles have to work for that. Please, sit. Wine for my cousin, Lord Angus."

So, they were to be cousins. Good. Angus had assumed that was the point of the meeting. He sat and was introduced to Guthred's scribe—a half-brother called Donald Ban—and his "young friend, Prince Liam O'Neill of Ulster."

By the time they had toasted each other's kin, Angus felt the hairs on his arms rise. "I understand you have a proposal," he said abruptly. And please God, let it be what they had imagined, a request for MacHeth help in returning to Scotland and the king's peace.

"A discussion," Guthred corrected, smiling. Affrica would have hated his smile, warm and yet calculating. "One we should have had long since, except that your family and mine aimed—separately—at the same thing."

"My family has long abandoned its pretensions to the throne. We have accepted the King of Scots."

"And an earldom." Guthred smiled coyly. "As my father discovered twenty years ago."

Angus smiled back. "The earldom was always ours. The king chose to acknowledge the fact and we to honor the agreement."

"Does he still acknowledge it?" asked the Irishman, Liam, insolently.

Angus turned his gaze on the young man who was little older than his own sons, probably skilled in arms, certainly full of himself. And the O'Neills were the most powerful family in Ulster, if no longer quite the force they had once been in Ireland as a whole. Liam reminded him of Kenneth who needed, occasionally, to be put in his place. So, without troubling to answer, Angus let his gaze return to Guthred.

"Your proposal?" he reminded gently.

The Irishman's smile faded. His eyes narrowed. But at least he was too old or wise for tantrums.

Guthred said, "Without going over ancient history, with which you are as familiar as I, you know I represent the senior line of King Malcolm III's issue. My grandfather was his eldest son *and* chosen by the people. By the old laws and the new, I am the true King of Scots."

Angus inclined his head, covering his increasing unease. "Sadly, by the laws of reality, you are not."

"And if I was in a position to make it a reality?"

"Are you?"

Guthred smiled. "Yes. With the help of Prince Liam here, I have an army capable of defeating the King of Scots and taking the whole country."

Angus's spine hurt with the effort of remaining still. "Then why are you here talking to me?"

"Because this time, I invite the MacHeths to join me. To share in my fortune."

"A divided kingship?" Angus said in polite disbelief. "Really?"

Guthred scowled. "No, of course not. *I* will be king. But the MacHeths would find their fortunes improved. An important court position of his choice for your cousin the Earl of Ross—hereditary if he wishes—and of course his title confirmed in perpetuity. Another earldom for you and your heirs."

Angus sat back, thrusting aside emotion to concentrate on knowledge. *Liam O'Neill, a prince of Ulster.*

"You are generous," he observed. "Recognizing, I assume, that my family has connections by marriage to most of the other great families of Scotland and the Isles, ancient and new. You want our influence—and the harbors and beaches of Wester Ross, so convenient for surprise invasion from Ireland."

"It would be the perfect solution," Guthred said, his previously dull eyes beginning to sparkle. "The MacHeth name has never been forgotten. It still strikes terror into the hearts of people and armies alike. Join us and march south, and the king's armies will melt before us. Bring back the glorious days when the sons of Malcolm MacHeth held the kingdom to ransom!"

Angus stared at him. "Cousin, you have lived too long in exile. Even in Scotland, life has moved on."

"You have grown too comfortable, perhaps, in your earldom?" Liam suggested.

"And in my country." Angus looked from Liam to Guthred and spoke deliberately. "Scotland will not rise for you, Guthred mac Donald. Nor will Ross."

"You speak for the earl?" said the clerkly brother unexpectedly.

"I do." Angus had the impression his refusal had surprised no one—in which case, why had they bothered to ask? Why drag him here at all?

"No matter," Guthred said briskly. "You need not join us. We will do the work. All you need do is turn a blind eye while we march south through Ross and Moray. Your rewards will be the same. You have nothing to lose."

*Except peace. Except our people and our animals and crops to an invading army of mercenaries.* Angus stood. "On the contrary, Ross has everything to lose by such madness. I was there when the last MacWilliam tried to use Ross for his own ends and turned our land into battlefields.

Cousin, I will keep our agreement. I will not betray this meeting or your plans at this time. But know that any ships you send to our coasts will be refused, and any soldiers you manage to land will be treated as enemy invaders. We kicked your father's army out of Ross two decades ago, and we will do the same with considerably more ease to anyone who tries the same tricks. I have to thank you for the wine and excuse myself. I have plans to make for visiting my brother."

"Ah yes, your brother the French prior," Guthred said, smiling. He had not risen, though Liam did. "Does your daughter go with you on this visit?"

Ice slid down Angus's spine, freezing his blood. "My daughter?"

"A pretty, adventurous little thing, I understand. Pure MacHeth. I am surprised you chose to subject her to the dangers of travel and foreign cities."

For an instant, fear paralyzed him. He saw the triumphant knowledge in Guthred's eyes and the smile on Liam's lips. Angus had always been the thoughtful MacHeth who weighed every decision with knowledge and common sense. But now he acted from pure instinct.

As Liam's hand hovered near his sword, Angus stepped right up to him, jostling his sword arm without even looking while he ground his gaze into Guthred's.

"Never threaten my daughter, Guthred. There is no army in the world, no king or even God that will save you or yours if one hair of her head is hurt. I will kill you. And if I fail, my brothers, my sons, my cousins will take my place. For her, we would see Scotland *does* rise, and it will be against you. I trust we are clear."

Beside him, a shudder went through Liam. Angus hoped it wasn't laughter. The clerkly Donald Ban shifted uncomfortably, perhaps because Finlay had moved closer, ready to make a fight of it if necessary. Guthred's trapped gaze widened, perhaps with shock. Certainly, a sheen of sweat had formed on his forehead. And then the man, inevitably, smiled.

"Relax, Angus," he said jovially. "How can you imagine I could—or would—threaten any child of yours? Let alone one so well guarded! Sit, man, and drink another cup of wine."

<hr />

WELL-GUARDED SHE MIGHT have been, but not impossibly so. By the time her father entered *Le Soleil*, she had already crossed to the left bank of the river, quite alone apart from Wolf, who was given an understandably wide berth by the natives.

Affrica loitered in what she guessed was the university quarter, in a narrow street of tall, cramped houses and loud, passing youths arguing in Latin. Her attention had been caught by one particular young man who sat in a low window, dangling his legs over the sill into the street. Apparently lost in the book spread open on his knees, he wore no hat or coat, merely an unremarkable, faded blue tunic and far-from-new shoes. A long dagger and a battered scrip hung from his belt.

Perhaps it was the way the sun glinted off his untidy, dark blond hair, but he reminded her of Ferchar Maccintsacairt, the son of the coarb of Tain, whom she had not seen for three years.

She didn't expect to see him now, for his studies were finished, and his father had been awaiting his imminent return even before she had left Ross. But still, this older youth had something of Ferchar's features—the long, full mouth and deep-set, hooded eyes, although this man's face was longer, finer, and somehow better hung together. Despite the gently waving leg, this man had a stillness she did not associate with the priest's son.

As though sensing her scrutiny, the young man glanced up from his book, scanning the street around him. Someone called a greeting in the distance, and he raised one hand in acknowledgement, even as his gaze moved on and found her.

Her breath caught. *Was* it Ferchar?

No, his attention passed on without recognition, and she breathed again. Then his head bent toward to the dog sniffing at his dangling feet. With a jolt, Affrica realized that Wolf had found him, too. And knew him, for his tail wagged and he thrust his great shaggy head against the man's knee.

Abruptly, the youth's gaze flew back to her. There was a long moment, when neither of them moved, and her heart tried to beat its way out of her throat. Then he closed the book, tossed it through the window to the room beyond, and crooked his finger.

No one outside her family had ever crooked a finger at Affrica MacHeth. With a flood of relief, she remembered her disguise. If this was Ferchar—and surely there was no longer any doubt—it was Wolf who had caught his attention. She was merely a curious, ill-dressed urchin boy.

Such a boy would surely respond to the command of his betters, even if only in the hope of earning a coin. So, with silent excitement bubbling inside her, she ran obediently up to him. She even tugged her cap.

His lips twitched. This close, he was taller, broader in the shoulders, and much more solid than she recalled. Temporarily, this unfamiliarity confused her. Until he said, "Affrica MacHeth, what mischief are you in now?"

Delighted laughter spilled out, because he *did* know her and did not seem remotely shocked. Since he moved to make space for her, she turned and hauled herself up beside him on the windowsill. "None, yet," she said happily. "No one knows I've gone."

"Gone from where?"

"A house my father borrowed in the merchants' quarter. On the other side of the river. I brought Wolf."

"He's better than *no* protection. I hesitate to ask what you've done with the rest of your guard."

"Sinead—my governess—went to sleep when she had promised we would go out this afternoon. I wanted to see the churches, Notre Dame and St. Denis and—"

"You could have wakened her up."

"I could," Affrica agreed. "But a grumpy companion is worse than no companion, don't you think? And the men-at-arms would not take me without her."

"You didn't ask them, did you?"

"Not exactly." She hesitated, then confessed. "I climbed out of the back window and hid behind a cart in the lane. But I am much safer as a boy—my father said so, though Sinead thinks it improper—and Wolf is worth two men-at-arms. You should have seen what he did to the thieves who tried to rob us on the road to Paris."

"And can you and Wolf find your way back to this merchant's house?"

"Of course," she scoffed, then grinned. "Well, to be honest, I'm relying on Wolf."

"Come on, Wolf can take us both, and you can give me all the news on the way."

"Can we go via Notre Dame?" she asked hopefully.

He laughed with what seemed genuine amusement. His gaze shifted beyond her, and before she could even smile back, he flung himself on her, knocking her backward through the window, just as something flew past her ear and buried itself in the shutter frame. Even before she saw what it was, she recognized the noise it made. Like the arrow which had once struck a laden tree at Tain and shaken apples onto her brothers' heads.

"*Run*," said Ferchar Maccintsacairt.

# Chapter Four

*Paris, summer 1207*

FERCHAR SHOULD NOT have been there. He should have already gone home to face the music. Despite that, he was ridiculously glad to see Affrica MacHeth in her hopeful disguise that would *not* please her father. In her boy's clothes, hair stuffed under a fortunately roomy cap, she was funny and curiously sweet.

But when he knocked her backward through the window into the house that happened to belong to his lover, what terrified him was the possibility that he would not save her.

As he sprang up, Wolf leapt through the window, and a fair young man rushed at him just before he slammed and fastened the shutters.

"Run!" he commanded, reaching down to haul Affrica to her feet.

Though her eyes were wide and frightened, she obeyed without question, seizing his urgent hand and rushing with him from the room. Someone was already battering on the front door of the building as Ferchar flew toward the back of the house, the dog bounding after them.

"Is this *all* your house?" she asked breathlessly, bolting with him through the several rooms that led to the kitchen.

"None of it. I'm just visiting." Throwing wide the kitchen shutters, he saw that the attackers had not yet discovered the back entrance, although they would.

"Ah," she said as he hurled himself through the window. "You are troubling other men's wives."

A breath of laughter took him by surprise. He seized her by the waist, hauling her after him. "Widow. Singular. When did you become so worldly wise?"

"I have eyes." With a trust that scared him, she took his hand, and they ran together across the yard to the gate, which flew open just as they reached it.

Ferchar didn't recognize the burly man who filled the opening, but he could not hesitate. Retaining Affrica's hand, he barged the intruder with enough force to hurt his shoulder and get them all to the other side of the gate. By then, he had his dagger free, and so did the other man, but Wolf stood between them, snarling and slavering, poised to leap, and inevitably, the attacker froze.

In the circumstances, Ferchar had no pride. He ran, tugging Affrica with him.

"Why is someone trying to kill me?" she asked raggedly, trying to look over her shoulder at Wolf. As though distress had been delayed.

"No one is trying to kill you."

"They shot an arrow at me! If you hadn't—"

"They shot an arrow at *me*."

At the end of the narrow alley, with both Wolf and the burly man catching them up, she tried to turn left. Ferchar yanked her to the right, knocking over buckets and barrows and barrels as he went. Wolf bounded over them.

"Because of the widow?" she asked anxiously.

"I suspect because of you."

The bowman he had first glimpsed at the window opposite Denise's house, appeared suddenly on top of the garden wall ahead. Ferchar fled through the nearest gate on the other side, into a carpenter's yard.

"*Me?*" Affrica squeaked with indignation.

"If I were disabled, you would be easier to seize. When we fell into the house, a second man was already coming for you."

"But why?" she demanded. At least she didn't slow her pace to argue, though she did call heartfelt apologies over her shoulder to the angry carpenter as they blundered through his shop. "Why would they kidnap a boy of the streets?"

"So worldly wise," Ferchar muttered, charging down the street. "And still so innocent." He doubted she understood all the implications of that, but he still wished he hadn't said it.

However, she was silent, running at his side while she apparently grasped the salient point. "They know who I am," she breathed. "They followed me from the house." Her hand tightened on his. "Oh, Ferchar, my father! We have to warn my father."

"Indeed, we do. But first, we have to… Damnation, they're still after us."

They dodged through closes and alleys and yards until Affrica was clutching her side and Ferchar's throat was parched. Changing tactics, he swerved across the street and into his favorite tavern.

Inevitably, several of his friends were there, greeting him with surprised ebullience as he pushed Affrica onto a bench among them and collapsed beside her. The barriers between their stations and genders had dissolved somewhere in the hectic flight. She didn't appear to mind being squashed into his side, and yet he felt the rapid rise and fall of her ragged breath, the drumming of her heart vibrating through him like a captured bird's.

A wave of protectiveness washed over him, as though he only just understood what he had been doing for the last twenty minutes. But somewhere, he grasped that this was more than simply defending the family of his lord. He was protecting *Affrica*, and always would.

A cup of ale was sloshed down on the table, and he pushed it in front of her. She lifted it in both hands, gulped once, and set it down before him. Wolf laid his head on her knee while, wide-eyed, she took in her surroundings and her company. Disreputable students on a spree, largely, with a scattering of even more disreputable women twined around them. He supposed he should be sorry for exposing her to that sight, too, but he had other things on his mind.

"What are you about, Farquar?" his friend Louis demanded in some amusement. "Are you the hunter or the hunted?"

"The former," Umberto guessed. "He has brought his own hound."

Which was when the fair man and the burly man walked slowly past the tavern window. The hairs on the back of Ferchar's neck stood up, and he knew at least one other of their pursuers would already be at the back door, blocking his escape.

"The hound," he repeated. "Of course. They always find us by asking after Wolf."

"So, the hunt*ed*," Louis said irrepressibly. "Why do you care? It's the middle of the day."

"That's true." So, there were people, witnesses who could be made to see, barriers to hide behind and attack from... "Affrica, introduce Wolf to Louis, here, make him stay. Louis, look after the dog and I'll come back for him this evening. Umberto, if you would be so good as to start a riot, I would be forever in your debt."

He sprang to his feet but had to all but drag Affrica away from Wolf and up the tavern's wooden staircase. For the first time, she jerked her hand free of his, demanding, "Where are we going?"

"Don't be grumpy. You're finally getting your wish to play on the roof—and Paris has much better rooves than Tain." Though he kept the words light and cheerful, she flung her arm across her stomach.

Stopping had been a mistake. It allowed her to think too much, to grasp the full, bewildering horror that strangers wanted to take her from her family for ends that could never be good. To understand the precariousness of their position.

And then a shout went up in the taproom below. A table crashed on its side among breaking crockery and cries and cheers. The front door burst open, and his friends spilled through the doorway into the street, fighting in fun and probably in earnest, too, making it impossible for the hunters to get through. With luck, Wolf and Louis would hold the other exit long enough.

"Affrica," he said urgently, and she ran past him up the rest of the stairs.

"You've done this before," she accused in the first room under the eaves while he opened the shutters and climbed out the window before reaching in to help her.

"Not sober."

Breath hissed between her teeth, and he was so relieved to discover it was laughter, however desperate, that he grinned back and refastened the shutters from outside. A shout went up below, but he ignored it, crouching on the narrow sill and holding his linked hands out as a step. Without hesitation, she placed her booted foot on his palms and sprang up onto the roof.

He clambered up behind her, his spine tingling as he kept his body between her and the man below who still carried a bow on his shoulder.

On the ridge, he risked a glance back down. There were far too many people around him for the bowman to risk another shot, but he stood apart from Ferchar's rioting, laughing friends who were now splashing ale from a barrel at each other while the tavern keeper yelled in justifiable fury.

The bowman stared directly at him, his mouth a grim line of determination. Three other men broke from around the side of the house. One pointed angrily upward.

Affrica crept round beside Ferchar. Putting her thumbs to her ears, she spread her fingers and wiggled them, sticking out her tongue at her enemies—so childish and yet so right for the moment that Ferchar let out a shout of laughter, seized her arm, and slid with her down the other side of the roof.

On the beach, that long ago day at Tirebeck, she had been spry and athletic, running and climbing among the rocks and the gaggle of older boys with no thought for her dress let alone the dangers of hurting herself. It was the same now. As sure-footed as he and considerably more graceful, she slid and edged, climbed, jumped, and ran, keeping up with his longer legs and rarely needing his help.

Of course, the enemy caught on. There was no point in them climbing, but they kept pace on the ground, finding their quarry almost immediately whichever direction Ferchar took over the rooves, because they knew, as he did, that sooner or later they would run onto a roof that had no way off. And then they would come.

The first time Ferchar and Affrica skidded to a halt with nowhere to go, they simply ran back the way they had come. But the chase could not go on forever. He needed to lose them.

The second time, there was a handily long plank of wood left behind, presumably, by builders, which enabled them to cross the space between houses. Ferchar drew the wood after them and briefly contemplated taking it with them for future eventualities. But since the wretched thing was too awkward to carry while clambering over rooftops, he elected to hurl it instead at their pursuers on the ground.

They scattered, though it caught one on the edge of the shoulder, knocking him to the ground. Affrica crowed with delight, and, discovering a loose tile, hurled that at them, too. Ferchar joined in enthusiastically until the enemy ran for cover, arms over their heads. Unfortunately, by then the local residents were running into the street, yelling at such wanton destruction and violent behavior. Worse, the window almost directly under their feet crashed open, and a man's jowled face, red with fury, threatened them with the law, execution, and hideous if anatomically impossible tortures.

Ferchar, his hand raised to hurl one last tile, thought better of it.

Bending, he dropped it into the man's gesticulating hands. "Quite right, monsieur. If I were you, I wouldn't tolerate it, either." After which, he snatched Affrica's hand and slid down to the next roof, the girl positively snorting with mirth.

"The MacHeths are coming!" Ferchar yelled in Gaelic, and she laughed harder, making it impossible not to join in. Which was when he realized he didn't have the control he needed to stop them flying off the edge of the short roof. He could only twist so that with luck, he would fall under her and give her some chance.

He did, landing on his back rather sooner than expected with Affrica's weight barely noticed on top of him. Winded, he could only gasp for breath and pray he'd broken no bones, while Affrica stared down at him wide-eyed.

Something soft and damp batted against his face and his hair. An enraged, middle-aged female face blocked out Affrica's.

"What are you doing on my balcony, imbecile? Beast! Turd! *Student!*"

Ferchar wheezed in laughter, and Affrica smiled dazzlingly, climbing off him, and offering him her hand to rise in a much-appreciated spirit of equality.

"I suppose that was you," the woman raged, "throwing poor Georges's roof into the road? By God, the law will have your neck for this and Georges, your hide!"

"Oh, Georges has stunning plans for my hide," Ferchar assured her. "I can only apologize to you both and…" He broke off, realizing two things. Footsteps were running covertly up a staircase at the side of the building, leading, presumably to this very balcony. And the wet, soft object he had felt against his face, was a large, freshly washed bed sheet.

In front of the sheet, which she had presumably just hung, the woman clutched a huge basket full of washing. A line was stretched across the road to a matching balcony on the house opposite, where a few clothes already hung in the afternoon sunshine. Ferchar's recovered breath caught once more.

"Forgive me," he said resignedly, and swiped a large apron from the top of the basket. Outraged, the woman struck him hard across the shoulders.

"Oh, please don't," Affrica begged seriously. "He hasn't got time to laugh. Ferchar, they're coming!"

"I know," he said, twisting the rolled-up apron about her waist and hauling her close against him while he tied it around both their bodies, and the woman continued to hit him. The laughter came anyway, impossible to hold back, even when he bunched the sheet on the line and the woman screamed in fury.

"Hold on to me," Ferchar gasped. "Arms and legs. Do *not* let go."

Astonished by his antics, Affrica flung her arms around his neck only just in time for him to loop the twisted sheet around the rope and, holding either side in his hands, launch them both off the balcony.

"Sor…ry!" he yelled back at the woman as they hurtled along under her washing line. His arms were almost jerked out of their sockets, but he hung on for dear life. It would have been so much easier if he hadn't been convulsed in hilarity and if Affrica's whole body, wrapped like a vise around his, hadn't been vibrating with it, too. By the time they landed on the opposite balcony, his neck was wet with her tears of mirth.

On the first balcony, the angry woman was now belaboring four harassed looking men with what might have been a laundry pole.

"You had a lucky escape," Affrica said in such an awed voice that she set Ferchar off again. Somehow, he managed to draw his dagger, cut the washing line, and then free them from the apron that bound them. They all but fell down the outside stairs of the house, helped on their way by two squawking old women with brooms.

Crying with laughter, they tumbled into the street and fled.

Ten minutes later, with no sign of their pursuers, they were safe in the heart of the university. Ferchar collapsed beside Affrica in the middle of a quiet flight of steps. The vast majority of scholars had left for the summer, so they could recover, probably, in peace.

Affrica wiped her still streaming eyes and hiccoughed.

Ferchar drew in a deep, satisfying breath. "Well. That's the most fun I've ever had fleeing for my life."

A giggle erupted and was still. Smiling, she gazed down the steps to the river shining in the sun and the king's palace which looked like an illuminated manuscript against the background of the merchant city.

He nudged her with his shoulder. "So how do you feel about rooftops now?"

Her smile broadened for an instant. She even nudged him back in a friendly way that still somehow snatched at his breath. But for some time, she sat in silence, just breathing.

She said, "That day, in Tain, I wasn't coming to play with you and the other children on the church roof. I saw you from the beach, and I knew something was wrong."

"How?"

She turned her head and met his gaze. For the first time ever, it seemed to be hard for her. She swallowed. "Your smile was wrong. It *hurt* me."

"Hurt you?" he repeated, bewildered. "How?"

"Because you didn't mean it. You were telling the world this would be fun, that you were enjoying yourself hugely, when inside you were furious at the injustice, hurt by the way they—my cousins and my brothers—had turned on you."

Three years ago, he would have walked away from such unbearable truths. Today, painful as they might be, he recognized she was not so much reading his secrets as confessing something to him.

A frown flickered across his brow before he could stop it. "And from that, you knew there could be serious trouble?"

"At his worst, Kenneth is a bully, and my brothers will always follow him." She dropped her gaze and swallowed audibly before raising it to his face once more. "The point is, I can feel the same emotions when you do. Not just you," she added hurriedly. "Anyone I choose to pay attention to. I know when they lie, when tears are false, when happiness is faked. It pains me here, in my stomach." She wrapped her arm around her middle and tried to smile. "It doesn't matter. I know you don't believe, let alone—"

"Don't," he said fiercely. "Don't pretend, not after that."

The happy-go-lucky if lonely child he had always imagined was anything but. She felt people's pain, real or imagined, and she *cared*, even for him, a relative stranger.

"Do you dream?" he asked steadily. "Do you *see*? As they say Adam mac Malcolm sees?"

Her lips quirked. "Not like him, not like my grandfather. But sometimes I do see pictures in the fire. Or dream something that comes true."

And she never told anyone.

"Only my grandfather," she said, just as if she had heard the thought, "because he understands. But I don't have his gifts, or his strength."

He took her hand in his and gripped. "Oh, you have his strength, Affrica MacHeth, never doubt that."

Her eyes widened. "I know you are…skeptical. I want you to know the worst of me if we are friends."

"Affrica, there is no worst."

She clung to his fingers, as if they were again flying along that washing line between the houses. He couldn't help bringing up his other hand to cup her cheek, so childishly soft and innocent as she pressed against his palm. She was not so trusting after all, this small, self-contained young being. Yet she *did* trust him, and that was humbling.

"Then we *are* friends?" she asked shakily.

"Always."

With a sound halfway between a sob and a laugh, she jumped to her feet. "Let's go to Notre Dame…"

## CHAPTER FIVE

*Paris, summer 1207*

THEY DID GO to Notre Dame on their way back to her father's borrowed house, but only after Ferchar had arranged some changes to their dress. After vanishing into one of the college buildings, he emerged wearing a large-brimmed hat and a light, sleeveless coat the color of mud.

"Dull," Affrica pronounced when he returned to her hiding place in the college out-building.

"That's the plan." He struck a pose that made her giggle. "Though I like to think the coat gives me the dignified appearance of a brilliant but horrifically poor scholar."

"Well, the hat hides your face. I could pull mine lower or dirty my cheeks a bit?"

"No, I have a different plan for you."

Quicker than thought, he whisked the boy's now-very-squint cap from her head, dragging several artfully arranged pins with it. Her hair tumbled free and thick, shrouding her like an unmanageable curtain.

"Ferchar!" she all but wailed.

"They're looking for a noble girl dressed as a boy," he said patiently. "So, you shall be a poor girl." He shook out the large apron purloined from the angry woman's washing line and dropped it over her head like a gown. While he pulled and tied it into some kind of shape, she grabbed some of the fallen pins from her hair and tried to tame it to at least keep it out of her face.

"Kitchen maid?" she said doubtfully. "To the horrifically poor—"

"But brilliant," Ferchar inserted.

"…scholar. Or perhaps your nagging, even more brilliant little sister."

"With luck no one will speak to us, and we need never decide." He stood back, surveying her critically from beneath the wide hat. For an instant, his eyes rested on her face, unblinking.

She stuck out her tongue, and his lips twitched.

"Insolent maid," he said, reaching for the door. "Out."

As they made their way through the narrow streets toward the river, her flagging energy began to revive, along with all her interest in this new country, in all the sights and sounds and colors of the packed, teeming city. And the man beside her, the friend enjoying it with her.

"You are at home here," she said suddenly. "No wonder you are reluctant to leave."

"It has been fun," he allowed. "But perhaps it is time to move on."

She glanced at him. "You don't sound very sure."

"I'm not."

"You could always stay here, make your life here," she said, although she didn't really want him to. "My uncle did. In fact, I have uncles all over the world, but I was thinking of Uncle Peter, the prior. But perhaps you should see your father first."

His lips twisted—not the kind of smile that hurt, but one that spoke of difficult answers. "Absolutely, I must see my father, whatever I do. And that is the thing I am avoiding."

"Why?" she asked blankly.

He looked straight ahead. "Because I have not done as everyone intended. I have not graduated. I have no degree."

She took this in. "The widows and wives?" she hazarded.

A breath of laughter hissed between his teeth. "And the tavern friends. I suppose they didn't help, but no one can say I have not studied. I have attended every lecture I could cram into the day, read every book I could lay my hands on. I have listened and discussed and argued. I have written essays by the score and even won occasional praise from my teachers and scholars I respect."

She frowned up at him, bewildered. "Then why won't they give you your degree?"

"In what?" he said ruefully. His head turned and his gaze bent to hers. "I came to study theology and canon law. And I did. But I also branched into civil law. And the arts. And medicine. I found it all…irresistible. But the result is, in my three years in Paris, I have not completed any one course of study."

She considered that with a certain amount of sympathy and understanding. No one cared much about her learning, so they let her absorb whatever was being taught to her, her brothers, her cousins, and even the clerks. She had had choices.

"Will it matter?" she asked at last.

He blinked.

"I mean, you already have more learning than most priests and clerks. I doubt either the earl my cousin or even Bishop Reinald will notice or care about the rest."

"I will know," he said ruefully. "*My father* will know that I failed, despite the money spent on my scholarship."

She nodded slowly. "Is there a solution?"

"I could obtain a degree, they tell me, if I stayed another year, focusing entirely on theology and cannon law." His lips quirked. "Or on the arts or civil law. Or even medicine. If I could pick one."

"And can you?"

He didn't answer.

She said, "Perhaps you should pick what they sent you to study. I'm sure my father would deal with the cost."

His shoulder jerked involuntarily—pride and honor, no doubt, getting in the way of good sense.

"You could pay him back later," she said impatiently. "But to all intents and purposes, you saved my life. That is a debt he will not forget. None of my family will."

"I saved my own life," he muttered. "And risked yours across the rooftops, which might have seemed like a good idea at the time, but..."

She grinned. "But it was fun."

His face cleared and he laughed. "Yes, it was fun."

⸻

ANGUS MACHETH STARED at Sinead, the harpist's daughter who served as governess to his own. "What do you mean, *she is not here?*"

Sinead wrung her hands in unconscious, very genuine anxiety that only fueled his own. "She is not in her room, my lord, nor anywhere in the house that I can discover, and yet no one has seen her go out. There is worse," she added, closing her eyes. "The boy's suit you had her wear on the journey, it's not in her chest."

Angus groaned and yet no sound came out. "Dear God, how can an entire household lose my daughter?" He strode to the door and raised his voice. "Finlay!" He swung back on Sinead. "When did you last see her?"

"This morning," Sinead whispered. She seemed to have to force herself to look at him. And no wonder. "Just after you left. She was nagging me to go out and look at the city and the churches. I agreed we should go after noon, but I was so tired, and it is so warm here... I fell asleep," she finished with shame.

Angus glared at Finlay—unjustly since the man hadn't even been in the house. "And no one else saw my daughter leave? Or even noticed she was not here? *All afternoon?*" He dragged his hand through his hair. "Summon the men. I want the city scoured from end to end until she is found. And I want my horse at the door in five minutes." He swung back on Sinead as Finlay bolted to do his bidding. "And you will wait here and pray to God she returns before I do."

Even as he raged, he knew he was being unfair. He had not been here either. He had whiled away the afternoon in a tavern with Guthred MacWilliam of all people, trying to grasp the root of his slippery, incomprehensible character. He had left, in the end, only because they had seemed too eager for him to stay. As though they had imagined the wine and good fellowship would make him change his mind about their idiotic invasion. He had made sure they understood it hadn't and it wouldn't.

But none of that mattered beside Affrica's disappearance. Nothing else mattered if she was harmed, if she was—

"Lord Angus."

Finlay stood at the door. Angus stared at him, lowering his hands from his face in unprecedented fear, for he should never have taken Affrica out of Scotland. It was just that he hadn't trusted anyone else to look after her properly while he was gone, and she had *wheedled*...

Finlay stood aside, and Angus's daughter rushed in, looking like a hoyden with her black hair flying free and some hideous, grubby garment clinging to her legs. She had never been so beautiful, and it paralyzed him.

"Father! Oh, Father, we have so much to tell you, and you need to know at once..." He lost the rest of her babble, which had never been so welcome, so musical, as he realized a very young man had followed her into the room.

Of no great degree, he wore an ancient, mud-colored coat and shoes that were all but falling apart, and he carried a ridiculously large, battered hat in one hand. He was a tall, loose-limbed boy with broad shoulders, a tangle of ill-cut light hair and forceful features that looked vaguely familiar. Angus had an instant to worry what influence this youth had exerted on his unworldly daughter, before Affrica herself distracted him with her enthusiastic hug and it was all he could do to keep his knees straight.

His arms wrapped convulsively around her for one precious moment of gratitude, and then he forced himself to push her from him and frown down at her.

"Well?" he said severely.

She wasn't fooled. She never was. Smiling sunnily, she said, "Father, you remember Ferchar? The son of the priest?"

And abruptly, he did. Even though Ferchar was a young man now, with something vaguely rakish about him, Angus's nasty suspicions fell away like a cloak from his back. No one of Ross, for any number of reasons, would harm a MacHeth.

"Ferchar! Of course, forgive me, I should have known you at once except we heard you'd gone home." Releasing Affrica, he went forward to greet his guest, noting at the back of his mind that even in the unprepossessing clothes, he bowed now with far more grace than the clumsy lad he had been three years ago. "Am I to understand you have rescued my daughter and brought her home?"

"Oh, he did, Father," Affrica said fervently before Ferchar could do more than open his mouth. "That is what we have to talk to you about."

"Well, why don't you go and change out of…" he waved one distasteful hand at her bizarre gown, and she giggled. "…out of *that*. While I talk to Ferchar." He could see her about to argue, though this was one fight she would not win.

But this time Ferchar beat them both to speak. "With respect, sir, I believe she needs to be here. She needs to properly understand the dangers, not least to prevent her taking more risks."

Angus's retort died unspoken. "What dangers?"

"Someone shot an arrow at Ferchar," Affrica said in a rush, "and tried to abduct me, and they chased us all over the left bank before we lost them. That's why we are in disguise."

The boy's breath shuddered. Stunningly, it might have been mirth, swiftly cut off. Angus moved blindly toward the table. "We had better sit. Send to the kitchen for wine and food, Sinead. Now, daughter, tell me exactly what happened, beginning with how you came to meet Ferchar."

The salient points of the tale were told succinctly by Ferchar himself, with excited embellishments from Affrica, who seemed to have thoroughly enjoyed the whole hair-raising experience. If Angus hadn't felt so sick, he might have insisted on some of the suppressed details that caused the pair to avoid each other's eyes and try not to laugh. But the implications of this threat were too huge, too appalling.

When their tale ended with Affrica's enthusiastic delight in the still-incomplete cathedral of Notre Dame, Angus was silent for a long time.

*"Does your daughter travel with you? ...I am surprised you chose to subject her to the dangers of travel and foreign cities..."*

Ferchar said, "They followed her, sir. She was their target."

His eyes refocused on the priest's son, who could not have known why Angus was in Paris, but who clearly recognized the breadth of the danger. And God knew, Angus needed all the help he could get to keep his family safe now. *All* his family.

"Do you know why, Father?" Affrica asked. The excited laughter had vanished from her eyes, leaving them too serious, too adult. And yet she was thirteen years old, a young woman by most standards. She could be married with a household and responsibilities of her own.

"I came to France to visit my brother Peter," Angus said slowly. "The first time I will have seen him in a decade. But I had another reason." He turned his gaze on Ferchar. "Have you heard of Guthred MacWilliam?"

"The son of Donald MacWilliam," Ferchar said evenly, "who sought the crown of Scotland by invading Ross and Murray."

"Guthred is a distant cousin of ours," Angus said. "His father Donald once married the daughter of Malcolm MacHeth's brother, the Earl of Angus. The families lost touch after Malcolm, my grandfather, accepted the king's peace. When Gilchrist's brother Adam—"

"He was named for my grandfather," Affrica interrupted, "though it gets confusing to have so many names the same."

Angus frowned at her. "When this younger Adam was earl in the 1180s, Donald MacWilliam took advantage of the relationship to invade Ross and try to take the whole kingdom—a rebellion, in which the MacHeths took no part, although poor Adam suffered for it. When the MacHeths and the king united and pushed the MacWilliams out, the remaining family lived in exile, mostly in Ireland, and we never communicated. Until a few months ago, Guthred sent a discreet message to Earl Gilchrist asking to meet and restore friendship as well as kinship."

Ferchar cut straight to the point. "What did he mean?"

"That is the question we asked ourselves," Angus said heavily, "and we came up with the wrong answer. We decided he wanted to return, to be accepted into the king's peace, no doubt on terms as advantageous to them as possible. We imagined they wanted our support with the king, to intercede for them and smooth the way. I discovered my error today."

The MacWilliam brothers and Liam O'Neill had persuaded him to stay with them in the tavern. But the wine and good fellowship they had pressed on him had not been to persuade him to their alliance, but to give their ruffians time to capture Affrica and force his hand. He shuddered.

"Guthred MacWilliam wants to land an army of invading mercenaries from Ireland and the Isles in Wester Ross in order to take Scotland and the throne. He wants alliance with us, but if he can't get that, he would settle for our complaisance."

Ferchar threw himself back in his chair, the gesture unexpectedly violent, the hazel eyes hard. "You are to sit by while an army ravages its way through Ross and sets the kingdom alight? Again?"

"Apparently. Though it would be best if we did a little ravaging of our own. For the good old days of Malcolm MacHeth and his sons."

At his savage tone, Ferchar's fingers loosened on his cup. His eyes lightened. "They *need* MacHeth help. They would force your hand if they can."

"They know they will get help no other way. I'm afraid I made that abundantly clear. What I don't know, is what they will do next. If they are set on this, if they *need* Ross—"

"Why would they?" Affrica interrupted. "They could land anywhere on the west coast or come in from Caithness in the north."

Ferchar said, "If they land further south, the king's army will be upon them before they are ready—likely a repeat of Somerled's failed invasion of 1168. From Caithness, they would still have to get through Ross, again giving the royal army time to meet them. If they land in a complaisant Ross, at the very, least they have time to gather, prepare supplies and march before the king even knows they're there. At best, they have the Ross host behind them."

The boy's instant grasp impressed Angus, though Affrica said, "A *reluctant* host ready to stab them in the back."

"No one would stab them," Ferchar said, catching her gaze. "Not if they held you."

"They don't," Affrica pointed out.

"Nor will they," Angus said flatly. "They will know by now they've missed their chance, that you'll be too well guarded for them to get anywhere near. So, what will they do next?"

Ferchar met his gaze and held it. "Look for another hostage. Or change the leadership of Ross. Quickly."

Angus inclined his head, like a teacher pleased with his pupil, just as though his blood wasn't boiling and freezing at the same time. "I will leave tomorrow to warn Peter of this before I return to Scotland and Gilchrist." Because without Gilchrist, Kenneth would be earl, and that would be disastrous. He shuddered. "I won't have time to warn my uncle and brother, who are with the crusading army in Thessalonica, though I suspect they are not safe from this treachery either."

He was only thinking aloud, wondering how best to get the urgency of his message out speedily enough.

"I can do that," Ferchar said.

Angus blinked. "I was going to ask you to join my daughter's protection." To distract her and keep her close, since she seemed to regard Ferchar as a friend.

"She won't endanger you by straying now," Ferchar said simply.

"I won't," Affrica whispered, wide-eyed. Ferchar didn't look at her.

"Can you protect yourself on such a journey?" Angus asked doubtfully.

Ferchar's smile was lopsided, though this time he did spare Affrica a glance. "That is my other confession. In the last three years, I have studied more than books."

# Chapter Six

*Ross, spring 1209*

Affrica accompanied her father from his duties in wester Ross to the earl's hall at Dingwall, in the southeast of the earldom. In the absence of a lady—the earl showed no desire to marry again—she occasionally steered the running of the household, a little like the light hand of a sailor at the helm.

"What do you think of this, sir?" Breezing into the main hall from the kitchen, while her father was closeted with Kenneth, she approached the earl's chair at the fireside.

The earl looked up and smiled, and her heart twisted. He did not look well. He hadn't looked well last month either, and as the steward's wife had told her, he was too thin and drawn, and he didn't eat enough. Nor was it like him to sit so close to the fire on what was essentially a pleasant spring day.

"What have you brought me?" he asked indulgently as Affrica presented him with the cup.

"I made it from a secret recipe, and my brothers were rude about it, but since their palates are as sensitive as a boar's…"

As she had hoped, he sipped to please her, and blinked with some surprise. "It's soup."

"I don't call it that," she said firmly, "for it's too thin and, I think, sweet." The work of the onions which had been grated to crumbs, along with spring vegetables, herbs, and the juices from beef. "I hear Kenneth wants to build you a castle as big as a palace and as secure as Roxburgh."

The earl smiled. "He's showing the plans to Angus." He took another distracted drink. "It's good for him to be involved in something of his own. Since he came back from court, he's been restless. He wants to rejoin the king."

"Should he?"

"If he saw more of the king and less of His Grace's worthless acolytes." He took a larger gulp from the cup. "He should be married. I would give him Dingwall and remove to the old hall at Brecka. It would be good for him."

"Then why don't you?" she asked lightly.

Since Paris and the MacWilliam proposal, Kenneth had been kept deliberately busy and well away from Wester Ross and anywhere else he was likely to run into Guthred's creatures. The country had remained quiet, and, forewarned, the scattered MacHeths had remained alive and free. Guthred, more closely watched than he probably knew, had eventually left Paris with his brother and his tame Irish prince, and returned to Ireland, no doubt to intrigue and fight another day.

"A matter of bride choice," the earl said with a crooked smiled. "Kenneth's and mine rarely overlap. But perhaps your father will talk sense into him. At any rate, I'll go to Brecka next month."

The earl lapsed into silence, and since he seemed to drink more of the soup when he was conversing, Affrica asked lightly, "Is there news? Anything I might do for you at Brecka or elsewhere?"

He smiled before he drank. "You are a good child. Like Angus, I thank God for you every day."

Affrica flushed and shifted uncomfortably. She liked to be busy, needed to be, now that she was too old to fill her days in lessons and playing with Wolf. She always found purpose and, mostly, a sense of contentment, although lately she had thought more about a conversation she had once had with her great-aunt Gormflaith, the Lady of Orkney.

In a moment of reminiscence, Gormflaith had told Affrica how she spent the early years of her adulthood *waiting*. For her father Malcolm MacHeth to be released from prison in Roxburgh; for her brothers to come home from whatever raid they were engaged in on the king's lands; for marriage. In Orkney, Gormflaith had found her purpose and her happiness in life, although she was dead now, poor lady, along with her honorable though turbulent lord.

Affrica did not yearn for marriage, though she had begun to better understand that long ago conversation about waiting.

Fortunately, the earl was still talking. "You knew that Henry of Carron had died?"

"Yes, I visited Deirdre, his widow, before we went westward. She has two little girls and seemed…lost."

"Henry was a good husband to her. She has gone to Henry's people in Normandy."

"In *Normandy*?" she said, startled. "I thought there was little contact between the two branches of the family."

The earl shrugged. "There may be less than she thinks, but she has taken the children with her."

"Why?" Affrica asked blankly. "Surely, she has no need to beg of Henry's family? Carron belongs to her."

"She is not the sort of woman who thrives without a husband. And I gather the available locals don't live up to Henry."

Affrica's lips twitched. "They don't speak French?"

The earl grinned into his cup.

"Still, she cannot have been thinking straight," Affrica said with a frown. "Surely, she should at least have waited a few months until the first grief had passed."

"I expect Carron held too many memories without him."

Visible softness in the earl always took Affrica by surprise, and yet he was no stranger to grief. Or love.

The earl blinked and drank. "But yes, I mention it because Angus should look in on the house and land. She has left a steward, but..."

He broke off as a male voice could be heard shouting in the distance. He sighed. "Perhaps Angus did not like his castle."

"Let Kenneth go back to the court."

"Perhaps I should. If England marches against us this summer, he will want to be fighting..." The earl stirred and fixed her with an unexpectedly clear eye. "Would you like to go to court, Affrica?"

She laughed. "What would I do there?"

"Look after the queen, of course. And be decorative. Learn to tell a good man from a talkative one and give yourself a wider choice."

Affrica regarded him uneasily. "You have thought about this."

"We have been selfish, your father and I, keeping you immured here in Ross."

"I went to Paris," she pointed out, smiling. She could never help smiling whenever Paris was mentioned.

"A treat that was cut short by Donald MacWilliam's spawn. In any case, you were not there to be received by royalty and great families."

"I have no desire to go to court," she said lightly. Hadn't she? Did part of her not long for new people, new, intelligent conversation? To widen her short, closed horizons with new friends, new life? To see how and by whom a *country* was governed?

A door slammed. Kenneth strode furiously through the hall, looking neither right nor left, until he barged out of the far door to the yard.

The earl sighed. Affrica's father followed more slowly and sat on the wooden settle beside her before meeting the earl's interrogative if sardonic gaze.

"He wants me to act less for you," Angus said, "so that he can act more."

"He wants to be head of the family. It will come soon enough."

"What do *you* want, Gilchrist?" Angus asked evenly.

"You and I have steered this course for two decades, ever since Adam died and we pushed the invaders out. It is a good course. But my son is not no one."

Affrica, noting with satisfaction that the earl had drunk all of his nourishing soup, rose and left them. Her task was to cajole Kenneth back into good spirits.

She found him sprawled on a bench beyond the herb garden, glaring over the water of the Cromarty Firth. She sat beside him in silence.

Kenneth had grown into a strong, handsome man, his petulance leavened by occasional humor, his willfulness by basic good nature. Although they had had little enough to do with each other over the years, familiarity had been inevitable through simple proximity. And from that, she supposed, came the same kind of frustrated fondness she felt for her brothers.

After a few moments, he stirred. "Do you never get bored with this place, Affrica?"

"Only when I let myself."

His head turned toward her; his discontented mouth lifted in faint if derisory amusement. "What the devil does a girl find to keep her so damned busy?"

"You'd be surprised." He would. He would also consider what she did to be of no importance. Caring for the people, the sick and the poor, disentangling their daily problems and disputes, aiding their prosperity and well-being rather than his…

"Let's not test me," he sardonically, though his eyes, dark MacHeth eyes, remained steady on her face. "They tell me you are fifteen years old. When did that happen?"

"When I stopped being fourteen."

He grinned. "You always had too ready a tongue. You'll have to watch that when you're married. Or at least your husband will."

"I hope my husband, whoever he turns out be, has enough sense of humor."

"Like me?"

She blinked. "You don't even *hear* most of my jokes."

"More than you think. You've grown into a pretty little thing, you know."

"Kenneth. It's me. Affrica."

He laughed. "I'm not cozening you. It just struck me. You would make a good Lady of Ross."

She stared at him. "How?"

"By marrying me, of course. You could keep bloody Angus off my back to start with."

"But could *bloody Angus* keep *me* off?" she retorted. "Don't be an ass, Kenneth." She stood up. "Go back to the king. It's where you want to be."

⤜⤛

THE FOLLOWING DAY, Affrica and her father rode on to Tirebeck, in time to shelter from two days of massive storms that boiled the sea and felled grown trees. And the following week, with the storm damage dealt with in their own lands, she accompanied her father north to Carron, where he meant to look over the Lady Deirdre's estate at the earl's request.

"You don't need to come," Angus assured her. "There will be little enough for you to do, and my father would like your company."

"He hardly notices me just now," she said. As he often did, her grandfather seemed to have lost all connection to the real world, although physically, he was well enough. "I thought I would call on Father Ruadri at Tain."

"Ask him if he's heard from Ferchar," Angus commanded, as

though that wasn't one of her main reasons for going in the first place. She limited herself to asking every three months, and it was true that only eight weeks had passed since her last visit, so her father had provided the excuse.

Not that she expected anything to have changed. Ferchar had found her crusading uncle, Gregor, and great-uncle Eochaid, and stayed with them. As far as she knew, he had never returned to Paris. A handful of letters had made their way to Tain. A few had come via more devious routes to her father, but those were never discussed with her.

"He is well," was all Angus ever said.

If something in Affrica hadn't blossomed that distant day in Paris, she might have imagined that wonderful afternoon had never been. As it was, she had learned to see their adventure through Ferchar's eyes. He had protected the daughter of his lord by unconventional means, and the genuine fun he had extracted from it was not lost on her. But to Ferchar, who had crammed so much into his years in Paris that he could scarcely have slept—formidable learning, wenching, drinking and, apparently, a little arms training thrown in—the adventure was one of many escapades. Perhaps with a rare edge of seriousness.

But she could not fool herself that to him it had meant anything more. Nor, she hoped, had he any way of knowing that to her, sheltered and lonely, it had been the happiest, most exciting day of her life.

Leaving her at Tain with her woman and a man-at-arms, Angus rode west immediately. "If I don't return by nightfall, stay with Bethoc or at the sanctuary house if it's empty. I'll find you there."

She nodded, impatient to reach the priest's cottage by St. Duthac's Church. The unease was already twisting through her as she made her way through the village. When she reached the path to Rhuadri's house, the blackness seemed to gallop on her, shrouding the watery sun and icing her bones.

She all but threw herself from the horse, abandoning it to her attendants as she hurled herself at the front door. It opened before she reached it. Bethoc, Father Ruadri's housekeeper, stood there, pale and distraught.

"Oh, lady, it's bad. So bad."

The black web around her tightened, swirling, trying to drag her down the spiral of oblivion.

"How bad?" she managed, though even her legs shook as she forced herself over the threshold into what she knew without question was a house of death.

"He was out all the time, during the storms," Bethoc said, all but charging through the main room of the cottage toward the bedchamber at the back. "Never paused to change into dry clothes. *What's the point?* he said, *when I'll just get soaked again?* I'd have been more surprised if he didn't catch a cold, but oh, lady, it only got worse, into his chest, his very lungs..."

By this time, Affrica had finally grasped that the bedchamber ahead was Ruadri's. That the story Bethoc told was Ruadri's. Conflicting emotion swept through her like a tide, unbearable in its intensity, in its dissonance.

The cottage was indeed a house of death. But it was Ruadri who would die. Not Ferchar.

---

SOMEHOW, SHE WALKED through the pain and lowered herself onto the side of the bed next to the sick man. There was water in his lungs. She could hear it bubbling when he breathed.

"Father, the Lady Affrica is here," Bethoc proclaimed with the terrible false cheer of the hopeless sick room. "You know she always makes you feel better. Makes you take your medicine, too!"

Affrica would have thought he didn't hear, for his eyes remained closed, but when she covered his hand with hers, it clasped her fingers, hot yet surprisingly firm.

"It grieves me to see you so ill," she murmured.

His eyes opened. "I'm holding on," he said clearly, "for my son."

"Is Ferchar coming?"

It was Bethoc who answered, a handkerchief to her face. "We've sent for him, lady, but God knows where he is or how long it will take."

"You're exhausted, Bethoc," Affrica said. "Go and rest. I'll sit with him—if you'll let me, Father?"

The priest smiled through a burbling breath. "I will insist, since I'm probably dreaming anyway."

"No, I'm here."

She bathed his hands and his face, helped him drink a little water, and he seemed to fall into sleep.

*Oh, please come home, Ferchar, please, because you will never be free of this if you don't. He needs it, and so do you...*

She sat in the chair that Bethoc had set beside the bed and curled among the cushions to sleep while Ruadri did. She must have drifted off, for when she next opened her eyes, the lamp was lit, and the shutters were closed. Bethoc had clearly been and gone.

"He won't come," Ruadri gasped out. "I drove him away."

"Of course, you did not," she said, distressed because he believed it.

"He is not a priest. It is not in his nature. But I pushed and pushed because I wanted him to have this. St. Duthac's. I wanted to give him something."

"You gave him everything," Affrica said vehemently. "And he knows it."

"And I knew it wasn't enough. I've always known. Ferchar always wanted more. He always will."

"He wanted you to be proud of him," she whispered. "That was one reason he couldn't stop..."

The hot, suffering eyes opened. The lamp's glow emphasized the harsh hollows of his skull. "I *am* proud of him. You will tell him? For doing what he has done, for saving you, for learning, for all of it.... You will...tell him?"

"I will tell him."

His eyes flickered closed again.

Her throat aching, she said, "He is proud of you also. He valued what you did at Tain, was afraid he could never equal your goodness."

Although his eyes didn't open, his lips stretched into an approximation of a smile. "You are good to lie."

"It's the truth," she insisted. "Though he may not recognize it yet. He is young, Father. But he will come home to you, to Tain."

"Not to me. It's too late." His eyes flew open again. "There are letters. In the cabinet beside you. For Ferchar, and for Bishop... and the earl."

"I'll see to them."

His fingers seized hers, and he held her gaze in something very like panic. "And you'll tell him? You'll write to him? You'll *help* him?"

"I will," she whispered, clasping his hand in both of hers while the blinding tears ran down her face like rain. His fingers relaxed, and she heard his awful breathing even into sleep. By the time she could see again, his eyes were open, and his striving breath had stopped.

※

WHEN ANGUS ENTERED the cottage at Tain, he knew of the priest's death, and was sorry for it. Ruadri had been a good man and a caring priest, as well as a conscientious coarb, the keeper of the sanctuary of St. Duthac. But Angus's main concern was that he had let his daughter go alone to deal with it. It was hardly the first death she had encountered, but still, he knew she was fond of Ruadri.

He was not prepared, however, for the white-faced, upright figure who rose from the table, holding a sealed document out to him before she had even greeted him. "Father, you will send this to Ferchar?"

Slowly, Angus took the parchment from her. "I'll send it with my own."

"Father Ruadri asked it of me. His last words."

Angus nodded cautiously and looked about him.

The priest's house was quiet as it had never been. Curiously empty, despite the presence of the people of Tain paying their last respects to the priest who had cared for them, and for all who needed refuge. Was that what his daughter felt?

"Bishop Reinald will put one of his own priests here," she said dully. "It won't be Ferchar."

He stirred. "No, it won't be Ferchar. But the new priest might look after the shrine and spiritual needs while a temporal coarb supervises the girth, the place of sanctuary. That post needn't be religious, so it could be hereditary. Gilchrist will allow it. But Ferchar will need to come home."

She turned away. "He no longer has a reason to come home, and all the guilt in the world to make him stay away."

Angus could not see the reasoning for that, although she was probably right that Ferchar had decided to make soldiering his chosen career. Uneasily aware that she *felt* things he did not, things that he generally did not want to think about, he said only, "Come. We need to go home."

When they eventually reached Tirebeck, the first thing he saw was a letter with a royal seal.

"Brought by a royal messenger," his steward said with awe. "I took it to Adam mac Malcolm, but he said to wait for you, that it wasn't important."

Angus's lips twisted as he took the document. "Not important and not important to my father are two different things." Having no need of clerks to read his letters for him, Angus broke the seal at once and spread the document out on the table. "Is the messenger waiting for an answer?"

"No, he just left again. It isn't...war, is it?"

Angus shook his head impatiently, for although his heart twisted, it was for other reasons entirely. He lifted his gaze to his daughter's distracted face and spoke bluntly to get it over with.

"Her Grace, the queen, requests your presence at court to serve her. You can travel with Kenneth if you wish. Do you want to go?"

A gasp shook her body. That sudden flash of longing hit him like blow. She drew in a steadying breath.

"Yes," she said, breaking his foolish, fatherly heart. "I want to go."

# Chapter Seven

*The North Sea and Edinburgh, summer 1209*

DEIRDRE, THE LADY of Carron, had been at sea for three miserable days before she noticed the other passenger. She had felt too numb and too hopeless to pay attention to her surroundings, beyond wishing the sea would calm so that her daughters and her servants would stop being sick.

When, finally, those simple prayers were answered, she was too exhausted to do more than sleep. And when she woke, the girls were gone.

She sighed, though she didn't really fear for their safety. The sides of the vessel were high and the sea calm. Bridie, the maidservant whose primary duty was their care, was presumably with the children. And the sailors Deirdre had encountered, at least on the outward voyage, had been kind in their rough way. Still, she knew she should be looking after her daughters. Since Henry had died, it was all she knew, all she clung to, although the burden of it seemed impossible.

Incomprehensibly, Henry's family in Normandy hadn't wanted to know them. They didn't care that Henry's flesh and blood were fatherless and alone. In fact, they seemed to have difficulty working out exactly who they were.

She heaved herself off the mattress they had been given in a curtained-off corner below the deck, pleased that she could stand without the ship trying to throw her about. Snatching a shawl, she tied it around her golden hair, fastened her cloak, and emerged from the curtain.

A man sprawled on the nearest bench, his back against the wall, one knee carelessly under his chin. Surrounded by weapons and armor, he appeared to be a soldier, although he had a piece of parchment grasped in his hand and was gazing at it. He radiated violence, roughness, everything she most hated and feared.

Yet when he glanced up, she saw that he was young, probably several years younger than she. He pointed to the ladder. "They went onto the deck."

"Thank you," she murmured hastily, hurrying away from him, and hauled herself up.

The girls and Bridie, the maid, were like completely different people in the sunshine, skipping about the deck with the sea breeze in their hair, and laughter on their lips. Deirdre was conscious of both relief and resentment, though the former won. She went and sat on a bench by the side, and they clustered around her, chattering about food and other passengers and games they had played, and a sailor who had climbed all the way up to the basket balanced precariously at the top of the mast.

She let it all wash over her while the sun warmed her numb skin, and she wondered what on earth she was going to do now. If she were honest, she wasn't quite sure anymore why she had gone to Normandy in the first place. Henry had had closer kin in Scotland, all of whom were happy to help her, though they had land and families of their own.

Well, she still had Carron. It had always been hers. And she had always known that the land would ensure she would marry again, give the girls a father again. And then things would be comfortable.

At least *one* of Henry's distant Norman family had admired her. He had been young and handsome, refined and courtly... and, sadly, married to someone else. There were not many men in Ross like that—educated, French-speaking, courteous. Except the earl and his family, of course, who were too far above her.

Two fellow passengers, merchants by their dress, bowed to her in passing, and she inclined her head. With a jolt, it came to her that she had traveled from home all the way to Normandy. It was hardly impossible for her to spend time in Inverness, Stirling, Dunfermline, Edinburgh. Somewhere, there would be a marriageable man of courtesy and refinement. And then she could relax.

She began to see why everyone had tried to talk her out of going to Normandy so soon. She had not been thinking straight, or she would have seen that there was no point to the foolish journey.

She smiled, laughing at herself. Christina, her eldest, caught her eye and smiled back. And then she saw the young soldier again.

He had emerged onto the deck, without his weapons or armor, his youthful face turned up to the sun, and for some reason, she could not look away. As the merchants passed him, exchanging a greeting, she realized that he was tall. The wind blew at his tunic, for he wore no coat or cloak.

He was not refined. His face was too strong, large-boned, with a hawk-like nose, and long, full lips that were surely more sensual than courtly. For one so young, as she had already noted, he looked rough and violent, the antithesis of the man she sought to replace her Henry.

And yet, as she stared, it struck her that he, too, was vulnerable at this moment. His face was just a little too thin, as though he had been ill or had not eaten enough. She wondered if he had been wounded in battle, if he was going home, and where home was for him. The ship would go as far as Leith, but it would make several stops along the English coast and Northumbria first.

The soldier's head turned, but not to her. He was looking downward at her daughters, who had accosted him. He blinked, as though adjusting his mind to their presence. *Take them away!* Deirdre shouted at Bridie in her mind, and indeed Bridie reached for them, but the soldier's lips moved, addressing the children, who laughed with delight, and his gaze lifted to the maid. Bridie blushed, replying coyly to whatever he had said to her.

The girls laughed again, and without waiting for Bridie, danced back to Deirdre. She thought his gaze flickered over her before he turned back to the sea, but she couldn't be sure.

"Who is he?" she asked Bridie. "The young man the girls accosted."

"Oh, he didn't mind, lady. He was quite friendly."

"A rough soldier," she said discontentedly.

"Not rough," Bridie assured her. "And more of a captain, I'd say. Talks like a gentleman."

"In what language?" Deirdre asked, surprised.

"English. But then, it's an English ship, isn't it? And the girls spoke to him first in that language."

Deirdre cast him another glance and saw that he was again staring at the piece of parchment held by both hands on the rail before him. An idea came to her, born of boredom and inexplicable curiosity.

Having sent the girls below with Bridie to eat, she stood and approached the soldier as though merely following the others. But as she reached him, she paused and said with pretty hesitation, "Your pardon, sir."

She wondered if he had known she was there, for he did not turn with any jolt of surprise. Instead, he straightened and said deliberately, "For what, lady?"

"For my daughters importuning you."

"Hardly that. I didn't mind."

She saw that he didn't. More than that, Bridie was right. His voice was not rough, and he spoke English like a native. "You are very good," she murmured. "Children are difficult to keep busy on a journey."

"I imagine they must be."

There was nothing but politeness in his expression. He showed no inclination whatever to keep her talking. If he had, she would have disdained him, and yet, perversely, his obvious indifference made her desperate.

"Forgive me," she said again. "I could not help noticing that you look frequently at some document. Should you need help reading it, you need only ask."

At that his eyes gleamed, although whether with gratitude or amusement she could not tell. "You are very kind, lady, but that is a service I need ask of no one."

"Oh." Deflated, she nevertheless realized at once that a man who could read was by definition refined, and that now she had no conversational gambit left.

Unexpectedly, he came to her aid. "Am I mistaken in hearing Scotland in your speech, lady?"

"Why, no, you are not mistaken. I am the Lady of Carron in Ross."

"Carron?" he repeated, his eyes sharpening with genuine interest for the first time. "Near Tain?"

"Why, yes," she said, her heart sinking. "Never tell me you know it?"

"I was born and reared in Tain." He bowed. "I am Ferchar Maccintsacairt."

The son of the priest, the coarb, who had kindly advised her to postpone her journey. An old-style priest who had been married, though she could not remember his wife. The son, she very vaguely recalled running wild with other local children. He had gone to the university in Paris and never come home.

His gaze had grown intent, which had the odd effect of depriving her of breath.

"I think I remember you," he said slowly. "Fergus of Carron's daughter. Did you not marry one of de Norman's sons?"

"Henry." She groped for her handkerchief. "He died this winter, just as the first new, green shoots began to speak of spring, which seems so wrong, does it not?"

"It always seems wrong," he said flatly. "I am sorry for his death and your loss, lady. Have you then been on some pilgrimage?"

She smiled ruefully through her tears. "A foolish one. An unworthy one. I took Henry's daughters to meet his family in Normandy. I'm not sure what I wanted or expected from such a meeting, but it was entirely unsatisfactory. I should have stayed at home, not dragged them across the sea among strangers."

"Sometimes," he said after a pause, "the sea and strangers seem to be the only solution. Do you return now to Carron?"

"I suppose I must, if only to make plans. And you, sir? I know your father will be wondrously happy to have you home. He speaks of you often."

Which was when the soldier's eyes closed, however briefly, and she saw that he was not rough at all, but sensitive and in pain. "My father is dead. And I was not there."

There was nothing to do but take his hand in hers, the parchment crinkling and awkward between them. "Grief is eased when borne together," she said in a trembling voice, even while she peeked curiously at the parchment and the creased, half-visible words, *...ever... friend, Affric...Heth.*

A priest's son trained at the finest university in Europe, a courteous man weighed down by grief. One who was on terms of correspondence with the Lady Affrica.

"I thought you were a soldier," she said in wonder at her own stupidity.

"I am. Or at least I was. God knows what I am now." His lips quirked unhappily. "Apart from the temporal coarb of the girth of Tain."

FERCHAR DID NOT think of it at once. Mainly because the woman's intrusion was annoying. The children, even the maid, he could disregard or amuse with little more than a word or a trick. The mother, the dignified Lady of Carron, expected attention when what he needed was peace to rediscover his strength, some kind of stability that had been rocked off its once powerful hinges by the news of his father's death. And God knew he needed both strength *and* stability to face what must be done. To take his father's things, few as they were, yet everyone associated with memories suddenly vivid and painful, and his father's legacy, the sanctuary of Tain.

It was time, more than time, for him to go home.

He had even been on his way when he had run by chance into the MacHeth messenger. How eagerly he'd unsealed the packet for news of home, uncaring then that he had no plan for his future, just a desire, once more, for something new. And for home.

Home had been his father. And Ruadri was dead.

He had nearly turned around and gone straight back to the crusading MacHeths. Except war—or at least *that* war—had turned sour with the sudden coalescing of his doubts during the previous few months. Where was the justice in this cause? Why was he fighting other Christians and a mere handful of Muslims to keep land that was neither holy nor the crusaders' to begin with? Why was he fighting for those who had already betrayed everyone's trust by taking the Christian city of Constantinople rather than Egypt, let alone Jerusalem, which had always been the stated goal of the crusade? Not that he had ever seen the justice in taking the Holy Land if he were honest. He had just been interested in the science of war, in honing his skills with weapons and tactics and strategy. It was the adventure he had loved, not the purpose. Just as, in Paris, it had been the learning, not the purpose of obtaining a degree and a position within the church or state.

He didn't want to turn back, even to Eochaid and Gregor MacHeth, whom he loved as older, wiser brothers. He could not bear to go home. And yet here he was, bound for Scotland and an uncertain future that did not contain the massive, necessary presence of his father.

Home held only grief and old friends he had forgotten. And Affrica MacHeth, who had been the one with his father at the end, where he should have been. Nor could he quite shake off the suspicion, however skeptical, that Affrica knew the depths of the grief he had caused his father by staying away.

*Guilt.*

He had been running headlong into guilt since he had arrived in Paris six years ago, and then he had run *from* it. Now he had to face it, and the wretched woman from Carron would not give him the quiet to prepare. She spoke of her grief, constantly, as though she was the only one ever to suffer it, and of her husband, whose description on her lips bore little resemblance to the amiable, earthy man Ferchar vaguely recalled. She asked intrusive questions about his life in Paris, about his friends in Scotland, even how well he knew the Earl of Ross's family.

Somehow, during the days at sea, barely held patience turned to tolerance and then acceptance. And with the realization that her basic kindness had indeed stabilized him, came gratitude. And, abruptly, out of the blue, another idea, novel and daring.

*I could marry her.*

The thought came to him as the ship eased out of the harbor at Berwick, buffeting this way and that in the wind as the sailors battled with the position of the sail. The town had seemed uneasy, as it often was, the greatest prize in never-ending border wars with England. The captain of their ship had not lingered.

Slowly, Ferchar turned his gaze from the vanishing town to the woman at his side. She was aware of him, of his gaze, for her skin blushed becomingly beneath the veil she wore around her head. She was beautiful, he saw, almost with surprise, and though some years his senior, she could only have been twenty-five or six.

Ferchar was nineteen years old, penniless save for the coin and a meagre share of booty which he had stashed in his chest below deck. And a tiny patch of land in Tain from which he could scratch subsistence in a good year if he worked hard. He had weapons and armor, experience in war, and considerable learning. He had skills but no kin to use them or sponsor him to great positions. He could, finally, go the bishop, hat-in-hand. Or to the Earl of Ross who would give him some kind of position. He could, perhaps, rise in time to captain the earl's host, except there were swarms of lesser MacHeths, younger sons and nephews and cousins, who would be before him in any contest for command.

Without kin, without decent land, he would always struggle to rise, to make his father posthumously proud.

The Lady Deirdre said nervously, "Why are you looking at me like that?"

Feeling his way, Ferchar took her gloved hand, the first move he had ever made to touch her, although she had often touched him, light pats that he had to steel himself not to shake off. What had been the matter with him?

"I was just thinking," he said with truth, "how glad I am to have met you on this journey. How kind and patient you have been with my…detachment."

"You have been kind also," she said with a hint of breathlessness. "To my daughters and to me, providing us with your protection onboard this ship."

He wanted to laugh suddenly because she hardly needed protection from two merchants and a few respectful sailors. This was not exactly a pirate ship or one full of rough soldiers desperate for women. Though now he thought of it, female companionship of that sort would be hugely welcome to *him*.

He smiled with self-deprecating mockery as he bent and lightly kissed her hand. Her glove pushed delicately against his lips, and with a surge of triumph, he knew he was right. She wanted him.

Deirdre had land, close to Tain. And if her land could be his, he would be noble and could begin something great.

He meant only to think about it, to mull the possibilities for later, but she turned into him, standing too close so that the softness of her breast pressed against his arm. Physical desire swept him up, tangled with yearning of other kinds, for newness, as always, and for the possibilities her standing could bring. She gazed at him with such flattering need, and she was lovely…

"It is a particular joy to me," she almost whispered, as though taking her courage in both hands, "at this sad time in my life, to encounter so unexpectedly, a man of such courtesy and refinement."

A quick glance showed him only a few sailors on deck, busy with the sail and paying the passengers no attention. When she lifted her face to his in mute invitation, he only hesitated a moment before he gave in to the clamorings of his body and kissed her.

By the time the ship came into Leith, he knew she was his.

⇛⇚

To Ferchar's astonishment, he did not have to coax her to marriage. He had assumed the loneliness of widowhood weighed heavily upon her and that she wanted his physical attentions, that it would be up to him to make those attentions so enjoyable as to be indispensable. But it seemed the lady was virtuous as well as urgent, and before he bedded her, they were married quickly and quietly the day after they landed.

The day after that, as a married man, he walked up to Edinburgh in search of accommodation for his new family. His bride desired to spend some time in the town before heading north to Ross, and with that, Ferchar could have no quibble.

Until he saw the troops marching out of the castle in a long, glistening column that prickled with pikes and lances, flanked by knights on restive, skittish horses. Royal banners and those of the other great families of Scotland ruffled in the wind, and Ferchar knew this was more than the king moving his residence for the next few weeks.

This was an army going to war.

"Ferchar? Ferchar, it *is* you!"

A man in half-armor loped over from a row of wains being loaded with supplies of animals, grain, leather, and steel. He seemed quite delighted to see Ferchar, who, grasped by both shoulders, gazed at him for a long, blank moment.

Ferchar's breath caught. "*Lulach?*" Lulach, his old childhood friend who had once sat on the church roof at Tain, hurling apples at the MacHeth boys. And then yelling in fury as the same MacHeth boys had done their best to beat Ferchar to a similar pulpy substance as that which littered the yard.

Lulach laughed. "Of course, it's me! Are you coming to fight?"

His discontent fled in an instant. "Fight whom? Where?"

"You really have been away, haven't you?" Lulach said jovially. "Well, the English are marching on Northumbria, and we're off to kick them out and back over their own border! Are you coming?"

The answer was never really in doubt.

# Chapter Eight

*Edinburgh, summer-autumn 1209*

AFFRICA'S DUTIES AS lady-in-waiting to Ermengarde, the Queen of Scots, were not arduous. Most difficult was remembering her own appearance so that she did not disgrace the Lady of Scotland. On her second day, when she had entered the queen's chamber, Her Grace had stared at her. "You look like a kitchen maid who has slept in her clothes. Again. Wake up, girl, and return properly dressed."

Her cheeks flaming under the French-accented rebuke, Affrica had bowed from the presence while the other ladies had giggled and watched her departure with glee or sympathy, according to their character. Only the Lady Marjorie of Buchan had slipped out after her and caught up with her before she reached her own small chamber.

"We are the setting for the central jewel that is our queen," Marjorie had said, taking her arm with a quick grin. "Don't feel bad. She tells us all off when she is in a mood, and you will outshine us all with just a little care. I should have warned you. Or one of us should."

"It would have made no difference," Affrica had confessed. "I never pay attention to what I wear or how I look."

"From now on, you do," Marjorie had said, throwing open the chamber door. "I will help you until you're comfortable."

Affrica, who hadn't imagined ever being comfortable with making herself a decorative setting for anyone, quickly found it became second nature. All it took, really, was a few, simple tasks. She kept her gowns and coats ironed, her hair washed, anointed, and brushed until it shone. She learned to match her dress with discreet jewels in the daytime, and in the evenings, to choose something bolder. She even discovered that attention to the smallest details of grooming made a difference to her appearance—like softening the skin of her hands and face with oils, taking a tiny brush to her eyelashes, and better defining the arch of her eyebrows with a few deft plucks of the tweezers.

She eschewed the heavy perfumes that most of the court employed and that tended to give her headaches. Until by chance, she came across a delightfully soft, light scent in a market stall. It smelled of Ross in summer, of flowers on the breeze and rain in the hills. And foolishly, tears sprang to her eyes. On impulse, she had spent precious coin on it and had worn it sparingly. She thought no one noticed until she caught one of the queen's gentlemen *sniffing* her. And when she glared at him in outrage, he only smiled with heat in his eyes and asked her to dance.

Affrica snorted with laughter as she relayed the story to Marjorie of Buchan. "The truly annoying thing is that I have grown used to the scent of it, and now I shall have to stop wearing it."

"You shall not," Marjorie declared. "It is *you*, and you are winning quite the court within the court, which can only be good."

*Am I?* "How?" Affrica asked dubiously. Marjorie was only a year or so older, but in such matters as these, she seemed lifetimes ahead of Affrica.

Marjorie sighed. "You and I will make dynastically important marriages. We are tools of alliance. *But*...we can be more. We can be an enticement, the honey that sweetens the meal. And that is also what gives us power within the marriage."

Affrica's lips quirked. "So, if I smell well enough that I don't give my husband a headache, I can lead him around by the nose and make my cousin the earl proud?"

"In a nutshell."

Affrica regarded her with curiosity. "You welcome such a fate?"

"I do, for it is the only way for women like us to make even limited choices. We have to go to our fate, but we can control how we manage it."

Affrica considered. "You are an earl's daughter. His heir. Whoever marries you will be the Earl of Buchan. My father is only an earl's cousin, and though he is not a poor man, he has sons also."

"It makes you no less valuable," Marjorie insisted. "Since the earl has no daughters, and your sisters are all married, *you* are now the family's best enticement to alliance."

"Then God help the MacHeths."

Marjorie laughed, and Affrica thrust the conversation aside. But it came back to her periodically as she drifted through the days and evenings at court, and she saw that Marjorie was right. The courtier who had sniffed her was not the only man who looked at her with covetous eyes.

After the first realization, it didn't even make her uncomfortable. Very subtly, she experimented with looks and smiles—flirting, she realized, trying not to laugh—while they talked to her, and she discovered how best and how easily to distract them. Not that she changed the style of her conversation. She doubted she would have known how.

"You are popular," Kenneth said to her the night before he left for Berwick with the king. "I am besieged by men asking to be introduced to you." His eyes raked her critically. "And I have to say, I've begun to understand why. You don't look much like the hoyden tumbling around Ross with that great, dirty dog."

"He is not dirty," said Affrica, who missed Wolf almost as much as her father and grandfather, and her annoying brothers, and Sinead, and... She swallowed. "You will take care with the king and come safely back."

"After giving His Grace of England a pasting," Kenneth said cheerfully.

One did not, of course, give the King of England a pasting very easily, and once the army had departed for Berwick, a distinct knot formed in Affrica's stomach. William the Lion, King of Scots, was old, no longer the force he had once been. And he had misjudged the English and his own strength before. It had led to a humiliating twenty years of subjection to King Henry of England. Affrica feared for King William, for his army, for Kenneth and the other soldiers in his train. Everything could go horribly wrong. Not that she dreamed like her grandfather was probably dreaming back at Tirebeck. But she *felt*. The knot in her stomach grew, not just with dread but with some strange, incomprehensible excitement.

The queen was uneasy, too. Much younger than her husband, French by birth though very distantly related to King John, she drove her husband's officials to fury by interfering in domestic government and spent much more time with her children. And she needed to be constantly entertained. Affrica read for her and played the harp. She and Marjorie talked to her for hours, sometimes on learned matters of religion or history, sometimes mere witty banter or empty chatter, though all of it was exhausting in its intensity.

They dined with guests every evening, although the male compliment was depleted, and there was often had music and dancing afterward. In fact, it was one such evening when, out of the blue, her father appeared.

Affrica and the other ladies accompanying the queen had just walked into the little ante chamber off the dining room to greet the evening's guests. By then, she had learned how to smile vaguely at no one in particular, to give the impression of gracious contentment that the queen wished to convey.

"Affrica," the queen said with unusual smugness, and Affrica hastily followed her mistress's gaze to the man just rising from his bow.

She had time to realize that the queen had known he was in Edinburgh and had chosen to give her a surprise, like a gift. And then she had hurled herself into his arms as though she were a child again, uncaring how or why he was here, just that he was.

Her father laughed. "I never hoped for such a welcome! Certainly not before I had greeted Her Grace, the queen!"

Still, she felt the strength of his embrace before she stepped back, blushing and apologizing.

"There, we all appreciate family affection," the queen said indulgently, holding out her hand. "My Lord Angus, you are welcome. And we thank you for the loan of your charming daughter."

Angus knelt to kiss her hand. "I thank you for your care of her." He rose, and after a moment's more conversation, bowed and stood aside. "Allow me to present to Your Grace the Lady of Carron in Ross. Her husband is in the south with the king's army."

Taken by surprise once more, Affrica saw Deirdre curtsey and accept the queen's gracious welcome.

"I thought she went to Normandy," Affrica murmured to her father. "But she has another husband already?"

"She has," Angus replied with a smile in his voice, "and you'll never guess who." He broke off as Deirdre of Carron joined them. "Lady, I'm sure you recall my daughter, Affrica."

"Of course." Deirdre smiled dazzlingly. "And court life clearly suits you, my lady. You must find it a huge change from the rigors of Ross."

"Yes," Affrica admitted. She accepted a cup of wine from the servant. "And I'm glad to see *you* looking so well. What brings you to Edinburgh?"

Deirdre took a sip of her own wine, while Angus returned to the queen's side. "My husband and I were on our way home when he felt compelled to join the king. So, I wait here for him. By purest chance I ran into Lord Angus this afternoon, and he invited me to be presented to the queen."

"Then you went to Henry's family? Did you marry again in Normandy? In France, perhaps?"

Deirdre smiled. "That is the silly thing. Everyone advised me not to go to Normandy so soon after Henry's death, and of course they were right. If I had waited another few weeks, I should have known not to go. Such a silly waste of time and trouble."

Affrica raised one humorous eyebrow. "Apart, one assumes, from your marriage."

"Oh, apart from that," Deirdre agreed, her eyes sparkling. "For I married a Scotsman in the end—in Leith only a few weeks ago."

"I am very happy for you," Affrica said politely.

"My daughters adore him, and he is a wonderful father to them. A man of great courtesy and refinement and, I believe, a friend of yours."

"Oh?" Affrica, in fact, was more interested in the health of the earl and the other news Angus would have brought from Ross. "Tease me no longer, if you please. Who is this paragon of a husband?"

Deirdre beamed. "Ferchar of Tain. Now of Carron."

Affrica's wandering gaze flew back to hers with a crash. "*Ferchar?* Ferchar came home?" Some tension she hadn't even been aware of seemed to release with a whoosh of relief. *He did come, he did...* She didn't know whether to laugh or to cry, because only a couple of months earlier would have meant so much to both his father and himself. In this company, she could only smile while delight and excitement swamped her.

"We met onboard the ship coming home," Deirdre was saying. "We married the day after we landed. The day after that, he installed us in a house close to the castle, and the following day rode south after the army."

Laughter bubbled up. "That sounds like Ferchar! Never still. How is he?"

She looked surprised. "Is he not in correspondence with you, lady?"

"Lord, no."

"Oh. It's just... I saw a letter you had written him."

Affrica cast her a closer glance, but there appeared to be no foolish jealousy or any other hidden emotion behind her words. Just a disappointment which rang oddly in Affrica's ears. "I told him of his father's death."

Deirdre nodded, almost as though uninterested, and said nothing more.

So, Affrica asked again, "How is he?"

"Well." Deirdre smiled. "It is so comfortable to have a husband again."

Affrica regarded her. "Comfortable? Are you sure you married Ferchar Maccintsacairt?"

"He does not care for that name, and of course, I am sure."

"Don't be offended," Affrica said with a quick smile. "It was only a joke because I don't recall Ferchar ever being a comfortable companion! But we all grow up. You will excuse me? The queen summons me."

⸻

BY THE TIME she sat down to dinner, Affrica realized she now had to worry about Ferchar as well as Kenneth and his men of Ross. Was Ferchar under Kenneth's command? He should be, she supposed, and yet she could not imagine it. But other questions took priority as soon as her father gave her his attention.

"How is the earl?" she asked.

"No better, but I think no worse. The king summoned him to help guard the queen and the children, but he could not travel."

"So, you came instead. I am glad of that at least. And all is...quiet in Ross?"

He knew she was asking about the coasts, if there were any signs that Guthred MacWilliam might take advantage of the crisis in Northumbria to invade. "Ranald and your brothers are keeping a close watch."

"The men must be stretched thin for such a huge task, with Kenneth's host in Northumbria, yours here with the queen…"

"We should manage. There is no movement from Ireland or the Isles. The men will be harvesting and unwilling to fight."

*Like ours.* Still, the earl and her father had spies everywhere. And this was a dangerous subject for the dinner table. She nodded further down the table to where Deirdre sat beside a very young courtier. "And what of Deirdre's sudden marriage? To Ferchar, whom she finds *comfortable!*"

He cast her a glance. "Do you mind?"

Affrica blinked. "Mind?"

"About his marriage. I know he made an impression on you, that you might have imagined a bond that could not be there."

A peel of laughter escaped her. "Not *that* kind of bond," she said with derision, and yet as her mind veered hastily away from any such ridiculous idea, a fresh knot tugged at her stomach. "But at least I know him well enough to realize he is not a comfortable person. My worry for Deirdre is that she doesn't know him at all."

"Or you don't," Angus said, lifting his cup. "Everyone grows up, Affrica."

"I know." She just hoped Ferchar hadn't grown too staid, for she dearly longed for a taste of the wild fun of Paris. Just to see him again, to know he was well and happy with his bride and new daughters. That the guilt over his father did not consume him.

He had come home.

LONG BEFORE THE king's return to Edinburgh, everyone knew that his cause had not prospered in Northumbria, which had been lost in its entirety and in perpetuity, so it was said, to the English. Rumors abounded about the terms of peace William the Lion had been forced to accept. Some whispered about previous occasions when King William had underestimated the English, and it had never worked out well for Scotland. Everyone recalled, but didn't speak of, the humiliating decades following the Treaty of Falaise when, thanks to William's carelessness in getting captured in battle, Scotland had had to place itself under England's thumb. William had wriggled out from under that burden in time and at some cost. Now, even the Scottish church was no longer subject to an archbishop in York, only to the Pope in Rome.

But now it seemed those dark days could come back. As the days grew shorter and cooler, Edinburgh waited with eagerness and fear for the return of the king. Affrica thought it ominous that no messenger came to the queen.

When, at last, the king rode into the town with his troops, the cheers of the populace were muted by unease. Affrica, watching him intently, thought his once vigorous figure somehow diminished, and knew it boded ill. Even so, she was not prepared, an hour later, for the screams of the queen.

⸻

"THE KING GAVE his two eldest daughters as hostages to the English," Affrica said flatly to Angus and Kenneth when she managed to visit her father's lodgings and found them both there.

"He had no choice," Kenneth said. "And at least it was only the princesses Margaret and Isabel, not Prince Alexander."

She stared at him. "Do you imagine that makes it more acceptable to the queen?"

"No," Angus said, "but rightly or wrongly, it does make it more acceptable to the country. The King of England will have control of their marriages, so he'll try to bind Scotland closer. But as long as Alexander lives, we have a king and a free country."

"And the queen loses her daughters to John of England. Would you give *me* to such a man?"

Angus shrugged impatiently. "I am not the king. And though my ancestors might turn in their graves to hear me say so, I thank God for it."

Affrica scowled at him, and then at Kenneth. "You look well and unhurt," she said grudgingly. "I am glad of that, at least."

"I can tell you are jumping with joy," he said sardonically. "Underneath."

She ignored him. "Is Ferchar Maccintsacairt with you?"

"Lord, no. He's playing messenger boy for the king somewhere. Still," he added thoughtfully, blissfully unaware of Affrica's disappointment, "he can fight these days and knows no fear. I'll give him that." He grinned. "And damned if he hasn't beaten us all to the altar. Decent marriage, too, for a priest's son. You must introduce me to his poor wife."

"She would like that," Affrica said with just a trace of malice.

Nevertheless, she found that she was annoyed with Ferchar on his neglected wife's behalf. And on her own, for in this mess of tragedy and discomfort, all that could have made it bearable was the return of her friend.

But when he did finally return, she was not so sure of that either.

# Chapter Nine

*Edinburgh, Dunfermline, and Ross, autumn 1209*

THE YOUNG PRINCESSES left the castle with their entourage, escorted south by the stiff-backed English commissioners, who had to be protected by the king's soldiers from the angry populace.

The queen, wan and listless, saw nobody but her ladies. The king, loud and furious with shame, was already plotting how to get his daughters back. After all, in the past, he'd got Scotland back. He'd got the church back. But time was no longer on his side.

The royal couple, determinedly depriving each other of the comfort they might have found together, were not speaking.

"My lady," Affrica said to her in desperation one day, "you could not prevent their departure, but you are not without influence in England. You can make plain your views with regard to their care in the south, act in mediation to help the king reverse this."

Queen Ermengarde glared at her and waved a dismissive hand, though a more thoughtful look seemed to have pierced her grief.

Meanwhile, the king had had enough of gloom. Like a whirlwind, he swept the entire court, including any of the queen's ladies who didn't hide in time, into a massive hawking expedition. Which at least gave Affrica the opportunity to ride beside her father.

Grim-faced on the fringes, Angus clearly did not want to be there.

He wanted to return to Ross and needed the king's permission. Affrica felt she should be with the queen. Kenneth, on the other hand, was in the thick of things, eager to show off his big, fierce new bird chained to his falconer's wrist.

"He is high in the king's favor," Affrica observed.

"Not as high as he thinks. Since he will be the next Earl of Ross, it behooves the king to keep him close."

"But Kenneth likes being at the center of power," Affrica pointed out. "He could become a great man at court."

Angus's smile was crooked. "If his surname were not MacHeth."

"So is yours." She frowned. "The king summoned you here to protect the queen."

"He summoned Gilchrist, the Earl of Ross. To forestall us fomenting trouble in Ross while he was engaged elsewhere."

"But you wouldn't! The earl wouldn't."

"No, but the king is never sure of that. Previous generations have made the MacHeth name synonymous with rebellion. And it would not surprise me," Angus added, lowering his voice, "if word reached him somehow of my meeting in Paris with Guthred MacWilliam."

Her stomach twisted. "Is that why I am here, too? A hostage in a gilded cage?"

"The king might imagine you are."

"And Kenneth…" She gazed ahead at the gaggle of boisterous young men around the king. "He is binding Kenneth to him."

"So far as he can."

Affrica shivered. She had enjoyed being at court—the company, the music, the witty banter, and the learned conversation of visiting scholars. She had grown fond of the queen and even pitied the king his impossible decisions. But now she pitied him more for the thousands of threads he had to hold together, of loyalty and suspicion and force, just to keep his kingdom whole. And that was before he dealt with the outside threats.

"Why would anyone want to be king?" she blurted.

"Power," Angus said. "Some men thrive on it. Some women, too."

She opened her mouth to argue, but in the end, she couldn't. Her own family wielded power in Ross that was as absolute as they chose to make it. They regarded such authority as their right, and they would not give it up to anyone. In the past, in her grandfather's youth, they had sought more, the kingdom itself, for, further back, their line had held that power, too.

As they pressed forward to catch up with the royal party, now ambling up the slope of Blackford Hill, she realized more. That even wielding no power, just being close to the center of it, was beguiling, too. For her as much as for Kenneth.

The day was bright and crisp, the best kind that autumn could bring—the warning nip in the breeze, the reds and golds and browns of the falling leaves surrounding them and the woods beyond. A nearby stream glistened in the sunshine, trickling its way downhill. In the distance, beyond the mighty Edinburgh Castle, the Firth of Forth gleamed a deeper blue than the sky, allowing clear views across to Fife.

The king flew his falcon, sending it soaring upward to find and target its prey and swoop downward for the kill.

The court applauded, and the lesser hawks were allowed to try their skills.

"You don't indulge in hawking, Lord Angus?" the king asked, approaching him unexpectedly.

"At home I do," Angus replied. "I did not bring any birds with me, but I'm content to admire the skills of others."

"Sire," someone said urgently. "A horseman approaches from the north. Riding fast, straight toward us."

"Messenger?" the king barked.

"Not obviously."

Without orders, everyone moved as though in some rehearsed,

complicated dance, the men closing in on the king, casually surrounding him.

For Affrica, the world suddenly tilted, not in fear of one man, but in some shadowy dream that was almost memory. *Which of you is the Lady de Lanson?* The distant voice echoed in her head, almost drowned out by the noise of a battle and the whimpering of the women who surrounded her.

Her horse moved beneath her, restive, and she realized she was gripping the reins too tightly. With an effort, she relaxed her hands and blinked away the inconvenient vision. There was no battle, and she was not surrounded by women but by the men protecting their king, who included her own father and her cousin Kenneth.

Her heart thudded in her breast, for such waking dreams were rare for her and left her disoriented and uncomfortable, and wary in the extreme of the horseman she glimpsed between the hunters' shoulders.

He galloped over the breast of the hill and straight toward them. Just a little too close, he reined in his mount with one deft hand. The horse danced a little, but he held it firmly. His light, plain cloak hung from one shoulder, revealing that he was armed to the teeth with sword and daggers, bow and quiver. Yet he sat at ease in the saddle, facing the hostile force in silence.

Slowly, he reached up and removed his hat, and Affrica saw with a relief she didn't yet understand that he was young and...

"Sire. I understood you sent for me." The low, deep voice, tinged with genuine amusement and absolutely no fear, carried clearly to the king, and straight into Affrica's heart, which soared with shock and laughter.

"*Ferchar!*" exclaimed the king. "Get over here and forgive my brave warriors. They are as jumpy as old women watching for rain on wash day. As for you, you're late."

"Your Grace's pardon," said this new Ferchar without noticeable apology. He walked his horse forward through the throng. Men and mounts scattered from his path, some with reluctance, while Affrica drank him in with unnoticed curiosity.

The big, half-wild youth she had last seen two and a half years ago had reached manhood with a vengeance. Not yet twenty years old, he rode with all the poise of a mature nobleman and the self-discipline of a soldier. Still clean-shaven, his large-boned face would never be conventionally handsome, and yet his features had grown together and smoothed somehow into a dramatic, oddly attractive visage. Like in Paris, only…*more*.

When he halted and bowed to the king, it was with an elegance she would have imagined impossible in the clumsy boy who clambered onto the church roof at Tain. Nor was this self-assurance studied, as it had *almost* been in Paris. Now, it was merely the natural grace of a man in control of his body, of which he was in complete and probably lethal understanding.

In gawping, she missed the few words of greeting between the king and Ferchar, though her attention snapped back when William said casually, "You will recall Lord Angus of Ross."

The hairs on her neck stood up, because she saw now that her father was right in his suspicions. The king *was* watching, smiling yet unblinking, as Ferchar turned to Angus. There was warmth in the hazel eyes she remembered so well, and a genuine smile on his long lips as he bowed to her father. "Of course, I do. I have been away too long."

"And his beauteous daughter, of course," the king added before Angus could speak.

She forced her hands to be still as Ferchar's gaze swept over her and over Marjorie of Buchan and the other ladies who had appeared miraculously around them. Looking, no doubt, for the "beauteous" one. The thought made her lips twitch and abruptly, the hazel gaze came back to her and smiled.

"*Affrica.*"

She never knew if he had said the name aloud, or if she imagined it, just that his instant of attention was dragged away by the king, and the whole group changed shape again, leaving her inexplicably shaken.

Kenneth and a couple of his friends were between them, talking hawks.

"What do you think?" Kenneth asked Ferchar, raising his thickly gloved hand where his new falcon perched, eating from his arm its share of the prey it had just killed.

"It's big," Ferchar said.

Kenneth smiled, his teasing smile, only half-malicious. "Want to try him?" He moved his arm next to Ferchar's as though to encourage the bird to change perches to a very unprotected arm—which it was unlikely to do while it was still eating off Kenneth's. Still, everyone seemed to be watching avidly to see if the newcomer would be brave enough or foolish enough to have skin rent by those ferocious claws.

Ferchar did not move. The bird, having finished its meal, straightened.

Kenneth's smile broadened. "Or shall I give little Affrica a turn instead?"

The taunt was clear, and inevitably someone tittered, while the eyes of the two men met and held.

"Oh, *little Affrica*, certainly," Ferchar said at once. "If someone will lend the lady a glove."

She would have turned the suggestion graciously aside, except for her annoyance at Kenneth's disparaging "little Affrica." Although she had been hawking with her father and her cousin the earl, she had ambiguous feelings for such sport. She loved the power of the falcons, their beauty in flight and pure instincts to prey. She admired the skill involved in training the creatures. But she disliked the gore and the avid, pitiless rending of flesh.

"Will you?" Marjorie murmured excitedly beside her.

"Why not?" Affrica said carelessly and looked around to see who would be first to offer her a glove. Several noblemen, whose birds were with their falconers, competed to reach her first. Without looking at Ferchar or Kenneth or even registering the donor, she took a proffered glove with a smile of thanks and turned expectantly to Kenneth.

Characteristically, her cousin was annoyed. His only intention had been a mild jibe at Ferchar's lack of a nobleman's skills. He hadn't actually meant to lend anyone his falcon and now had no choice.

*Ha*, thought Affrica unkindly as the bird was hooded and chained and enticed to flap onto her borrowed glove. It was heavier than any she'd flown in Ross. Averting her gaze from its still bloody claws, she gave it time to settle, then nodded to the falconer to remove the hood once more.

Along with the rest of the king's court, the bird looked about it, fixed its gaze and flew, its weight jolting her arm. She kept her face serene and her gaze upward, as though pleased to see it rend and kill for her. Her left hand tightened again on the reins, and her horse danced backward in annoyance. Hastily, she relaxed her hold, murmured something soothing. Everyone else's attention was fixed on Kenneth's falcon, which had swooped unerringly on its prey. Only Ferchar's gaze might have grazed her face. What did he see?

"Where is it going?" someone asked, amused, for, far from coming back with its catch, the bird was dropping down toward the forest.

"Damn it, Affrica," Kenneth fumed.

"You shouldn't have let anyone else fly the bird when it's so new to you," Sir William Comyn observed.

"It might just be taking a long way back," Affrica said hopefully.

"Over the treetops," Ferchar murmured, and she wondered if he was remembering the rooftops of Paris. She could not quite bring herself to look and see, though she didn't know why, just that his voice thrilled down her spine like music sometimes did. And her heart beat and beat with some strange, new awareness.

⋙⋘

Having done the king's bidding and reported to him all he had managed to survey of the English troops and fortifications in Northumbria, Ferchar was anxious to be home to Ross. The king, however, kept him kicking his heels in Edinburgh, allowing him home to his wife that night but summoning him to the castle again the following afternoon, though for what reason, he could not discover—until he was sent to the queen.

"You are a glorified messenger boy," Sir William Comyn, the Justiciar of Scotland, told him in malicious amusement "Comely enough to appeal to the queen."

Ferchar bowed ironically.

"And unknown to her," Kenneth MacHeth added. "So, you are not too much associated in her mind with His Grace and the loss of her daughters."

"You are, in effect, much more than the bearer of the king's news," Sir William added. "You are the mender of the king's marriage."

"Then I am doomed," Ferchar said—which might just see him banished to Ross and the rescue his own marriage.

Thrusting Deirdre from his mind, he found his way to the queen's apartments, where the smells of good food made his stomach rumble. He was taken directly to an antechamber crowded with people and beckoned imperiously to the royal side.

"I don't know you," uttered the angry lady who was his queen.

"No, Your Grace." He bowed. "My name is Ferchar, of Carron in Ross, and the king sent me to tell you he intends to depart for Dunfermline two days hence."

Her sudden dismissive hand gesture looked involuntary and turned out not to be aimed at him, for while some of her ladies tittered, presumably at his bluntness, the queen said, "And do you go with His Grace, Ferchar of Carron?"

"I plan to go on to Ross, if the king permits."

"The court does not please you?"

"I am no courtier, as Your Grace has discovered. I am a mere soldier."

Her lips twitched. "Of course. Ross, you say? Another MacHeth, like the Lady Affrica, who serves me?"

For some reason, the discovery that Affrica MacHeth was at court had astonished him. Though it shouldn't, for she must have been almost sixteen and could not remain a tomboy forever. In fact, his brief glimpses of her at the hawking had revealed her to be surprisingly elegant as well as adult. And brave about Kenneth's bloody falcon. A quick glance about the room showed him, disappointingly, that was Affrica was not present.

"No, Your Grace, I am not so exalted."

"Not so humble as you pretend either, are you?"

He smiled. "Force of habit, lady."

"Then you may join us for dinner since we have a spare place."

There was no way out of it since the king had not commanded his immediate return. He didn't even know if Deirdre would be annoyed by his absence or delighted by the queen's notice. He could only bow his thanks, and certainly his stomach appreciated the invitation.

An inner door opened, and a dazzling young lady darted into the room in a glittering mist of jet-black hair and shimmering golden silk. The wild locks once stuffed under a boy's cap had been artfully tamed with combs and a wispy veil. Dainty splashes of gold and emerald dangled from her ears and clung to her slender throat.

He wanted to smile because she was not merely grown up and elegant. She was lovely.

"May we go in to dinner now, Affrica?" the queen asked with heavy irony.

"Sorry, Your Grace," Affrica said humbly, dipping a courtesy along with a quick, unexpectedly sweet smile.

*She likes her.* But then, Affrica liked everyone, even him. Her eyes widened as they caught him. He thought, intriguingly, that she might even have begun to blush, though, to his annoyance, the queen distracted him before he could be sure.

"Your arm, sir."

It seemed he was to have the honor of escorting the queen to the dining room. As he left, he was aware that behind him, at least two men were competing to take Affrica.

⟫⟪

THE FOOD WAS excellent, and the event not nearly as tense as he expected when presided over by an angry, grieving queen. Her Grace, however, seemed willing to be entertained by the banter of her courtiers.

As Ferchar always did in new situations, he watched and learned. He allowed his tongue to loosen only gradually, letting wit and humor to find a level that was entertaining as well as acceptable. And the queen was unexpectedly charming.

On his other side, the Lady Marjorie of Buchan helped with his education. Bright eyed and pretty, she was happy to explain everyone to him in a way that was informative and amusing.

"And, of course, you already know my friend, the Lady Affrica," she said at last.

"When she was a child," Ferchar said. She was not a child now. She was listening with dancing eyes to the nonsense of the young nobleman beside her, not remotely put-out by his flirting. In fact, she actually flirted back, however decorously. He would have laughed with delight except that he was too surprised, and yet impressed, because she kept it so light, and turned frequently to the older gentleman on her other side who conversed with her in obvious pleasure.

"You find her much changed?" Marjorie asked guilelessly.

"I hardly know. She doesn't have a dog with her at court, does she?"

"Wolf's in Ross," Affrica said, missing barely a beat of her own conversation.

Marjorie laughed. Ferchar didn't, but for some reason, his heart warmed because, all appearances to the contrary, Affrica was paying enough attention to him to hear.

When the meal was cleared away, the queen lingered, demanding music and poetry. The wine flowed again, and Ferchar enjoyed interesting conversations with several people and flirted elegantly with Marjorie of Buchan. From time to time, he was sure he felt Affrica's gaze at least glancing off him, but she never approached him, and that caused him an unexpected pang. The old Affrica, the child Affrica, would have bounced up to him, chattering and questioning, her eyes bright with friendly interest.

His gaze followed her to the harp, which she went to play at the queen's command. Her eyes were no longer childishly bright, they were large and luminous and brilliant, which should have been impossible when they were so meltingly dark. The soft curve of her neck was beguiling, her definite womanly shape a discreet delight as her breast rose and fell and her slender fingers placed themselves delicately upon the harp strings.

Laughter tugged at his breath once more as he wondered if she could actually play the wretched instrument, and he looked hastily back at his companions to distract himself.

It was a long time before he could make himself look again, for she *could* play. Of course, she could. The great Muiredach's son, a respected musician in his own right, had probably taught her. It didn't matter. Her music raised the hairs on his neck, stole their way inside him, and seemed to bind around him every tragedy and every joy he had ever felt, turning them into a lump in his throat that he feared he could never dislodge.

He did, with difficulty, once the harp was silent. And when she was begged by many voices for more, he was better prepared. He could smile, even turn and watch her admiringly, while conversing with others.

Her companion from dinner joined her at the harp as the piece came to a close. Her hands, graceful as the wings of a bird, lifted from the strings and descended to her lap. It came to him that this was not really a game, this waiting to see how long it would take her to come to him. *If* she would. There were things he had to say to her.

When he could excuse himself, she had a different male companion, although she still sat by the table with the now silent harp. As he approached, a delicate flush rose beneath her creamy skin, either because of her companion's compliments or because she knew Ferchar was coming. Perhaps he imagined, too, that it took courage for her to raise her eyes to his face, for surely, he had never been frightening to her.

But she smiled, once more the familiar, friendly Affrica he knew. "Ferchar. I haven't driven you away, after all."

"Hardly. I came to ask if you also sing."

"Not where anyone can hear me." Although her expression was humorous, he thought it was probably true. He would make a point of hearing her sing one day.

Marjorie of Buchan swept by, not to corner him again, but to sweep away Affrica's admirer.

And now, it seemed, she had nothing to say. And he didn't know where to start.

Almost in desperation, he leaned over to touch one of the harp strings and drew in a breath. "I have to thank you," he said abruptly.

Her eyebrows, perfectly arched, flew up. "Why?"

"For being with my father when he died, when I was not. For writing to me."

Her eyelids drooped, perfect almonds. Her black lashes fanned against her cheek. With a whirl of impatience, she tugged her skirts aside, revealing a stool, which she kicked wordlessly toward him.

His lips twitched with appreciation. Hiding the stool was clearly how she discouraged her admirers from staying too long. As he sat beside her, he positioned his head to block his face and hers from the rest of the room.

"You were kind," he said. "I appreciate that, too."

She shook her head impatiently. "I was not kind. I did as he asked, told you what he said in so many words."

"You were trying to assuage my guilt," he said bluntly.

"What would be the point? One lives with guilt as part of life. He spoke the words, Ferchar. He was proud of you for everything. He knew by then he'd been wrong to try and make a priest of you. He knew it wasn't your nature, and he was glad of your strength in going your own way. But he wanted you to have as much of Tain as he could give you."

He stared not at her but at his fingers, abstractly stroking the harp strings. He dropped his hand before he drew attention by an unintended sound.

"Will you keep the office of coarb now you have Carron?" she asked.

"Yes, I'll keep it. And God willing, so will my sons." He paused, realizing something else. "You know about Carron?"

"My father met Deirdre, brought her to meet the queen."

Had Deirdre told him that? Had there been time? Behind them, someone plucked a lute or something similar, and in a rush of pleasure, people began to mill about forming into a dance set, he suspected, as the music grew lively.

"Your marriage was a surprise," Affrica said lightly. "A happy one.

I wish you both well."

They would need all such wishes they could get. "Thank you. What of your own marriage, now that you are grown? Do any of these fine fellows find favor?"

She laughed. "These fine fellows are playing. I will be married as a MacHeth not as Affrica. And, please, God, not just yet."

His lips quirked. "I almost didn't know you. You have found a new place and new ways to shine."

A faint pinkness stained the skin over her cheekbones. "I almost didn't know you either. And so have you—found new ways to shine, I mean."

"For that, I would ask you to dance, except I don't know the steps and would embarrass us both."

"Get Deirdre to teach you," she said warmly. "I will dance with you in Ross."

"I will hold you to it." With odd reluctance, he rose to his feet. "Good night, Affrica MacHeth."

"Good night, Ferchar Maccintsacairt."

⇻⇺

WITH THOSE UNINSPIRED words, she let him go. Although she gazed at the dancers, hiding behind the vague smile she had learned at court, it was Ferchar's large, retreating frame that seemed to be stuck to the backs of her eyelids. Still, her heart seemed to beat in that odd, excited way, and the knot in her stomach was not pain.

He was taking his leave of the queen, bowing over her proffered hand, and yet just before he turned, he flicked one glance at her and she stuck out her tongue, just as if she were still ten years old. Even as the laughter flashed across his face and vanished, she wanted the world to swallow her.

Why had she done such a thing? To remind him—or herself?—of

old friendship? Stupid, because she didn't want him to see her as that child anymore. She wanted him to see her now. She wanted to know *him* now.

Her mind drifted back to his arrival on Blackford Hill this morning. The faint dream that had imposed itself on the reality of sights and sounds around her. *"Which of you is the Lady de Lanson?"* Just a story, often told at Tirebeck, of how her grandfather, Adam mac Malcolm, had first met her grandmother, whose name had once been de Lanson.

Why should this, whether vision or memory, impose itself now on her mind? Because Christian de Lanson had loved Adam MacHeth, even when she shouldn't have?

Slowly, Affrica's arms crept across her stomach, but not in pain. Her smile was no longer vague. For an instant at least, it was wild with joy.

※※※

FERCHAR WAS NOT surprised to find few MacHeths in their hall at Tirebeck. Neither Angus nor Affrica had returned from court, although Angus was expected imminently. Nechtan, Angus's elder son, was at Dingwall, and Colin was out somewhere on Tirebeck land.

Ferchar didn't mind. His business was not with any of them. With reluctance, he turned his feet toward the guest house where Adam mac Malcolm MacHeth stayed. He wasn't particularly looking forward to his interview with the old charlatan, who seemed to have little care for anyone, even his own family. But on the other hand, Ferchar had made promises when he left Adam's son Gregor, who clearly loved and missed his strange father. Even Eochaid MacHeth, Adam's much younger brother, seemed to hold the old man in considerable affection.

He found Adam asleep before the fire. Or at least, his eyes were closed.

"My lord," Ferchar said into the silence. "Lord Adam." Since nothing happened, he was about to speak again more loudly, when the filmy eyes opened and focused at once on his face. "We met once before, years ago. I'm Ferchar Maccintsacairt."

The old man sat up. "I remember."

Ferchar, who doubted it, produced Gregor MacHeth's letter from inside his tunic. "I promised your son I would give you this, along with his love and obedience."

Something unexpected flared on Adam's face as he reached for the letter, almost as if he couldn't help it. Ferchar stepped forward and thrust it into his hands.

"You have seen Gregor?"

"I fought beside him and your brother Eochaid in Thessalonica. Eochaid also sends greetings. I believe he might have scrawled something on Gregor's letter."

A smile flickered on Adam's lips. He held the letter in both hands but didn't break the seal. "Of course. You went there at Angus's behest and stayed to fight."

"You saw that in a dream?" Ferchar said carefully.

The old eyes, still dark as Affrica's, held a hint of mockery. "No. Angus told me. I thank you."

"There is no need," Ferchar said stiffly. "I am glad to be of any service to Gregor, who has been a good friend to me."

Adam's eyes drifted. "He was always the most... *surprising* of our children. I thought at first, he would be like me... But he wasn't, just himself. He was the peacemaker in a turbulent house, the one who broke up fights between his brothers, the one who comforted his mother when she was distressed, and was kind to all. And yet he chose war. Is he happy?"

The question took Ferchar by surprise, not least because Adam's eyes pinned him like twin skewers, no longer remotely vague. It wasn't a casual question. He really wanted an answer, one without platitudes.

"Mostly. He has purpose and contentment in his personal life. He misses you. And his brothers and sisters. And Tirebeck."

Adam smiled, and yet Ferchar was sure his eyes glistened. "But he will never come home." A shudder seemed to pass through him. He wiped one hand across his face. "Will you sit, Ferchar? And tell me tales of Gregor's exploits with my reckless little brother?"

To his surprise, Ferchar was tempted. He began, reluctantly, to understand why the other MacHeths so cared for this strange, detached old man, who was not detached at all. In his own way, he loved them all, and not carelessly but with intensity. For Gregor's sake, Ferchar was glad. "I can't. I am needed at home. But I will come another day, if I may."

The old man nodded. "Is Affrica not with you?"

"Affrica?" Ferchar blinked. Perhaps Adam was confusing this with his previous visit. "She is still with the court as far as I know."

"Of course," Adam said vaguely. His head turned away, toward the flames.

"I'll take my leave," Ferchar said, a touch awkwardly.

The disturbing eyes returned to him. "Come again. If you wish."

"I will," Ferchar said, and meant it.

# Chapter Ten

*Ross, spring 1210*

THE DAY THAT Kenneth was proclaimed Earl of Ross was auspicious.

The rain of the last week vanished into clear sky and calm sea, leaving the land green and sweet-smelling and the people hopeful and proud. The important men and women came from all over Ross, from the rugged west to the gentler east that was the earl's true domain. Some guests were packed into the hall and outbuildings at Dingwall, their retinues into the wooden barracks beside the massive foundations of Kenneth's new castle. Others were scattered among nearby houses as everyone seemed glad to give and receive hospitality in honor of Kenneth's ascent.

The open enthusiasm of all was partly a reflection of Kenneth's own, partly a relief at throwing off the anxiety and grief over Earl Gilchrist's long illness and death.

Affrica had returned to Ross with Kenneth, as she had left it less than a year ago, and yet everything had changed. The steady, careful rule of the last two decades was gone, and Kenneth now stepped out of his father's shadow, free of Angus's iron grip if not his advice.

But Affrica, too, had hope. She rose early, escaping from the cramped hall at dawn to walk with Wolf across the moor toward the gentle hills and thought of Kenneth as he had been on that strange silent journey north. It had still been winter and the road from Perth, where the combined court had lain since before Christmas, was difficult and bitterly cold. Dealing with her own grief, she had been very aware of Kenneth's greater loss, and she had never seen him so grave or so thoughtful. As long as she could remember, everyone had worried about Kenneth's succession, but it seemed to be the making of him, a cruel jolt from his old, selfish rebellion, into duty.

She hoped it would last. She thought it would.

Wolf bounded along beside her, behaving like a puppy again, and Affrica let the calm happiness of the new day wash over her. Birds' song mingled musically in her ears, blackbirds and thrushes and chirping sparrows, for once without the plaintive wails of sea birds drowning them out. She breathed in the sweet-smelling air of Ross and was glad to be home. Bombarded by a thousand memories, some vivid, some intangible, she began to run, to dance and spin just to release the unbearable mix of happiness and loss.

Wolf rushed and bounced around her, joining in as he always had until, close to a stream, she let herself fall in a dizzy heap, with the dog on top of her licking her face while she pushed him off, laughing. And became aware of another figure only a body length away, sitting in the long grass, watching her.

Her heart jolted. Holding onto Wolf's head, she dragged herself into a sitting position and blinked. Ferchar Maccintsacairt didn't disappear. In fact, Wolf pulled out of her grip to greet him casually, as though the wretched animal had always known he was close. Perhaps he had. Perhaps he had driven her this way.

"I wondered," Ferchar said, "if you would still play like the child on the beach."

Embarrassment surged, heating her skin, but she tilted her chin and tried to look haughty. "And do I?"

"Not quite."

"Because I forgot to throw stones for Wolf? Or for you?"

His lips curved into a fleeting smile, and she swallowed, totally unprepared for this meeting so soon. "No. You move differently."

Before she could even register that properly, he rose and took a pace closer, stretching down his hand to help her rise. Almost like the boy Ferchar had done on the beach at Tirebeck, when none of her family had troubled. It had seemed a rather delightful courtesy then. Now, she suspected he was mocking her.

Ungloved, his hand was large and calloused and mostly clean. A hint of stubble across his chin and upper lip reminded her, as though she needed reminding, that he was no longer a boy. But he wore old, comfortable clothes, as she did. Neither of them had expected company this early in the day.

She took his hand and rose with what dignity she could summon. A lost cause.

"I don't always feel grown up," she confessed, dropping his hand at once because of its hard strength. Not the hand of the priest's scholarly son but of a soldier.

"We can allow ourselves a few moments," he said lightly, beginning to walk along the stream. "Since we'll have to be grown up for the rest of the day." He bent, picked up a fallen twig by the old willow, and threw it for the dog, who chased happily after it.

Watching him, she said, "How come you are here? You can't be just arriving at Dingwall."

"We came last night. Lulach has a hall a mile or so over there." He pointed vaguely, away from the sea.

"I hoped you would stay with us, with Kenneth." In fact, she had thought he had chosen not to come at all.

"I knew the house would be full." He dropped his gaze to her face as they walked. "I am sorry about Gilchrist mac Donald."

She nodded. "Thank you. My father feels it deeply. They had been friends forever."

He nodded in return, and their eyes met in some silent acknowledgment that they had said what they needed and could now, with relief, move on.

"Tell me," she said in a rush, "about the crusading."

He took the stick from the dog's mouth and threw it again. "I'll tell you about the fun, if you like."

The next hour wasn't like the crazy scamper over rooves and washing lines, with a few difficult confidences thrown in at odd moments. But it was fascinating and beguiling all the same and made her laugh. She drank it all in, reading between the lines of what he did say to guess at what he did not, following the trail of his memories with thoughts and quips of her own that he answered in kind.

When they parted, it was suddenly, as she saw the height of the sun and had to scamper back to the hall at speed to avoid the scolding of her aunts and sisters, who had returned to Ross, it seemed, for the sole purpose, as she told Ferchar, of "out-ladying" her. He laughed, which made her smile as she ran.

She was almost at the hall before she realized she had not asked after his wife. And he had never mentioned her.

⸻

THE DAY WAS largely one of celebration before Kenneth would begin his progress around Ross with more serious intent. There was to be music and dancing, feasting, drinking, and contests in archery and manly sports. People of all walks of life milled around the hall, the gardens and the yards, spilling as far as the foundations of Kenneth's new stone castle. Men and children seemed particularly interested in the building, which was replacing the wooden castle the king had built here twenty years ago when Donald MacWilliam had been ejected from the country.

Kenneth was happy to discuss his pet project, especially with those familiar with the great castles further south—Stirling and Edinburgh and Roxburgh, and those in England and Europe. Affrica saw Ferchar there, inspecting, asking questions, and pointing. She smiled as she turned away, and for the first time saw the Lady of Carron, standing with a couple of other wives. Two little girls leaned into her skirts, perfectly still apart from their wide, darting eyes.

Affrica walked toward them, and all three ladies curtseyed to her. So did the children. Affrica smiled, including the girls in her greeting.

"My daughters," Deirdre of Carron said proudly, "Euphemia and Christina."

"I'm so glad you came," Affrica confided, lowering her head to the children. "Do you think you could help Gilla keep the younger ones out of trouble?"

Gilla—or Devorgilla—was her sister Joan's daughter and at least as mischievous as the boys, but she was a friendly girl and ran over at Affrica's bidding, sweeping Deirdre's daughters away with her. Deirdre looked gratified.

"They have more fun without us," Affrica observed.

"No rushing off to join them," Joan said, appearing behind her. "Though I have to say, Affrica, you do look alarmingly elegant. Court has been good for you."

"It made me pay attention," Affrica admitted. "But I can still climb the oak tree faster than you."

Joan laughed. "I don't doubt it and beg you not to prove it!" She bustled off again.

Deirdre said, "I was sorry not to see more of you when we were in Edinburgh. My husband was desperate to get back to Ross."

"I suppose he had been away a long time. Do you still live at Carron now that you are married again, or do you divide your time between there and Tain?"

"I stay mainly at Carron, though my husband divides his time between the two. He is very conscientious about the girth at Tain, as with everything."

Affrica began to walk with her toward the archery yards where the men were forming up for the competition. "Then he is settled into land stewardship after his adventures abroad?"

Deirdre looked surprised. "Perfectly. I am so glad I married him."

She spoke with a fervor that was clearly genuine, and yet for some reason, it grated on Affrica.

"The girls adore him," Deirdre added. "They are fortunate to have him as their father and protector."

"I can imagine he would be a fun stepfather."

Another of those faintly surprised and yet speculative looks. "We would be glad to receive you should you care to visit in the north."

"Thank you, you're very kind."

"And will your own marriage be soon, my lady?"

"I doubt it."

"Why?" Deirdre regarded her, brows raised. "You could have anyone in Scotland. Oh dear, is that Christina? What is she doing to that gown?"

"Scraping it on tree bark," Affrica said in some amusement. "That is the oak tree that Joan and I were talking about."

"She's stuck!"

Ferchar appeared, plucking the child out of the tree and onto his shoulders instead. Euphemia and Devorgilla appeared to sit on his feet while he tried to walk. Affrica let out a snort of laughter and watched him shake the children off like sand from his boots, to the sounds of their shouted laughter.

>>><<<

"Do you remember Deirdre of Carron from when we were children?" Affrica asked Joan while they retreated to organize the feast and the men shot arrows and fought each other with blunted weapons.

"Only as a name. Why, do you?"

"Not before she married Henry de Norman. I remember the wedding."

"She is an odd wife for Ferchar Maccintsacairt," Joan remarked.

"In what way?"

Joan shrugged. "Every way. He was always clever, curious, intellectual, even. Physically, he may have been a clumsy boy, but he always found ways of doing things. But she… I would have said she was dull witted except that she chose Ferchar and somehow got him to choose her."

Affrica closed her mouth at this casually devastating opinion. "I hardly think he could have been browbeaten into it."

Joan laughed and leaned closer. "How about seduced?"

Affrica flushed and slapped her outrageous sister's arm before hurrying off to organize the outdoor seating. She wished she hadn't begun the conversation, and she resolved to keep her nose out of Ferchar's personal life.

⟫⟪

BY EVENING, THE ale and the wine had been flowing freely for several hours, but thanks to plenty of sport and food, high spirits had never broken out into fighting. It had been a happy and successful day, and Kenneth well acclaimed by the nobility and people of Ross. Messages had arrived all day from other earldoms throughout Scotland, and yet, as she passed Kenneth in a quiet moment, she caught a moment of bleakness in his eyes.

"What is it?" she asked quickly. "Are you not enjoying your day?"

"Of course, I am. It's just…" He sighed. "The world has acknowledged me. All but the King of Scots."

"He never formally acknowledged Gilchrist as earl either," Affrica reminded him. "But he treated him as such."

Kenneth brushed that aside with an impatient waft of his hand. "I was at court, Affrica. I fought for him."

"So did Gilchrist." She nudged him on her way past. "Be patient."

Patience, of course, was not Kenneth's greatest virtue, but he did seem to have accepted reality. There had been no unseemly gloating over wins on the field, no taunting of lesser talents. He had been all grace and compliments, even when Ferchar, wearing Deirdre's token, had beaten him in the archery contest, and he himself had won the mock melee.

The lesser men and neighbors departed as the sun lowered—along with the rain—leaving only family and the great men of the earldom to feast and dance in the evening. The fighting men changed into their silks and finery, and Affrica, seated by her father at the end of the raised table on the dais, joined in the traditional family banter that spread around the hall. Even Angus, who had been morose since the old earl's death, began to smile and to joke with Kenneth.

Further down the room, Ferchar smiled faintly at something Deirdre was saying as she gazed worshipfully up into his eyes. And Affrica's arm closed across the pain in her stomach before she wrenched her gaze free.

After the feast, the tables were cleared away by an army of servants, and the musicians began to play. Kenneth bowed elaborately before Affrica and held out his hand to her. Laughing, she took it, and they joined the forming circle.

As they danced, she was impressed by the number of other men who could still acquit themselves reasonably on the dance floor, including her own brothers and her cousin Ranald, who was dancing with the beautiful Lady of Carron.

Ferchar, she saw, did not dance, but was propped against one of the wooden pillars to the right of the hall, talking with Bishop Reinald and Robert de Norman.

After that, in a more courtly dance that frequently broke the circle into couples, she partnered an old friend of her father's and then, laughing at his final joke, she spun away a little too fast and found herself face to face with Ferchar Maccintsacairt.

"Don't tell me," she said breathlessly, "you still don't know the steps."

"Not well enough to be sure of avoiding your toes, but if you're brave enough—" he bowed and held out his hand, "...I'm inviting you."

"And what an irresistible invitation it is." She laid her hand on his silk sleeve, and the embroidered folds of his coat swirled around her gown.

"If you would prefer to merely walk, talk, eat, or drink," he offered, "I—"

"No, I feel you should suffer."

"But should *you*?"

"I'll let you know after we dance."

The music began in courtly fashion, and they moved sedately around the circle, and broke into couples, stepping forward and back from each other, circling and turning while the music grew mischievously faster. In Ferchar, there was no sign now of the clumsy boy. He was in perfect control of his flexible limbs and danced with the graceful confidence of a courtier. A smile even played on his lips, and if it came with a faintly ironic, even challenging glint in his eyes, somehow that only added to his charm.

Something odd happened to her body when he surged toward her. Her breath wobbled, and something inside her stomach dived. After the third time this happened, she realized she rather liked it. She savored all her new awareness as they wove behind each other, and when she turned beneath his arm and came up breathlessly close to him, happiness blazed within her.

Their steps quickened with the music until most of the circle had broken up into laughing couples performing simple jigs or just leaning on each other for breath. But she and Ferchar would not give in. Her whole being was laughing and yet joyfully, physically aware of every touch, every glide, every movement. She stepped and spun, pulled back and threw herself forward with abandon until the music ended from sheer exhaustion. Only then did Ferchar fling a protective arm around her, and she was glad of it holding her up.

A huge, laughing cheer had gone up, like an echo within her. She wanted the moment to freeze, to never change, because the same knowledge she had felt in Edinburgh last autumn was galloping on her once more, and this time, she didn't think she could ignore it.

"You see?" he said breathlessly. "There are alternatives to risking life and limb on rooftops." His arm dropped, and she tried desperately to school her features into the bland court mask she had learned. He bowed elaborately, and as she curtsied in return, she saw her father striding toward her, grim-faced.

Her heart lurched. Had she made a fool herself? Was she in trouble for dancing? With Ferchar? But no, Angus wasn't even looking at her. He rushed right past. Without a word to Ferchar, she followed her father and grasped his arm.

"What is it? Where…?"

Her father's frowning gaze swept impatiently over her to Ferchar who, amazingly enough, was right beside her.

"Liam O'Neill," Angus said, low. "Guthred's Irishman in Paris. He's here."

# Chapter Eleven

*Ross, spring 1210*

"Where?" Ferchar, unlike Affrica's brain, did not waste time asking how this could be or if it was likely, just went straight to the point.

"Here, in the hall, milling around among everyone else. He was going *this*—" Her father broke off as Affrica dug her fingers into his arm, warning him not to shout or point or cause any upset to Kenneth's day. Apart from anything else, word would quickly travel that an enemy had penetrated the Earl of Ross's hall, or, worse, that a creature of Guthred MacWilliam's had been a guest here.

"Heading over there," Angus said more moderately, nodding casually to the other side of the hall. "Burgundy hat and coat, heavily embroidered over the shoulder, black hair. If you find him, bring him quietly to the earl's room."

Ferchar nodded once and swung off in the opposite direction to Angus, who continued his own purposeful prowl, leaving Affrica to follow one or the other or go her own way.

It struck her that if this man really was Liam O'Neill and not some unknown friend of Kenneth's, then if he realized Angus had recognized him, he would simply leave. Accordingly, Affrica walked toward the hall door, exchanging smiles and the odd word with people she passed on the way. After her exertions on the dance floor—delight bubbled up again, quickly squashed as she reminded herself of the dangers Liam could present—no one could be surprised if she sought some fresh air.

She slipped out of the door into the cool of the night. Torches blazed on either side of the door and at various points around the yard, which was not empty. A few young men were drinking and shouting with laughter only a few yards away. She knew them all. From somewhere in the gardens, she heard a female giggle and a sigh and a soft male voice. And from somewhere close to the back of the hall, the inevitable, unmistakable splash of someone relieving himself.

She moved away from the door, circling the yard, past each of the outbuildings that tonight housed many of Kenneth's guests. Inside, they were all in darkness, and outside, the torchlight threw changing shadows across the walls and shuttered windows. The doors were not locked from the outside. Anyone could hide there until the guest spilled out of the hall to sleep.

Affrica was not brave or foolish enough to enter each house in search of her quarry. But she did pause very slightly at each door or window to listen intently. At the first three, she heard nothing save the soft scurrying of mouse or rat across the floor within. The hairs on her neck stood up as she walked to the next. Anyone could also hide in the darkness between the buildings.

She paused by the first window, her heart thundering as she tried to listen for footsteps or a stranger's breath.

"Dare I hope you're looking for me?" came a light, male voice from behind her. It spoke in Gaelic yet with an unfamiliar accent.

She turned very slowly, ready to call for help, but no one stood in the darkness, threatening or otherwise.

"I can't tell until I see you," she managed. "Show yourself."

"*You* show yourself," the voice said playfully. "I'm down here."

In the dark space between the buildings. She had sensed it. "Then you may stay there until I send in the dogs to flush you out."

"Cruel. Look, here I am."

He emerged slowly to the corner of the house, where the torchlight played across a very handsome, male face, black, curly hair and a heavily embroidered burgundy coat that came to his knees. He smiled. "Dare I hope you like what you see?"

"I can't stop anyone hoping, but if you're so pleased by your own delights, why are you hiding?"

"My, you have a sharp tongue for such a beautiful lady." His Gaelic, though perfect, did indeed bear faint inflexions. Irish inflections. "I was watching you dance and hoped you had seen me, too. Only then your father came charging after me, and I thought I was dead."

"You probably are," Affrica said. She took a step closer, to better see and remember his features. "Since you were not invited."

"I was invited," the Irishman said with mock outrage. "By the great Lord of Ross himself. Are you thinking me some kind of peasant? A ruffian of no account? I assure you the blood in my veins is as royal as yours. More so. I would make a most acceptable husband, especially for a noble lady all of sixteen with no suitors to her name."

The words were contemptuous, though the tightening of her stomach told her they were also dishonest in intent. His reason intrigued her, which may have been why she didn't spot his movement until it was too late. He had meant to shock her.

With the speed of an arrow, he shot forward and seized Affrica by the arm, spinning her hard against him and trapping one of her hands between their bodies. Her other hand was already caught behind her back, and something cold and sharp was held along the side of her neck.

She made herself stop the panicked scrabbling of her hand against his chest. She felt sick.

He said softly, "Goodness, but you are lovely, are you not? Be still now, and silent, for I would hate to mark that beautiful face, especially if I do decide to marry you one day. But needs must, my dear. Needs must."

"As you say," she managed as her heart seemed to hammer into her throat. "With you being such a handsome, gallant prince of royal blood, and me being an aging spinster with no suitors."

His teeth flashed in what might have been genuine admiration. "I heard you had spirit, but there's no need to lay it on so thick. Rankled, did it?"

She elected to stare while he loosened his grip enough for her to flex her cramped fingers. When they closed into fists again, her knuckles brushed what was surely a dagger hilt.

"If you want to keep the earl as a friend," she said coldly, "you should let me go now."

They stood in the shadow of the building, yet there was no one here to see. The drunken young men on the other side of the yard were fully engrossed in themselves. The music seeping from the hall was another lively dance tune. Could she scream and pull free before his knife cut into her? Unlikely.

"Does he want to marry you himself, then?" the Irishman mused. "I wouldn't blame him."

She gave an annoyed little push. "Why do you harp on marriage? Your conversation is dull." *Yes.* She got her fingers around the dagger hilt before she stilled as though suddenly remembering the knife's presence at her throat. If it pierced her skin, she didn't feel it.

"Don't you want to know who I am before you continue your rudeness?"

"Oh, I know who you are, Liam O'Neill, and I won't be your free passage out of Ross." She tugged hard at the dagger hilt and threw her body weight backward at the same time to avoid Liam's knife if she could. Her fist holding the dagger connected painfully with his chin, and she brought the blade sweeping down to stab his arm.

He let out a short grunt of pain and shock loosened his hold long enough for her to stumble out of his reach into the wall of the building, holding his dagger before her. Her breath came in pants as she wondered wildly what to do now. If she called for help, she would bring down on them all the dangers she had warned her father about. Yet she couldn't fight him alone, not for long.

Not for any time at all, it seemed, for his right, uninjured arm, the one holding the first dagger, lifted. The blade glinted in the torch light, and she knew without doubt that he would throw it and that his aim was true.

"What a foolish little girl," he uttered between his teeth. "A couple of feet won't save you."

And they wouldn't, for another figure loomed from the alley behind him.

---

FERCHAR MOVED AMONG the milling throngs in the hall with massive relief. A task. One to distract him from feelings he could not allow or even contemplate. He needed, badly, to banish the vision of Affrica MacHeth that consumed him, and searching for a very different face seemed to be the perfect way to do it. Why that should be the strongest motive for hunting down Guthred MacWilliam's ally, he refused to imagine. Instead, he concentrated on the task.

He knew almost everyone by sight, and if he didn't, they were the wrong age, with the wrong coloring or the wrong clothing. As he approached the front of the hall, he knew that either he or Angus should have come across the man by now. If he was still in the hall.

His skin prickled. Why would Liam stay in the hall if he knew Angus had recognized him? Wouldn't he bolt?

And where was Affrica? He had been so consumed with escaping her presence that he hadn't paid any attention to where she went. She hadn't followed him, and neither, he saw, was she with Angus, who was making alone for the earl's private rooms at the front of the hall, some distance behind the dais.

Also at the front of the hall was the door that led to the kitchens. It was, Ferchar suspected, a convenient means for the earl to come and go at night without disturbing his men sleeping on the hall floor. Without compunction, Ferchar walked through the door. He glanced in at the kitchens, where, while the ale flowed, the servants were still cheerfully busy, washing massive pots and silver plates and an endless supply of cups. Others were sorting leftover food which would be distributed among local families. No one but Ferchar stood around looking out of place.

He moved on, past clucking chickens and snuffling pigs, meaning to head for the stables in case Liam was bent upon escape. Which would at least save Angus and Kenneth from having to deal with him, although they needed to know what the devil he was doing here. And, more to the point, who had come with him.

As he turned left toward the stables, something caught his eye to the right, and he swung back. All was quiet in that direction. Over the lively music and thumping of feet from the hall, he could hear occasional unsober voices in the main yard, on the other side of the buildings that surrounded it. There was no reason for anyone to be here at the back of the houses. And yet something had moved, something had blocked, for an instant, the pale, distant glow of light that filtered up the alleys between the buildings. An animal? A cat jumping between the rooves? An owl or a bat?

In his arms training in Paris, and even more so with the crusading army in its interminable fight with the Bulgarians, Ferchar had learned to trust his instincts. They had saved him in tavern brawls, in battle, and in avoiding ambushes. He drew the dagger from his belt and, light-footed, he swarmed down behind the buildings, one, two...

Voices. Voices that made the hair on his neck stand up. For one of them was Affrica MacHeth's, speaking in Gaelic. *"Oh, I know who you are, Liam O'Neill, and I won't be your free passage out of Ross."*

Shadows danced wildly across the alley between the houses as Ferchar sprinted up it, unsure if he should be shouting or silent. A sound of scuffling and gasping breath froze the blood in his veins, but still he kept moving.

"What a foolish little girl," said a quietly savage male voice as he broke from the passage to the front of the house.

The man stood less than a yard in front of him, his arm raised to throw a blade that shone in the nearby torchlight. Facing him, her back to the building, stood Affrica MacHeth, his brave, beautiful warrior, a jewel-hilted dagger held threateningly before her. Much good would it do her when the bastard's blade hit her first.

"A couple of feet won't save you," Liam O'Neill sneered.

"Depends on the feet," Ferchar said and kicked the Irishman hard enough to swipe both legs from under him. And then Ferchar was on him, his own dagger to Liam's throat to preempt any attack with the blade Liam had somehow managed to retain as he fell.

Liam bucked once with ferocious strength. Ferchar, almost dislodged, let his knife bite. "Drop it. And be still or I'll spit you."

Liam sighed and released his knife.

With his free hand, Ferchar took it and spun it across the ground in the direction of the house and Affrica. "I should have known you would be the one to catch our prey. Your trophy, my lady."

He had one glimpse of her, pale and shaken. She needed someone to embrace her, comfort her, tell her she was safe, and praise her undoubted bravery. But even if he did not have Liam to contain, he was not that someone.

"Ferchar, is that you?" came Angus's voice. "What have you got there?"

"Intruder," Ferchar said tersely, hauling Liam to his knees and then his feet.

"Liar," Liam complained. "Why does no one believe I am a *bona fide* guest of the earl?"

"Perhaps because the earl is here with me," Angus said dryly just before his eyes fell on his daughter and widened. "Affrica?"

But Kenneth's irritable voice stayed them all. "Ferchar, what in hell are you doing? Release my guest immediately."

"Guest?" Angus exclaimed. "Oh, dear God, tell me you jest."

"I don't," Kenneth retorted. "Nor do I want or need your approval. What I do expect of you is basic courtesy. *Ferchar!*" The last was snarled as Ferchar still had not released the Irishman, who now showed no inclination to fight.

Ferchar gave his captive a shake. "It's your house, of course. But personally, I wouldn't give even basic courtesy to someone who aimed a dagger at my lady cousin."

Angus made a furious lunge at Liam, but Kenneth caught his arm and hauled him back. "Don't be ridiculous, man. Why would he do such a thing? In any case, Affrica seems to be the one with the dagger."

"Only because Ferchar disarmed him," Affrica said coldly.

"For the love of God," Liam said piously. "It was a joke. The lady only takes it seriously now you are all here to witness her presence. Of course, I would never have hurt her."

"There you are," Kenneth said. "And now the subject comes up, Affrica, what *were* you doing out here alone."

Liam smiled. "Looking for me," he said with simple, devastating truth.

Affrica's mouth opened to retort and closed again. Her wide eyes clashed with Liam's merry ones. Ferchar, who still had hold of Liam's collar, began to twist it, until Kenneth surprised him by snatching his friend free.

"It's not a discussion for out here," Angus said, tight-lipped but controlled. "Your rooms, Kenneth."

"Tomorrow," Kenneth said. He met Angus's gaze, a battle of wills that had been forming, erupting, and reforming for years. And at last,

Kenneth had the upper hand. He was the Lord of Ross and the chief of the family.

Ferchar was not his family. "Tonight," he barked. "Unless you want the discussion in the hall, where I guarantee you'll find all the support is all for the lady. And the king," he added, striding off across the yard.

Behind him, Kenneth swore. "Damn it, Liam, how do you manage to antagonize so many people in one night? Are you *trying* to cause a brawl in my house?"

"Oh, I think it's your man—Ferchar?—who wants to brawl," came the Irishman's amused voice. "A little sweet on a young lady far above his reach, wouldn't you…"

Ferchar strode on, furious as he hadn't been since he'd first discovered the injustice of the world through the acts of the same damned MacHeth who'd made a friend of bloody Liam O'Neill. And furious was no condition in which to meet this particular situation. He'd won the argument for immediate discussion by means of a threat he would never carry out—though Affrica might. A breath of laughter took him by surprise, steadying his anger and allowing him to control it.

Allowing him to prepare to meet her after she'd heard Liam's poisonous words.

He entered the hall by the same door he had left it. The music had paused, though only temporarily, he hoped. He didn't want Kenneth distracted by hostly duties like farewells while Liam slipped the net. He moved toward the table where wine was set out, took a cup, and let himself into Kenneth's rooms.

No servant accosted him. Presumably, they were all celebrating in their own way elsewhere. He found an oil lamp and lit it from the nearby tinder box, and then lit two others to cast enough light to look about him.

It was a large room, with a comfortable, upholstered chair on one side, and a table and stool, perhaps for Kenneth's scribe, on the other.

Weapons hung on the walls. A large space in the middle of the room suggested Kenneth might practice swordsmanship in here on occasions. A wooden partition, with a curtained arch in the center, led to his bed and chests for his clothes.

Ferchar paced to the shuttered window, through which a pleasant draught cooled the remains of his temper. Rather than open the shutters, he turned his back on them and raised the cup to his lips. The MacHeths always had good wine.

The door opened abruptly, and Affrica walked in, closely followed, fortunately, by her father, whose eyebrows flew up at the sight of Ferchar waiting for them.

"Where is he?" Ferchar asked abruptly, setting his cup down on the table.

"Coming."

"Do we know if Liam has allies here?"

"Kenneth says not. He met Liam in Dumbarton last winter. They caroused together, no more."

*Do you believe him?* Not a question he could ask Kenneth's kinsman, though Affrica was more likely to know the answer.

She moved restlessly about the room. "Kenneth sees no ill intent or enmity in him," she said, throwing herself into the chair and then immediately springing up again. "He's shocked by our... excessive reaction."

Angus snorted. "Ferchar, I owe you again for my daughter's life."

"He wouldn't have killed me," Affrica said before Ferchar could wave away her father's thanks. "He just wanted me under his control, a shield if he needed one. Beyond that..." She frowned, not looking at either of them. "Beyond that, I think he was making my acquaintance, testing the water, if you like."

"Why?" Ferchar asked.

She shrugged and glanced up, meeting his gaze. "He seems to want MacHeth friends, doesn't he?"

*Again, why?*

The door opened, and Angus moved closer to his daughter. Ferchar imagined lead weights on his feet to weigh them down and keep them still. But Kenneth entered alone.

"Where is Liam O'Neill?" Angus demanded.

"In the hall, dancing," Kenneth retorted, "which is where we should all be. I don't even see why we need to discuss it further. I've told you he is my guest. The offense, such as it is, can be solved with Ferchar's simple apology."

Ferchar laughed, which attracted Kenneth's glare.

"And Liam's to Affrica, for the misunderstanding." the earl added shortly. "I saw no purpose to putting him in the same room as Ferchar. Now, can we return to the hall?"

"Do you know that he is an ally of Guthred MacWilliam?" Angus said.

Kenneth shrugged impatiently. "*Was* an ally of the MacWilliams. They met in Ireland, but Liam hasn't seen him in years. He finds Guthred embittered and unamusing if you want the truth."

"He found him amusing enough in Paris," Angus said.

"Paris?" Kenneth repeated with a quick, distracted frown.

"I met him in Paris," Angus said patiently. "With Guthred. While their thugs tried to abduct Affrica to force my hand. To force your father's hand. You know this story. Do you really see no parallel with what happened here tonight?"

Kenneth stared at him, his fingers tapping against the engraved gold buckle on his belt. "No," he said thoughtfully, at last. "I can't. But I can see why you do, and why Ferchar felt compelled to intervene—as he did before in Paris. But Liam had nothing to do with the attempt in Paris. He was shocked when I told him about it."

Angus cast his eyes up to the ceiling as though looking to heaven for strength.

Affrica said, "Did he know it was Ferchar who saved me in Paris?"

Kenneth blinked. "Not from me. He just knows the attempt against you was unsuccessful. Why?"

"No reason," she said vaguely.

Angus scowled. "You understand I won't have Affrica staying here while Liam O'Neill is in your house?"

"White Christ, Angus, she is perfectly safe!"

"That decision is not yours to make," Angus said. "I'll warn the men, and we'll be ready to leave in an hour."

"Don't you think," Affrica suggested, "that might cause the talk we are trying to avoid?"

"You will not stay here," Angus said flatly.

Ferchar stirred. He didn't want this. Yet he longed for it with an excitement that threatened to swamp him. For no reason. And yet it was a simple solution. "Deirdre and I are staying with Lulach. The Lady Affrica could come with us tonight, and you can collect her on your way home, whenever you choose to travel. My wife will be glad of the company."

Angus and Kenneth exchanged glances. "It's a solution," Angus allowed. "I'll give you a few of my men as added escort."

Kenneth sighed and tried for dignity. "If you feel you must, Angus. I understand, though I can't help being insulted by your lack of trust."

"It's not you I distrust. But for God's sake, look after my sisters and my other daughters."

"I will." Kenneth strode to the door. "And I will look after your sons and the rest of my family, household, and guests. You are an old woman sometimes. Shall we go? I, for one, need wine."

Ferchar lifted his cup in a silent toast to no one in particular. It gave him something to do and somewhere to look as Affrica walked away, escorted by her father. He followed more slowly. Time to tell Deirdre of her felicity. And poor Lulach of course.

But when he got to the hall, there was no sign of Liam. A discreet inquiry to the stables elicited the news that he had ridden off in a westerly direction.

# Chapter Twelve

*Ross, summer 1210*

Deirdre, the Lady of Carron, was not dissatisfied with her second marriage. How could she be when her husband was always so civil, appreciated good taste in matters of dress and ornamentation, and treated the girls as if they were his own daughters? In fact, Deirdre found it hard now to remember that they were not.

Having a husband again released such a massive weight from her shoulders that it was several months before she admitted even to herself that he might have a few tiny, less-than-refined faults. However, by the nature of the beast, he was a man, and she could hardly complain about that. His delights massively outweighed such minor inconveniences, and if the thought crossed her mind once or twice that she could have aimed a little higher, at one of the MacHeth family, perhaps, she quickly banished such notions. There were other ways to intimacy with the earl and his kin.

On the day the note came from the Lady Affrica, she could not wait for Ferchar to come home from the hills, where he had been sheering sheep. This was not a refined task, and certainly not one suited to a gentleman. When she had told him so, he had only laughed and gone anyway. He was civil, but he was not…biddable.

Henry had been biddable. But she could no longer see his face clearly. Ferchar's was everywhere she looked.

When he came home, in time for a late afternoon meal, he went immediately to wash and change. She appreciated the courtesy, although today she was desperate to tell him her news. Eventually, clean and properly dressed, he reentered the hall and hugged each of the girls as they ran to him, babbling about their games and a broken doll.

Without waiting for Bridie to come and take the girls away to the nursery, Deirdre said, "I had a message today from the Lady Affrica."

Crouched on the floor, examining the injured doll, he didn't look up. "Oh? Is she well?"

"Oh, yes. In fact, she intends to accompany her brother Colin when he comes to see you."

Ferchar glanced up, frowning. "Why? Colin's coming to look at sheep."

"*I* am at Carron, too," Deirdre reminded him. "I expect she misses female company. As I do."

"We're females," Christina pointed out.

"Of course, you are, dear, but you're not yet grown-up. Your father knows what I mean. In any case, even Colin will want to do more than look at sheep. They will stay for a few nights and then—"

"No," Ferchar said.

This was so rare, so downright, that Deirdre blinked. "I beg your pardon?"

He was scowling and impatient. "Carron is not so large that they need stay for more than one night."

Deirdre stared at him in outrage. "You want me to write to the Lady Affrica and tell her that she and her brother have to leave the day after they arrive, because you have run out of sheep to show them?"

With an effort, it seemed, his scowl retreated. He even smiled reluctantly. "It does sound rude when you put it like that."

"It sounds nonsensical. Which it is."

He gazed down at the doll and its broken leg held between his fingers, but she had the impression he wasn't seeing them. "Of course. They are welcome to stay, and I know you will enjoy the company."

"Won't you?" she asked lightly.

He stirred and rose to his feet. "Of course. Is supper ready?"

<hr />

AFFRICA HAD NEARLY refused Deirdre's invitation. She wasn't sure she wanted to be so close to Ferchar, whose very presence seemed to churn her up in ways she neither liked nor understood. Partly, that was due to the new feeling that had sprung up since their encounter in Edinburgh. And partly it was due to the knowledge that Ferchar was not happy.

She missed the carefree, adventurous boy who had made saving her life into a game. There had been odd glimpses of the old Ferchar, of course, such as when she had danced with him, but then the music had stopped and so had the fun.

She wasn't sure she liked the new, secretive, responsible Ferchar, whose presence at Dingwall had troubled her, excited her, and *hurt* her. As had his absence. She worried about him. And she wasn't sure she cared for Deirdre.

Up until the last moment, she had hoped a summons from the queen would take the decision out of her hands. But no such summons came. Angus was busy on other matters. Her grandfather seemed to have retreated from the world altogether, and Affrica was bored.

So, accompanied only by her tirewoman and her brother Colin and his men, she set off for Carron.

"Why do you want to see his sheep?" she asked.

"They're bigger. More wool. Breeding them with our own stock might be good."

She smiled. "Colin, are you becoming a *farmer?*"

"Don't you think we have enough fighting MacHeths? Especially with no one for us to fight. Peace is good for Ross."

"You'll still have to fight for the king if he summons you," she pointed out.

"He hasn't even summoned Kenneth, either to court or the army."

"He probably thinks Kenneth is too busy grappling with his new earldom."

"Then he doesn't know Kenneth," Colin said dryly. "Kenneth thinks the king doesn't trust him or any of the MacHeths, even now."

"Kenneth and I were both at court until the beginning of the year."

"But no one has asked for you since."

That was indisputable, but riding across the country in the sunshine, with her brother as her main escort, the illusion of freedom cheered her. She was no longer bored or disappointed, merely contented.

Inevitably, of course, it rained before the end of their journey, so they arrived at Carron like drowned rats.

Servants spilled out of doors to take Affrica and Colin's horses and show the men where to go. Deirdre's concerned voice apologized for the weather and urged them to come inside, though through the rain, Affrica could see only two blurred figures at the door of what might have been a fine hall. One of the blurs, larger and male in shape, came right out into the rain, and without a word, lifted her from the saddle.

The blur was only too solid to the touch—strong arms and warm, firm hands, the brush of hard muscle, and the scent of Paris. Awareness jolted through her, along with a wild, intense happiness that must always remain secret. And yet she smiled because just for a few rapid heartbeats she could lie against him, sheltered, hidden, and yet truthful, at least to herself.

Then she stepped back, and his arm hurried her forward to the door and inside the hall, where Deirdre waited to welcome her, and she gaily apologized for dripping all over them both. She allowed her cloak to be removed—not by a servant, but by Ferchar again, his fingers deft and barely touching her. He took Colin's cloak, too, and spread them before the fire, which was not long lit she suspected, against the sudden chill of the rain.

"Come, I'll show you to your apartments," Deirdre said, "so that you can change out of those wet things. You must be soaked to the skin." She led them to an internal staircase, like the one at Tirebeck, but there the resemblance ended. The loft in Tirebeck was used by the housekeeper and the most necessary house servants. Here, it had been made into two rather grand bedchambers, each with their own bed and chests and hangings on the walls.

"This is lovely," Affrica said warmly. "I hope you haven't moved out of your own room on our account…"

"Oh, no, my room is downstairs. We designed these as guest rooms—so much more convenient than separate buildings, especially in weather like this. The chest by the bed is empty if you wish to store things in it while you are here."

"Thank you."

The Lady of Carron seemed to live in more luxury than the earl. Affrica wondered if she should have brought her court dresses.

"I'll show you the rest of the house later, if you like," Deirdre offered.

"I look forward to it."

"And here is your woman, so I'll leave you for now. Come down when you are ready. It won't be long until supper."

As Deirdre made her graceful way back downstairs, Colin, from the passage, met Affrica's gaze and grinned. Gently, she closed the door on him, and, with the help of Eta, her maid, peeled off her wet clothing.

Her formal gown had at least remained dry in its saddle bag, though in appearance it was somewhat crushed.

"Oh well, no one will notice when I'm sitting down," Affrica said philosophically, attaching the elegant pink glass earrings. She remembered, too, it was the gown she had worn at Kenneth's celebration. The peony red suited her coloring, and she rather liked it, but she suspected Deirdre's was new. The woman had a lot of gowns. Carron was no bigger than the demesne of Tirebeck, but Affrica suspected it must yield considerably more. She would ask Colin.

The Lord and Lady of Carron were waiting for them when they descended the stairs, and a servant presented them with cups of wine. The hall here was more like one of the queen's private dining rooms. No household clerks or housekeepers or men-at-arms necessitated extra tables or sleeping spaces at night. An eastern carpet rather than rushes graced the flagstone floor.

"This is a lovely hall," Affrica said warmly. "Will your daughters not be joining us, lady?"

"No, they dine in the nursery when we have guests."

"You must have a lot of space here."

"We built on to the original hall," Deirdre said. "A little like Tirebeck. But we'll show you when the rain goes off."

Ferchar had not contributed to the conversation, and yet his presence, silent and strangely tense, dominated the room, like a dark shadow over the bright nothingness of his wife's chatter. Occasionally, Deirdre deferred to him, and he smiled faintly, as though he understood no more was expected of him, and it didn't appear to be, for she would ask Colin or Affrica something else.

When they sat down at the table, Ferchar and Affrica were placed opposite Colin and Deirdre. The wine, like the food, was excellent, and Colin led Ferchar into a discussion of wine making in southern Europe, which veered somehow into amusing stories about their crusading MacHeth kinsmen.

"Will they ever come home, do you think?" Affrica asked Ferchar.

"I don't know," Ferchar replied. "Not for a while. They have both made lives out there."

Affrica's eyes widened. "Are they *married*, Ferchar? Do they have children?"

His lips quirked. "Sort of. And yes. The children are delightful."

"Oh, I would love to go and see them one day," Affrica said wistfully.

Colin laughed. "It will take you more than one day! Were you not tempted to stay, Ferchar?"

"Yes. In some ways. It was fascinating, but it was not my fight."

"Ferchar is not really a soldier by nature," Deirdre said.

"Actually, I am," Ferchar said, and a frown of annoyance crossed Deirdre's face.

"*That's* what I meant to ask you about," Colin said, setting down his wine cup. "Nechtan said you were training men in Tain."

"To guard the sanctuary," Ferchar said mildly. "To be sure it is safe and used as St. Duthac intended."

"Was it being misused?" Affrica asked.

He met her gaze. "I thought it might have been."

*By Liam O'Neill?*

"Ferchar is most conscientious," Deirdre said proudly.

"So he should be." Colin smiled at her. "And if he gathers enough men, perhaps you will have an escort suitable for a great lady."

This clearly struck Deirdre for the first time, for an awed look came into her eyes. A sardonic smile curved her husband's lips and vanished almost immediately. His eyelids came down, hiding any expression.

Not for the first time, Affrica wondered with distress if all was well with Ferchar's marriage. Did he *love* Deirdre?

After dinner, a servant brought a lute, and on Deirdre's request, Affrica played a little. She meant it as accompaniment to talk or to playing cards, but Deirdre listened, rapt, and Ferchar gazed at his big hands and said nothing. Even Colin listened with critical approval.

"My father saw no reason to teach me music," Deirdre said sadly.

"Or anything else, really."

"But you read and write," Affrica said quickly, passing the lute to her brother. "Which is more than most women, even those of birth."

"She taught herself," Ferchar said. "With very little help from the local priest."

At the pride in his voice, Affrica smiled with relief. It had seemed a long time coming.

And yet later, as she lay in her comfortable bed, listening to the rain still pattering on the roof, she thought of her hosts and let other, less palatable feelings assail her. She was glad he admired his wife—she was—but somewhere a tiny, corrosive hint of jealousy tugged, for she would have liked him to admire *her* for something, too.

Impossible to know or understand what went on inside a marriage. But something told her all was not well with Ferchar's. They were wrong together, and she thought he knew it. That was no worse than most marriages, which were made for political gain, or for land or influence, only she had never imagined Ferchar would marry for such reasons. He was too honest, too loyal.

But if he had made a mistake, if he didn't love Deirdre, did it not mean his heart was free?

Affrica hated the flash of hope, of unkind pleasure that sprang up. Ferchar's marriage was no business of hers. He was her friend. Deirdre *wanted* to be her friend. And that was all there would ever be. She would not weep for that.

※

WHEN SHE WOKE, shards of early light peeped through the tiny cracks in the shutters. She could hear no movement in the house, though the sounds of animals and poultry and human voices drifted in from outside. She rose and padded to the window, throwing the shutters wide to a beautiful, clear morning. The yard below seemed to be at the back of the house, which jutted out at odd angles on the ground floor. A roof overhung a cushioned bench and table, just to the left of her, perhaps designed to let one watch the sea in the distance, and any approaching boats. She sat on the chest beneath her window to enjoy the view.

To the right, the blue, clear water of the Dornoch Firth shone a deeper blue than the sky, stretching over to Sutherland in the north. Fishing boats bobbed near the coast. A bigger ship sailed tranquilly toward the open sea. Similar and yet different to the more familiar scene at Tirebeck.

The gentle clopping of horses' hooves drew her attention straight ahead to the ridged farmland spreading inland and rising to gentle, forested hills. Some were dotted instead with sheep and goats. Cattle lowed close by.

Two horsemen picked their way along a track leading away from the hall, their backs to Affrica. But she knew who they were: Colin and Ferchar making an early start, without servants or escort. She wished suddenly that she were going with them, then scolded herself, because it would be entertaining at the house, too.

She rose from the chest, dangling out the window as far as her waist to see further left. As though sensing her, one of the riders turned to look back over his shoulder. Ferchar. He raised one hand, and, embarrassed at being caught hanging out the window in her shift, she threw herself back inside, landing with a bump on the chest, her knees under her chin. Her whole body felt hot.

Which was stupid. He could have seen nothing at that distance, not even who she was. Except that he presumably knew which window was hers.

Still warm, she bounced up from the chest and threw it open to decide what to wear, before she remembered that her few clothes were in the other chest. This one was full of someone else's things.

The late Henry's, perhaps, she thought as she lowered the lid again. But no, that was the deep blue coat, surely, that Ferchar had worn at Dingwall. Her hand paused, holding the lid still half open. She touched the coat, as though to be sure, even dragging it up to sniff it.

*Oh, Fiend seize him, why does the smell of him make me… Why do I even notice it?*

She dropped the coat back in, folding it neatly as it had been, only as she spread it, something rustled beneath. She lifted the coat to smooth whatever she had disturbed, and saw it was a piece of parchment with Ferchar's name written on it in her hand.

Her breath caught. He'd kept her letter.

Well, of course he did. It told him his father's last words of forgiveness, understanding, and blessing. He had packed it away with the clothes he rarely wore. She set the coat carefully back on top of it and closed the lid before trotting guiltily to her own attire in the other chest.

Eta, her tirewoman, came in then, bearing fresh water to wash in, and helped her dress in the comfortable, all-purpose blue gown she had brought with her—respectable enough to receive well-born visitors, yet stout enough to bear the attentions of Wolf or the accidents of children or kitchen staff. It would just have to be respectable enough for the Lady of Carron.

"Is the Lady Deirdre up yet?" Affrica asked.

"She rises late," Eta replied, gazing about her with interest. "What's this?" she added, reaching for a curtain that hung on a rail across part of the wall. She pulled it open to reveal a door and glanced back at Affrica, who shrugged and nodded. Eta pulled back the bolt.

The door opened onto an outside staircase down the side of the house.

"Excellent," Affrica said happily. "I'll go out that way and disturb no one."

"Your veil, lady!" Eta said scandalized, holding it out to her with a pile of pins and a head dress.

Affrica seized the veil but skipped down the stairs without the rest.

# Chapter Thirteen

*Ross, summer 1210*

DEIRDRE FOUND HER an hour later seated on the cushioned bench she had first seen from her bedroom window.

"Ah, there you are," Deirdre said, smiling. "They told me you had gone for an early walk."

"I did, but not a very long one. It's still very muddy out there. But this is a lovely place to sit."

Deirdre nodded and sat down beside her. "My husband likes to sit out here and think."

"Do you not?" Affrica asked lightly.

"I am more of a practical person. I have the house and the girls and my needlework."

"Needlework? Did you make the hangings in the hall?"

"And those in the bedchambers. Do you sew, lady?"

"When I have to," Affrica said with a grimace. "Which, fortunately, isn't often. I'm not much of a needlewoman."

"You lost your mother early, though, did you not? It was my mother who first taught me. It was the one thing my father thought a girl should learn."

"My father just gave me governors and governesses and let me learn what I liked. And the rest of the time I ran wild or followed my father about. Or the boys if they didn't notice."

"Didn't you mind?" Deirdre sounded shocked.

"Not at the time." She shrugged. "Nor now, to be honest."

"I suppose you would always have had servants to do your needlework of all kinds."

Affrica, who had never really thought about it, nodded, and watched the flight of a heron over the sea.

"I wonder what men think about," Deirdre mused.

Affrica, with the benefit of two brothers and several male cousins who barely noticed her existence, had a fairly good idea. "You should ask Ferchar," she said diplomatically.

Deirdre's gaze rested on her face. "Will you marry the earl?"

"No, I won't marry the earl." That, at least, was clearer to her now than it had ever been. "I don't believe I shall marry anyone."

"I don't believe that," Deirdre said earnestly. "You are only sixteen years old. You mustn't give up hope."

She was almost seventeen. But it was not a matter of hope. It was, she had long suspected, a matter of love.

⸻ ❖ ⸻

AFFRICA FOUND HER day with Deirdre pleasant if slightly frustrating as she tried to understand her hostess. This self-imposed task was a little like trying to grasp a bar of wet soap in a basin full of water—as soon as you thought you had it, it would slip from your grasp and shoot off beneath the water.

Deirdre showed her the rest of the house, including her own, very feminine bedroom. Affrica could discover nothing of Ferchar there. She visited the nursery and played with Deirdre's mischievous-eyed yet extremely well-behaved daughters. She wanted to take them for a ramble over the moors and hills but managed a game of hide-and-seek in the garden. She admired Deirdre's needlework with genuine awe and gradually came to realize that the older woman was just as curious about her—and probably just as mystified.

Colin and Ferchar returned in time for the evening meal, their maleness erupting into the feminine territory of the hall like an invading army. Ferchar was relaxed and smiling, Colin bright-eyed with enthusiasm for more than sheep. Both were spattered with mud and smelled of horse, and Deirdre shooed them away to change their clothing. Since she rose to do the same, Affrica realized she would have to don the red gown again.

Ferchar, without hurrying to do his lady's bidding, was pouring ale into two cups, one of which he handed to Colin. They clinked cups and drank the ale down while Affrica made her way to the stairs. A moment later, Colin bounded after her. They were in the little passage outside her bedchamber door when the door of the hall opened and closed and Ferchar's deep voice could be heard faintly calling to someone outside.

The realization swept over Affrica like a wave. He did not share Deirdre's chamber. *This* was his chamber, with the chest full of his clothes and his things. And since she was in his room, he slept for the time being in one of the despised guest houses in the yard.

Why?

Eta would not let her wear the red gown again but was lacing her into the green court gown before she noticed.

"Where did this come from?" Affrica asked. "I never packed it."

"I did. Can't have you shown up by the Lady of Carron."

Affrica's gaze fixed on her. *Does everyone understand Deirdre but me?* "Don't be silly," she said aloud. "But certainly, they tend to formality here, so I'm glad you brought it." She moved away until Eta caught her again.

"Your hair, lady—be still!"

Her veil and her jewels were affixed before Colin stuck his head in the door.

"Aren't you ready yet? I had to scrub an inch of mud off me, and I'm still dressed before you."

"But you don't look half as pretty," Eta retorted.

Colin grinned. "I'll give you that. Come on, Affrica."

"Why the impatience? The lady will be there for you to ogle all evening."

Colin flushed. "I do not ogle. It would be disrespectful to her and Ferchar—who is great company, you know. Funny and yet utterly serious, and he has done so many things, been so many places while Nechtan and I have rarely been out of Ross! And he knows our uncles in the east better than we *ever* will—he has such stories!"

With an unusual spurt of jealousy, Affrica realized she wanted those stories. She wished she had been with them, learning Ferchar the Lord of Carron—*funny and yet utterly serious*—instead of the lady whose surface she could not even scratch.

Ferchar had made a friend of Colin, that much was obvious. And his friendship had always been beguiling.

"We're off to Tain tomorrow," Colin said cheerfully over dinner.

"More sheep?" Affrica inquired, and Deirdre smiled over her knife.

"No, men. Ferchar's going to show me the girth guard."

The evening, while similar in shape to the one before, felt considerably more relaxed. The boyhood differences and quarrels, which had probably weighed on Colin more than Ferchar, must have vanished in the growing bond of new friendship created during the day, for they bantered and laughed together with the ease of longer acquaintance.

Affrica again played the lute, but this time as she made to lay it aside, Ferchar's big hand closed over it. He loomed for only an instant, when she could not breathe, and then he sat down beside her on the cushions, examining the instrument.

"Could you teach me?" he asked.

"To play? Yes, if you like." With relief, she showed him the basics of how to hold the instrument and place his fingers, moving his digits prosaically and without embarrassment since she had a task to perform.

He glanced up from his hands to meet her gaze, a lazy smile in his hazel eyes. Then they slipped beyond her to the others. "Don't worry, I shan't ruin the evening by forcing you to listen to my discordant efforts."

"Play on your own," Affrica said lightly. "Listen and experiment, and I will give you lessons at more suitable times." It was a reason to be with him. And if she taught him, they could play together... *We are friends,* she thought, almost in panic. *We have always been friends.*

Yet still, she stood and moved away from him, as if to safety.

⸻

LYING IN BED was worse. There was no safety there either, for once the knowledge that this was his bed had entered her head, it would not leave. She imagined she could smell him—she couldn't—or thought of him lying there, passing the time by carving the images she found hidden just behind the chest. By the light of the lamp, she couldn't even tell what the carvings were, though they were intricate, for someone had scraped over them with a broad knife, obliterating everything except that they had been there.

Of course, anyone could have made the carvings. Anyone could have destroyed them. It didn't have to be Ferchar who had done either or both, and yet she couldn't lose the conviction that he had.

This obsession with Ferchar, with her friend, with another woman's husband, was wrong in every way known to her. And yet her body was hot as she lay in his bed. She ached and not with dishonesty but with intense longing. She imagined him lying beside her and tried to thrust the vision from her. He should be lying beside Deirdre. Why wasn't he? Could she somehow fix that? In reparation for her thoughts of...?

With an impatient gasp, she threw herself out of the bed and began to pace the room, forcing herself to stop only when it entered her head that she might be disturbing Deirdre below. She halted, resting her forehead against the window shutters. The wood was too warm to cool her skin, so she reached for the shutters before a better idea came to her.

She needed to run into exhaustion, preferable in company with Wolf. Since she couldn't, in strange country without the dog, she could probably manage a brisk walk without disturbing a soul.

Returning to the bed, she pulled on the soft shoes Eta had placed neatly beneath it, and then swung around her shoulders her old wool traveling cloak, which was well dried and cleaned after its soaking on the journey north. The bolt on the door to the outside staircase slid back easily, as though it was often used. Her shoes made no sound on the stairs as she flitted down them and veered right, toward the sea.

"Affrica."

She stopped and closed her eyes. Had she known when she came out here? Had she hoped? Movement came from behind her, from the cushioned bench beneath the awning where, according to his wife, he sat to think.

"Should I be shocked?" he asked. "Are you off on some secret assignation?"

"Only with my mind."

"Then you had better come back, or you'll destroy these slippers."

There was nothing else for it. Running would not calm her now. She turned and walked back. "You can't possibly see that I'm wearing slippers."

"Your feet made no sound on the steps and even you cannot be foolish enough to run about barefoot at night."

The banter was a relief. "Even me? Whatever happened to the new, courteous Ferchar?"

"He's had too much wine. Would you care to join him?" He did not weave as he stood beside the little table. His words were not slurred, or even enunciated with the particular precision of the inebriated. But by the light of the almost full moon, his eyes definitely glittered.

He had never asked for her company, never needed to, so far as she knew. And yet she thought he needed it now, and she could not refuse him.

She took a step nearer until she could smell the wine in the jug, or perhaps on his breath. She sat, and so did he, not touching. He reached for the jug and poured a full cup, which he passed to her.

"Now you don't have one," she pointed out.

He clinked the bottom of the jug against the cup and a breath of laughter caught in her throat as she lifted the cup and sipped, watching him drink straight from the jug. He didn't spill any. Neither did he gulp. He set the jug back on the table and together they gazed up at the stars and out to the silver-glinting sea and the low hills beyond.

Her stomach unknotted into calm. And yet she was no less aware of the man at her side.

She said, "Are you happy, Ferchar Maccintsacairt?"

"Are you, Affrica MacHeth?"

"Usually," she said honestly, and felt him smile.

"That was always what fascinated me about you, even as a child. How could anyone be so constantly content while those about you seethed? While I seethed. Were you born knowing that happiness is just a moment? To be savored and enjoyed to the full because in another moment, it will be gone, only to come again when you least expect it."

"You make it sound rare."

"Isn't it?"

"Not for me."

His gaze came back to her face and held until she turned her head to meet his eyes. "Perhaps not. But I'm not talking about general contentment—I think that is your nature as general restlessness is mine. I mean the moments that soar above that." A breath of laughter stirred her hair, invading her with the scent of wine and Ferchar. "Like sliding across a precarious washing line in Paris."

She smiled, warmed to her core because he brought it up, because it had meant happiness to him as it had to her. Even now. "I sent the angry woman a new apron," she offered.

"Not just the old one back?"

"It was too abused." And it lay in her room at Tirebeck.

"And now you are a young lady of beauty and style and fascination."

"But no suitors," she pointed out. "While you are married."

"I am." More words seemed to start to his lips, but he never spoke them, merely shifted in his seat, and she raised the cup to her lips. The cup he had already drunk from. *Why did you marry her? Do you love her?*

"So, *are* you happy?" she repeated, almost in desperation. "Do you find your *moments* more frequently?"

His gaze rested on her face, and she took another drink before setting the cup down and pushing it away from her. He said deliberately, "I won't discuss my marriage with you, Affrica MacHeth."

The heat of embarrassment surged through her. "Did I ask you to?" she retorted.

"I think perhaps you might have." His lips twisted as he sipped from the jug. "So many things we cannot talk about now that we are adults. I thought you would go back to the queen this year."

"She did not ask for me. Nor the king for Kenneth, even though he succeeds his father. Kenneth finds both sinister."

"Kenneth looks always for drama. The king is old and doesn't want to be surrounded by the young and enthusiastic and troublesome."

"Like you?"

"He'll have forgotten me by now."

"Do you mind?"

"Why should I mind? I have this." He waved his hand to the land and the coast, all his, more or less, as far as Tain.

"You have this," she agreed. "Colin is impressed." Since his lips quirked, though he said nothing, she added. "He likes you."

"I aim to be liked."

She regarded him with a hint of relief among the stirrings of excitement. "What are you up to, Ferchar Maccintsacairt?"

"Finding the fun in my new position. I like Colin, too. He is a good man, emerging from Kenneth's shadow."

"You don't think Kenneth a good man?" she asked quickly.

"Kenneth...has a good enough heart but bad impulses. In my experience. Our task is to preserve the former and limit the latter."

She blinked. "Is that not rather beyond you and me?"

He raised the jug to her in a silent toast. "Probably. It remains to be seen."

"It still isn't enough, is it, Ferchar?"

He held her gaze. "You sound like my father."

"I know."

Everything went still, and then his breath came out in a rush. "I'm damned if I know why I like being with you, Affrica MacHeth. But I am glad you're here."

Her whole being ached, not with dissonance but with the pain of truth. *So am I.*

"How do I help?" she asked when she could speak. She was no longer talking about Kenneth, and it seemed he knew it.

"Teach me the happiness of music." He paused with the jug halfway to his mouth. "We had no music in Paris."

"I heard the odd strum, and a pipe practiced somewhere below. There were birds, most of them in very startled song. And Wolf howling in the distance. You can always hear music if you listen."

He smiled. "How is Wolf?"

She told him a story about the dog guarding the standing stone at

Tirebeck, and the locals beginning to wonder if he was a god reborn, until he dug up the pig's bone he had buried right beside the stone. And he told her about the goose who shared his guard duty in Bulgaria, and how he woke the entire camp by chasing after the man who tried to take the bird away to cook it.

She laughed at the vision he conjured, and then said, "Why did you say the crusaders' fight was not yours?"

To her surprise, he told her. He did not laugh at her questions, and she was not shocked by his answers. Instead, she mulled his novel arguments in her mind and tried to apply them to Scotland.

"You are raising men to protect the holy sanctuary at Tain. Is that not the same as protecting Jerusalem?"

"No. Not even if we *were* protecting Jerusalem rather than land we had opportunistically seized from other Christians. Here, it is my given task, inherited and requested by my lords the bishop and the earl, to protect the shrine and the sanctuary of St. Duthac. I will always protect Tain and Carron. And Ross. And Scotland. Although I might try to run from them occasionally, they are my home."

He nudged her shoulder, much as he had done in Paris, and she realized that they had moved and that their bodies touched at arm and hip. She pretended not to notice, so that she could treasure that nearness for a few moments more.

"I am not denouncing crusades or crusaders. It is an ideal taken to its logical extreme, even if it falls down, like most religious enterprises in the hands of men. But I could not be part of it. Even if I hadn't needed to come home."

She nodded. "You have much here worth protecting."

"More than you know."

She glanced at him for clarification and found his gaze intent and unreadable on her face. In desperation, she raised her cup to her lips. "It's empty."

"So is the jug. I could go and get more, but I suspect I have bored you enough that you will sleep until well past sunrise." He rose, still steady on his feet, and drew her up beside him. Her heart thundered as he lifted her hand and dropped the lightest kiss on her fingertips. "Thank you for my moment of happiness. Good night."

And he walked away, leaving her nothing to do but walk up the staircase back to her bedroom, which was his. She bolted the door behind her and lay down in his bed, listening to her heart beat, and holding her fingertips to her cheek.

---

"WHAT HAPPENED IN Paris?"

Deirdre's quiet, casual question took Affrica by complete surprise. Ferchar and Colin had left for Tain before she had risen, and the women had spent the day much like the one before. Until now, when, walking in her garden of sweet-smelling herbs, Deirdre asked about Paris.

"In Paris?" Affrica repeated. "When?"

"When you met my husband there. I know he performed some service for your father, one that took him eastward and prevented him finishing his studies, but he never explained what happened."

Affrica leaned to smell the rosemary that grew almost to head height. "It was all kept quiet for the sake of my family. The…difficulty was really my fault. I was both too adventurous and too ignorant, and I left the house alone without anyone's knowledge. I was thirteen, I think, old enough to know better, you might imagine. I went to look for the great churches and found myself in the university quarter, where my dog discovered Ferchar. Which was fortunate, because when someone tried to abduct me, he saved me. After which my father asked him to warn my uncles of the danger to the family."

Deirdre fixed her with a steady gaze. "There is more than that."

Affrica said nothing, merely held the suddenly accusing gaze.

"I did not sleep well either," Deirdre said impatiently. "I heard you and my husband talking."

There was no reason to feel guilt at that, and yet Deirdre's tone irritated her even as she understood it.

She raised her eyebrows. "I'm sorry to have disturbed you. I could tell you every smelly street we ran through, every house and tavern and every roof we crossed—if I could remember such details three years later. It was the most exciting thing that had ever happened to me in a single afternoon. I was a child, Deirdre, with a child's sense of adventure. Ferchar never saw me as anything else, and if you heard us talking, you know that."

Deirdre's eyes never wavered, though the faintest frown tugged her brow. Affrica walked on, wondering how to change the subject and wishing Deirdre had never brought it up because she didn't want either Paris or last night mauled by anyone else, least of all his wife.

"I don't understand men," Deirdre said, coming up beside her. "I thought I did. When I met Henry, I knew I would marry him, and I did, and I knew him. Ferchar is… different."

"Of course, he is," Affrica said, startled. "Men are no more alike than women."

Deirdre's eyes lightened a little. "You don't want to marry, and I cannot exist without a husband."

Somewhat lost but trying to help, Affrica said, "You chose two good husbands. Ferchar is utterly loyal. If he were not, my father would never have trusted him. You should, too." *Share his bed, share his life. He needs you.*

"You must forgive my odd humors. I believe I am with child."

# Chapter Fourteen

*Ross, autumn-winter 1210*

In November, an early but severe fall of snow blocked most of the roads and hill passes into Wester Ross. On impulse, Ferchar rode over to Tain to see if this inconvenience had thrown any unlikely characters into sanctuary.

"A couple," his sergeant told him, huddling into his cloak for warmth. "Claim to be messengers from Wester Ross."

"Messengers? Then why do they need sanctuary? Why aren't they looked after by whoever sent their message or received it?"

"Apparently, they're too far away. But I'd say they know this place. They've been here before."

"Before we started guarding it?" Ferchar asked.

The sergeant nodded.

"I'll have a word."

He found them in the sanctuary house with an aged pilgrim and a shifty looking, hairy character, who no doubt hoped to escape justice for another few days. They sat together at the old table, all eating the food provided by the community.

"Gentlemen," Ferchar said pleasantly as he walked in.

The pilgrim rose and bowed. The thief, or whatever he was, stuffed some more food in his face before nodding. The messengers merely looked at him, although their hands strayed to their belts, where their weapons should have been, and their eyes were on Ferchar's.

"You can't carry weapons here," one of them said by way of greeting. He spoke in Gaelic, perhaps with an inflection of the isles. Neither young nor old, they had a seasoned look about them. Wiry old warriors. Mercenaries, no doubt.

Ferchar stood at the head of the table, "Actually, I can. I'm Ferchar Maccintsacairt, the keeper of the shrine and the girth of St. Duthac."

"Ah." The two strangers exchanged glances. "Then it is you who's turned the holy sanctuary into a fortress?"

"Hardly," Ferchar said mildly. "But, yes, I grew concerned by its misuse. We provide sanctuary and charity, not free meals and shelter to those who neither need it nor deserve it."

One of the strangers stood. "Are you accusing us of something, keeper of the shrine and the girth of St. Duthac?"

"Not yet," Ferchar said gently. "Though I question such a poor master as yours who sends you across the country without money for lodging. I ask you for his name, so that I might explain the rules of sanctuary to him."

The standing man took a belligerent step forward, though his friend restrained him by gripping his arm.

"There will be no need of that. We'll make sure the master gives us more coin the next time."

"More than is already rattling in your friend's scrip?" Ferchar said politely. "A donation to St. Duthac would be most welcome upon your departure."

The belligerent messenger sat down. "You're throwing us out? On a night like this?"

"How un-Christian that would be," Ferchar said as though shocked. "No, I'll be throwing you out in the morning and escorting you to the harbor at Tain."

"That will not suit," the belligerent man ground out. "We need to be on the west of the country."

Ferchar smiled. "You may sail there eventually. Enjoy your supper, gentlemen. Good evening."

The sergeant at the door, who must have heard everything, was grinning. He turned and walked with Ferchar from the house.

"They won't come this way again," he said with satisfaction. "But what poor sod's going to sail with them in this weather?"

"None, probably. I fully expect them to decamp during the night."

"You want them captured?"

"No, I want them followed."

※

THE EARL OF ROSS was known to be at his old family home at Brecka, although the word was, he intended to spend Christmas at Dingwall.

"I want to catch him before he goes south," Ferchar told his wife the following day, as he stuffed clothing into saddle bags. "That way, I shall be back more quickly."

"But you will be gone days as it is!" Deirdre stood at the door of his room, her hand over her stomach in a gesture that reminded him unbearably of Affrica.

"Only a few. I may go to Tirebeck also."

Some rare fury spat from her eyes, quickly hidden, although the emotion left her breathing more quickly than usual. "And what if you are trapped there by the weather?"

"I won't be."

"Will she be there?"

Ferchar cast her an impatient glance. Once, this sign of jealousy would have pleased him, proved there was a spark of feeling there. Now it just annoyed him. "If you mean the Lady Affrica, I have no idea. No one keeps me abreast of her movements."

"And if I am ill? If the baby is born while you are away?"

With difficulty, he kept a lid on his temper. "Deirdre, you are nowhere near your time. You have your women and even a midwife in the house with you. If you are ill, they are more competent to help than I. I rejoice in your good health, as you should. And I will back before you have time to miss me."

She came then and put her arms around him in a rare show of affection, something she only did when she wanted something of him. Like marriage.

"Would you not prefer to stay here with me?" she wheedled.

He had fallen for that one twice before. And learned that the affection, if one could call it that, would be withdrawn as soon as he agreed to stay. That was how their child had been conceived.

"I would," he said patiently. "But it is my duty to go to the earl and to speak to Angus mac Adam." He dropped a chaste kiss on top of her head. "You will take good care of yourself and our child."

Gently, he moved out of her embrace and went to say farewell to the girls. He thought she might continue to sulk, but in the end, she waved him off from the door of the hall, looking so beautiful and so grieved by the parting that he wondered desperately why they didn't love each other.

With relief, he rode away, leaving the pain of his home life behind him.

※

KENNETH WAS DISCOVERED in Brecka's huge hall, which was blissfully warm around the fireplace, along with his brother Ranald and his cousin Nechtan, Affrica's brother, planning their journey to Dingwall.

"Son of the priest!" Kenneth greeted him jovially. "I thought you would be trapped in Carron."

"No, the first snows have already melted, even in the hills, which makes the ground horrible but passable. I'm glad I caught you here."

"Sit," Kenneth commanded before calling to a serving girl. "Wine, girl, for the Thane of Carron. What can we do for you?"

"Tell me, if you would, if you know anything about two tight-lipped islesmen who claim to be messengers and yet who abuse the hospitality of the girth of Tain."

Kenneth's lips curled. "Why come to me? You are the keeper of the girth, and you are hardly short of men to enforce the rules."

"Because the men in question refused to say where they had been or where they were going, and I had it in my head they might have been here."

Kenneth scowled, then sighed. "Go and warn the men we leave in an hour, Nechtan. Ranald, round up the servants. I'll join you in ten minutes. Now," he added when his kinsmen went off to do his bidding, "spit out whatever accusation is eating at your self-righteous soul."

Ferchar took the cup from the serving girl and took a welcome mouthful. "It is only a request for information," he said mildly.

"Such information is not concerned with the girth of Tain."

"It is when they hide there to avoid lodging in respectable houses."

Kenneth swore, pushing to his feet. "What do you know about running an earldom? I have spies everywhere, as my father did, and his father. If I choose not to have their work or even their presence shouted abroad, that is my right, and I do *not* answer to the son of the priest, whatever petty lordship he holds these days. Be easy, for God's sake. I will instruct them to avoid Tain in the future."

"I believe they are already clear on that point." He took another mouthful of wine and set down the cup. "And, of course, I am aware that you protect Ross by such means. I just thought Hebridean mercenaries an odd choice of messenger."

From the swift narrowing of Kenneth's eyes, he could see at once that his instinct was right—the messengers were professional soldiers of the Isles, the fearsome, organized troops who moved from master to master and war to war.

"They were not my choice," Kenneth snapped. "They came from someone else."

"No one...dangerous?"

"That is not your concern."

"With respect, it's everyone's concern. My aim is to help if I can, not thwart you."

Kenneth sat down again and poured himself wine from the jug. "You are a good man, Ferchar. I know that. But I walk a very thin rope as earl, balancing this way and that to do what is best."

Ferchar inclined his head and waited. His lips quirked. "But you will not confide in me."

Kenneth laughed. "Trust me, I have a surfeit of MacHeths to confide in and to advise me. Was there anything else?"

"Yes. My girth guard is stretched. I was hoping every lord in Ross would contribute a man or two to the task. Do I have your blessing to proceed?"

Kenneth regarded him warily, then let out a laugh. "Of course. I'll even give you four of mine. Now, if you'll forgive me, I want to reach Tirebeck before nightfall. You're welcome to rest here before you go home."

"Thank you." He had every intention of going to Tirebeck himself, just not when Kenneth was there.

※※※※

AFFRICA WAS WORRIED about her grandfather. For weeks, months even, he had seemed completely divorced from the real world and barely acknowledged her presence. At least he ate or drank whatever was put into his thin, old hands, which held none of the tremors common to old age. Without much hope, she wrapped his fingers around a cup of warm, spiced ale.

To her surprise, his face turned away from the fire, and he looked directly at her. One of his rare, sweet smiles broke out.

"Affrica," he said as though her presence was unexpected.

She smiled back. "There you are. I was afraid you had left us altogether."

"Not yet."

"Do you *like* being old, Grandfather?" she blurted when he had taken a few mouthfuls of the ale.

His white eyebrows with their odd strands of raven black, shot up. "What a very odd question. No one likes it." He appeared to think about it. "I suppose I don't miss the activity of youth, as most do at my age. I still run and ride and even fight in my mind. It's real enough."

"Wouldn't you like to be with us more?" she asked. "We miss you in the hall."

"You might. Even Angus might. Everyone else would be horribly uncomfortable. I can't control the dreams anymore."

"Can't you?" she asked with sudden insight. "I think you could if you tried."

"I never could, not really." He blinked and sipped his ale. "But you're right, I've let them consume me."

"Why? There is life here and now, Grandfather."

"There is something I have yet to see," he said vaguely.

Before he slipped away again, she took the ale from him and set it down, then thrust the bowl of stew onto his knee. Obediently, he lifted the spoon to his mouth. Then he lowered it again. "I see you often, and I'm glad of it. The last of the MacHeths."

A frisson passed through her veins, along with a tangle of grief-stricken images that vanished with the thud of the door opening. From her crouching position at her grandfather's knee, she stared at Ferchar Maccintsacairt.

He wore his forbidding face, though he bowed and said briefly,

"Your pardon. May I come in?"

"Of course," she managed, rising and trying to control the rapid beat of her heart. "Grandfather, you remember Ferchar? Of Carron and Tain."

Her grandfather actually smiled, inclining his head in greeting. "Have you come to speak to me or to Affrica?"

Ferchar gave a crooked smile and pulled up two stools, waiting for Affrica to sit before he did. "Actually, I was looking for Angus mac Adam, but they tell me he won't be back until later."

"He and Colin are traveling some of the way south with Kenneth," Affrica said. "Can you wait?"

"Gladly."

"How is Deirdre?" Affrica asked brightly.

"She is well, if a little nervous. She asks to be remembered to you."

"And I to her," Affrica returned. Since Deirdre's announcement about her pregnancy in the summer, she had given up trying to understand their marriage. The unhappiness, the lack of empathy between them that she would have done anything to bring right. She had assumed—wrongly—that they eschewed physical intimacy. Now, she assumed that if they did, it was because of Deirdre's condition. She had misunderstood everything at Carron and couldn't trust her judgment on anything to do with Ferchar.

She pushed aside the riot of thoughts and emotions that his appearance always brought her and realized that he and her grandfather were actually conversing, if not as old friends, then at least as people pleased to see each other.

Inevitably, of course, the old man turned his gaze back to the flames, and she caught the empty stew bowl before it fell from his knee. Standing, she pressed a quick kiss on her grandfather's head and moved toward the door.

Ferchar opened it for her and followed her outside into cold drizzle. As one, they hurried toward the hall door.

"You've visited him before," she said curiously.

"When I first came back. I had messages from Gregor and Eochaid. And he was eager to hear everything I could tell him."

"He can concentrate when he wants to," Affrica said, not knowing whether to be pleased or annoyed. "According to my father, my grandmother's death crushed him. I was only three when she died. But from then, he stopped paying attention."

"I think he might have begun again."

"Perhaps," she said doubtfully. "He rarely notices me anymore, though my father still goes to him every day and discusses things with him. I'm not sure how one-sided the conversation is. But…something *worries* him."

Ferchar pushed open the hall door. "Did he ever act as lord here at Tirebeck?"

"So I believe. For years, when he was little older than you, he and his brother between them ruled all of Ross and campaigned across most of Scotland against the king, too. That was before Earl Malcolm came home and brought peace. Then my grandfather retired here to Tirebeck, for the most part. It was my grandmother's land, and he was content with that, though the family still relied on him—his brother, Earl Donald, and Gilchrist, too."

She smiled a little as they walked the length of the hall toward the fire. "The men still tell stories of him, crazy stories that must be at least half-myth. He could rule if he wanted to." Not just Tirebeck, but Ross. And yet Kenneth discounted him, as he discounted Angus her father…

"Gregor misses him, I think."

"He misses all his children, though he never shows it. My aunts love him and visit when they can, but it is not the same as them living here."

"It is life. One day you won't live here either."

She wrinkled her nose. "Maybe not." A shiver passed over her.

"My grandfather is afraid. We should all pay attention to that." She took his cloak from him and spread it by the fire.

"Are you?" he asked.

She felt his gaze on her face but didn't look up from fussing with the cloak. "I don't have his gifts."

"But?"

She shrugged. "I feel something ominous." She glanced up and smiled. "No doubt my father and Kenneth are discussing my marriage."

She meant it to be funny, but he didn't smile or release her gaze. "Will you have a say?"

"If I do, I will stay here."

"Why?"

She moved to avoid his unbearable scrutiny. "My grandparents married for love."

"Perhaps you will, too."

She shook her head, and with relief saw Wolf trotting toward them from her bedchamber where he had been asleep. "Lazy dog!"

Even with the distraction, she thought for a moment that Ferchar would pursue the old conversation and searched desperately for a new topic. She found it in Sinead, who appeared sleepily after the dog.

"Sinead is a better musician than I will ever be," she told Ferchar. "Her father was the great harpist, Muiredach. She should be the one to give you the next music lesson."

There had been only one, at Carron, a secret delight that had somehow smoothed the discomfort of her odd conversation with Deirdre the day after she and Ferchar had drunk wine together in the moonlight.

While the lute was brought, he fingered the harp which sat permanently on a side table, plucking each string to listen to the differences in sounds. Sinead began little tunes on the lute with each note he struck, and the lesson became more of a game that had all three of them laughing by the time Angus and Colin strode into the hall arguing about something trivial that was instantly abandoned.

"Ferchar! Kenneth thought you were on your way back to Carron. Have you come to wheedle men for Tain out of us?"

"If I can," Ferchar said, bowing and shaking the hands instantly offered to him.

"How many?" Angus asked suspiciously.

"I'm asking for one from each lordship, but since your name is MacHeth, I thought you might give me two. The earl has promised me four."

"To give him more eyes on what you're up to," Angus said dryly.

"It doesn't matter. The men will be useful."

Without Affrica having to issue specific orders, food and wine were brought to the table. Sinead departed for her own house, leaving Affrica alone with the three men.

"Kenneth might have given you four men," Colin said through a mouthful of food, "but he doesn't trust what you're up to. He doesn't want anyone leading a force of men that could rival his own."

"It doesn't," Ferchar pointed out. "The earl can call on every able-bodied man in Ross. I cannot. Nor do I need to in order to protect so small an area as the girth."

"I believe what puzzles Kenneth is why you should need to," Angus said wryly. "He suspects you of wheedling the men out of him to provide your wife with an impressive bodyguard."

Ferchar waved such nonsense aside. "Did he tell you the other reason I called on him?"

"Something to do with messengers, not even his abusing the sanctuary?"

"They weren't his," Ferchar agreed. "But I'm fairly sure their original message was *for* him, and that they were carrying a reply back from him."

Angus shrugged. "They had no reason to be at the girth, perhaps, but Ferchar, my father and my uncle Donald received messengers all the time. No one sneezed in Ross without them knowing, and they had spies reporting from all over Scotland and the Isles. Even I receive news by unconventional means."

"I don't doubt the right or the wisdom in doing so. I just..." Ferchar threw down his bread. "They were islesmen, mercenaries. Is he in touch with Guthred MacWilliam?"

Angus stared at him. "I should hope not. Especially not after the trouble with Liam O'Neill in Dingwall."

"He said something about walking a narrow rope. I understand he needs to keep everyone happy, including powerful exiles with support at home. But Guthred is a step too far for me."

"And for me," Angus admitted. "The man isn't interested in peace. And after Paris..."

"He does not care for the people or the land," Ferchar interrupted. "How could he? He's never lived here. He follows some entitled ambition of his own."

"Ferchar, you've never met him," Colin pointed out.

"No, but my assessment isn't groundless."

"It isn't," Angus agreed. "I wouldn't trust Guthred—or his too amiable, scholarly brother—further than I could throw them. But they carry a beguiling message of nostalgia to the discontented, inspire a longing for the old ways before foreigners were placed over us, a time when the King of Scots was chosen for more than his position as eldest son, whatever his age or ability."

"A time of constant warfare and instability," Ferchar retorted, "that kept Ross and every other part of Scotland in poverty."

"I'm not disagreeing with you," Angus said mildly. "But Malcolm MacHeth fought for these things, and he is part of folk memory. My own father is a hero of *living* memory for pursuing the same dreams. You can't change people's ideals overnight. There are thanes in Ross who would be happy to see Guthred MacWilliam on the throne, and a return to the old ways. Not that it would happen, for we can never go back, and like you, I don't believe we should. But Kenneth has to consider these discontented men, to listen to them and their advocates. It doesn't make him a traitor to the current King of Scots."

Ferchar shifted restlessly. "I know that." He drank his wine, perhaps mulling over Angus's words.

Angus asked, "Have you no idea where the messengers were returning to?"

"Not yet, but I'm hoping to find out before Christmas."

"You will let me know?"

"I will."

Angus nodded. "I'll speak to Kenneth again if I need to. In the meantime, it's too late in the year to worry about war. Spring will be time enough."

# Chapter Fifteen

*Ross, winter 1210-1211*

As usual, the weather saved its worst for the new year, allowing everyone to become hopeful of spring before letting loose its most savage attack. Even Tirebeck, so close to the coast that it was often spared the worst of the snow, saw blizzards that piled the snow high against the sides of the hall. Icy winds tried to batter open the shutters, and even the skins hung over the doors and windows didn't prevent the drafts whistling through the bedchambers and the hall.

Once it stopped snowing, the sun came out occasionally, and Affrica threw open all the shutters to capture the brief warmth. With the old joy of childhood, she wrapped herself in layers of gowns and furs, gloves and stout boots, and went bounding through the snow with Wolf, admiring their weaving footprints in the pristine whiteness. They clambered and slid their way down to the beach, where the snow was less, but considerably icier. Wolf skidded, and Affrica all but fell onto the large rock from where she liked to watch the sea and the boats when the weather was fine.

Today, land and hills were all white. Only the Black Isle, on the other side of the firth, lived up to its name, like a different country.

It was too cold to linger. She began to trudge back up from the beach toward the road and the village to see that everyone had enough food and warmth to stay alive. For an instant, the snow blinded her, as though with a sudden flash. She halted, reaching for the trunk of a bare, wispy tree to steady herself and weather the storm of grief that assailed her.

And then it was gone. Only the half-glimpsed vision of Ferchar, riding too fast through the snow, remained behind her eyes.

>>><<<

FERCHAR WAS IN no hurry to go home. Having toured what he could of his frozen lands in Carron and Tain, and solving what problems he could in such weather, he sat back in the saddle to enjoy his rare solitude.

Christmas hadn't been so bad. Lulach and his household had joined them at Carron, and there had been warmth and laughter, and Deirdre had seemed happy. But with Lulach's departure and the worsening of the weather…

He was not cut out for marriage. He should not welcome these moments of solitude with quite such fervent relief. Nor should he feel such impatience, such temper, toward his pregnant wife, whose discomforts and discontents were constant and vocal. He had never shouted—yet—but escaping her demands and her carping, even the sound of her voice, had become his prime focus. And that was wrong.

But in truth, he could not think in her presence. She gave him no peace, and he was clearly no comfort to her. But he had to go back, with the strength and calm he had surely possessed in the past. The English, the Bulgars, charging into battle against him, had been easier to deal with than his frail little wife, who asked for nothing but the presence of her husband.

A husband who finally realized he would rather be anywhere else in the world. Who needed to think and plan and watch for the messengers who had fled from the sanctuary at Tain had gone back to

Guthred MacWilliam. He had told Angus mac Adam, though he had no idea what Angus had done about it. Nothing *could* be done until the spring, except tie and gag Kenneth MacHeth.

While his shaggy little horse picked its own way through the snowy path, he allowed his mind to drift back to his last visit to Tirebeck, when he had talked with Angus and Colin about the dangers facing Ross. And had almost played the lute with Affrica and her old governess. He smiled faintly, recalling her piquant, laughing face, the beauty and grace that had somehow slid over the being of the sunny, reckless child and made her…incomparable.

He had risen early to return to Carron from Tirebeck, meaning to call at other lordships on his way home. But as he had led his horse from the stable, he had heard Affrica singing.

Lively and happy like birdsong at dawn, her voice had drifted through the half-open shutters at the back of the house where the family slept. He had no doubts it was Affrica. It wasn't a performance. She was singing to herself as she had told him back in Edinburgh that was all she ever did. If that was so, it wasn't because her voice was unpleasant or even untrue. Her song was like the essence of Affrica herself—a little secretive, yet joyous and sweet with just a hint of uncertainty. Its beauty had bombarded him, halting him and his horse in their tracks, washing over him with an emotion at once unbearable and uplifting. He had actually smiled before his horse had nudged him ungently, reminding him of the task in hand.

He smiled again now on his reluctant way home to Carron. Did Kenneth realize what a powerful prize he had there to barter in marriage? Ferchar shied away from that thought, concentrating instead on the peace and pleasure of her company. Of the fun dancing in her eyes, so reminiscent of the fearless child and yet overlaid, now, with the mystery of the woman.

Another rider was approaching him, urging on his horse, who was clearly reluctant to risk his footing. Frowning, Ferchar kicked his mount forward, recognizing the rider as one of his own people.

"My lord, you have to hurry!" the man panted. "It's the lady. The baby is coming, and the midwife is afraid…"

Ferchar waited for no more but spurred forward in desperation, his mind suddenly full of very different and terrible visions. Deirdre, afraid of being alone, his child…

Of course, she was not really alone. She was surrounded by women experienced in birthing. There should be no greater fear for them than before. And yet, when he burst into the hall, the screams of agony and the soothing pity of other female voices tore at his heart.

The midwife scurried out of the bedchamber at the front of the hall and paused. Their eyes met, his furious with fear, hers resigned and full of pity.

*No. Please, God, no. I will do anything if you let them live…*

>>><<<

AFFRICA COULD NEVER remember waiting for a thaw with such impatience. But when it finally began and her father suggested she come with him and Colin to Dingwall, she refused. For the next two days, she wished she hadn't, for the chaotic variety of the journey would have distracted and soothed this anxiety she had no name or reason for. Instead, she had little company but Sinead and Wolf's, and that of the local people who sought her help or judgment.

She even suggested to Sinead that they could set out for Dingwall after all, which Sinead flatly refused to do. Her mother, who was even older than Affrica's grandfather, was unwell, and Affrica could not be so cruel as to drag Sinead away at such a time.

Instead, she sat with her unresponsive grandfather. "Mairead is ill. Muiredach's wife. Sinead is afraid she will die."

Her grandfather nodded, as if this was not unexpected. If there was grief there for so old a friend, it was hidden behind all the rest that clouded his unquiet, unfocused eyes. When she had made sure he ate and drank, she stood up to leave him to his dreams.

"You should go," he murmured.

"To Dingwall? I suppose I could go without Sinead, if I took Eta. Two men-at-arms would be enough, don't you think?"

Adam mac Malcolm did not confide what he thought, so she sighed and departed.

Back in the hall, she found the welcome distraction of a messenger from Father Stephen at Tain. Although he was begging sustenance on his way to Dingwall and the earl, Affrica brightened. She would have the messenger's company as well, so two men-at-arms would definitely be enough, even for her father.

"Is your message urgent?" she asked.

"Not really. Father Stephen keeps the earl informed of life in the parish. He has not written since before Christmas, so when the thaw came, he sent me southward."

"Do you have news from the Lord of Carron, too?"

The messenger, settling by the fire with his mug of warmed ale, grimaced. "Not directly, lady. The lord is not up to reports, but Father Stephen will have written it down."

Her stomach twisted in knots. "Written what down?"

"The Lady of Carron is dead, and the child with her. Ferchar Maccintsacairt has taken it hard."

"Oh, dear God," she whispered. "The poor..." Words fell apart in grief. She knew now what that odd vision in the snow had meant, what her anxiety since had been all about. Childbirth was a danger no one could do anything about. Save take the path of celibacy.

She gave herself a shake, trying to think through the tangle of thoughts and emotions. "Is someone caring for the little girls?"

"I imagine the servants are, and the neighboring women will keep an eye on them."

But Deirdre had no other living family, and neither did Ferchar.

"You should go."

―――※―――

SHE TOOK HER maid, Eta and two men-at-arms and journeyed not south to Dingwall but north to Carron, following the coast roads as Father Stephen's messenger had recommended. They had to spend one night in a cold shepherd's cottage, then slogged on through mud and slush to Tain and along the coast of the Dornoch Firth to the hall at Carron.

It was dusk when they arrived. Affrica, though relieved that a stable lad came to take their horses, could hardly dismount for the waves of emotional chill that seemed to emanate from the house. A house of death, past the first days of shock but deep in mourning. And yet as she walked into the hall, she had to hold her stomach to control the pain.

The hall was not empty. Euphemia and Christina were on the rug at the front of the hall, squabbling over a wooden toy on a string which they both abandoned at sight of Affrica and ran to her.

"Lady! Lady Affrica!" Christina cried.

"My mother isn't here." Euphemia's lips wobbled pitiably.

"She's gone to God," Christina whispered, "and we can't go with her."

"Our little brother went with her," Euphemia confided.

Affrica swallowed. "Then she has company while she watches over you."

"Do you think she does?" Christina asked doubtfully. She glanced at the toys and cups scattered about the hall. "We forgot to curtsey to you, too."

"I think your mother would allow all these sins for once," Affrica managed through her aching throat. "Where is your stepfather? Is he away from home?"

"No, he's up there." Euphemia pointed to the staircase.

"No, he isn't," Christina murmured, nodding toward the outside door.

Affrica jerked around. The unmistakable figure of Ferchar strode across the hall. She had half-expected a man broken by grief, unshaven, unkempt, uncaring, his body bent, his face a mask of grief. But this man marched straight-backed toward them, little expression but irritation in his clean-shaven face. His dress, though not new, was cared for, clean save for the odd splash of mud.

Then he stopped in his tracks, his gaze searching the hall, skimming over the children before coming back to her. "Christ. What are you doing here?"

Her arm tightened across her stomach.

He saw the involuntary gesture, for his gaze flickered to it and back to hers. His face didn't soften. "Where are your people?"

"My men are caring for the horses. My woman is in the corner waiting for instruction."

"You came alone?" He stared at her. "Why? What is wrong?"

*You have lost your wife and child!* She wanted to scream the words at him, but settled for a mild, "With me? Nothing. I came to see your daughters."

"We forgot to curtsey," Christina said, "but the lady thinks Mother wouldn't mind."

"I'm sure she's right." Only as he walked past her to the table did she realize that he had neither bowed nor greeted her. He might not have been stricken by grief, but he was rattled.

She watched his straight, broad back and listened to the sounds of liquid splashing into cups.

"Please, sit," he said curtly.

She did, lowering herself to the cushioned settle while he loomed over her, offering her a cup, which she took with a word of thanks. He did not sit but stood frowning down at her.

"Even you must know you should not have come here without

any of your family or at least another lady."

*Even you.* It was a familiar insult, but she had never heard it without humor before. "Well, I *am* here, so might we move on? Who is caring for the girls?"

The children had drifted back to their game.

"Bridie," Ferchar said, lifting his cup to his lips. "As she always has."

"None of your neighbors?"

"They took it in turns to look in for the first week or so." He walked back to the table to refill his cup.

In desperation, she rose and followed him, for nothing here was right. He swung around, cup in hand, and halted so suddenly that the wine slopped over the side. He was too close, much too close. She could smell the wine, smell him. And yet neither of them moved.

"Ferchar, I'm sorry," she said urgently, for some things had to be said if only to bring them into the open. "So very sorry."

"I daresay Angus will forgive you if you return at once. But I wouldn't tell Kenneth."

For an instant, she couldn't comprehend what he was talking about, and then she wanted to hit him.

"I am sorry about the death of your wife and child," she said deliberately.

"A letter would have been sufficient." His face didn't change, but the pain in her stomach nagged on. Ignoring her closeness, he raised his cup, and his arm brushed against her shoulder as he drank. The insolence was curiously deliberate, for he held her gaze the whole time. And at last, she saw the tiny veins of redness in his eyes.

"A letter would not have collected Deirdre's daughters and brought them to Tirebeck. We will leave in the morning."

His eyebrows flew up. "Fighting talk," he observed. "But I am their guardian, and they stay."

"Why?" she demanded.

"Carron is their home. I hold it for them." He moved away at last, calling to the hovering maid servant. "Make the guest room ready for the Lady Affrica. She will dine with us." He refilled his cup, nodded curtly and walked away.

Without a word, she followed the servant to the inner stairs. The hall door banged shut as she climbed. The woman led her to the first bedchamber, the one Colin had occupied on her last visit. Which meant, presumably, that Ferchar still used the other.

*I cannot be up here alone with him. That is even more improper! Is he trying to drive me out this evening, or just make me uncomfortable?*

"You have a separate guest house, do you not?" she said to the maid. "I would be more comfortable there."

"Oh, no, lady. That's where the lord has gone. There will just be yourself and the girls in the hall."

Affrica stared at her. "He has slept out there since the lady died?"

The maid nodded. "He's taken it hard, lady. Doesn't show it for the sake of the girls. But he's not eating, and we can't keep the wine jug full enough."

Affrica sank onto the bed, digesting this.

"He's still kind to the girls," the maid said anxiously. "Talks to them, plays with them even and takes them for walks. It's only himself he's damaging. And him so young, too, but he won't let us *mother* him."

"You mean he won't let you take his jug away and insist he eats the food you've prepared."

A smile flashed across the woman's lips by way of reply.

"Was he with her when she died?" Affrica asked abruptly.

"Yes. He came back in time, though only just. Her time came early. The neighbors have been kind, calling to see the girls and bringing their own children for an hour or so."

*But who has been here for him?* The snow had prevented even news of the tragedy from spreading. "Have any of his friends come? Lulach?" Who else did she even call a friend? She had no idea.

"Father Stephen came over from Tain. And Father John from the parish church."

"I see. Thank you." He was dealing with his pain alone, as he always did. And his hostility to her was as false as his smile from the roof of St. Duthac's Church when they were children.

To her relief, Christina and Euphemia ate with them. Their childish chatter seemed perfectly normal, even their sudden silences as they mentioned Deirdre and realized she was no longer in their world. To her relief, Ferchar spoke to them at such times, saying how much their mother would have enjoyed such a game or outing or appreciated the improvement in Christina's needlework, and moved on to other easier subjects.

To Affrica, it seemed healthy. He did not make light of their loss but made sure they would remember their mother openly and with fondness. How much pain it cost him to talk of Deirdre, she could not tell. But he drank steadily throughout the meal, eating little.

After, at the girls' request, Affrica went with them to the nursery and helped them prepare for bed. She told them the magical stories that her mother and her nurse and even her father had told to her.

"Bless you, lady," Bridie whispered as Affrica left them at last.

Returning to the hall, she found that the table had been cleared and most of the lamps had been doused. There was no sign of her host, who was presumably drinking himself to sleep in the guest house. She thought of bearding him there, but from experience, she suspected that even if he understood her, he was unlikely to remember whatever agreement she wrung out of him. Morning would be better. When he was weak and defenseless.

Accordingly, she picked up the lamp and walked toward the stairs. She had just set her foot on the first when the outer door opened, and a blast of cold air blew Ferchar in. This time, he was not quite steady as he made his way to a cupboard at the front, from which he extracted a jug.

He stilled.

"Affrica. Why are you always there?"

"Often, years pass without my being there. From your point of view. Are you going to crash in and out of the house all night? Perhaps you should take two jugs to keep you going."

"You will make some poor sod a wonderful wife."

"I barely notice swearing. I live in a house full of soldiers."

"Soldiers," he said. "Uncouth. Not refined. Apart, apparently, from me. You should go to bed, Affrica. I have a tendency to gibber in my cups."

Her head knew it was foolish, but she didn't hesitate. She took her foot off the step and walked across the hall to him. "I know. I am happy to gibber with you for an hour."

"Why?" He eyed her suspiciously as she appeared beside him at the table.

"I came all this way. I might as well talk to somebody. And at least you're awake."

His lips twitched. He waved one slightly too expansive hand, and she sat at the table on the nearest chair. He rummaged in the cupboard again and plonked himself on the chair next to hers, slapping the cups and jug onto the table. "And at least you're dressed this time."

Refusing to let him rile her, she picked up her cup and clinked it off his. She sipped.

"I don't want to take the girls away from you," she said.

"They need me, just for a little…continuity."

She nodded. "They do. But not like this, Ferchar."

"Are you saying I cannot hold my wine?" he mocked.

"You can hold the wine, but not much else, and not for much longer. You are barely held together."

"I'm drunk," he said deliberately. "In the morning, I shall be sober."

"Until breakfast?"

"Ouch." He sounded merely amused.

"They have no one else. Neither do you."

His wine slopped as he lowered it to the table too quickly. "Do you think I don't know that? For God's sake, give me another week of self-indulgence. If it wasn't the middle of bloody winter, at least there would be something else to do."

She leaned forward, grasping his wrist. It jerked as though he'd pull free, and then lay still between her fingers and thumb. "Come with me, Ferchar. Bring the girls to Tirebeck and from there you can escort us all to Dingwall. My father and brothers are there. Being alone here is not good for you, or for the girls. Not anymore."

"Give me a week," he repeated.

"For what? To wallow in your own loss? Your own grief?"

He stared at her and then, almost frighteningly, a hoarse bark of laughter escaped his lips. It should have more than hurt her stomach. It should have tied it in knots. And yet it didn't.

"Loss. Grief," he said breathlessly. "Is that really what you think?"

Bewildered, she hung onto his gaze with desperation. "What else is *this?*"

"Guilt, Affrica." Tearing his gaze free, he raised the cup and drained it. "You, who soaks up emotions like rain on starved earth, should recognize *that* when you see it."

"Guilt for what? You could not save her or the child. It's a risk, a tragedy, that everyone faces. She loved you!"

He set down his cup and met her gaze with defiance. "Deirdre did not love me. I'd be surprised if she had ever loved anyone. It wasn't in her nature."

In a blinding moment, Affrica saw that it was true. She and Deirdre had never got near understanding each other because Deirdre did not love.

"That is not your fault," she whispered.

"No. My fault was that I did not love her either. I married her for her land and her favors, just to return to Scotland *with something*." He wrenched his wrist free of her tightened hold. "And there I will stop," he added, pushing to his feet, "before I tell you about the favors, too. You will forgive me if I go and wallow now in private."

He didn't lurch, not quite, but she couldn't bring herself to watch him as he weaved down the hall with whatever was left in the wine jug.

*There is more. There has to be more.* He was twenty-one years old, ridiculously clever and a talented soldier. So, he had married for personal gain. Why should he castigate himself for doing what all ambitious men did?

Without consciously meaning to, she was out of her chair and reached the hall door before he did. She flattened herself against it, blocking his way. "You share such guilt with most of the country," she said furiously. "What is your problem, Ferchar?"

His unfocused eyes were suddenly very focused indeed. He moved, taking her waist between his hands. Her body flamed in his grip, and she could not breathe. He lifted her so that for an instant their bodies touched, and his face was a mere inch from hers. Everything in her tangled and ached.

And then her feet landed on the ground once more, a foot to the left of the door.

"You, Affrica. You are my problem," he said and went out.

※

HE HAD ALMOST told her the truth.

He woke with the knowledge, along with the pounding head and the sick heaviness that had given him something to fight against for the last two weeks. Or was it three? He licked his dry lips and sat up, pausing to let his head get on with swimming while he felt blindly for the water jug.

Affrica MacHeth was an innocent. It was one reason there had always been friendship between them, because she had inspired nothing but innocent affection until…until the feast in Dingwall. Or perhaps before, in Edinburgh. He had taken it for shock at the time, that his little friend had grown into a lovely and fascinating young woman. But he hadn't been immune. Only his marriage had kept him safe, and now that was gone. And when he was drunk, *she* was not safe.

He had to get rid of her.

*"You, Affrica. You are my problem."* He hoped to God she hadn't understood that. She probably imagined he simply wanted her to leave. Which he did.

Even though the prospect of seeing her this morning shone like a beacon on a dark road. And the temptation to see her again tomorrow. If he were sober, he would be good, and she would never know…

Longing washed over him in waves that made him shiver.

*For God's sake, be a man. You are the Lord of Carron, with daughters and responsibilities, not some silly, love-sick youth who thinks with his nether regions.*

Which was funny, considering why he had married Deirdre.

He stumbled naked from the bed to the washing bowl and poured a jug over his head, letting the cold shock him into proper thought, which finally came as he scrubbed his body dry and threw on clean clothes. Shaved and decent, he left the guest house and the yard and took himself for a short, very brisk walk. Then, ready to meet her at last, he strolled into the hall.

She was laughing at something the girls said, her whole face lit up with utterly unconscious beauty. He bore it, even when she glanced up and the smile instantly faded. Wondering, no doubt, what she had to deal with.

"Good morning," he said pleasantly, using the embraces of the girls who ran to him to avoid looking at her. He straightened and met her grave eyes. "Do you mean to go to Dingwall?"

"I don't know. I didn't, and then I was bored and thought I might, and then I came here instead."

"If you are still in Tirebeck in a week, and of the same mind, send to me to invite the girls, and I will bring them. If you are not, we will be fine here."

Her brow twitched. "You are getting rid of me," she said flatly.

"Yes. But be reasonable. You need to be got rid of. You know you should not be here."

"Why not?" asked Euphemia wide-eyed.

"Because too many people worry about the lady," Ferchar said adroitly. "A word, lady, if you please?"

She rose without fuss and walked with him to the table.

"You are right," he said lightly, "and I shall wallow no more."

"It wasn't so much a criticism as a plea. You are too alone here, Ferchar. Come with me to Tirebeck now. If you are worried about the proprieties, my grandfather is there, and Sinead, most of the time."

"I am better here," he said steadily. "And I don't want another sudden change for the girls. We can plan our journey and make it more fun than bewildering." He read the doubt in her eyes without difficulty and gave her a twisted smile. "I will remain sober and respectable. I will even sleep in the lord's bedchamber. Now, please, will you sit and eat and leave before the entire MacHeth kindred comes and kills me?"

It won a reluctant laugh from her, which shouldn't have pleased him as it did.

An hour later, he helped her mount, and rode with her and her tiny escort almost as far as Tain.

"The fewer people who see me with you the better," he said. "Safe journey, lady."

"Thank you." Her horse sidled, and he wondered if it was deliberate so that she could speak to him without the others overhearing. "I'm not really a problem to you, am I?"

She looked so genuinely anxious that he was able to smile as though she were still that thirteen-year-old child. "Of course, you are. But one I hope never to be without. Farewell, Affrica MacHeth."

He had time to see her face smooth and soften before he wheeled his horse around and rode back to Carron.

# Chapter Sixteen

*Ross, spring-summer 1211*

WITH THE FIRST signs of winter's wane, Kenneth journeyed south to Dunfermline and the royal court.

"Did the king summon him after all?" Affrica asked her father, who had brought the news back with him from Dingwall. She had been delighted to welcome him and Colin home to Tirebeck, just in time to eat. The hall was full again, of noise and soldiers and laughter. Beside her, Euphemia and Christina were wide-eyed, almost shocked.

"No," Angus answered her. "Though he will bow to the king if he can. He's gone primarily in search of a bride, or so he says. He wants Marjorie of Buchan."

"I think Marjorie likes him," Affrica said with a quick smile for the memory of the friend she hadn't seen in more than a year. "To flirt with at any rate. She would be a good Lady of Ross."

"And company for you, who are too much alone. Although we seem to have inherited two children. Please tell me they do not belong to your brothers?"

On his other side, Colin snorted with laughter.

"They are Deirdre of Carron's daughters," Affrica said.

"Are we fostering them?" Angus asked dubiously.

"No. I invited them to stay for a while, to give Ferchar more freedom. And because they miss their mother. Has Nechtan gone with Kenneth?"

"He has taken a large following," Angus said without emphasis. "Someone has to keep the men in order while Kenneth is courting."

"He is showing off his power and wealth?" Affrica asked with a hint of amusement. *Like a bird puffing up its feathers.*

"Clearly."

"You don't approve," Affrica noted.

"It leaves Ross short of men for one thing. For another…" He broke off and sighed. "He's up to something. I know he is, but if I try to inquire, he laughs at me as if I'm a senile old man."

"He laughs at everyone like that," Affrica soothed.

"He does," Colin confirmed, from Angus's other side. "Don't worry, Father. He just wants to strut in front of the king and the ladies. And marriage will be good for him, you'll see."

"Gilchrist always thought so," Angus said broodingly. "But then, he wanted it to be Affrica."

"You didn't?" Colin asked, surprised. "To be Lady of Ross is no small—"

"I favored an alliance with one of the indisputably loyal families," Angus interrupted. "For Kenneth and for Affrica. And for you and Nechtan, if you must know."

Colin grinned. "Maybe Nechtan can cut Kenneth out with Marjorie of Buchan, though I don't fancy my own chances. Who do you want for Affrica? She is all of seventeen after all."

"There are a few poss—*Father!*" On the word, Angus leapt to his feet in startlement.

Adam mac Malcolm MacHeth strode into the hall like a man half his age, and all over the hall, the noise died, and the men rose to their feet in respect.

In all her life, Affrica could count on one hand the number of times her grandfather had entered the hall—a couple of Christmas feasts and family celebrations. But not for years now. Yet as she jumped up in delight to go to him, to order a place set for him, dread hit her in the stomach like a blow.

He hadn't come to celebrate the reunion. His steps were too determined, and yet his eyes were unfocused and wild. If it wasn't for the fact that he moved easily between the tables, she would have assumed he didn't know where he was. She forced her feet forward, all but running around the table to get to him, but even so, her father got there first.

Angus stood in front of him, placing a hand on either side of her grandfather's head. Sometimes, it was the only way to gain or keep his attention, and even then, it wasn't guaranteed. "Father."

"Angus." The briefest of smiles flickered on the old man's lips, relief, perhaps, and pleasure. Then his thin fingers gripped her father's wrist. "Angus, you must stop it. You must try. Bring him back and save the east though the west is lost. Don't let it happen again."

Affrica's stomach knotted tight.

"What did you see?" Angus asked. The words seemed forced from his lips, like old belief shattering modern rationality. "What has happened?"

"I thought we had time, but it's too soon. He is not ready…"

"Who is not ready?" Angus demanded.

Adam frowned as if it was obvious. "Ferchar."

"You want Ferchar brought here?" her father asked dubiously. "Ferchar Maccintsacairt? Of Carron?"

The old man shook his head impatiently. "Kenneth. Bring him home, bring the men. Or it will be too late, and the east will burn. It will all burn again."

The strength seemed to go out of his legs, for Angus seized him by the waist. Affrica took the other side, and together, they took him to the place he never occupied anymore, the lord's place at the table.

"You'll do it?" Adam kept his fierce gaze on his son. "You'll bring them home?"

"I'll send for them."

He could send, but there were no guarantees that Kenneth would come at Angus's behest or even Adam's.

"How long do we have?" Angus asked, and at that, the reality of her father's belief in the danger washed over Affrica like an icy sea.

"Not long," Adam said. He rubbed his forehead, and now his hand shook. "I don't know."

As it turned out, it was not long enough. Angus sent his man after Kenneth in the morning. But only two days later, another messenger galloped exhausted into the courtyard of Tirebeck with the news that Wester Ross was in flames.

⇉⇇

"GUTHRED MACWILLIAM," FERCHAR said grimly while he pulled weapons and armor from a chest and threw them clanking on the hall table. "From Ireland via the Isles, on almost the first spring tide. How is it we've expected him for years, and yet he still took us by surprise?"

"He was smart," Angus replied, dropping onto the nearest chair for a moment's respite. "And wellinformed. Killed our watchers, so it took another day to get the word out. The king is ill, but his army will march north immediately, though God knows how long that will take. And in the meantime, the bulk of our own men are in the south with Kenneth."

Which was suspicious in itself, though Ferchar kept his mouth shut on the accusation. "Some will favor this," he warned. "Just as you said. Some men of Wester Ross in particular will join Guthred. Even here, without Kenneth to order otherwise, they will fight against the King of Scots because it's in their blood."

"That's why I need to summon all the men I can to my side. If they're with me, they can't be with the MacWilliams."

"Are they marching east?"

"Inevitably. They'll want to goad the king into marching and then destroy the flower of his army. I've sent your daughters with Affrica and my father to Brecka. It's better hidden, and Donald MacWilliam was never there. But my aim is to hold Guthred in Wester Ross long enough to let the king's army come up and smash them."

Ferchar rose and faced him. "With so few men, *can* we contain him in Wester Ross?"

Angus gave a crooked smile. "If Kenneth returns swiftly, maybe. From what my brother Gregor wrote to me, I was hoping you would have some ideas."

"I might," Ferchar admitted. More than tension screamed inside him. He wanted to fight, *needed* to, and not just for the good of the realm.

"Then bring the girth guard, rouse every man on your way, and I will meet you two days hence."

⇶⇷

FERCHAR WOKE WITH a start from the deepest sleep he'd enjoyed for more than a week. His fingers had lost their grip of the dagger, but at least lay on top of it so he could grasp it easily as he shot bolt upright, glaring into the startled eyes of a man he knew.

"Ferchar. It's me, Colin."

It was daylight, just, so Ferchar could see exactly who he was. He lowered the dagger. "What are you doing here? I thought you were at Brecka."

"My father needs to know this. Where is he?"

Ferchar looked about him, then up at the cloudy sky through which he could barely make out the sun's position, and pointed. "Eight miles or so behind that hill. What's your news? Has the earl reached Brecka?"

"Kenneth isn't coming," Colin said flatly, all but falling onto the grass beside him. "The king is keeping him and my brother at Stirling, but Nechtan managed to get one of the men out with a message. The king doesn't trust them, so he's sent the Scottish host without the men of Ross. The Earls of Fife and Mar are in command, but they won't be here for days."

Ferchar swore. "We haven't got days. The MacWilliams are getting wise to us. We've forced them to divide and chase their tails and even each other for more than a week. But unless they pursue your father's force now, they're going to come together again and march east over the hills."

"And if they do pursue my father?"

"We'll harry them and distract them, giving your father time to regroup elsewhere."

"And if they march east?"

Ferchar's lips twisted. "We'll do much the same and try to pick them off in the hills. But we can't hold them. There are too many of them, and good troops at that. A lot of them know the land, too. The only thing in our favor is that they have a lot of baggage slowing them down."

"Baggage?" Colin repeated. "They brought their own food? They're not just robbing the locals?"

"Enough for a siege," Ferchar said.

Colin stared at him.

"Bad news," Lulach said, loping silently over a tussock to drop beside them. "They haven't taken the bait. There's movement on the other side of the loch, so it looks as if they're going to join forces and go through the passes."

"Then we'd better get into the hills before they do and pick them off," Ferchar said without surprise. "Send word to Lord Angus."

"I'll go," Colin said eagerly.

Ferchar hesitated, for he had more questions for Colin, but in the end, he merely nodded and told him exactly where to find his father.

>>><<<

IT WAS THE dusk on the following day before he saw Colin again. A day of swift movement and hard climbing, followed by a day of slaughter—fortunately slaughter of the invading forces as they tried to cross the hill passes. They had let so many through, then, from their vantage points, annihilated them with arrows. After that, the enemy had tried to flush out their positions by sending just a few men as bait.

"Shoot them," Ferchar had ordered. "And then move—fast." And so, when the enemy fired their arrows, they landed on empty ground, and when the enemy marched, they met a hail of arrows coming from different places entirely.

It was grim work and tiring, so he was glad when, at dusk, Colin found him again with the news that Angus was now in position, too.

"I don't suppose you managed to shoot Guthred MacWilliam?" Colin said hopefully as they watched the enemy make camp around the foothills, posting plenty of guards to warn of attack.

"We almost got him in the first attempt," Lulach said cheerfully, "but his men sheltered him and got him out of the melee. Still, we know what he looks like now. And Donald Ban, his brother."

"Get some food and some rest," Ferchar ordered. "Because tomorrow, we'll have to be prepared for anything."

Once he had set the guards, which he did while eating, Ferchar unrolled his blanket beside Colin and asked the question that had been preying on his mind since the day before.

"What else did Nechtan say?"

Colin sighed. "That Kenneth was appalled by the king's lack of trust, by the way he was being treated. They really don't want to know Kenneth with a grievance, but it seems no one told His Grace that."

Ferchar said nothing, merely lay down and hoped it wouldn't rain before the morning.

"But then," Colin murmured, "I think you have suspicions of your own."

"Suspicions are not facts, as the king will have to acknowledge."

He felt Colin's stare on his face.

"Seriously?" Colin said. "You imagine Kenneth would ravage his own lands?"

"No. But he's pursued a dangerous policy, combining loyalty to the king with sympathy for the discontented thanes. He calls it balance. Others might call it ambiguity. Others again, like Guthred MacWilliam and possibly the king, might misunderstand. And here we are."

There was silence. "You blame Kenneth."

"I pity Kenneth. I blame the MacWilliams."

⟫⟩⟨⟪

THE FOLLOWING MORNING, in fine drizzle, they could tell by the screams echoing around the hills that the enemy were being assaulted by Angus and his men.

"Should we join my father?" Colin asked eagerly as they watched the movement of the troops below.

"No, if we wait, you'll probably see them try here again. The more—" Ferchar broke off as one of his scouts slid down the slope to land beside him.

The man was grinning. "Royal army's here," he said laconically. "We're saved."

Relief poured off Ferchar in waves, for he knew only too well that all they were doing here was delaying the invaders. It was only a matter of time until they broke through. "Not if you don't keep your eyes open," he said severely as several men began to leave their posts to hear the news. Hastily, they jumped back to their positions.

About an hour later, much as he had foretold, the enemy began to sneak up the path, a few at a time, covered by larger movement at the next pass, and then more.

"Steady," Ferchar warned. "Let's get as many as we can before we slip away and join the royal army."

But, bizarrely, it was more than scouts who were approaching from the east side of the mountains. A large detachment of king's men was coming their way.

"They must intend to join battle in Wester Ross," Lulach said doubtfully.

"In the bogs and glens where they don't know the land?" Ferchar returned. "Besides, a detachment won't be enough for a pitched battle."

He returned his gaze to the enemy filing up the hill below, more piling up behind. He lifted his hand in warning, aware that the royal reinforcements were advancing noisily behind him but determined to make this last attack by his own men count.

"Jesus Christ, you're letting them through!" a furious voice exclaimed. "Archers, loose! Men form up behind!"

Suddenly, Ferchar's position was overrun. He was shoved aside, so that his arrow fell at his feet. Hardly any of his men got a chance to fire, displaced as they were by the new arrivals who had no time to judge their aim. Moreover, the shouting had alerted the enemy, who hastily brought up their shields so that the few arrows that did shoot true only hit a roof of shields.

Irate, Ferchar turned on his ally and found himself staring into the face of the Earl of Mar—or at least one of the feuding claimants to the earldom. Worse, among those crowding behind the earl, he recognized Angus MacHeth and some of his men being shoved out of the way, too. The other passes were unguarded.

"Two more seconds and they'd have been halved in number,"

Ferchar said between his teeth.

"Is that right?" Mar sneered. "Looked to me like you were letting them through! Who the devil are you, anyway?"

"Ferchar. Of Carron. We've met."

"And I am Colin mac Angus MacHeth," Colin announced, drawing himself up to his full height after being ignominiously shoved off his rock.

"MacHeth!" Mar snarled. "Another one! I might have known. Get all the MacHeths and Ross men out of here! We'll deal with them later."

Appalled, Ferchar realized they really did mean to march down the mountain. Since most of the enemy were retreating out of arrow range once more, they'd probably make it, too.

"There are nearly three thousand men down there!" he said urgently, catching Mar's arm. "And while you go after them and get slaughtered, most of them will march through the other passes!"

Mar shook him off with contempt. Short of cutting the earl down, there was nothing Ferchar could do. Swarms of men covered the hills already, flying downward toward their doom. The men of Ross, who had been harrying the enemy for days were knocked aside by sheer numbers.

Over their heads, Ferchar met Angus's gaze. He lifted his arm, a signal to his own men, and together they slipped away, heading over the hills for a clearer view.

"White Christ," Angus whispered two hours later as they looked down on the enemy swarming up and over the hills into Easter Ross. "There are too many. They're in."

"Surely there are more effective royal forces to meet them?" Ferchar said.

"One would hope so," Angus said grimly. "But we'd better go and see. Not that the Earl of Ross's loyal men appear to count for much."

By the time they found Sir William Comyn and the rest of the royal army, a battle had already been fought and won, and the Scots were cock-a-hoop.

"Four thousand men," scoffed Sir William when Angus finally managed to get to him in his luxurious tent. "There were less than half that! A quarter, even allowing for the stragglers the Earl of Mar should be cutting down."

Ferchar's skin began to prickle. "How many?" he interrupted. "How many did you fight?"

Sir William scowled at him. "I didn't stop to count. I was busy. What does it matter?"

"Oh, it matters. *How many?*"

Sir William shrugged. "Maybe a thousand. Why?" An uneasy look had entered his gaze as it traveled from Ferchar to Angus and Colin and back. "*Why?*"

"Because that is only a fraction of the MacWilliam army," Angus uttered. "I suggest we find out where the rest of it went."

They didn't have long to find out, for the enemy left a trail of destruction eastward toward the Black Isle, collecting some of the local thanes as they went.

"Eddirdour Castle," Ferchar said.

Angus said nothing, but spurred on faster, for only the Cromarty Firth separated the royal castle from Tirebeck.

They never got as far as Eddirdour, in the end, because they met the king's men coming the other way. "The castle's in MacWilliam hands," said the captain of the tiny garrison who had been allowed to march out in return for handing it over. "We were overrun and couldn't hold it. But there's more, and worse. Half of them are marching north to Dunscaith... And...they've got a siege engine."

"Well," Colin said into the silence. "Now we know why they had so many wagons."

# Chapter Seventeen

*Ross, autumn 1211*

In his young outlaw years, Malcolm MacHeth had built the hall at Brecka not as a fortress but as a hide-out. Halla, his lady, had added to it during the long years of his imprisonment and made it a comfortable home. Affrica knew it well but had never spent so long here at a time. She suspected she was not the first MacHeth lady to climb the hill behind the hall from sheer boredom. Wolf, ambling gamely by her side, was her only companion, while the wind whipped at her shawl, and misty rain damped her face and clothes.

She would see little from up here, she realized as she neared the top. Not that it mattered. Scouts guarded all the approaches to Brecka and the enemy wouldn't get close before the occupants melted away.

Or so she thought.

But as she stood on the summit of the hill, Wolf sitting on her foot, the column of men marching out of the forest to the south was perfectly clear. Mist hid their banners, but not the bristling weapons or the horses.

The fear that had never left her for months sharpened into terror. If the enemy was at her door, what had become of the watching guards? Of her father, Colin, and the men of Tirebeck? Of Ferchar?

With a gasp, she spun around and bolted back down the hill, slipping and sliding, half on her bottom in her haste. Wolf galloped at her side, keeping a wary eye on her as though he sensed her panic. As she bolted across the yard to the hall, another runner came from the southern gate—one of the scouts. She called to him urgently by name, and was astonished to see him grin.

"Did you see the soldiers?" she demanded. "We have to evacuate now. There is no time to—"

"Lady, it's the earl!" the scout interrupted. "It's the earl, home at last!"

She almost sagged to her knees. As it was, she needed to lean one hand on Wolf's great head. *Kenneth*. That was why there had been no warning. Thank God.

"Then we had better prepare a feast," she managed calmly.

She had no sooner given the orders than Eta dragged her away to change her muddy dress.

"It's Kenneth," Affrica said crossly, "not the king!"

"You don't know that," Eta said direly. "You don't know who's with him, and in his absence, you have been the Lady of Ross. You have to act the part."

Eta made a good point. She had no idea who Kenneth might have brought here, and one thing she had learned at court was the importance of appearance. She was only too aware that the king's suspicions had kept Kenneth and the men in the south when they were desperately needed up here, so if he came, it could well be with some kind of guard.

Decked in one of her better yet more severe gowns, without jewels, a dark, unornamented veil covering her hair, she stood outside the hall with only Eta and the sergeant of her guard. Kenneth rode in, scowling, no doubt because no one had cheered his homecoming. There were few men to make any noise at all, since they were all with Angus, fighting.

At his side rode the familiar figure of Sir William Comyn, the Justiciar of Scotland. She had been right to change her dress.

"At least it's not the king," she murmured to Eta as she went forward to greet her cousin.

Kenneth slid from his horse and enveloped her in a bear hug. "Affrica, thank God."

"I thank Him for your return, too. Is all well?" She barely breathed the question after the formal greeting and received only a terse nod in return before he released her.

"You remember Sir William Comyn?"

"Of course." Affrica curtseyed. "Welcome to Brecka, sir. You have our thanks for coming to Ross's aid."

"Scotland's aid," Sir William corrected, though he bowed low over her hand and added. "My honor as well as my duty."

"Come inside. Your men will be taken care of along with our own. Allow me to show you to more private quarters."

As she conducted him to Kenneth's old room, one of the other doors in the narrow passage opened. Her grandfather stood there, his unquiet gaze moving from Affrica to their guest.

"Grandfather. Kenneth is home. And here is Sir William Comyn, the Justiciar of Scotland. Sir William, my grandfather, Adam of Tirebeck."

Sir William's eyes widened. "Adam MacHeth? You are legendary, sir. I count myself honored to meet you."

"Do you?" Adam asked with more curiosity than rudeness.

"You will join us at the feast?" Affrica asked hastily.

Adam didn't answer, merely stepped back to let them pass.

※※※

ALTHOUGH THERE WAS no time for private conversation with Kenneth before the feast, he told her of the latest events while they ate.

"The king brought us north with him in the end. Comyn vouched for Angus, since he's had more success than the royal army who, as you know, not only managed to let the MacWilliams into Easter Ross, but let them take the royal castles, too."

"Have you seen my father?"

"Briefly. I left Nechtan with him. They're chasing Guthred MacWilliam into Moray now. I think we might have him on the run from Ross. You have been safe here?"

"Quite safe. Where is the king?"

Kenneth grinned. "Gone to get his castles back. William and I will leave again in the morning to help him."

Affrica frowned. "I'm delighted to see you, of course, but why did you come here?"

"I wanted to be sure you were safe. So did Sir William." Kenneth lowered his voice. "You could do worse, little cousin."

Her eyebrows flew up in astonishment, but her attention was needed elsewhere, and she never got the chance to pursue this ill-timed statement with him. Instead, she set out to be the perfect hostess, hospitable and entertaining. But clearly, the men were tired, and she retired as soon as she could with civility.

For some time, she waited for Kenneth to come and tell her what was really going on, but after an hour, it was clear he wouldn't. She gave up and went to bed.

In the morning, she rose early to see the men on their way. Leaving them to break their fast in the hall, she was surprised to run into Sir William Comyn in the courtyard.

"My lady," he greeted her civilly, although his gaze was a little too curious for her comfort. "You have been looking after all this alone?"

"Since the spring, when my father sent me here from Tirebeck."

"But you're not just hiding, are you? You are caring for the wounded."

"Those that can be sent here or make their own way," she said evenly. "It is a tradition." Which didn't stop her blood running cold each time more injured men arrived, in case they were her father or Colin or Ranald. Or Ferchar, of whom she had heard nothing for months…

Sir William said, "It is quite an undertaking, stewarding the land, feeding your own people and the refugees, caring for the injured and sending them back to fight."

Slightly needled, she retorted. "Do you believe I have failed in some way?"

To her surprise, his serious face lightened. "On the contrary. I am all admiration for your capability. How old are you, lady?"

She tilted her chin. "Eighteen."

His brow twitched.

"Nearly," she amended. "There was no one else."

His lips quirked. "You would make a formidable Lady of Ross."

"Only as an emergency substitute. I will never be the Lady of Ross."

"Oh, I don't know." Sir William's eyes moved beyond her to the hall door, where Kenneth was emerging. "Ross is unstable."

"It wouldn't be if Kenneth and his men had been available months ago to fight the MacWilliams."

"Are you criticizing my own efforts in that regard?" He sounded more amused than offended.

"I'm sure you did your best," she said kindly. "It's not your fault that you don't know the land."

He inhaled sharply, then said with a rather appealing hint of ruefulness, "We are all servants of the king. I am glad he brought Kenneth north."

She inclined her head. "I wish you good fortune, Sir William."

To her surprise, her grandfather came out to see the men depart. After a few moments, he raised his face to the sky.

"Will they live?" she asked him. "Will they win?"

"Yes," he said after a moment.

She blurted, "I think Kenneth is trying to arrange a marriage for me with William Comyn, the Justiciar."

"You don't like that?"

"I don't understand why Comyn would consider it. I will never be Lady of Ross. I would bring nothing to such an alliance."

Adam smiled at the clouds. "There will never *be* such an alliance, not through you, though the lines will join one day. You may be easy."

*Easy?* In a country torn by war and hunger and tragedy? She forgot sometimes that he was used to those things. Her grandfather patted her hand and walked back inside the hall.

⸻

IT WAS ALMOST a month later when she was called from tending the wounded by news that a loan rider approached. By then, she knew that Kenneth's optimism had been misplaced. Neither his arrival in Ross nor the king's had seen the immediate defeat of the MacWilliams, although it seemed the king would wrest his castles back.

Affrica washed her hands and emerged from the makeshift infirmary. She could almost ignore the permanent knot in her stomach since her own fears made no difference to what happened in the country. But when she saw the gates open and her brother Colin ride through, the reins held in one hand while the other hung useless and bloody at his side, her throat constricted.

She started toward him involuntarily. He threw himself off his horse, stumbling slightly, and swung around to face her. She stopped in her tracks.

Emotion poured off him in waves, though his grim face gave little away. The women had emerged from the houses around the yard to gawp. A couple of the walking wounded sprawled in the wink of autumnal sunlight. Bridie emerged from the hall with Ferchar's stepdaughters, ready for the forest ramble Affrica had promised them.

Affrica swallowed and closed the distance to her brother. "You're hurt. Come into the hall and let me see to it while you give me your news."

He nodded, letting her take his good arm, and they walked together into the hall. One of the women rushed after her with a bowl of clean water. A medicine box was already open on a table near the fire.

She pushed Colin gently onto the bench and began to unwind the grizzly bandage.

"I don't think it's bad," he said, then abruptly, "You're not safe here. You have no house guard."

"They're fighting, along with everyone else. Colin, what's happened?"

His Adam's apple wobbled. "Father," he said.

*Oh, no, oh please no...*

At long last, Colin met her gaze, and she knew it was true. "How?" she managed, though it didn't matter. Their father was dead.

"Ambush," Colin said with bitterness. "Donald Ban MacWilliam. We put up a fight, though we were outnumbered. But they *knew*, Affrica... He—Donald—drove straight at Father before he could even draw his sword. We had to flee. I had to drag Nechtan away to save him, to save any of us. He was beside himself. He still is."

She cleaned Colin's wound in silence as though the too-familiar actions could blot out the terrible emptiness opening in her life. "Where is Nechtan now?"

"I left him with Kenneth, but I'll have to go back, or he'll fight for revenge alone, whatever the cost, and lose."

"Tomorrow," she said, anointing the wound and reaching for clean bandages. "Tomorrow, you can go back. Tonight, you rest and recover." Another terrible weight was crushing her. She, Colin, Nechtan, and their sisters had lost their father. But she still had to tell her grandfather that his son was dead.

She drew a shuddering breath. "Eat, Colin, and then sleep." She turned and walked to the end of the hall, and through the passage that led to her grandfather's room. He had slept there in his boyhood, and it had always been his whenever they had come to Brecka.

She knocked and went in.

The old man sat by the window, tears running down his face. He already knew.

---

IN THE MORNING, Colin hugged her convulsively before he left.

"Go and save Nechtan from himself," she said as lightly as she could manage. "He has strong shoes to step into."

"He has." Colin released her, mounted slightly awkwardly because of his injured arm, and rode away.

Over the next week, Affrica kept almost feverishly busy. She could not give in to grief while she had all these people to look after. She took Deirdre of Carron's daughters on long walks and played games that delighted them and distracted her. She cared for another batch of wounded who had arrived together on a cart, victims of the same ambush that had killed her father. She made sure everyone was in a position to depart instantly, even her grandfather, although he did not speak. He didn't even look into the fire anymore.

And then came another lone rider, this one a messenger, bearing word from Nechtan. He had fought and lost, as Colin had been afraid of.

"A bigger force than us, led by Donald Ban MacWilliam," the messenger said tiredly. "If fury could have won it, we'd have been victors twice over. Everyone wanted to kill the man who'd killed Angus mac Adam."

The tears she so feared began to weigh her down, clogging her head and her throat, but somehow, she kept them from her eyes.

"To our shame," the man said, "we didn't. We lost too many men, and Lord Nechtan is afraid we've left the way open to Brecka. He wants you to go the sanctuary at Tain. Be ready in a day, he says. He'll get an escort to you while he holds up the MacWilliams."

"Thank you," she managed, and sent him to eat and sleep, while she told everyone to be ready to leave the following day.

She was glad to go. She was bored with Brecka, tired of being stuck in the same place with the same few people. She hated saving men's lives only to send them back to die somewhere else. But she wouldn't think of that.

She fell asleep that night crossing off items on her mental list of necessities, and woke the following morning, going over it all again. By the time she had seen that the wounded were fit to travel, their escort had arrived, and she went straight to the stables to saddle her own horse.

And for some reason, just as she opened the stall door, it hit her.

She was leaving Brecka and would probably never see it again, this beloved home of the MacHeths for almost a century. And even that loss paled into nothing beside the massive, irreparable loss of her father.

She gasped, burying her face in the neck of her pony, and since she couldn't stop the tears this time, she opened her mouth wide and let them come—huge, wracking and almost silent.

She should have been alone, but life was not so kind. Through her grief, she heard the quick footsteps, heard them pause, and then the stall door opened. She threw up her head and turned, glaring, daring whoever had come to utter one word.

"Affrica," Ferchar Maccintsacairt said, and reached for her.

There was a moment when she didn't know what to do and held herself stiff as a board. And then, with as much relief as anguish, she collapsed against him, pushing into him as though she could hide there from all the grief and pain she could not bear.

He held her tightly, his arms strong and secure, his rough cheek against her hair, while she cried into his chest. Her sobs died slowly to shudders, and she realized she was clutching his shoulders as though she would never let them go. One of his arms had wrapped around her back. His other held the back of her head as though she were a baby.

She inhaled the scent of Ferchar, mixed now with horse and faint sweat. For the first time since Colin had arrived a week ago, she felt safe. Strength began to seep into her as though Ferchar lent her his.

"Thank you," she whispered into his chest and slowly, reluctantly, released his shoulders. Only then, as his arms began to fall away, she realized she would have to look him in the eyes and let him see her like this.

But it seemed she didn't have to after all. Someone in the yard was calling her. "Lady, you need to come. The old lord won't leave."

Hastily, she wiped her face on her shawl and strode out of the stable. She still hadn't saddled the wretched pony, but at least she had another task to complete.

Striding through the chaos in the yard, she was vaguely aware of Ferchar behind her, following her into the hall and along to her grandfather's room.

"He says he's staying here," Eta said flatly. "Shall I send the men to carry him? Oh…" She caught sight of Ferchar with sheer relief. "*He* can carry him."

"He isn't a child," Ferchar said mildly. "Lord Adam can walk."

"But I won't," the old man said. "Not yet."

"Grandfather, it isn't safe here," Affrica said urgently. "We have to leave, and I need you with me."

He smiled, a moment of genuine amusement. "No, you don't. Affrica." He took her face between his gnarled old hands. "I will slow you down. And I don't want to leave. I was born here, and I would die here rather than fleeing through the hills with strangers."

"I am not a stranger," Affrica said firmly. "Neither is Ferchar."

"No," he allowed. "But all the same, I will not go. Ferchar will see you safe. Affrica," he said, gently chiding as she opened her mouth to issue more orders, "I have had a long, happy life. Leave me the dignity of dying as I choose."

She stared into his unusually focused eyes and caught at his wrists. "What have you seen?"

"That it is time to go my own way at last. I want you to know you are the joy of my old age." He dropped his hands from her face and placed her hand in Ferchar's. "You will look after my joy."

Ferchar's fingers curled around hers, though his eyes were locked with Adam's. "I will."

"Then go with my blessing, and leave me with yours."

"But Grandfather, we've taken all the food!"

"No, you haven't," he said, gently. "Farewell, Affrica."

She had to dig in her heels, for Ferchar was sweeping her from the room. "We can't leave him! It is just his grief…"

Ferchar looked at her, his eyes almost helpless. "He wants it. Allow him this gift."

*Gift?* She peered back over her shoulder to see her grandfather sitting on his chair once more, his unfocused eyes staring into the distance. She had already lost him.

It was more than grief, more than not bearing the world as it had become. It was about foresight and his own death.

And she would not cry again.

⁂

ADAM'S EARS WERE not as weak as he sometimes pretended. Besides which, Brecka had never before been a silent place. As he ate his cold stew, he could have heard a pin drop. The arrival of so many armed men in the vicinity of the hall was easy to hear.

He pushed his bowl away and rose to his feet. They were waiting now, waiting to see how stoutly the MacHeths old home would be defended. Adam smiled sourly. Even Donald MacWilliam, in his rampage twenty years ago, had not come here. But his sons had.

After half an hour, as dusk fell, they began to set up camp. They meant to live here, then, not burn it to the ground. Adam, who had already made preparations after his own people had gone, left the hall with his flint and tinder box, and lit the dry brush he had piled against the wall. He felt the ghosts of his parents at his shoulder as he worked, and those of his dead brother and sister. They would understand. Fire made such a dramatic background for a prophecy.

He had to open the gate himself, which was when he judged he was most likely to be shot by a nervous guard. But he didn't hurry. He let them see that he was old and took his time opening and even closing the gate behind him.

He could see their army now, spread out around the perimeter in an arc. Not a huge force, certainly not the entire MacWilliam army, just, he hoped, the men commanded by Guthred's brother, Donald Ban MacWilliam. As he ambled down the path, memories assailed him. Riding this way so often with his brother as they went to harry the King of Scots and home again, hiding their wounds in bravado. He smiled because they had come once with a galley, hauled overland from Tirebeck. Findlaech, his old friend, had lain in it at one point while someone poured welcome ale straight into his mouth.

And there was the hill on which he had killed the Norman de Lanson after defeating him in battle, the act by which he had both made it possible to win Cairistiona or to lose her forever. Cairistiona… Warmth suffused him. He felt her presence, strengthening, relying.

He remembered the time they had come home with the huge host that had gone to meet his father, freshly released from prison. He hated to think of his mother's face that day when she discovered her husband was not with them…

The smell of smoke assailed his nostrils.

"It's only one old man," someone called in the distance.

"Can you smell burning?" came a voice from farther back.

Adam kept walking, steadily, veering off the path toward the camp. Darkness was falling fast, but the glow from campfires and from the hall behind him, lit up the sort of scene that had once been so familiar to him. Although, to be sure, tents were a luxury he had rarely bothered with. They had slept wrapped in blankets under the stars and whatever shelter they could find in tree branches or caves or huts...

"It's the hall! Who fired the hall?" someone demanded into the faint rush of confusion around the hall. "Did we do that?"

And there was the biggest tent, with men emerging to stare over at the hall.

"Here, where do you think you're going?" A soldier grabbed his arm.

"To speak to Donald Ban, son of Donald," Adam replied, as though surprised.

"Don't be stupid, old man, why would he bother with you?"

"Because I have a prophecy for him," Adam said, making sure his voice carried. He was fairly certain he looked the part of the mad prophet, too, never allowing his eyes to focus or the dreams to take him. He had given in to the dreams for too long, without the anchor of his wife. Now, it was time not to see, but to act. "He'll want to hear this. He needs to hear it."

"Halt where you are," the soldier commanded, though uneasiness dripped from his voice.

"Search him!" ordered a voice that filled him with rage and grief, even though he had never heard it before. On some level, he recognized it. "Then bring the old fool to me."

They pushed him around a bit, took his dagger, which was a pity though not an insurmountable problem.

"Sir, the whole hall's alight—outbuildings, too—but no one's running out. I think it's empty."

"Then for God's sake put it out and save what you can. Did you fire it, old man?" Donald Ban MacWilliam strode right up to him—a florid man with ink stains on his fingers. Adam smiled because Angus had described him thus. He wore no armor save a loosened breast plate, though sword and dagger hung at his belt.

"I have no interest in the hall," Adam said with perfect truth. "Though there is prophecy in the flames, Donald Ban mac Donald."

"Amuse me, old man." The younger man stood too close, glaring at him. A bully. The sort of man who would abduct a child or ambush an enemy and see no dishonor in either. A man who would ruin a country for mere ambition. No one had learned from Malcolm MacHeth, except, perhaps, the MacHeths themselves. Some of them.

"I have seen your defeat," Adam said clearly. "And your brother's death. Yours also."

Donald Ban's lips sneered. He even seized Adam by the back of his tunic, perhaps to show his listening men that he didn't believe in such nonsense. "And who are you, old man, to pretend to be God to your betters?"

"I?" Focusing on the muddy eyes, he snatched the dagger from Donald Ban's scabbard with his left and thrust it up under the breast plate and deep into flesh. "I am Adam, son of Malcolm. And you killed my son. The king will kill your brother as I have killed you. And in your defeat will be the end of your line."

By then, he was on his knees as countless weapons cut into him, but he didn't release Donald Ban's eyes which widened with astonishment. By the fierce glow from the burning hall, his mouth opened and closed like a fish before his own people caught his falling body.

Ignoring the pain, Adam turned his head toward the fire and smiled as the world, and the blows faded around him and he let himself fly beyond the flames at last, to Cairistiona and Angus and all those he had loved who were waiting for him.

# Chapter Eighteen

*Ross, autumn-winter 1211*

Affrica thought she saw a plume of smoke from the direction of Brecka. But she did not mention it, or even think about it, beyond being glad that the men who had killed her father and, presumably, her grandfather, would not live in their house.

Ferchar led them through the hills by a very indirect route, luring any trackers away from their goal of Tain, which was a little too close to Dunscaith Castle, reputed to be still in MacWilliam hands. Ferchar's plan was to mislead any pursuit into believing they fled into Wester Ross.

"Would they trouble to follow us?" Affrica asked doubtfully.

"Oh yes," Ferchar replied. "In their hands, you would be a powerful weapon to make your brothers and even Kenneth lay down their arms. Come to that, the king would not rejoice in any MacWilliam-MacHeth marriage alliance."

"I'd cut my own throat first."

"Then let us avoid such an outcome."

She saw a good deal of Ferchar these days, though they there was little chance to speak to him. He was always busy, galloping ahead, directing scouts, organizing camps and guards. His energy was formidable and the men, who might have struggled to keep up, seemed to do so mainly by his will power.

Each day, his stepdaughters took turns sitting before him in the saddle for an hour, their childish voices high with excitement and pleasure. The men grinned but did not laugh. Most of them, probably, would have given anything to be with their own children. Affrica observed him with something of the same fascination she had first discovered in her childhood. Sometimes, she doubted she knew him any better.

But he was good at this. Leaving aside the incongruity of playing with his stepdaughters, it was as if he had born a soldier. A commander of soldiers. Occasionally, she imagined lines of fatigue around his mouth, exhaustion in the hazel eyes that were rarely still. He had told Deirdre once that he was a soldier by nature, and it seemed to be true. The new hardness she had first recognized in Edinburgh was more pronounced now. He never relaxed. Never rude, he kept them all, soldiers and servants, women and children under strictest discipline.

At night, they slept under the stars or sheltered in caves, and even close to a fire, with Christina and Euphemia huddled on either side of her, Affrica shivered with cold. Ferchar, if he slept at all, did so near his men.

Only once, in the middle of the day when they had stopped to rest and eat, did she come upon him asleep. They were moving down from the hills then, circling toward Tain, and he sat on the ground, his back resting against a tree as he gazed in the direction of the sea.

Or at least she thought that was where he looked as she approached with a hunk of bread and cheese that was his share of the meal. But his eyes were closed, his head resting against the tree bark. The fingers of one hand splayed across his dagger hilt, but his face had smoothed and slackened into sleep.

Emotion curled in her stomach, for in repose, he looked as young as he actually was. Not yet twenty-two years old. And yet it was a face of strength, of character and intelligence. She had barely scratched the surface of Ferchar Maccintsacairt, and that was both exciting and terrifying.

Wolf, who had accompanied her, licked Ferchar's face.

His fingers closed convulsively around the dagger hilt and his eyes flew open. Wolf backed off.

"You don't need to attack me for it," she said mildly, holding out the bread and cheese. "I meant it for you."

"Sorry," he muttered, taking it from her before he began to rise.

She saved him the trouble by dropping onto her knees beside him. For a while, she let him eat in silence, then observed. "There's been no sign of pursuit."

"No. I think we sent them the wrong way." He glanced at her. "And I suspect Lord Adam bought us a little time."

She swallowed. "Do you think that's what he intended by staying?"

"By all I ever heard, Adam MacHeth always had several plans and intentions in play at once."

She smiled. "Perhaps. Are we going straight to Tain now?"

"We'll see."

She looked at him directly. "Will men like Guthred or Donald Ban MacWilliam honor sanctuary?"

"If they want any claim to legitimacy, yes." He swallowed the last of his bread and rose to his feet in one smooth movement. He held down his hand to her quite casually, and yet as she took his hand, the simple act assumed quite inappropriate importance. To her. Only to her, for as soon as she stood beside him, he released her and without another word, he turned and strode to his horse.

⫸⫷

FERCHAR WAS WEIGHED down by more than the burden of responsibility for the safety of Affrica MacHeth and his stepdaughters. He had ached for her grief at Brecka, and then shattered because he was the one she chose for comfort. He defied any man to hold Affrica MacHeth in his arms and remain unmoved by the experience. Well, he was moved. Moved by her loss, by her strength, and her trust. Moved not to sleep or go near her in case he exploded, for God knew, he was also moved by her beauty, haunted by the feel of her in his arms.

Which was idiocy for any number of reasons, not least of them being that without his wits about him, he might miss the signs of impending attack and lose her, with all that entailed to himself, the MacHeths, and Scotland.

So, he kept her at a distance whenever he possibly could and maintained a cool reserve that she probably didn't notice—although, just occasionally, he imagined a spark of hurt in her melting brown eyes.

They emerged at last into forest that stretched along the other side of the coast road, within smelling distance of the Dornoch Firth. And there, at last, the scouts picked up signs of the enemy.

"Not a large force," he told Affrica, for once walking his horse beside hers. "Possibly scavenging, but enough to harry us. And they *might* have been placed to catch you on the road to Tain. We're in front of them, and I'm hoping they don't yet know it, but we need to move faster."

She nodded. "If we hide the rest of the women and the wounded with the supplies in the woods, would they ignore them and chase us to Tain?"

"They might, but on losing you, they might well take out their annoyance on anyone else they can find. At this stage, I'm reluctant to break up our group at all."

"Then what do you suggest?"

"That we move forward as fast as we can, prepared to meet any attack. If we do, I want you to keep going forward. We'll catch up as soon as we've scared them off."

She nodded, but as he spurred forward, she stayed him. "Ferchar? You will take care?"

"Of course." He spoke with impatience, covering the warmth that her concern touched in him. Yes, he had been become that pathetic and needed to be away from her.

The first warning came as the scout from behind came riding up at full tilt. "I was seen," he confessed. "And they're in pursuit. At least four of them."

"Then let's ambush the ambushers," Ferchar said wryly. "Lady, you keep going as we discussed. Four men will stay with you. The rest into the trees with me."

It was a simple matter to be rid of them. One was stopped with an arrow, two died in the subsequent fight, after which the fourth man bolted back the way they had come. As Ferchar took aim at him, he saw another horseman pulling in to meet him.

It was impossible to tell with any certainty. But something about the newcomer, the way he gesticulated, the smooth way he wheeled around his horse, and, most of all, the shock of black, curly hair, reminded him strongly of Liam O'Neill. Ferchar altered his aim and loosed his arrow, but the men were already in motion and the arrow fell harmlessly in the road where they had been.

"Bring him," Ferchar said briefly, nodding to the man with the arrow in his chest.

From there, it was something of a mad dash to Tain. Sweeping up Affrica and the women, the wounded, and the pack animals along with him, he galloped relentlessly along the road, swerving only to reach the first cross that marked the girth of Tain, the boundary of holy sanctuary. His fear was that the enemy would rush around and cut them off from the other direction.

As it was, once Affrica and the women and the wounded were inside the sanctuary, he sent one of the women to fetch Father Stephen and set his men around the outer perimeter of the girth.

As coarb, he was entitled to enter the sanctuary, so he did, marching straight up to his unconscious prisoner and slapping his face until he woke up. By the time Father Stephen bustled up in outrage, he had discovered all he needed to and took off his helmet to show his face to the priest.

"Oh," Stephen said, mid-rage. He swallowed. "Your pardon, lord, but who will believe in the sanctity of this place if you treat it like your own barracks?"

"I don't," Ferchar said mildly. "My men, if you'll notice, wait beyond the cross. Inside, I have brought the Lady Affrica to sanctuary along with wounded men of Ross, who are pursued by MacWilliams. And one wounded MacWilliam. I don't much care if he lives or dies."

"Company, sir," came a muffled report from beyond the girth boundary.

Ferchar stepped forward, taking the arm of the priest who seemed inclined to retreat back to his church. "No, Father," he said pleasantly. "I need you as a witness. These people claim sanctuary with you. As temporal coarb, I commend them to your care." He stared across the uneven land to where a close-knit group of men had paused. Then one, with a white kerchief tied around his lance, rode forward with another horseman.

Inevitably, Affrica came as close to the cross as Ferchar would allow her to see what was happening.

She gasped. "But that's…"

"Liam O'Neill. I thought so." He glanced to the nearest guard. "Keep him in your sights at all times. If he makes the smallest move toward a weapon or the sanctuary, kill him. Lady, step back."

Liam O'Neill, prince of Ulster, bowed gracefully in her direction. "Lady Affrica, we meet again at last. I have long carried your beauty in my heart. But though it grieves me, I cannot compliment you on your choice of escort. Armed soldiers wandering in and out of sanctuary? Why, then, I could do so myself."

"Not without my permission," Ferchar said. "Since I am coarb."

The blue eyes turned on him, gleaming with apparent amusement.

"Are you, by God? The warrior priest of Tain?"

"I am not a priest. And the lady with all her people has been granted sanctuary here."

Liam searched his face without obvious hostility. "Have we met before?" He slapped his thigh and the bow trained upon him twitched. He didn't glance at it. "I remember. The violent youth at the Earl of Ross's feast."

"I believe we just missed each other in Paris, too," Ferchar said, and that did merit the tiniest narrowing of the Irishman's eyes.

"Paris? What a very traveled youth you are."

"Is there a point to this discussion?" Ferchar asked. "Or are you about to withdraw?"

"Thank you for reminding me. I came to offer you an exchange."

Ferchar raised his eyebrows. "You have something I want?"

"I do," Liam said, apparently pleased. "One Lulach Macimantokell, or some such. At any rate, he is a friend of Ferchar of Carron. That *is* you, I take it."

With an effort, Ferchar kept his face bland. "Lulach is your prisoner?"

"Not so far from here. He had the effrontery to pursue us from…Brecka, do you call it? I am prepared to release him to you."

"Thank you," Ferchar said steadily, "but I doubt I have anything *you* want in exchange."

Liam's smile was dazzling. "The Lady Affrica, of course."

"The lady is in sanctuary."

"But she cannot stay there. She has committed murder."

"I have?" Affrica said, clearly startled. She had moved up to the cross once more. Ferchar stepped in front of her, blocking her from Liam's view.

"She has?" Ferchar repeated politely. "When has she had time to do that?"

"Before fleeing Brecka, of course. She instructed an old man to kill my friend Donald Ban MacWilliam."

Affrica's gasp was audible. Ferchar knew how she felt, and yet fierce elation fought its way to his heart.

"Adam mac Malcolm killed Donald Ban?" he uttered, just to be sure.

"Well, he wasn't quite dead when I left him, but I expect he is by now. So, you will give me the lady, his granddaughter who put him up to it."

Ferchar laughed.

Affrica said shakily, "You don't know my grandfather if you think anyone could *put him up* to anything. But if he killed an invader, I am proud of him."

"You see?" Liam said. He lowered his voice confidingly. "A little fiction for the men, only. I know Adam MacHeth's past and his motives as well as you do. But it gives you an excuse to release her to me and get your fierce friend back."

"My friend who would kill me for me giving up the lady?" Ferchar said wryly. "And rightly so. What do you take us for?"

Liam sighed. "Still sweet on her? Well, she's still not for you, and, in truth, you'll be doing her a favor. If Donald Ban lives, he'll marry her. If he doesn't, I will."

"I have it on good authority that the lady would cut her own throat first. It doesn't arise. She is and will remain in sanctuary that even the MacWilliams dare not break."

"I thought you would say that," Liam said cheerfully. "The lady, on the other hand, is likely to be more soft-hearted." He waved one arm down the road to where the rest of his men waited.

Nothing happened.

Ferchar began to smile. The injured prisoner he had taken had told him a great deal very quickly, and the orders Ferchar had subsequently issued had clearly been carried out.

"Are you looking for me?" Lulach limped past the stunned priest and Affrica and stood beside Ferchar.

"I had my own men fetch him," Ferchar explained, resisting the urge to hold up his unsteady, injured friend. "You have a count of ten to retreat. Be gone by nightfall." He turned his back on the prince and walked beside Lulach into the sanctuary. He didn't look back until he heard the horses' hooves thundering back down the road. Then he flung an arm around Lulach, whose body had begun to shake. Affrica appeared anxiously on his other side, and together they lowered him to the ground. Only then, with unspeakable relief, did Ferchar see that his friend was laughing uncontrollably. And then they all were.

He didn't laugh in the morning when he woke and saw the smoke and the line of refugees heading toward the sanctuary. Liam had indeed gone, but he'd stayed long enough to burn Carron first.

※

THE SANCTUARY HOUSE was so full of wounded soldiers and homeless refugees that Affrica doubted there was any room for those fleeing from the law. However, huts with braziers were flung up in the grounds to accommodate the extra bodies. The people of Tain and the surrounding area gave alms and food.

One of the wounded from Brecka died, largely Affrica feared, from the final, jolting rush to the girth. But others survived and improved, and some left to rejoin their leaders.

The people of Carron rebuilt their homes and, as the weather turned colder, went back to live there. Many of their animals came back, too, since Liam had had no time to drive them south. Deirdre's once beautiful hall was being rebuilt, too, and once everyone pronounced the area safe, Affrica occasionally took Christina and Euphemia to see the new building.

Ferchar had stayed only two days, most of which had been spent apart from her while he made arrangements with his guard, and with his people of Carron for work needed there. Only once had she had the chance to speak to him—when he came to her the evening before his departure. She was just leaving the kitchen and found him in the doorway.

"Is it an imposition to ask you to care for my daughters again?"

"You know it isn't." She held his gaze. "Where are you going?"

"To find the men I left with Nechtan. The assault on Brecka, the pursuit of you, was desperation. The war is going badly for the MacWilliams at last. We won't kick them out before winter, but they'll still be vulnerable in the spring."

She nodded, then said abruptly. "My grandfather is dead, isn't he?"

"It was inevitable from the moment he decided to stay. He knew that." He shifted his feet. "I think he *saw* it."

"Do you? It crossed my mind that…"

"That what?"

"That he was trying to change things."

"In what way?"

She waved one frustrated hand. "I don't know. Prevent some future tragedy by killing Donald Ban MacWilliam."

Ferchar considered. "Perhaps he did. I, for one, will rejoice when Donald is dead. And I hope he takes Guthred with him."

"And Liam O'Neill," she said with distaste.

"And Liam O'Neill," he agreed. He drew in his breath. "I want to ask if you are well, if you will cope, but I know that you are *not* well and will cope just the same."

Involuntarily, she flung out her hand to him. "As will you."

He looked at her hand, and for a moment, she thought he wouldn't take it and felt only blind hurt. Then his fingers closed around hers.

"Everything can be rebuilt," she said shakily. "Everything. Thank you, Ferchar."

He moved quickly, as if he couldn't bear to be still any longer, dragging her hand to his rough cheek for the barest instant before he let her go and swung away, striding to the door without even a farewell.

# Chapter Nineteen

*Ross, winter 1211-1212*

Just before Christmas, she was overjoyed to welcome her brothers. Since they brought with them pack animals loaded with supplies, no one said a word about abuse of sanctuary. Affrica clung to them as to her only family left—at least in Ross—and began to dread their departure almost as soon as they arrived.

But on Christmas Eve, while they were decorating the sanctuary house with berries and greenery, the door opened and Ferchar walked in as casually as if he'd only been for a walk. He was drenched with rain and let in a blast of cold air that made Christina squeal. And then, with a different kind of noise entirely, she and her sister ran at Ferchar.

He crouched to hug them, apparently uninhibited by the cynical observations of Colin and Nechtan who, from their ladders, had been winding greenery among the roof beams. Which at least gave her time to compose her face, if not her inner turmoil, before she had to greet him.

She set her vase—well, a chipped jug—of Christmas roses in the center of the table and came, smiling, to greet him, searching for any changes since she had seen him last. But as he rose to his feet and bowed, there appeared to be none. His smile was as friendly, as impersonal as the one he bestowed on her brothers.

"I heard about Carron," Colin said awkwardly. "I'm sorry."

"It's not the only land that suffered. It will be ready for spring planting, and the hall is already rebuilt."

"Then we can go home?" Christina asked eagerly, slipping her hand into Ferchar's.

"Not quite yet," he said ruefully. "It's only a shell, with no furniture or linen. It's not ready, sadly, for Yuletide feasts."

"We're having one," Euphemia said brightly. "You will be here, won't you, Father?"

"Of course, he will," Nechtan said, smacking him across the shoulders. "He has yet to meet Hairy Harry who stole the shears."

"I'm fairly sure I know Hairy Harry," Ferchar replied dryly, "and he steals anything that isn't nailed down."

"We thought he just meant to cut his hair and his beard," Affrica said, disappointed, and was rewarded by the flash of his real grin.

It was a strange Christmas, spent with a bizarre mix of people including a one-legged soldier called Giric, servants and farmers from Brecka and, of course, Hairy Harry, a thief who seemed to have been pursued across Scotland. Ferchar's stepdaughters were excited and ran wild around the house and the grounds with the other children. Ale and wine from Colin and Nechtan's plunder flowed, and the food, prepared in a good-natured guddle was plentiful and splendid, at least by recent standards.

After a few days, Affrica realized that she had stopped clinging to her brothers. More, for the first time since Brecka, she was no longer pretending to smile. Laughter had seeped back, not just into the house, but into her heart.

She thought it might have had something to do with Ferchar, who seemed to have recovered all the joy in life that had so infected her in Paris. He laughed easily, invented games for both adults and children, and threw himself wholeheartedly into every festive activity. It all brought a rosier glow to the faces of the cooped-up children, and to the adults, who had all been through their own different tragedies.

And then one day, at dinner, Nechtan's smile slipped. He said, "I wish Kenneth and Ranald were here with us."

"They probably wish we were in Dingwall with them," Colin said ruefully. "Why aren't we?"

"Because you'd had enough of the fighting men, and your sister is here," Ferchar said mildly. He cracked a nut and threw it into his mouth before sitting back thoughtfully. "On the other hand… perhaps we could find a gift for them. And for the king."

"A gift?" Nechtan repeated, uncomprehending.

"What would make them happiest?" Ferchar wondered, an infectious gleam in his eyes.

Nechtan answered obligingly, "To kick out the MacWilliams and return to peace."

"Well, then, let's go and kick out a few MacWilliams."

Colin blinked. "It's winter."

"If it's too inconvenient for you, I'll tell you all about when I come back."

"Back from where?" Nechtan demanded, leaning over the table with a hint of aggression.

"There are a few outposts scattered about the coast, places the enemy will abandon on their own as soon as its spring, taking animals and plunder with them if they can. If we scare them off now, without the plunder, we can concentrate on bigger fish, come the spring. Besides," Ferchar added, reaching for his cup, "it will be fun."

"How?" Affrica asked with interest, and quick laughter lit his eyes.

"Because we'll sail and take them by surprise."

"Sail?" Colin said, startled. "In winter?"

"We'll be fine, hugging the coast. And we'll be back before Twelfth Night."

"I'll come," said the old soldier, Giric.

Nechtan stared at him. "My friend, you only have one leg."

"He can row, can't he?" Ferchar said mildly.

Hairy Harry crashed his cup down on the table and wiped his mouth on his sleeve. "When do we leave?"

"First light." Ferchar set his drained cup down on the table, rather more gently, and Colin refilled it for him.

"Then we'll see you at first light," he mocked. "If you still remember…"

Affrica, relieved they would not really risk their lives on anything so trivial, left them to their increasingly more ridiculous planning, and went to bed smiling.

The next morning, however, she woke to muffled laughter and quiet voices in the grounds. She threw open her shutters in time to see nearly every man in the girth running or riding out of it. Hairy Harry carried one of the wounded soldiers on his back. The one-legged Giric rode behind Ferchar, other wounded behind Colin and Nechtan. And they were heading in the direction of Tain harbor.

Furious, Affrica almost called them back. In the end, though, she didn't. For one thing, they wouldn't have come. For another, she recognized that she was, largely, jealous of the adventure because it didn't include her.

⇶⇷

"I KNOW WHAT you're doing," she said, a week later.

The men had just returned in rare high spirts, full of laughter and stories. Of how, leaving the disabled in the boats to batter daggers on shields and shout, they had convinced each outpost that a much larger force was attacking. Meanwhile, the able-bodied had chased out the terrified defenders and put local people in their place. They didn't tell her how many had died, though she had already noted as many raiders returned as had set out.

She spoke during the first raucous meal after their return. Ferchar sat beside her, his arm all but touching hers while his head was bent toward Sinead. But he turned to her at once, a smile just dying on his lips, as his expression changed to one of innocence.

"You do?"

"I do. You're giving the wounded back their confidence so they'll be ready to fight again."

His expression didn't alter. "Will it work?"

"You're the captain. You're also...making friends of my brothers," she said in a rush.

"I have counted them my friends since childhood."

She waved that aside with impatience. "Not like that. You're...binding them to you. It's what you do." *It's what you did with me, all these years ago, without evening noticing, and I'm still tied...*

"It was fun, Affrica," he said deliberately. He reached for the jug and poured wine into both their cups. "Don't be grumpy just because you wish you'd been there."

She smiled reluctantly. "Part of me does wish that."

"Part of me does, too," he said unexpectedly. "But your brothers would never have let you come."

"Would you?"

He lifted his cup, gazing into it, perhaps giving himself time. His eyes lifted slowly to hers. A faint smile tugged at his lips, and her heart fluttered and dived. He drank without answering, and Colin shouted something to her from further down the table, distracting her, infuriating and relieving her all at once.

The following day, he took his daughters to Carron. The girls asked her to come, too, but she shook her head and sent them on their way. There was plenty to do for the Twelfth Night celebration—another feast, this time with music and dancing. Sinead had borrowed an ancient lute from Father Stephen, and a harp was discovered hidden beneath the stairs in the sanctuary house. Affrica wanted the girls to have this time alone with their stepfather. They were, perhaps, a little too attached to her, and she to them, for she was not their mother.

But as the women chattered around her, she found herself staring not at the table she was supposed to be decorating, but through the open shutters in the direction of Carron. Because it came to her that by refusing to go with Ferchar today, she had been punishing him—for not answering her last night, for not wanting to take her with him on the reckless sea raid. And because when he had looked at her last night, she had been afraid.

When had she started being afraid of Ferchar Maccintsacairt? When had the excitement and pleasure of his company, become so churningly uncomfortable? How could she yearn to be with him now and dread his coming back with this harsh, boiling whirlpool in the pit of her stomach?

*I don't know him. I never did.* From the boy who refused to accept the cruelty of his social superiors, to the youth who made fleeing from ruthless enemies into a game, to this self-contained soldier who could lead her brothers, whose experience was so far beyond hers she could never catch up. And yet that bond remained, intensified now into something both alluring and painful, almost terrible.

*If I love him, surely it should not be like this?*

When the war with the MacWilliams was past, she would be married to some close friend of the king's with unimpeachable loyalty. As her aunts and sisters had been. As Kenneth himself would be. It was the way of the world, and even when she had railed against it, she had accepted it in her bones. She would marry for the good of the family, Ross, and Scotland but hadn't given up hope of personal happiness in that marriage. And when she found it—she would *make* it happy, for there was something to love in everyone—she and Ferchar could be friends again.

Her lips twisted, and she turned her attention back to her task—for five minutes before she gave up again. Instead, she took Wolf with her out beyond the boundary of the girth, as if, in exercise, she could loosen the maddening, knotted tangles of her feelings.

>>><<<

SHE HAD NEVER been so beautiful as now, laughing, her delicate cheeks flushed from dancing with men who would never normally come within yards of her. Her thick, dark hair hung loose, confined only by the veil pinned to her crown, a bare nod to convention. Her red gown was old and mended, and yet it reflected her bright, indomitable spirit. Whether at the court of kings or among beggars, soldiers and thieves, Affrica MacHeth would always shine.

But never for him.

Everyone who could had taken it in turns to play so that everyone had the chance to dance. Ferchar had arranged matters so that when she danced, he took his poor turn on the lute. His playing caused more hilarity than admiration.

He built on that, making his stepdaughters howl with glee, and happily batted back insults with the men over the rhythmic but occasionally discordant music. In the end, Sinead left her partner—Nechtan—and wrested the instrument from Ferchar's hands.

Nechtan cheered, so Ferchar danced with him instead. Affrica's face flashed by him, wet with tears of laughter and fun, and the fierce ache within him grew unbearable. He could not trust himself to dance with her now, as he had at Dingwall. He could not trust himself anywhere near her.

His stepdaughters, gamely dancing with Colin and Hairy Harry, were exhausted. He chose to take them up to their bedroom himself, even though they shared it with Affrica.

"Another five minutes," Euphemia begged, although she could barely keep her eyes open. He laughed at her and swept her up to his shoulders, taking Christina by the hand. Bridie followed him, and everyone else waved and called a cheerful goodnight. It was a night they would always remember. So would he, although for vastly different reasons.

Their room was reached from the outside staircase, which gave him a welcome blast of damp, icy air. He thought it might snow. At least the girls' bedchamber was warm enough, and they had plenty of blankets for their own little cots.

He had been here before once or twice to say good night to them, trying not to look beyond their own little corner to the larger bed and makeshift chest that was Affrica's domain.

"Quickly into bed," Bridie scolded. "Before Lord Ferchar counts to twenty."

Deirdre had made her household call him that, he reflected as he began his count—which tended to veer off as he amused them by pretending to forget numbers and go back to the beginning again. By marriage, of course, he was the Lord of Carron, but it was not his. He held it for the girls, and he was no lord. He was the son of the priest of St. Duthac, and he should never forget it.

Because he couldn't be still, he paced as he counted. "Ten, what comes after ten?" he wondered, as he noticed a white, crumpled garment of some kind on the floor near the larger bed.

"Six!" Christina cried.

"Two!" Euphemia disputed.

"That must be it," Ferchar said, bending to pick up the fallen linen from the floor. "Two, three, four…"

The girls giggled happily and Ferchar straightened, tossing the garment on the bed, where it unfolded into something he suddenly recognized.

"Seven, eight, nine, ten, eleven, of course it's eleven!" A white linen apron purloined from a washing line in Paris to bind them together as they rode across the line to the building on the other side of the road. What in God's name had he been thinking of? "Twelve, thirteen, nine…"

She had kept it. She had never worn it, even here where her position as lady was less delineated. It was far too big for her. And yet she had brought it on the journey from Brecka, with only a few other things. He could almost believe it had fallen from under her pillow. It would smell of her, held close, perhaps to her warm, sweet body.

His ears sang. His heart was beating as though she stood before him.

Did Affrica MacHeth *care* for him? Was something possible here that he had never seen?

No. It was her last memory of freedom and fun, of winning over the danger that had threatened. She had been a child and he not much older. And yet there had been moments since, a warmth in her eyes, a blush, the dance in Dingwall. Even... When she had rushed to Tain a year ago, when Deirdre had died, had it been as much for his sake as for the children?

Could Affrica MacHeth *love* him?

"Twenty!" He spun around to find his stepdaughters tucked up in their beds, grinning at him with Bridie smiling proudly before them.

As he said the final goodnight, he realized afresh that love or lack of it did not matter. Lord of Carron or son of the priest, he could never aspire to Affrica MacHeth. She was too valuable to her family, to the king himself after the tragic divisions of this war. She would be given to Sir William Comyn or some other powerful lord of unimpeachable loyalty, another layer of rope binding Ross and the MacHeths to the king.

It made no difference. On the steps down the side of the house, he paused, leaning one shoulder against the building, giving himself time to gather his strength, to regain his balance. From below, music started up again, rhythmic but too rough to be made by Affrica or Sinead. He closed his eyes, letting the image of one graceful, laughing girl dance across his mind.

The inhuman brutality of battle, the mire of intrigue that was the king's court, had both begun to appeal far more than this torture. Pushing off the wall, he ran the rest of the way down the steps and strode back to the front door.

Affrica stood in the open doorway, as though she had opened it to air the hall and was about to close it again. But she had seen him. He could not take the coward's way and slip round by the kitchen door. Besides, she looked determined to speak to him, for she didn't stand aside to let him pass.

"I owe you an apology," she said unexpectedly.

"You do? What heinous crime have you committed now?"

"At supper last night, I was both unkind and intrusive. I'm sorry."

With an effort, he dredged up the conversation, which had somehow got lost in her eyes. "Binding," he said, and laughed. Dear God, and she thought she had offended him. "You needn't apologize, for you're right. Mostly. I'm just not quite so calculating about it as you think. Most men tell jokes to make their companions laugh. I get carried away and take them raiding." Or over the Paris rooves. Even then, he had wanted to bind the child to him in friendship, and not because she was valued kin of the Earl of Ross. "We all need friends," he finished vaguely.

Her tongue darted out, nervously licking her lips, drawing his eyes and his inevitable desire. He could not think about her mouth, could not look at it. Determinedly, he dragged his gaze back to her eyes, but it was too late. She had seen where he looked and even in the poor light seeping from the hall behind her, he saw the blush staining her cheeks, the warm desperation of her eyes.

*Oh, Affrica...* "I have to leave tomorrow," he said abruptly. "The king expects me in Dingwall."

She blinked. "In January? There's snow coming."

"Which is why I need to go now."

For an instant, her eyes searched his, then dragged free as she stood aside to let him in. "Are you taking my brothers?"

He shook his head. Did she know she was the reason he left? Did she imagine she was of no account? It was what she *had* to think and what he had to train himself to believe. But he could brush past her, inhaling the sweetness of her scent. He could sink into the chair by the table, cup in hand and watch her, listen as she played the harp, a soothing, moving lullaby rather than the jolly dances of earlier. He could keep the smile on his lips and pretend to be jug-bitten while he ached and longed for the last time. Surely the last time.

# Chapter Twenty

*Ross, summer 1212*

IN THE SPRING, the King of Scots went south to Durham with the queen, negotiating once more with King John of England. The royal armies, under the youthful Prince Alexander, joined now by Brabantine mercenaries supplied by John himself, had swept all before them before the summer and finally captured Guthred MacWilliam.

One rumor said Guthred had been betrayed by his own mercenaries who had had enough. Another said it was disillusioned thanes of Ross who had given him up to the king's men. Everyone said he was on his way to prison and trial before the king, that he was so ashamed of his failure that he was refusing to eat. And then that on the king's order, Sir William Comyn had executed him at Kincardine.

Affrica returned to Tirebeck with her triumphant brothers and Ferchar's daughters. Somehow Hairy Harry and Giric, the one-legged soldier, were also in her train. There was so much to do to set things right that she barely had time to miss her father or her grandfather, or to register the further changes that would occur. Nechtan was betrothed to a lady in Perth, and on his marriage, Affrica's place at Tirebeck would be supplanted.

Kenneth wrote, summoning her to Dingwall to act as his hostess when the king would be visiting. And then Colin heard from a returning soldier that the earl was at Brecka. Confused, Affrica and Colin decided to go to Brecka to make sure all was well.

At Brecka, the hastily constructed new gates stood open, and a new, much smaller hall had been built in part of the space once occupied by the old. One of the more distant outbuildings had survived the fire, though for some reason it made Affrica shiver more than the incongruous new hall.

"Where are the men?" Colin wondered.

"The war is over," she said uneasily. "Why should he travel with an army?" She could answer her own question, of course. *Because it adds to his consequence.*

A man Affrica didn't recognize appeared in the stable to look after their mounts. At least there were other horses here, if no obvious soldiers.

They found Kenneth in the main hall, instructing a house servant, though when he looked up and saw them, his jaw dropped with surprise. "Good God, what are you two doing here?"

"A pleasure to see you, too, cousin," Colin said wryly. "No one had heard of you in weeks, apart from Affrica's curt summons to Dingwall. We were worried."

"For God's sake, I'm not a child," he said testily. "I don't need nurses, especially not my younger cousins!"

"Then you'd like us just to go, without even unsaddling the horses?" Colin said, which at last made Kenneth laugh, although it was a poor effort.

"There, don't be so haughty. I'm just in a foul mood and you took me by surprise. Naturally, you are welcome, though you'll see we're not exactly ready for company yet. I'm afraid you'll both have to sleep in the loft, and there isn't much in the way of comfort."

"What about the guest house that's still standing?" Affrica asked.

"Unlivable, sadly," Kenneth said dismissively. "I'll have the servants make up beds for you and take up your things. How long can you stay?"

Despite the words, the question sounded more like, *When are you leaving?* "You have servants here?" Affrica asked cautiously.

"If I'd known you were coming, I would have brought the staff from Dingwall," he retorted. "As it is, you must put up with the inconvenience. It can't be worse than sanctuary all that time in the company of thieves and miscreants."

"There were others beside Colin and Nechtan," Affrica quipped in an attempt to lighten this very odd mood. "Talking of whom, is Nechtan with you?"

"No, I left him in Dingwall with the men. This was meant to be a flying visit." He gestured impatiently to the table and while they sat, he fetched wine and glasses himself.

"Have you got a woman stowed secretly up here?" Colin asked.

Kenneth shoved a cup at him. "If I had, I wouldn't tell you. At least, not in front of your lady sister."

*Someone else's wife, perhaps?* It would certainly explain Kenneth's unease and annoyance. She resolved to retire early so as not to spoil his tryst any farther. Though she couldn't help wondering if the woman was hiding in Kenneth's bedroom, which he clearly had no intention of giving up to Affrica, or in the guest house where he obviously didn't want them either.

She wished they hadn't come.

⋙⋘

SOME HOURS LATER, lying awake in her makeshift bed on the far side of the loft, she gazed into the heavy darkness, trying to unwind the knot of her unease. She was used to Kenneth's changeable moods and dislike of being thwarted in even the smallest things, but although he had exerted himself to be a genial host, his false graciousness had hurt her stomach. And if he had some gentlewoman concealed in his bedchamber, Affrica had no hint of it. No feminine perfume drifted out to her, no sounds of movement from the room at the back of the hall. Nor did Kenneth make any excuses to go there at any point in their visit.

A manservant she had never seen before had served their indifferent dinner. An untrained local girl had made up the beds and cleared the table—she was the same servant Kenneth had been haranguing on their arrival. He really hadn't brought any of his people with him.

*He is just grumpy. Probably the king has slighted him in some way, and he is licking the wounds to his pride.*

A door below closed softly. Was that a faint glow in the darkness, seeping through the shutters? She heard a male voice, too low to recognize let alone make out the words. Kenneth, seeking his ladylove in the guest house? She owed him some privacy surely and would not look.

All was quiet. A stone crunched in the yard just as she was nodding off to sleep, and the hall door opened and closed.

Not a very long tryst, then.

Affrica turned onto her other side and closed her eyes firmly. She drifted off to sleep at last, an uneasy slumber disturbed by dreams and imagined noises that woke her for the barest instant before she drifted off again, and then woke, finally, to silence.

This time, she definitely heard running footsteps, soft but unmistakable.

She threw off the blankets and walked across the jaggy straw on the floor to the window. Opening the shutters, she stuck her head out and peered down. A man stood outside, silently closing the shutters of the hall window below.

Her breath caught. Had he been in the hall? Robbing Kenneth? Assassinating Kenneth? She turned away in panic to rouse Colin, when the man's movement caught her eye. He loped away from the main building and as he glanced up at the sky, perhaps trying to gauge the time or the weather, a shaft of pale moonlight fell across his face.

*Ferchar.*

⟫⟫⟫⟪⟪⟪

FERCHAR HAD BEEN tracking his quarry for days. The king had given him the unenviable task of capturing or killing any remnants of the MacWilliam army. He had spent weeks in Wester Ross doing just that. Yet only when he'd returned with relief to Easter Ross had he picked up word of an amiable Irishman traveling north. Sometimes the Irishman had been a priest or a traveling monk. Sometimes, he had been a gentleman, but he journeyed alone, and Ferchar was increasingly sure that they were all Liam O'Neill.

The man switched directions, hiding and misleading as though by nature rather than with any purpose, and yet the direction became steadily clearer.

Ferchar felt sick. Liam could have only two reasons for going to Brecka. To assassinate Kenneth for fighting against him and the MacWilliams. Or because, despite everything, Kenneth was still helping the man he had called friend, even after Liam had held Affrica at the point of his dagger.

Neither was acceptable to Ferchar. And yet if it was the latter…

He sent his men to patrol the hill paths into Wester Ross and sped on to Brecka alone. It seemed the best of bad choices, and from brief words exchanged with innkeepers, shepherds, and other travelers, he was catching up with the elusive Irishman. On the other hand, Liam, if it was he, seemed to have given up all attempts to mislead. His path became swift and direct.

Stupidly, Ferchar still hoped he was wrong. He hoped Kenneth was nowhere near Brecka, as he had been nowhere near Ross when the MacWilliams had invaded. God knew Ferchar did not want Kenneth assassinated. He would lay down his own life to prevent it. But neither could he let the earl harbor such a fugitive, risk his family and his people and Ross itself for the self-serving ambition of one dishonorable man.

His best hope was that Liam merely went to *ask* for Kenneth's help. With luck, Kenneth would not even be there and Ferchar could kill or capture Liam. Or Kenneth would have done the capturing. That would be best of all…

It was night before he came to Brecka. A new, smaller hall had gone up since he had last seen the burned wreckage of Malcolm MacHeth's old headquarters. It stood black and still, almost blending with the trees behind it. Abandoning his horse with a pat, he went the rest of the way on foot. The gates stood open but the whole place still looked unlived in. No guards challenged him or even lurked around the minimal stockade. Anyone would think no one was there at all, until a faint snorting from the stables broke the silence.

A quick survey showed him several horses, including the earl's own magnificent chestnut and several sturdy ponies.

*Don't you dare be dead now, Kenneth MacHeth…*

The hall door was barred from the inside, with no lights shining beneath. Ferchar felt his way around the house to where he judged the lord's bedchamber to be and set about unfastening the shutters with his knife. Nothing stirred within, though he might have heard a sigh.

At last, he could peer through the window until he could make out the bed and the hump of blankets that might have contained a human. Probably the earl, but he had to be sure. He jumped, hauling himself over the sill as silently as possible, and crept across the floor. In the darkness, it was impossible to make out the features of the sleeping man. He reached into his scrip for the tinder box, knowing the flare of light was likely to wake up the occupant of bed. But he had to know.

The figure on the bed muttered in his sleep, and at the familiar sound of his voice, Ferchar relaxed. With relief, he dropped the box back into his scrip and left the way he had come in, closing the shutters over behind him. Kenneth could repair the fastening tomorrow.

If Liam was here, where was he? Camped in the forest? Sleeping on the hall floor? He glanced up at the sky as a thin shaft of moonlight peeked out from the clouds. He had time to search the one remaining outhouse before even the first servants were up and about.

Only why had Kenneth come with no men? Had he returned to his old home, the home of his kin for generations, to make some kind of farewell? Even Kenneth must feel the need for solitude and peace sometimes.

The outbuilding was in darkness, too. With one hand on his dagger hilt, he pushed open the door. Silence.

He stepped inside—and a point of cold, sharp steel pierced the skin of his neck. He froze.

"Good man," said the unmistakable tones of Liam O'Neill. "Now, back out again."

A flare of light blinded Ferchar as he obeyed. Fortunately, it blinded Liam too, for the prince swore and stilled, which gave Ferchar the instant he needed to leap out of reach of the blade and draw his own.

"Bring the lantern here," Liam ordered. "And kill him quickly."

Of course, Liam was not alone. In the lantern's glow, an older man with a fair beard, and two men-at-arms spilled out of the house, swords drawn.

Ferchar backed, circling to prevent them surrounding him, his sword in one hand, dagger in the other.

"You again?" Liam said in disbelief. "Were you put on this earth merely to plague me?"

"No, but it's an appealing bonus." He lashed out with his dagger, slashing the arm of the man who tried to come at him from his left, and swept his sword in a wide, vicious arc, preventing a joint attack by the other three. For Liam himself had deigned to join the advance.

The fair man lunged at him with his sword, and Ferchar parried, moving out of reach of the others and trying to fend off the first man-at-arms with his dagger, while defending himself from the fair man's sword.

"Mind your wound," Liam said abruptly. "Let me, for it will be a pleasure, trust me."

*"Mind your wound."* Abruptly, everything fell into place in Ferchar's mind.

"Donald Ban MacWilliam," he said, attacking so viciously so that the man could not disengage if he wanted to. "So, Adam mac Malcolm didn't quite kill you after all, and your own people left you here to die."

"To recover," Liam said. His voice gave Ferchar an instant's warning, and he threw himself aside, slashing someone else's flesh with his dagger as he felt Liam's sword bite into his shoulder. Now he faced the joint attack of Donald Ban and Liam, while the men-at-arms, circled behind. It was like dancing—advancing and retreating to the clashing of the swords, constantly skipping and spinning to avoid the lesser men's blades.

"So, you came alone," Liam said breathlessly after several minutes of this. "That was a mistake."

It was. And this was one fight he could not win. He dared not even yell for Kenneth, for he could not trust which side the earl would take. Blood ran down his dagger hand, between his fingers, making his grip slippery. The wound to his shoulder had begun to shriek with his every movement, but giving up, never in his nature, meant death.

"Get the horses," Liam flung at one of the men-at-arms, which at least reduced the numbers against Ferchar, though it was a lowering commentary on the enemy's confidence.

"Stop it!" cried a female voice in fury. "Stop at once! Kenneth, for God's sake…!"

He barely heard the words after the first cry for his blood ran cold. For the first time, pure fear surged through him, for now he *had* to win in order to protect her. Unfortunately, in his startlement, he'd lost sight of the remaining man-at-arms, who brought him down with a sweep of his boot, and in an instant, Donald Ban and Liam were upon him, swords raised for the kill.

Someone stood on his sword. Ferchar released it long enough to grab the ankle to his right and yanked the man down before snatching up his sword and swiping aside those that threatened him. It gave him another second, that was all, just in case it might be useful. He could not even look for Affrica. To have failed her…

Liam O'Neill staggered backward under a mighty push.

"Get off him," Kenneth MacHeth snarled at Donald Ban, his own sword held as a weapon. "Go, for God's sake. Now!"

Liam snatched Donald's arm and they loped together across the yard. Ferchar hauled himself to his feet, determined to pursue, but Kenneth caught him by his bloody arm.

"Be still man, and thank God and me you're not dead," he snarled. "What in the name of the foul fiend are you doing here?"

The men were galloping off through the open gates, and Ferchar's horse was up in the woods. He turned his furious gaze on Kenneth. "What am *I* doing here?" He laughed, a harsh, contemptuous sound and, in spite of everything, was aware of Affrica's arm falling across her stomach. Colin was beside her, wide-eyed and unarmed. "Trying to save your bloody earldom and prevent the next war, since you seem to be bent on the destruction of the former and the preservation of the other."

The silence was not friendly. "You," Kenneth said, "need to mind your tongue. If you can manage that, I'll speak to you in the hall. If you can't, get out now."

"And if he goes to the king with this?" Colin uttered, in apparent disbelief. "We are all dead."

"Nonsense," said Kenneth, stalking away to the hall. "I had no idea Donald Ban MacWilliam was here."

Ferchar turned from him, staring toward the gate once more. He couldn't see the enemy. He couldn't even hear them. It was all to do again.

But Kenneth was right about one thing. They did need to talk before Ferchar set off in pursuit once more.

"Let me see to your injuries," Affrica said. She spoke calmly, and yet her voice shook.

He couldn't bear it. He swung away from her. "I'll see to my own." And he strode after Kenneth without waiting for either Colin or the lady.

In the hall where lamps had been lit, Kenneth gestured toward his open bedchamber door. There was light in there, too. Ferchar walked past him and closed the door.

He cleaned his own wounds, which were not too deep, and tied them up with linen torn with some satisfaction from shirts he found on top of Kenneth's open chest. Then he washed his face, combed his hair, and hoped Affrica had gone to bed.

She hadn't.

She sat at the table beside Colin, facing Kenneth, who was repeating, "I didn't know. I came for solitude, you know that. I wasn't even pleased to see you two. It never entered my head there was anyone else here."

"Is that what I should tell the king?" Ferchar asked.

Everyone looked at him.

"If you have to," Kenneth said evenly.

"Such an unlikely tale on any level."

"The truth often is. So, it might be best to keep it between ourselves. If the king takes the earldom from me, he won't give it to Ranald or even Nechtan. It will be a foreigner, and it will be feudal, military rule."

"And still, you couldn't resist."

"I don't see why you insist—" Kenneth began in self-righteous tones.

"Yes, you do. Liam came here within the last day, two at the most, to take Donald Ban MacWilliam away to safety. While you just happened to be here."

Kenneth sighed and drew a jug of wine nearer him. Affrica took it from him and poured four cups. Ferchar neither drank nor sat.

"No one wants the royal armies here longer than they have to be," Kenneth said. "I want them gone, not chasing minor MacWilliams about. Or even executing them. There is ill-feeling enough over Guthred's death."

"And my father's?" Colin said harshly. "Adam mac Malcolm's? The hundreds of our own people who have died?"

"I did not cause this war, Colin," Kenneth said wearily. "But I do understand it. It's over, now. Finished. Liam and Donald Ban will be back in Ireland in a week. And the rest of the royal troops will be gone in two. And then we have peace again. If we don't start another hue and cry after Donald Ban. You must leave it, Ferchar."

"Must I?" Ferchar's fingers clenched and unclenched once. "Perhaps so. But I give you warning, Kenneth mac Gilchrist. There must be no more playing one side against the other to see who wins, to find out who will give most to the MacHeths. The price is too high, and I will not allow it."

Kenneth's eyebrows flew up. He tried to laugh. "*You*, Ferchar Maccintsacairt?"

"I, Ferchar Maccintsacairt." He spoke his name like an oath, and he saw the recognition of it dawn on Kenneth's face, though being Kenneth, he could not resist the taunt.

"And how will you do that, my friend?"

"I will kill you," Ferchar said. And in the lethal silence, he knocked over the cup of wine that had been meant for him. It flowed redly across the table like blood. Then he walked to the door and let it bang shut behind him.

AFFRICA'S LEGS SHOOK as she rose to her feet.

"Jumped up priest's son," Kenneth muttered, and took a gulp of wine. "Not even a thank you for saving his worthless life. Time he was cut down to size."

"But he is right!" Affrica uttered. "And you know it."

She ran after Ferchar without caring whether or not they followed her. Since she couldn't see him marching out of the gate, she hurried to the stables, and there came to a halt. Her heart bumped against her ribs.

She wished he was storming about the place, kicking things in his fury. Instead, he stood by Colin's horse. He had placed the saddle on its back and rested his forehead against it in what was, surely, a rare moment of weakness. Because there was nothing a man like him could do to prevent a nobleman like Kenneth from making all sorts of wrong decisions, decisions that killed people and brought the country to ruin. Because despite other successes, he had never managed to bind Kenneth to him, and in this part of the country, Kenneth was the man who counted. Nothing he ever did would change that, and for a man like Ferchar that was truly unbearable.

A lump formed in her throat. As though he heard her swallow, he jerked his head up and saw her.

"My own horse is in the woods," he said distantly. "I'll ride this one to find him and then send it back."

"Did you mean it?" she blurted.

He didn't ask what she meant. "Yes. This time he goes free. But never again."

"We weren't part of it," she said. "Colin and I."

At least a tired smile flickered across his lips. "I know that, too." He began fastening girths and lengthening stirrups.

"Why don't you stay until tomorrow?" she pleaded. "Give your wounds at least a few hours to heal?"

"Because they'll be far enough ahead of me as it is."

"You can't take on four of them, Ferchar!"

"I won't need to. Once I drive them toward my men."

"And a few hours' sleep will make a huge difference to that?"

He stilled. "What do you want of me, Affrica?" There was controlled savagery in his voice, and yet it gave her hope that she was reaching him.

Emboldened, she stepped closer and took his arm to draw him away from the horse.

But at the first brush of her fingers, he jerked away with shocking violence and spun to face her. "Don't *touch* me!"

Hurt washed through her, shriveling her heart, for there was no softness in his voice or his boiling, turbulent eyes, only fury and revulsion. With blinding clarity, she saw that at this moment, *she* was the cause of his pain. And that broke her.

She stumbled back against the door, wrenched around to flee.

"I cannot bear your touch." His voice, quieter now, was right behind her, as though he he'd moved with her, drawn that by that invisible string that bound her to him, even as his words lacerated her. Yet he *was* touching her, his hands light on her shoulders. "And I do not think you can bear mine."

Her eyes closed. "I'm bearing it now," she whispered.

His fingers gripped and slowly, inexorably turned her. Torchlight flared over the stall door, causing shadows to dance along the long bones of his face. What she had thought of as anger in his eyes looked more like desperation. A new suspicion, wonderful and terrifying, seemed to stop her heart. His eyes devoured her, searching. And that gave her the courage to reach up with both hands and touch his rough cheeks with her fingertips. His breath caught, but he did not move.

"So are you," she said huskily.

"So am I what?" he asked, as though he had lost the thread in her eyes.

"Bearing my touch."

Very slowly, his hand moved inward from her shoulder to her neck and her lips parted with sweet, delicious shock. "As you are bearing mine?" His palm closed over her nape, and she gasped. "I am beginning to wonder if what we need is…more."

"More what?" she managed, and the hand still heavy on her shoulder moved down her back and drew her suddenly hard against his body.

"Touching," he whispered, bending his head to hers.

Her whole body trembled. One wrong word, one wrong movement would end this. And that, she truly could not bear. She moved her fingers delicately across his face, drinking in the bristling stubble, the smoothness closer to his eyes and temples. In wonder, she ran her fingers through his hair and, her heart thundering, tugged his head downward.

"I am already bound to you," she said brokenly. "I always was."

His breath gave a mighty heave. For an awful instant she thought he would pull away from her, but then his head dipped the final inch, and his mouth sank on hers.

A sob of relief surged up her body and was lost in his mouth. She had wondered so often, when she couldn't stop herself, what his kisses would feel like on her lips, but nothing had prepared her for this overwhelming heat, for the intense, intrusive assault on all her senses. She met the first sweetness eagerly, opening to his urging with joy.

But one kiss was not enough, and the next bombarded her with hunger and pleasure. His hands drove through her hair, holding her steady for the onslaught of his mouth while his body pinned her to the door. The weapons at his belt dug into her and she didn't care because the rest of him was so hard and exciting. His arousal enflamed her as much as his hands wildly caressing her neck, her back and waist and hips. Everywhere he touched shivered with delight, and when he cupped her breast, she pressed into his hand, writhing.

His kisses spread fire from her lips along her jaw to her throat and lower over the swell of her breasts, and she held his head to her in bliss. His caresses made her gasp, and he kissed her open mouth once more.

He muttered against her lips, words that might have been, "I never imagined, never truly considered...You want this."

She smiled against his lips. "The touching?"

And his lips smiled back. "You always touched me, Affrica MacHeth." He heaved a breath that she felt deep in her own body, and his lips left her. He touched his forehead to hers. "But I have to go."

With aching slowness, he detached his body from hers, leaving a small, cold space between them.

"Why?" Even to her own ears, she sounded like a bewildered child.

"You know."

"To finish what my grandfather tried to do?"

"There is that. And honoring you." He dipped his head and pressed a hard kiss to her lips. "My lady. Tell them I've gone, and my lips are sealed."

It sounded like dismissal and yet his hand cupped her cheek, as if he didn't want to stop touching her now that he'd begun. More than that, she realized his hand trembled. As she did.

"You will take care?" she said helplessly.

"I will." His lips parted again, as though he would say more, but he only shook his head. His arms fell away from her, and he stepped back, reaching out to push open the stall door. But she could read his expression now. She could feel his emotion, and he was not hiding or pretending. He was happy.

And so, she *could* leave, glancing back over her shoulder to smile once more before the stall door fell shut, blocking him from her view.

As she walked, dazed, back to the hall, she found enough sense to right her veil over her tangled hair. She heard the unmistakable sounds of Ferchar galloping across the yard away from her and raised her eyes to see that dawn was breaking on a fine new day.

# Chapter Twenty-One

*Ross and Stirling, summer–autumn 1212*

By the time she and Colin left for Dingwall, they had heard nothing more of Donald Ban MacWilliam or Liam O'Neill. Affrica could only assume they had escaped, though she could not be sure since she had seen nothing of Ferchar. His only communication was a short, impersonal message of thanks when he sent for his stepdaughters.

The girls were excited to go home to Carron. Affrica had little time to dwell on missing either them or their stepfather, for the feast at Dingwall, where the king was to be guest of honor, meant a great deal to Kenneth, and strict formality was expected.

Affrica dusted off her court dresses which had somehow survived the depredations of war, cleaned her jewels, and set off with Sinead, Colin, and the men.

Colin was unusually quiet on the journey, although he often rode beside her, rather than with the guard, as if there was something he wanted to discuss with her. At last, he said abruptly, "Kenneth sheltered Donald Ban MacWilliam. For the sake of peace. I can almost understand that. Do you think he brought the MacWilliams here in the first place?"

"It's what the king suspected at the beginning," Affrica said. "He can't now. Kenneth *fought* the MacWilliams."

"It's what Ferchar suspects."

"Ferchar and Kenneth will never understand each other." Affrica hesitated, then, "I think it more likely that Kenneth suspected something *might* happen—he talks to everyone, after all—and stood aside to see what would unfold. He probably wanted to be the king's champion in the north and defeat the MacWilliams himself, but the king wouldn't let him go until they had too big a hold to easily dislodge."

Colin stared at her. "Nechtan and I are with him nearly all the time. We ride and fight and train with him. Father all but brought him up. We all ignore you, and you see everything."

"I didn't see it in time," she said bleakly. And yet they all should have. They'd known messengers came from Guthred MacWilliam to Kenneth. Liam O'Neill had been at Dingwall.

"You should have been Gilchrist's heir." Colin said bitterly.

"Don't hate him," Affrica said urgently. "Don't quarrel. It's our duty to keep him on a safe path."

He stared at her. "Can we?"

"Between us, I think we can."

Colin rode on beside her in thoughtful silence.

At Dingwall, she was astonished to discover a castle. Despite the war, or perhaps because of it, Kenneth had finally and proudly built his heart's desire. It wasn't finished yet but boasted a gracious stone hall and two stories of rooms around a large courtyard. Outbuildings of varied quality leaned against the inner walls of the courtyard. A tower rose above the sea, the harbor, and the town, and battlements ran all the way around.

Kenneth appeared to enjoy her awe, then left her to organize the reception of the king and his entourage, which was mostly military with few women expected, save the local ladies whom Affrica already knew. One pleasant surprise was the arrival of Marjorie of Buchan, who embraced her with enthusiasm and demanded details of her adventures in the late war.

The king arrived later the same day, in company with the Earls of Mar, Fife, and Strathearn, and Sir William Comyn. He greeted Affrica with kindness, and Kenneth and her brothers like old comrades, which was something of a relief.

As nominal hostess, she sat at the king's side during the feast. She didn't expect to receive much of his attention, and she didn't, which gave her time to study him. He had aged in the last two years. A slight stoop marred the soldierly bearing, and though he still spoke like a vigorous man, she had noticed he walked more slowly. He was too gaunt. Weariness stood out in his eyes. King William the Lion was an old man who just wanted peace in his turbulent realm.

Without warning, the king turned and met her gaze. She smiled at once, and to her relief he smiled back, as though he didn't mind her staring.

"Lady Affrica. A pleasure to my old eyes to find you here. The queen has missed you."

"As I have missed Her Grace. I hope she is well?"

The king's lips twisted. "Thoroughly. We hope you will join her court again."

"I would be honored." She would also be relieved not to be at home when Nechtan's wife became Lady of Tirebeck.

"You could travel with us to Perth," the king mused. "Lord Kenneth comes with us and could escort you."

*Lord Kenneth*, she noted uneasily. Not *the Earl of Ross*. "Thank you, sire."

He eyed her thoughtfully. "You are not yet betrothed, lady."

"There have been other concerns this last year," she murmured.

"A year which has made a good marriage for you more essential than ever. The queen and I will arrange it."

Affrica's heart sank. "I would not trouble—"

"Between ourselves," the king interrupted, leaning closer in amiable conspiracy, "you might think of your other neighbor." His gaze flickered beyond her, and she realized he meant the man on her other side, Sir William Comyn. "He thinks highly of you."

Affrica kept the faint smile affixed to her lips. Maybe going to court was not such a good idea…

The king straightened and addressed himself to his venison. "I met your grandmother once, did you know that?"

"Christian? I knew she had met the late king, your brother."

"He called her his eyes and ears in Ross."

Affrica knew that, too. She was also aware, as she hoped the king was not, that Christian's first loyalty had always been to her husband. And that her offer of service to King Malcolm IV had been largely to obtain the release of her father-in-law, Malcolm MacHeth, from his long imprisonment.

"Malcolm MacHeth was a man of his word," the king allowed. "He brought peace to Ross and the realm, as long as he lived."

"His descendants are equally loyal, sire."

The king smiled faintly. Impossible to tell if he meant it, or if he had just lost interest in the subject, for he turned away from her shortly after to address Kenneth on his other side.

"Do you stay in Ross, sir, or leave with the king?" she asked Sir William.

"I have duties elsewhere, now that Ross and Moray are quiet."

Affrica supposed that was a good thing. The evening passed, a little tense but in perfect good humor. The food and wine were excellent, and the servants performed admirably, as did the musicians and the tumblers who entertained the company afterward. But it was a mercifully short evening, since the king chose to retire early. The local guests departed, and the king's entourage broke up. Still, with sharp eyes and ears all over the castle, there could be no family conferences that might look like conspiracy. Ranald, Nechtan, and Colin all drifted away to their own quarters and Affrica, with relief, sought the chamber she was sharing with Lady Marjorie.

Before she got there, however, she came across Kenneth in the courtyard. He might have been waiting for her.

"What did the king say to you?" he murmured, strolling with her to the side of the castle set apart for the ladies.

"He wants me to return to the queen."

He nodded. "I think it's a good thing. I'm to go south with him, too." He bent his head closer. "Did he mention Comyn?"

"Yes, but archly. He might have been jesting."

"It would be a good marriage, Affrica. For all of us."

He meant it, which was curious. Whoever married her had a claim to the earldom, however flimsy. He sought Comyn's favor, clearly, which bode well for future peace. No more MacWilliam adventures.

"Well, Sir William has mentioned no such thing to me," she said. And wouldn't. Her grandfather had told her there would be no marriage with Sir William Comyn, and she did not fear it.

Until the morning, when, as she walked beyond the castle gates, Sir William himself fell into step beside her.

"You are abroad early, my lady," he observed.

"It's a habit of mine. I make sure all is functioning as it should in the household and then I escape for an hour, if I can, before everyone else rises. What of you, sir?"

"I saw you from my room," he said unexpectedly, "and hoped to speak to you in private."

She cast him a suddenly wary glance. "Oh?"

"I could not help overhearing some of what the king said to you last night."

She smiled comfortingly. "Don't worry. I didn't take him seriously."

"You should. He rarely says anything without purpose. And in this case, he supports—encourages—a marriage alliance between us."

This was not at all how it was meant to go. She gazed at him, perplexed.

"You'll forgive my indelicacy in approaching you," he said impatiently. "For I have already spoken to your cousin of Ross, the head of your family. He is in favor of the match, as is your brother."

She blinked. "You spoke to Nechtan?" How dare he keep such a matter from her? So that now she was taken by surprise, by this powerful nobleman whom it was dangerous to cross.

"He is your brother," Sir William said dryly. "Of course, I did. *He* surprised me, too. While supporting the alliance, he told me it was your consent I needed or there was no point."

"Did he say that?" Affrica was momentarily distracted.

"More or less. So here I am, lady, hoping for your consent to a marriage between us."

*Oh, the devil and damnation...!*

"I believe we could deal well together. You would make me an admirable helpmeet and be an excellent mother to my existing children as well to any granted to you and me. And in return, you would enjoy an unassailable position in Scotland."

He swallowed, and for the first time, she recognized that this was not easy for him. Yet how could she have stopped him?

"I can offer you also my deepest respect and affection."

She wished very badly that she had at least stopped him before that part. More stunning than all, her grandfather the seer had been wrong.

But then, her grandfather the seer had also believed in action. Nothing was written in stone. Her fate was in her own hands.

※

"You turned him down!" Unannounced, Kenneth barged into her bedchamber, where her brothers were already berating her. "Are you insane?"

"No," Affrica said patiently. She sat on a wooden chair with the three men looming over her, her head throbbing and her spirit wilting. "Such a marriage is not right for us."

"For whom?" Kenneth raged. "Whom do you expect to catch better than the Justiciar of Scotland? Do you realize the power he holds?"

"Then why give him more?" Affrica said tiredly. "I understand you want his favor, but have you really considered? If the king takes you in dislike again, he might well give the earldom to my husband, using me to claim legitimacy."

"Then it is up to you to see he does not! We need you, Affrica, and you have let us down. Come with me now and tell him you have changed your mind."

"I haven't," Affrica said.

"Now, Affrica!"

She had seen his anger before but never directed at her. She blinked at his hand, held peremptorily out to her, and lifted her gaze to his. She was shaking. "No."

Kenneth seized her by the wrist and hauled her to her feet. And suddenly, Nechtan's hand clamped over Kenneth's.

"She said no, Kenneth," Colin snapped.

Kenneth released her, throwing Nechtan off. "Oh, for God's sake, I wasn't hurting her! You are as furious as I am over this idiotic start. You know she must take Comyn!"

Nechtan drew in his breath. "I would be happier if she would. But my father and my grandfather both made us promise that Affrica would be allowed to choose. I will keep that promise, and so will Colin. We can't make her marry him."

Kenneth smiled unpleasantly. "But we can persuade her? I have the whole journey to Perth and several weeks after to persuade her to change her mind."

Affrica's heart sank still further. But she held fast to her mind's image of Ferchar and to her memory of those few passionate minutes in his arms. And knew she would never change her mind.

⸻

THE JOURNEY SOUTH was not pleasant. She did not even have the company of Marjorie to support her, for Marjorie had gone straight to Buchan, where her father the earl was reputedly dying. Kenneth used every means within his power, using every possible moment to nag, reason, threaten, and plead, so that the queen's court, when they eventually reached Perth, felt like a sanctuary.

The following day, she heard that Sir William had departed immediately for his lands in Kilbride in the southwest. And the day after that, the king left for Edinburgh, taking Kenneth with him, and Affrica breathed a massive sigh of relief.

⸻

THE HILLS WERE turning rust-red and golden as Ferchar left Ross once more and found the king's court at Stirling. Inevitably, he was made to kick his heels for some time before an audience with His Grace. Ferchar tried not to mind too much. He liked Stirling, surrounded by its gentle, rolling hills and gracious rivers, so he rode out each day, waiting for his appointment and wondering if he had time to ride to Dunfermline, where the queen's court and Affrica now lay.

After the third ride around the hillfoots, he was returning to his lodgings when he ran into the Earl of Ross. After their last meeting, he wasn't sure whether Kenneth would ignore him or draw steel. In the event, he did neither, merely halted in surprise.

"Good God, what are you doing here?"

"Waiting to see the king."

"Important matters in the lordship of Carron?" Kenneth mocked.

"Or the girth of Tain, perhaps."

"Perhaps," Ferchar said agreeably. "How is His Grace?"

"Grumpy. They're all quarrelling over who will control young Alexander when William turns up his toes."

"Who is your money on?"

Kenneth grimaced. "Not on me at any rate. There's nothing for me here. I've asked for the king's permission to winter in Ross."

"Will the Lady Affrica go with you?" he asked casually.

"God knows," Kenneth growled. "But I hope not. I can't bear the sight of her right now."

"I heard she had refused William Comyn."

"And her henpecked brothers let her," Kenneth fumed. "Despite their much-vaunted loyalty to me. And now she's lost the chance because Comyn's married Marjorie of Buchan."

And Kenneth had wanted Marjorie. It all suited Ferchar very well, and he had run out of sympathy for Kenneth MacHeth. Still, he gave him a commiserating clap on the shoulder, just as he spotted his servant running down the road toward him.

"You've got half an hour to get to the castle, lord!" the man puffed.

Ferchar swore, and Kenneth laughed as he walked away, leaving Ferchar to rush home, change and hasten up to the castle.

"Well, Ferchar?" the king said jovially. He had dismissed his scribe and his courtiers, as he had done the last time they spoke. He looked better than in the spring, better than Kenneth had led him to believe. "How are things in Ross?"

"Quiet," Ferchar said. "The crops were better than we feared, and everyone should eat. Which keeps matters calm. In Wester Ross, too, I believe."

"Then you have not come to warn me about unrest and disaffection?"

"No. I still think it will take more than a MacWilliam banner to get anyone to rise in Wester Ross again, either among the greater or lesser men."

"What about a MacHeth banner? No, don't answer that. I know your views and everyone else's. And yet I would be sure."

"Then show the Earl of Ross some favor."

"I would have given him Lady Marjorie of Buchan—if Lady Affrica had not turned down my Justiciar. Now William Comyn will be Earl of Buchan in his place."

"There are good lordships in the south. They don't have to come with heiresses."

The king regarded him sardonically. "And what of you, Ferchar? You still want no reward? Being Lord of Carron, and coarb of Tain is still enough for you?"

"Whether we call it reward or not, I still ask for the same thing. Lady Affrica."

"She has her brother's leave to choose. And she exercises it. Do you imagine she will choose the son of the priest over the Justiciar of Scotland?"

"I can only ask," Ferchar said evenly.

"You mean you haven't already?"

"Her family is likely to oppose it if I don't have Your Grace's support."

"Good luck to them," the king muttered. "I have it on good authority that Kenneth pestered her the whole journey south to marry Comyn and she did not budge. What will you do if she turns you down? Accept it? Or abduct her and make enemies of all her kin?"

"I don't know," Ferchar said, after a pause. "I can only give you my word—again—that if she agrees, I will be able to hold Ross for you against any and all eventualities."

"Her name is a powerful one in Ross," the king said slowly, "but she shares it with two male cousins and two brothers, to say nothing of the older sisters married elsewhere."

"She has something the others lack," Ferchar said, meeting the king's scowl. "The love of the people, high and low. She's the only one who has paid them attention throughout and asked for nothing in return. From Tain to Dingwall, Tirebeck to the Gairloch, everyone has cause to know Lady Affrica. As her husband, I would command that loyalty, and a force to protect her and the interests of Scotland if necessary."

The king stared at him for a long time. "How old are you, Ferchar Maccintsacairt?"

"Twenty-two."

"Whelp. God help us when you grow to maturity. Very well, ask the girl, but bear in mind the queen bears her a kindness and so do I. There will be no abductions."

# Chapter Twenty-Two

*Dunfermline, autumn 1212*

"I SWEAR TO you," Sir Simon de Beaumont drawled in his half-laughing, half-bored manner, "by a process of elimination, it has to be in this room."

"Because no one has ever used it?" Affrica said wryly.

"Well, if you're not brave enough to come in with me, I shall not share my win with you."

Affrica was not foolish enough go into a deserted room with him, even in an innocuous treasure hunt that was the evening's entertainment. The other ladies of the court envied her her partner in the game and would, no doubt, have gone willingly to their doom.

"I shall guard your back," she assured him, "and give warning if anyone else appears struck with the same brilliant idea."

"You mock me," Sir Simon complained and threw open the small chamber door with a flourish and a dashing smile that affected her not one jot.

"I am now guarding your back," she assured him.

After the queen had welcomed her return to court with open arms, Affrica had fallen quickly back into the familiar routines. She had renewed old friendships and made new ones, met interesting people, heard beautiful new music, and danced. As she always did, she made the best of her situation but as the weeks passed and she heard nothing from Ferchar, the brightness of her spring hopes had faded. Exactly what she had expected, she didn't know, but not this long silence, not this neglect that wilted her spirit.

Pride and self-preservation kept her smiling and dancing and playing silly treasure-hunting games. She tried to salve her pride on the admiration of some of the court gentlemen and visitors, some of whom flirted with her or watched her too closely. Some flirtation verged on courtship, and she had begun to relearn how to discourage with a light touch. Even so, she seemed to have acquired two suitors, even before the English envoy, Sir Simon de Beaumont, had appeared to discuss the future of the Scottish princesses in England.

Sir Simon was different. Young, confident, and handsome, he was related to the queen and much sought-after. To Affrica, he smiled too much, and yet there seemed no disingenuousness about those smiles for her stomach never knotted up in his company. He was genuinely amused by the Scottish queen's court and Her Grace's constant quarrels with her husband. He blatantly admired the queen's younger ladies and was a favored guest at the queen's dinners where he was witty and gracious and yet gave the impression of being immeasurably above even the highest ranked Scots. In general, he favored the company of the queen and other passing foreigners and as a result became an object of fascination to the women of the court. When he traveled to the king, who rarely resided in the same town as the queen, he was missed, and his return eagerly awaited.

Except by Affrica, who cared only for the return of one man. Perhaps her indifference was why Sir Simon always noticed her, and had, this evening, chosen her to be his partner in the treasure hunt.

He stepped into the dark room. "Hmm. Be so good as to pass me the lamp."

Obligingly, she picked up the lamp from the shelf in the passage and handed it to him. He took it with one hand, and with the other, gripped her elbow and spun her into the room as though they were dancing. In an instant, he had kicked the door shut with his heel.

"Now where," he said softly, "should I begin my search?"

"I could offer a suggestion, but you'd find it most uncomfortable." She reached for the door latch and had pulled the door open a crack before his weight thumped it shut again.

"Come now, we are alone at last, little bird, and no one knows but you and I. Let me show you a little courtly love." He reached for her, and she ducked nimbly out of his way.

"No," she said baldly, and waited for him to move away from the door. "Play your silly games with someone who is willing. I am not."

"But you present so delightful a challenge." He took a step forward. She took two back, and he followed.

"The queen does not take lightly any insult offered her ladies," she warned. *One step more...*

He laughed. "Insult? Can you truly be so innocent? Neither of us will tell the queen *my cousin*. Now come here."

She took another step back, feinted to the left, and when he moved with her, bolted to the right and lunged for the door. She almost made it, but his arm shot out, catching her around the middle. He hauled her back and spun her hard against his body.

"My playfulness is at an end," he snapped. "Now take your pleasure like a lady."

Affrica's flesh crawled, the complete opposite to her reaction to the only other time she had been this close to a man. Of course, there had been Liam O'Neill, too, whose intentions had hardly been amorous... *Liam.*

While Sir Simon's left hand closed painfully about her nape, his right began tugging at her skirts. Fear as well as anger broke through her paralysis. He laughed at her struggles, though as she wrenched the dagger free of its scabbard at his belt, his smile froze.

"Get your hands off me," she said clearly.

"God, you're arousing." He seized her wrist, squeezed it so hard she gasped with agony and the dagger fell to the floor. "*Now*, little bird..."

Without warning, he wrenched away from her and flew across the floor, and she found herself staring, at last, into the face of Ferchar Maccintsacairt. It was like one of those rare, waking dreams that overlayed reality.

Then, as one, they both looked at Sir Simon, who had landed with some force against the wall next to the open door. He clutched his head.

"Now, *little bird*," Ferchar said, drawing his sword and advancing on the man with clearly murderous intent. "Fly or die."

Simon scrambled to his feet, trying to draw his own sword, but Ferchar's was already at his throat, forcing him to stillness.

"Do you want to use that pretty dagger first?" he flung over his shoulder at Affrica.

"You can't hurt me," Simon said furiously between his teeth. "I am an envoy of the King of England and cousin to the Queen of Scots!"

"I don't care if you're the Archangel Gabriel."

Affrica, who had gathered her wits enough to prevent disaster, hurried to Ferchar's side and was appalled by the violence spitting from his eyes. She wasn't foolish enough to clutch his sword arm, but she grabbed the other, saying urgently, "He misunderstood, Ferchar. I don't think he's very bright. I'm sure Her Grace will ask for someone with more sense to replace him, but you probably shouldn't kill him. Here."

Simon's eyes widened. "Barbarian—"

Ferchar tutted. "You're right. Not very bright." He let the sword bite, just a little, before he lowered it, wrenched Simon around by the shoulder, and kicked him in the backside.

Affrica heard him hit the opposite wall of the passage as Ferchar shut the door and swung on her with eyes hard as agates.

"What the *devil* were you doing alone behind closed doors with such as him?"

"I expect I got bored waiting for you."

That stopped him in his tracks. Wariness entered his eyes, along with the hint of a smile that looked both warm and predatory. "Did you?"

"Goodness, no. As you see, there's no shortage of entertainment at the queen's court. Have you seen her yet, or do you want me to announce you?"

"I didn't come for her. I came for you."

Her erratically beating heart gave a prodigious thump. At the same time, her knees threatened to give out, so she sat down on the dusty wooden settle. "Why? Is everything well?"

"I hope so." He ventured closer but did not sit. "I'm sorry to have taken so long, but the king would not agree when I first asked and then there was…I wanted to have something…" He broke off, dragging a hand through his hair.

This was a Ferchar she had never seen before—unsure, all but tongue-tied. She patted the seat beside her, and he threw himself onto it, swiveling to meet at her gaze.

"You turned down Sir William Comyn," he said abruptly.

"I did."

"May I know why?"

This new formality hurt her. She had to will her arm to be still and not try to comfort the twisting pain in her stomach. She said, "Because I did not wish to marry Sir William Comyn. He is much better suited to Marjorie."

If he even heard that, he treated it with the contempt it deserved, saying immediately, "I have the king's consent to marry you. He would not give it when I first asked because he wanted Comyn to have you. I have just asked him again."

This was so far from any reunion, any proposal that she had imagined that she didn't know whether to weep or hit him. Instead, she said desperately, "Why?"

"I told you. He wouldn't agree in the spring."

"No, why did you ask him at all?"

A frown flickered across his brow. "Because of what happened between us at Brecka. Am I wrong?"

"No, but it seems I was."

Silence. His eyes went opaque. "Then you will not consider the benefits of an alliance between us?"

She wanted to laugh except the pain deprived her of breath. She didn't even know if it was his or hers. She gazed at her fidgeting hands, willing them to stillness in her lap.

"Christ, I'm making a mess of this," he muttered. "After months of silence I subject you to *the benefits of an alliance*. Affrica…" He took one hand from her lap. It jumped in his, and she hoped he couldn't feel the helpless racing of her pulse. "Did you turn down Comyn for me?"

She closed her eyes, letting the pain of her own protective dishonesty seep away. "You know I did," she whispered.

His fingers moved, threading between her. "I hoped you did. I hoped…" A breath of laughter touched her skin. "And I hoped." He raised her hand and kissed the backs of her fingers, then pressed another kiss into her palm. "Will we take on this adventure together, Affrica? Will you marry me?"

*Say you love me. Please, say it so that I know…*

His eyes were warm, compelling, yet with the same softness she had seen there when he kissed her at Brecka. He carried her hand to his cheek and held it there, a tenderness that moved her.

Why should he love her? She had long suspected that men did not love as women did. But he cared and she had been bound to him with invisible ties for so long that she could not send him away now, not from pique.

Her fingertips moved, gliding against his cheek in a caress. "I will. I always would have."

A smile tugged at his lips, relief among the gladness as he bent and at last pressed his mouth to hers. Her every nerve leapt to meet him, but it was a brief salute, containing more promise than passion.

"Then you had better take me to the queen," he said lightly. "And prepare for the deluge of family displeasure."

※

THE QUEEN SEEMED somewhat bemused by Affrica's choice of husband, but she wished them well and insisted they be married in Dunfermline.

Her family, in the person of the Earl of Ross, descended the next morning, all but dragging her from the queen's apartments to unleash the expected displeasure.

"You turn down the Justiciar for the son of the priest?" he railed. "What are you thinking of? Are you *trying* to make us a laughingstock?"

"I don't need to," she said tartly. "If you shout any louder, the king will hear you over in Stirling."

Kenneth glared at her, without pausing his furious pacing. "Good. Because you and I are going home to Ross, and if I have to, I'll burn him out of Carron and Tain!"

"You're being ridiculous," Affrica said calmly. "It is not a great match by the world's standards, but neither am I a great heiress or an earl's daughter."

"He is marrying your name," Kenneth flung at her.

"Of course, he is."

Something in her tone must have struck him, for he stopped pacing to stare at her. "Has he dared to *touch* you, Affrica? Because if that's the reason…"

"You insult both of us."

Kenneth kicked the nearest chair viciously, then threw himself into it, eyeing her resentfully. "You always liked him, didn't you? Even as children you defended him, fetched my father and the damned bishop just when he was getting his just desserts."

"Your memory is faulty. As I recall there were four supposed noblemen beating a younger boy, the son of their host, because he bested your swords with apples."

Kenneth had already moved on. "The man threatened me in your hearing. In my own home."

"Better him than the king," Affrica pointed out. "Look, you wanted me to marry a man unswervingly loyal to the King of Scots. Ferchar might not hold great office—yet—but the king trusts him. That can only be good for you."

"And do you remember your answer to me?" Kenneth retorted. "That Comyn, married to you, could challenge me for the earldom. Is that not equally true of Ferchar Maccintsacairt?"

She shrugged. "Why would Ferchar do such a thing?"

Kenneth knew the answer. Ferchar had warned him clearly enough. His angry color deepened. "Don't be naïve, cousin. He's using you to build an army, to give him legitimacy and power. He was quite clear on that score when he asked the king for his support."

Stricken at last, Affrica turned away from him. Something had been wrong between herself and Ferchar last night. Some truth he was not telling. They were friends, but... even Ferchar's father had told her that truth. *"Ferchar always wanted more. He always will."*

⊱⊰

THE MARRIAGE WAS set for the following week in the royal chapel, before both the queen and the king. In the circumstances, Kenneth had to seethe in silence and smile in public while he gave her hand in marriage to the man he despised as the mere son of a priest.

In a sudden fit of nerves, Affrica had suggested waiting for her brothers to join them, or to be married in Ross instead, but she was royally overruled. The marriage, it seemed, had taken on a life of its own, out of her control or Ferchar's. Even the wedding feast was being provided by the queen.

In the week before the wedding, she barely saw Ferchar. Which only served to remind her how little time they had ever spent together. A few encounters as children, an afternoon in Paris, and a handful of meetings as adults that were more enigmatic than comforting. And yet from this she had imagined she was somehow bound to him, that she loved him and that she could make him happy.

Kenneth's revelation about what Ferchar had said to the king—how did Kenneth know this, in any case?—should not have surprised her. It made no real difference. She would still marry him. It was just that she had imagined—hoped—that his unexpected embrace at Brecka betokened more than blind ambition. She hung on to that hope still, while the wedding preparations had gone on around her, and she went through the motions of serving the queen in something of a daze. After all, he had never mentioned marriage until after Brecka, never touched her until that fraught, emotionally charged night when he had been so angry. Angry with Kenneth, with the MacHeths, with a world that could give such people power over the well-being of so many others, could support them against all reason and in the face of all crimes, simply because of their blood.

*I am a MacHeth.* She had always known she would be a tool of politics between men. All noblewomen were. She had railed a little against such fate, but there had never been any real choice. Now, miraculously, she was being given to the man she would have chosen above all others. And she was afraid.

She reminded herself that Joan had made a good marriage that made her happy. It was not a *great* marriage by the world's standards, either, but in those times of stability, Angus's daughters had not been pawns of huge importance. And so, her sisters had had some say in their disposal, while Affrica had run wild with the boys when they'd let her, and with Wolf when they would not, which was most of the time. And now the King and Queen of Scots were giving her in marriage to the ambitious son of the priest.

In the teeth of the earl her cousin's objections. God knew what her brothers thought.

By the morning of the wedding, her nerves were in tatters. She had not been sleeping well and was afraid to look at her reflection. She let the queen's ladies and maids do what they willed with her. At least among them was Marjorie, now Lady of Buchan upon her father's death, who had returned to court just in time for the wedding.

Affrica let all their chatter and their teasing and their admiration for her heroic bridegroom wash over her while she smiled as she had learned to do at court. She came to herself only in the chapel when her hand was laid in Ferchar's.

In shock, she watched his large, strong fingers curl over hers, felt the physical thrill of his touch while the Bishop of St. Andrews himself intoned the words of the marriage. She turned her head slowly, gazing up at her husband's face. It was a familiar countenance that she had seen grow and change from childhood, big-boned and lean, confident and strong. Her friend. And yet she was not comforted, even when his gaze shifted and found hers.

Instead, the world tilted in that odd way it occasionally did and Ferchar's visage altered. His mouth opened in a mighty shout. He was covered in blood that she could smell, surrounded by terrifying noise, screaming... A bare instant later, he had aged twenty, thirty years, grey and lined and smiling. She thought she heard children's voices, and dogs... And then he was young again, his shoulders naked above her and his face rapt as she had never seen it.

The image, *all* the rapid images, vanished in a jolt, taking with them the sounds and scents that had nothing to do with the queen's chapel. There was only Ferchar now, a frown tugging his brow, and she realized she was gripping his hand so hard her knuckles had whitened. She forced them to relax, cast him the flicker of a smile in apology. The quirk of his own lips in response and relief, warmed her once more to hope.

But Bishop William was pronouncing them man and wife, and there was no time to think of what she had dreamed, only that she wished her grandfather were here. The bishop embraced Ferchar and stood back, and Ferchar bent his head to press a warm kiss on Affrica's cold lips.

At least the shock of it enlivened her. She could accept the royal congratulations with genuine smiles and face the ordeal of the wedding feast with new courage. And in fact, it was not awkward at all. A cup of wine calmed her jumping nerves. The chatter of familiar friends, even Kenneth on his best behavior, helped loosen her tongue and her wit.

Through it all, she was aware of Ferchar, large and solid at her side, an immovable presence at once welcome and disturbing, an old friend and a stranger into whose power she had just delivered herself.

Mercifully, the royal couple left early, if separately, and the guests could devote themselves to the serious business of drinking and entertainment. With a murmured apology, Ferchar stood and went off somewhere, leaving her in the throes of mingled relief and panic.

For no reason, she thought suddenly of Sir Simon, the English envoy, cousin to the queen, and realized she had not laid eyes on him since the night of the treasure hunt.

"Whatever became of Sir Simon de Beaumont?" she asked aloud.

"He was sent home is disgrace," said the Justiciar, Sir William Comyn, now Earl of Buchan through his wife. Casually, he took the vacant seat next to hers. "Apparently, he was trifling with the queen's ladies. I wish you every happiness in your nuptials, lady."

"And I congratulate you on yours," she said civilly, wondering if

Ferchar had a hand in Sir Simon's departure. "You will know by now that you got the better bargain."

His serious face relaxed. "I am content."

So was Marjorie. Affrica raised her cup in a toast to the laughing lady further down the table, and thought her old friend was rather outshining the bride of the day.

"Ferchar is a good man," the earl said abruptly. "It is a sop to my pride that your heart was engaged elsewhere when you rejected me. Though I wish you had told me."

"How could I?" she managed.

A maidservant bent over her, murmuring, "Lady, your husband requests a private word—in the antechamber."

Blushing, she rose under the earl's knowing smile and hurried anxiously toward the antechamber.

# CHAPTER TWENTY-THREE

*Dunfermline, autumn 1212*

SELF-CONSCIOUS AND WORRIED, she had closed the anteroom door before she saw Ferchar at the other door to the passage, issuing brisk orders.

He turned at the click of the door. "Affrica. Are you ready to leave?"

"Leave?" she repeated. "But I thought…the queen has given us rooms here."

"And we can use them, if you wish," he said at once. "But I have borrowed a merchant's house in the town in case you would like privacy. I thought you might prefer not to have me conducted to your bed by a crowd of drunks determined to watch and comment on the subsequent festivities."

Her jaw dropped. "Dear God, would they do so?" No wonder her sisters had left Tirebeck immediately after the wedding ceremony. She swallowed. "When can we leave, do you think?"

A smile flickered. "Now, if you wish."

"But my things—"

"Are about to head out the palace door, though I can call them back if that's your choice."

"God, no," she said fervently, marching across the room to him.

He grabbed her hand, drawing her behind the door as two courtiers ambled along the passage in drunken conversation. As their voices faded, he peered around the door, then pulled her after him.

Suddenly, it was easy, like a childish game of avoiding the adults to sneak out the house. And then they were running hand in hand through the corridor to a side door and down the path in the drizzling rain to a closed wain. He all but threw her in beside her chests, and she was laughing as he closed the doors and sat on the large trunk opposite hers. The vehicle began to bump painfully toward the palace gates and the town.

"Thank you," she said, breathless but fervent. "I had no idea of the nightmare in store for me. Marjorie might have warned me." Though perhaps Marjorie was not above a little mischief, especially since she probably knew her husband had first courted Affrica. "Won't they wonder where we are? They'll think us awfully rude."

"Do you mind?"

She thought about it until a particularly large bump knocked her against the side of the carriage, which was more a cart with a roof and no pretensions to comfort, let alone luxury.

"No," she said, righting herself before he could reach across to help. A few moments later, the vehicle halted and Ferchar jumped down, turning to catch her around the waist and lift her before she could climb out by herself. There was nothing loverlike about his brief hold, just efficiency. And yet it spread a pleasant, heavy heat through her whole body.

The merchant's house reminded her of the Paris lodgings she and her father had enjoyed, though this was on a smaller scale. It was comfortable, warm, and private, save for a scattering of respectful servants.

"Thank God," she murmured. "I was half expecting a dozen courtiers to pop out from under the stairs."

Ferchar grinned. "Come, I'll show you our private quarters where we can refresh ourselves, and then, perhaps, talk for a little."

She followed him upstairs and into a comfortable room with cushions on the settles. On an oak table stood a jug of wine and a plate of honey cakes. Ferchar opened another door, to show her a large bedchamber with a washing bowl and a large screen. A battered chest stood under the window.

"They'll bring your things up directly," Ferchar said, brushing past her toward the table. Relieved, she followed him, and accepted a cup of wine, just as her trunks were bumped into the room and hauled onward to the bedchamber. Helpfully, the manservant closed the bedchamber door, touched his forehead, and departed.

"Do you want to change your dress?" Ferchar asked.

"Not unless I look hideous."

His lips quirked. "You couldn't if you tried." The half-smile died into rueful curiosity. "Were you trying?"

"No, I just wasn't paying attention."

He took a sip of wine, perhaps to give himself time, then said abruptly, "I could see your doubts in the chapel. I thought you might have changed your mind."

She shook her head, yet the words she needed to explain eluded her. She sat on one of the settles, wondering whether or not she wanted him to join her there. He didn't. He drew the other settle a few feet nearer and sat opposite her. Intimate, yet respectfully distant.

He said, "I have hardly seen you all week. What have you been doing?"

"Whatever the queen told me to. I barely noticed. Oh, I quarreled with Kenneth. Or at least he quarreled with me."

Ferchar's lips twisted. "He came to quarrel with me, too."

"Did you let him?"

"I...deflected him. I think."

She said deliberately, "He believes you married me to obtain an army with which to take Ross from him."

"I know." His expression was rueful, not like a man caught out but one willfully misunderstood, which gave her a little surge of hope. "I pointed out all the ways I could be useful to him, with or without armies." He raised his eyes from his cup to meet her gaze. "He will always consider it an insult that I am a member of his family, but he is resigned to it."

"I'm sorry," she said with difficulty.

"Don't be. I expected it. In fact, so far everything has gone better than I hoped. Except my proposal. I messed that up royally, and I apologize. I had no idea how to make it right."

"Is that why you didn't come near me all week?"

He opened his mouth as though to deny it, then sipped his wine again. "Partly. I had a lot of ruffled feathers to smooth, arrangements to make concerning the girls and property." His lips quirked into the deprecating half smile that was so familiar and dear to her. "But if I'm honest, I…was giving you time to change your mind. I didn't want to make you marry me by browbeating you. Or seducing you, and I have never been confident in my ability to keep my hands off you."

Blood rushed up her body, suffusing her face. "You have a low opinion of my constancy."

He shook his head impatiently. "Never that." He drew in his breath. "I married Deirdre in a fit of lust—and greed for her land. I think I might have been drunk enough to tell you that once. She…*managed* that. Used it. She needed the validation of a husband, a man she could manage, who would protect her without sullying her, and arrange the dull matters of life without subjecting her to its dirty mundanities. For some reason, she saw those qualities in me, so we were both wrong. I could not be managed. I was not *refined*. And she did not want me in her bed."

Affrica had guessed some of this, felt the rest. She said, "Were you hurt?"

He nodded. "I knew by the morning after the wedding, when she all but kicked me out of bed to find her better lodgings that things between us were not...right. That's part of the reason I went with the king to Northumbria. And then I thought she might miss me, and I could make things right when I got back. I couldn't, of course." His eyes refocused on hers. "I'm sorry. I didn't mean to talk about Deirdre on *our* wedding night. I suppose I tell you this so you might understand my...neglect. What must have seemed like neglect. With you..." He trailed off and retreated to his wine cup, leaving Affrica to mull over what he had told her.

"Did you back to the widows and other men's wives?" she asked curiously.

A hiss of laughter broke from him. He shook his head.

"Then you mean to be faithful to me, too?" she said. "Even if I don't please you?"

"Affrica..." For an instant, he looked almost helpless. "Every moment with you pleases me. It was never vows that bound us."

Her heart beat harder, because he acknowledged that bond, *felt* it. A wave of awe swept over her, and some raw, powerful emotion. She wanted to lean across the space between them, which was suddenly much too big, and touch him, embrace him...

The thought brought his earlier words to mind. *"I have never been confident in my ability to keep my hands off you,"* she quoted.

His lips curved into a slow smile that she felt in the pit of her stomach. "Didn't you know? When you and Colin came to Carron? Surely it was obvious at Tain last winter?"

"I misunderstood. I *feel* so much and understand nothing..."

"Such as?"

Her breath caught. "Such as why you are sitting over there if you cannot keep your hands off me."

Something leapt in his eyes, something hot and exciting. "Self-denial has become something of a habit." He set his cup on the floor and rose to take hers, which he set beside the first. Deliberately he held out his hand. "Come with me. Let me show you the gifts we can bring each other."

She didn't hesitate to take his hand, to rise with him. But still he waited, letting her grow used to his closeness, while his thumb softly circled her wrist, spreading shivers of excitement through her veins. He bent and kissed her mouth, a long, achingly tender kiss that surprised and enchanted her all over again.

Then he led her to the bedchamber and stepped closer. He spanned his fingers from her neck to her cheeks and took her mouth once more. From need, she leaned into his body, slid her arms around his waist and gave herself up to the sweetness of his plundering. She barely noticed as her gown and undergowns spilled around her feet. She was too taken with the smooth heat of his skin, which she had found by pushing under his tunic and shirt.

And then she was on the bed, his naked skin gliding against hers in ever more intimate caresses until all she knew was *him* and delight and unendurable arousal which he taught her, gradually yet stunningly, how to assuage. The invasion into her body overwhelmed her, but only for the moment it took him to recover his breathing, and then he showed her everything he had promised, and gave her his ultimate gift before accepting hers.

※※※※※

"THEY'RE NOT COMING back," the Lady of Buchan said in clear amusement as she sat down beside Kenneth. "The antechamber is empty, and so is the bridal bedchamber. Ferchar has spirited her away in secret."

Kenneth, who had drunk too much wine and intended to drink considerably more yet, curled his lips. "Of course, he has. It was always an abduction, but no one recognized it except me."

Marjorie regarded him with her knowing eyes. "Then you did

want her for yourself?"

"Don't be silly. I wanted you."

"You wanted me for Buchan," Marjorie said without rancor. "Affrica is more personal."

"Affrica is my family. And now so is he. You married a foreigner, but at least he is a noble one of high office. Now I'm supposed to acknowledge the priest's son as my equal."

"You are still the earl," Marjorie pointed out.

He shot her a brooding glance. "Am I? The king does not call me so."

"Nor does he deny it. And he certainly calls no one else Earl of Ross. He dangles it before you like a carrot which you have to deserve."

"I *fought* for him in Ross!" He glared at Marjorie, knowing he should be silent and yet unable to stop the resentment fighting its way out.

"So did Ferchar," she murmured, maliciously he thought.

"I led hundreds of men. How many did *he* bring? A couple of peasants! Yet he is given my cousin over all my objections, and I am given what? The sight of a carrot always out of my reach."

She stared at him. "You have *Ross*. You have an ancient name and a loyal family. Those things are not nothing."

"Loyal family? She married him when she might have had Comyn. And I might have had you."

"Actually, my lord," Marjorie said, rising to her feet. "You would never have had me. My advice? Make peace with Ferchar. He is a better ally than most. And I would not care to be his enemy."

She walked away, leaving Kenneth to glare resentfully after her. No sympathy there, then. No sympathy anywhere, but then he had almost forgotten that this was the bastard's wedding. Well, Ferchar would serve *him* in the end. He had offered, and Kenneth would make sure he took it in full.

Ferchar gazed down at Affrica MacHeth, lying smiling and replete in his arms, her raven-black hair tumbling decadently across his naked chest.

Her wonder had enchanted him; her delight fed his own. And here was yet another new sweetness, holding her after pleasure, enjoying her contentment, as he had earlier reveled in her joy.

God, had he reveled. Never had he found such intensity in passion than with this virgin girl who had become his obsession. And who now, his wife and lover, had grown into something altogether more dangerous. His weakness.

Though her eyes were closed, she was not asleep. The smile played about her lips as her fingertips lazily teased the skin of his stomach.

"I like being married to you," she murmured, moving to kiss his skin through her veil of hair.

He cupped her face caressingly. "I like being married to you."

Ferchar had tortured himself only too often by imagining Affrica MacHeth naked in his bed. The reality of her beauty and her desire had almost undone him long before he had even entered her body.

In the church, at the feast, she had been wound so tightly he had thought she would shatter if he touched her. Her skin had seemed too finely drawn across the delicate bones of her face. The smile on her lips had not been honest, for it was not reflected in her eyes. She had not been his warm, laughing Affrica but some distant, icy beauty.

He had brought her here to this house to grow used to him. He had meant to be so patient, to wait to consummate the marriage if that was what she wanted. Meant to court her properly, woo her as she deserved. But somehow, she hadn't given him the chance to make the offer.

At Brecka, her kisses had tasted of untutored passion and an eager delight that had enflamed him. Here, she had added instinctive, profound sensuality and learned from his every caress. More than that, he learned from hers, and from Affrica herself. In her body he had found not only blazing pleasure but peace. In her whole person, he had found…happiness.

She turned her face into him, her arm creeping across his chest to hold him, her mouth muffled against him. "I love you, you know. I always have."

Emotion flooded him so quickly, he was afraid he would weep. As it was, his arm tightened around her convulsively.

"I don't want you to say anything back," she whispered. "I just need you to know. Now, go to sleep."

"Sleep?" He rolled over her, taking his weight on his elbows while he held her face between his hands, forcing her to look at him. "How could I sleep in the face of courage that puts my own to shame? I have been so concerned with hiding the truth from you, from the world. *Of course*, I love you. God, I have no words for this…"

He took her mouth to convey his love, until that was no longer enough for either of them and then he took her body again, like a vow.

※※※

HE WOKE TO broad daylight and a deep, luxurious wellbeing. He didn't want to open his eyes in case she had gone, but after a moment, when he was sure he felt her breathing, he looked.

She sat on the bed, gloriously naked save for the sheet casually draped over her for warmth. And she was watching him.

She smiled as he opened his eyes. "Look what I found," she said, indicating the checked board and carved pieces set up between them. "Would you like to play chess?"

Laughter rumbled up from deep inside him, half-amusement and all happiness.

# Chapter Twenty-Four

*Moray and Ross, spring-summer 1215*

"This time will be different," Prince Liam O'Neill said dreamily, gazing out over the Moray hills from his perch atop the highest hill for miles. "I shall be in command of my own Ulstermen. Donald Ban will bring more mercenaries than before. And you will bring the men of Ross."

Kenneth did not ask how Donald Ban MacWilliam was paying for so many mercenaries. He was fairly sure Scotland would pay in the end, once the crown was back in legitimate hands. Under King Donald, Kenneth would be Earl of Ross *and* Moray, and his brother Ranald would become Lord of the Isles and Argyll. A sweet fantasy, but one that this time he would throw his all behind.

"Won't you?" Liam said, peering at him from beneath his windblown hair.

"Won't I what?" Kenneth asked testily.

"Bring the men of Ross to march on the King of Scots."

"What sort of question is that? I've already agreed I will."

"Then there will be no trouble?" Liam said. "From other noblemen of Ross? To say nothing of your cousin the coarb of Tain."

"My men will see to Ferchar." Leaving his widow free to remarry. Kenneth smiled wolfishly. "He was obliging enough to train them for me. But their first loyalty is to me."

"And your other cousins? Of Tirebeck?"

"Colin may be his," Kenneth admitted, "but Nechtan has always been mine. And he commands the men. Stop worrying. As soon as you land, the men of Ross will march into Moray to join you. We'll smash the king's troops before he can draw breath. Alexander is a child. He's not the man, let alone the soldier, his father was, which leaves the kingdom weak and ripe for the taking."

A rare moment of curiosity assailed him, and he glanced at Liam. "What of you, my friend? What do you hope to gain from the venture?"

"Oh, whatever I can," Liam said vaguely. His eyes refocused on Kenneth. "We will have to wait and see who lives and who dies, won't we? I'll never be a king in Ireland, but by summer's end I hope at least to be an earl in Scotland."

※

DESPITE THE BREEZE, the spring sun was warm on Colin's face as he rode through the gates to Carron Hall, accompanied by Nechtan and his wife, Anna.

Euphemia and Christina erupted from the hall with their usual ebullience, little hoydens at ages eleven and nine. An instant later Affrica walked out into the yard, smiling her sunny smile, her little son holding her hand as he toddled along beside her. Colin felt a rush of affection and pleasure for her sister. If anyone deserved this peace and happiness, it was Affrica, although somehow, he had never imagined her settling into such quiet domestication.

Colin dismounted in time to receive the full force of both little girls' welcome, before Nechtan slid down beside them and was similarly accosted. Even Will, only nineteen months old, tugged free of Affrica's hand to waddle in their direction. Old Wolf roused himself to amble protectively beside the baby.

Colin and Nechtan had come to regard the girls as their own nieces, so they swung them boisterously around, before Nechtan crouched, his arm still around Christina, to greet baby Will.

"Can this big fellow be my nephew?" he marveled.

"Will, son of Ferchar," came the proud answer.

"And who am I?"

Will grinned. "Uncle Nechan," he said and ran back to Affrica, holding onto Wolf's fur. Affrica laughed, taking his little hand once more to walk across the yard to greet her more reserved sister-in-law.

"Anna, welcome!" she said. "Apologies for the chaos! I hope your journey wasn't too awful."

"Remarkably pleasant," Anna replied, allowing Nechtan to lift her from the saddle to the ground, now mercifully free of flying children. "And your chaos is always more delightful than anyone else's *tidy* hospitality."

Affrica laughed, for she and Anna had long since reached an amiable understanding. Much to Nechtan's relief.

"You're looking well!" Colin said, embracing Affrica. He stood back, frowning. "Are you with child again?"

She wrinkled her nose. "Do I have a bump already? The baby shouldn't be born until the autumn."

"Felicitations, sister!" Nechtan said, dropping a careless kiss on her cheek. "Where is the proud father?"

"Out on the land. He'll be back shortly. But I thought Kenneth was coming with you?"

"So did we," Colin said cheerfully. "But I suppose the earl is by nature, a busy man."

Inevitably, the subject came up again over dinner.

Dinner at Carron was a very different affair from the quiet, refined suppers once hosted by the Lady Deirdre. Now, as at Tirebeck, the household ate together as far as possible. The hall was full of soldiers, stewards, servants, and their families. Ferchar and Affrica sat at the high table, with Colin and Anna, Nechtan and Sinead on either side of them. Nor was there a great deal of formality. Conversations were exchanged with those at the lower tables, and yet it was possible to speak privately, too, still within the warm ambience of a contented household.

Ferchar glanced at his wife, brushed her hand with his as though to attract her attention. In fact, Colin had the impression Ferchar always had her attention, whether she was apparently engrossed in anyone else or not. They had been married for about two and a half years, but Colin was still fascinated by the looks and touches of a communication that was beyond him. Their relationship was so much less comprehensible to him than Nechtan's with Anna, and yet on some level it ran deeper, smoother, while subject to unexpected turbulence.

Proving Kenneth wrong—again—Ferchar always showed her public respect.

"Where is Kenneth?" Ferchar asked, as though he had just noticed the earl's absence.

"Moray," Nechtan said reluctantly. "He didn't tell me where or why, just that he would return in a week."

Ferchar looked toward him. "I have spies in Moray."

Nechtan scowled. "Am I supposed to pass that on to him? I'm fairly sure he knows and knows who they are, too."

Which meant, Colin suspected, that he could avoid them more easily. Kenneth had ever been slippery.

"Besides, he's the earl," Nechtan pointed out. "Chances are, he has more spies than you do."

"Why are we talking like this?" Affrica asked. "After the last time, Kenneth would *never* risk another invasion."

"Before he died," Ferchar said conversationally, "King William promised him a certain heiress of Lanark."

"Which King Alexander has conveniently forgotten," Colin said.

"Along with his promise to confirm Kenneth as Earl of Ross. One can understand his frustration."

"He's not a child," Ferchar said mildly.

But in some ways a child was exactly what Kenneth was, despite his pride and his dignity. While Ferchar, despite his mad starts like the New Year sea raids with a largely crippled crew, and last year's hilarious summer hunt that had reduced even Kenneth to tears of laughter, had always been an adult.

※

A WEEK LATER, Ferchar rode into the castle courtyard at Dingwall. Kenneth kept him waiting in the hall for almost half an hour, but then he always did.

He entered the great hall from the chamber beyond, yawning. "Ferchar. You're always so damned early. What can I do for you?"

"I was about to ask you the same question, since I'm bound to the market at Rosemarkie at Affrica's bidding."

"You're a bit off course," Kenneth pointed out.

"Deliberately so. Affrica missed you at Carron last month and asked me to make sure you were well. Commissions at the market are an excuse."

"I recognized them," Kenneth said with the hint of a return smile.

Such hints, like the brief bonding of the crazy summer hunt, kept Ferchar hoping, but he was never foolish enough to let down his guard. To him, Kenneth was a weird mixture of the son you could never reach and the drunken wastrel of a father you desperately wanted to look up to and never could. The strain of it, or perhaps the tragedy, made Ferchar ache.

"Give Affrica and Will my love," Kenneth said, pouring himself a glass of wine from the jug and offering it silently to Ferchar, who shook his head. He had already drunk a mug of ale waiting for his host. "And my apologies for failing you last month."

"Nechtan said you were called to Moray."

"I was," Kenneth said blatantly. "I greeted your man there. He looked well."

"He said the same of yours," Ferchar said, and Kenneth laughed.

"Between us, we will keep my earldom safe," he said, raising his cup in a toast.

"Ross is safer," Ferchar said, "than it has ever been since the latter days of Earl Malcolm MacHeth. I am happy to help you keep it so."

He knew Kenneth understood him, for the corner of one eye betrayed the tiniest twitch. But the earl smiled and drank. "You are such a comfort to me, Ferchar."

"You are such a liar, my lord."

Kenneth laughed. "I hear Affrica is breeding again. You must be very proud."

"Actually, I feel guilty. To be the cause of birth pain is humbling in the extreme."

"Old woman," Kenneth said cheerfully. "Come on, I'll ride with you to the road."

⇶⫸⫷⇷

BLOOD AND SLAUGHTER. Bodies and unattached limbs lay scattered. Men and horses screamed and died and suffered. In the thick of it, the commander of this carnage rode his horse among it, sword swinging, face contorted in battle cry, hacking, thrusting, killing. At his horse's feet lay severed heads. While another sword swung accurately at his exposed neck.

"Affrica."

She woke to Ferchar's concerned embrace, his hand stroking her hair, his voice soft.

"You're dreaming. Wake up."

For the first time ever, the dream still vivid, she pushed him away in horror. And then, with a soundless sob, seized him convulsively, pressing her wet cheek to his. "I'm sorry. A horrible dream, and you…you were there."

"What was I doing?"

Her fingers dug into his naked shoulders, and she had to force them to relax just a little. "Fighting."

"It wouldn't be the first time," he pointed out.

Her heartbeat had calmed, along with the sharpness of fear. But the ominous foreboding remained. She swallowed. "I think…I think it was more vision than dream."

His hand stroking her hair stilled. "Should I be worried?"

She nodded. "We should all be worried." She drew back a little. Dawn had broken and light was seeping through the shutters, though rain pattered relentlessly against them. She let her fingertips wander over his familiar, beloved face as though relearning all its blades and hollows, the warm skin and rough morning stubble. "It is not written in stone. My grandfather told me that."

Her grandfather who had tried to change the future by killing Donald Ban MacWilliam. And failed.

"Then why worry?"

"Are you a *ruthless* soldier, Ferchar?" Men fought and boasted and told stories that could be funny or heroic. Ferchar told only the funny ones. And she had never asked him what he had done in the late MacWilliam war. But men followed him. They didn't follow milksops or refined gentlemen who couldn't wield their swords to good effect. Her soldiering uncle and great-uncle had been his friends when he was little more than a boy.

"When I have to be," Ferchar said steadily. "What did you see?"

"Battle," she whispered.

He laid his forehead against hers. "Battles are ugly. And yet the sheer violence brings a terrible euphoria. It's not the side of me I would bring to you."

He was naked, her husband. So, she kissed his broad, scarred shoulder. "What side would you bring me?"

His hands swept up beneath her shift, over her hips and waist and breasts, tossing the garment over her head. She pushed him back against the pillows and kissed him, a teasing, provocative kiss that quickly became something deeper and more urgent. She needed his love to blot out those other images and fears. And then she just needed his love.

<hr />

She was singing as she finally rose that morning. But then she sang most mornings, her body and soul happy in her husband's love. She no longer had to make happiness for herself within a world of boredom or danger or intrigue. She lived her life with laughter and fun, the joy of her child, the companionship of Ferchar, which was alternately exciting, sweet, hilarious, and provoking. To say nothing of the private moments when she could lose herself in physical pleasures that were constantly new.

Life was good for Affrica, idyllic even. She did not miss the court although she would enjoy going to Perth next month with Ferchar, the first time she would meet Prince Alexander since he became King of Scots. And probably the last time she would venture very far before the baby was born.

She already went on fewer journeys with her husband. In the last two years they had traveled a good deal within Ross, for Ferchar had much to discuss with the local nobility and Affrica's presence as his wife gave him an importance, a gravity he hadn't had before. There were several new lords, replacing those who had followed Donald MacWilliam, to become acquainted with. And old lords to aid and placate. There was much to do to bring Ross back from the wasteland of 1211.

From these journeys had grown a network of trained fighting men, ready at a moment's notice to follow where their captains led. They trained separately and together, with the earl's blessing and occasional participation. But it was Ferchar who spoke to them and to their lords, and who, with Affrica, kept abreast of their opinions and anxieties, and helped find solutions to their problems. To her, it was natural. She had always done so, from duty and from choice and she was glad to have Ferchar's partnership.

Ferchar's motives were many. He was learning lordship and command and he wanted prosperity and peace for the people. He wanted and received a modest increase in his guard for the girth of Tain and, from the earl, for his household. Kenneth's men were sent, she was sure, as spies and, probably, insurance against Ferchar's "betrayal." But however they started, she sensed their devotion now, not just to Affrica, but to Ferchar.

Without huge lands or an ancient name, Ferchar had become an important man in Ross. One who might not have accrued the vast armies Kenneth had feared, but who knew how to bring them together.

Affrica was aware of all of this. She knew that since the old king's death last year, her husband had been wary and waiting. Perhaps that had been the cause of her dream last night. And yet she was still taken by surprise when, grim faced, Hairy Harry had ridden into the yard, yelling for Ferchar.

Harry no longer stole. He had stopped at Tain and never touched anything at Tirebeck. Now he followed Ferchar and did his bidding elsewhere, often acting as a collector of messages and information.

Affrica steadied herself against the door jamb, for she knew at once this was the worst sort of information, and it was. Ferchar came and stood behind her, his hand heavy on her shoulder, both a comfort and a warning.

"MacWilliams," Harry said tersely. "Boatloads of them, more than before. Donald Ban and some Irish princeling. They landed in the south of Wester Ross and are headed for Moray."

Affrica closed her eyes. It was happening again, despite her grandfather's best efforts.

But Ferchar was calm. He shouted for messengers, giving each curt, simple messages and sent them out into Ross. And when he finally turned to her, she saw the blaze of determination in his eyes, so intense it was almost joy. He had been waiting for this, planning for it, and now he would see it through.

"It won't be like last time," he said an hour later in their bedchamber. He was dressed in mail, weapons at his belt, helmet in his hand, saying farewell. "I will finish it, before the king even hears of it."

"You sent to my brothers," she managed. She was shaking. "But not to Kenneth."

"Oh, I think Kenneth knows. In any case, I'm riding to Dingwall immediately."

"And if he won't lead you against the MacWilliams?"

Ferchar's eyes didn't waver. "I warned him."

Affrica, overcome by a sense of the world falling apart before her helpless eyes, reached up and grasped his shoulders. "Ferchar…"

"I know."

"Come back. Please, come back."

"You know I will." He took her in his arms and kissed her mouth with the same focus he did everything. She couldn't bear for it to be the last time, hardly noticed the discomfort of his weapons and armor as she pressed desperately against him. And then he released her and was gone, calling to his men as he strode through the hall.

All over Ross, all over Scotland, probably, the same scene was being enacted, as it had been throughout the ages. Women saying goodbye to their men, who rushed off to kill and die. The weight of her mother, of her grandmother Christian, and her great-grandmother Halla seemed to press on her shoulders as she watched her husband ride away. Curiously, it was some comfort.

THE LANDING OF the MacWilliam army already felt like victory to Kenneth. He seemed to come alive with a vigor he hadn't known in years, not since before the last rising and the clipping of his wings by the late, suspicious King of Scots. The new king, his ears full of whispers was suspicious, too—and rightly so, as it happened, for Kenneth had every intention of deposing him in favor of Donald MacWilliam, who had the better claim and the better grasp of the old ways, to say nothing of the better army.

Or so it seemed to Kenneth as he sent far and wide for the men of Ross, whom Ferchar Maccintsacairt had conveniently trained for him, and rode out of Dingwall with his own guard to join the MacWilliam host.

As he left the castle, he saw the glint of armor to the north—men marching to his banner. Oh yes, this was how it was meant to be. Grinning, he gave the signal to move forward. The men of Ross would flood after him in time to impress his allies, Donald and Liam.

A little way on, he glanced back, and could no longer see the distant column of men.

"Where are they?" he demanded.

"They stopped, my lord," his captain said uneasily. "At Dingwall."

Kenneth halted. With a sudden twinge of unease, he reined his horse around and galloped back down the column of his men until he could peer over toward the castle. There were men on the battlements, far more than the handful he had left behind.

"Who?" he uttered. "Who is in my castle?"

"It's a MacHeth banner, my lord," he was told, and then one of the rear scouts ran up, panting.

"It's just Lord Ferchar of Carron," he panted. "With Nechtan and Colin of Tirebeck."

*Just.* Ferchar wasn't holding it to guard Kenneth's back. He was too damned quick. And Kenneth's orders had been to follow him. Ferchar, damn him, had taken it for the King of Scots. Kenneth's hope lay in Nechtan who would, surely, do the right thing. Take the castle from his sister's husband and rush the men to Kenneth in Moray.

In the meantime, they could not risk disaster.

"Send into Moray," he snarled. "Donald Ban must march back to Ross until this is resolved."

---

"I DON'T EXPECT you fight him," Ferchar said patiently to Nechtan and Colin, who were pacing the hall at Dingwall like caged animals. "You were brought up almost as his brothers and your allegiance to the earl is unquestioned. But the earl's allegiance is not to Ross or to Scotland. He is allied with invaders."

"You don't know that," Nechtan snapped. "He could be marching to fight them and need our support."

"He would certainly need our support," Ferchar retorted. "And would have waited for it. Who would oppose an invading army with little more than his house guards?"

Nechtan stormed to the other end of the hall, then swung around to face him. "Ferchar, I can't! He is the earl, the Lord of Ross, and my friend."

"And that justifies another war, another rising for nothing, just when we are recovering form the last MacWilliam depredations? There comes a time to say, *No. Enough.* This is that time. I don't ask you to follow me. I ask you to hold the castle, while I pursue him. I will give him every chance to change sides, to surrender his arms. Fighting him will be my last resort."

"It will be the only resort." White-faced, Colin stood beside him, staring at him. "He won't give up, will he?"

"Probably not."

Colin swallowed. "I'll come with you. Nechtan—"

Nechtan swung around and thumped the stone wall with his fists.

"Hold the castle," Ferchar said. "Will you do that much?" It had no strategic importance to Ferchar's plan, except to save Nechtan's agony of divided loyalties. But for himself, for his friendship with his brothers-in-law, for Affrica, he found he needed Nechtan's compliance, that one small sign of support. Like a justification his heart needed while his head was already miles in advance. His very bones seemed to ache with the strain.

Nechtan didn't look around, but he nodded once.

Before he sagged with relief, Ferchar swung away to the door. "Thank you."

"Ferchar?" Nechtan's voice stayed him only a pace away. "Don't kill him."

Ferchar swallowed. "If there's a way not to, I'll find it."

⸻

KENNETH FUMED, INVENTING in his mind increasingly horrific ways for his cousins to slaughter Ferchar Maccintsacairt. On the other hand, he would really prefer to kill the bastard himself.

And suddenly, he had the chance. Men, lots of men appeared on the hill to their right. And their banner was not MacHeth or MacWilliam. It bore the lion of Scotland. And yet these men had clearly come from the north. There had been no time for the royal army to march...

Thoughts raced through his head as he halted and barked out orders to wheel around and form up to face the enemy. And as he rode up and down the lines of his men, he saw others behind—the men who had stopped at Dingwall. They spread out across the ground, and he saw the banner of Scotland again. And MacHeth.

*Ferchar.*

Enraged, Kenneth almost charged straight at them, and in fact did urge his horse several paces nearer before he reined in. A horseman detached himself from the lines and rode slowly toward him.

*Ferchar.*

And he kept coming. "My lord! Fall back to Dingwall," he called. "Leave the MacWilliams to us. We've brought the army to fight them for you."

Dear God, was he really trying to give Kenneth a way out? To protect him? Why would he do such a thing? Because of Affrica? Or because Nechtan and Colin would kill him if he didn't? Kenneth grinned. *Or because of the men of Ross would not fight against Kenneth MacHeth, their earl?*

He lifted up his voice and bellowed, loud enough that he hoped everyone would hear. "Men of Ross! Join me in this last great bid for the ways of our fathers, for Ross itself. Join me and our allies! Let us march across the realm and put the true king on the throne of Scotland! King Donald mac Donald!"

His voice echoed around the hills, swept across the plain—and was greeted by silence. Bewildered, Kenneth glanced back at the still figure of Ferchar. He looked somehow...tragic. And alone, as Kenneth was.

Then, slowly, Ferchar raised his hand. No one shot him. No one knocked him off his horse. For Ferchar, it seemed, was not alone after all.

"My lord!" yelled Kenneth's captain in panic. Ferchar's arm fell, and a massive shout shattered Kenneth's ears. Ferchar and his men were running toward him while the men on the hill charged downward.

Kenneth and his men were trapped. He could order them to throw down their arms. Or he could fight and pray that the MacWilliam army was closer than he had thought.

He had always been a man of risks.

He drew his sword. "MacHeth!" he shouted, and let the carnage begin.

# Chapter Twenty-Five

*Ross, summer 1215*

F ERCHAR HAD ALWAYS known it would come to this, even while he had warned Kenneth three years ago, even while he had tried everything he knew to win the earl's trust, to make him see things through Ferchar's eyes, how he could be a great lord and win fame without this.

As his forces closed in on Kenneth's from two sides, part of him still hoped that Kenneth would lay down his arms, or at least return to Dingwall. It might have saved his life, though nothing would save his earldom now. Even when Ferchar gave the order to attack, some hope existed that Kenneth might live, or at the very least that someone might kill him before Ferchar had to.

For it would not be a difficult battle to win. Men of Ross did not want to fight other men of Ross, their families, friends, old comrades. Kenneth was outnumbered, attacked on two sides, and Ferchar's troops were better trained.

And Kenneth, inevitably, came straight at him, screaming like a madman, sword swinging wildly if savagely. Ferchar knocked him off his horse with one blow of his shield, then leapt from the saddle to face him.

Kenneth bounced back to his feet, a stream of invective spilling from his mouth. Ferchar made out the words *traitor* and *priest* and let it all wash over him. He had to concentrate on staying alive, for Kenneth was no novice fighter. He had always been quick and accurate and vicious, and while the battle raged around them, he did his very best to kill Ferchar. Steel clashed and slashed. None of the men battling around them would intervene.

They exchanged heavy blows with shields and feet as well with swords. Each of them wanted it over quickly, and Ferchar knew he could expect no mercy.

And he gave none. When Kenneth pushed him back and he stumbled, he was ready, knocking aside Kenneth's sword, even as he fell backward, and then, before Kenneth could thrust again, Ferchar did, pushing his sword deep into Kenneth's neck.

Kenneth's sword fell as both hands clutched his throat. Somehow, Ferchar caught him as he fell and wanted to scream with the rage and tragedy of the whole thing. And still, something in him wanted to apologize.

"It couldn't go on, Kenneth," he said, his voice a husky pant. "It couldn't. It wasn't *right*."

Some glimmer of intelligence might have greeted this, some faint twitch, though whether of acknowledgment or anger or simple pain, Ferchar would never know, for the earl's eyes glazed and his hands stilled.

Ferchar drew in his breath on a harsh sob. "Kenneth mac Gilchrist is dead!"

His shout echoed around the battlefield in yells and whispers, whether in fear or triumph. "The earl is dead." "The Lord of Ross is dead." "Kenneth is dead." Whatever they called him, he was gone, and with him, their reason to fight.

Ferchar might have imagined the relief with which weapons were thrown down and withdrawn. But he didn't think so.

Ferchar rose to his feet, for there was more, much more to do. He turned his face south, to march on Donald Ban MacWilliam and Liam O'Neill.

>>><<<

AFFRICA SHOULD HAVE been used to the waiting. She had done enough of it in the last war. But as the women before her knew, one didn't ever grow accustomed to such fear. It stayed with her, at the front of her mind, twisting inside her body while she went about her daily tasks and played with the children. They ate meals in the hall that was too quiet with nearly all the men gone.

She lived for news. For a time, she knew only that as Kenneth had marched out of Dingwall, Ferchar had walked into the castle, and that Nechtan remained there while Colin went with Ferchar.

Later the same day, came another, briefer message from Nechtan. "Kenneth is dead."

She took time to weep for that, even though she had known it was inevitable. Kenneth had drawn his sword once too often, and this time Ferchar had struck back with something more lethal than apples. God knew what would come now. Ranald was earl by right, but who knew what right would count now. Would the king allow any MacHeth to rule here after this? She didn't even know where Ranald was.

She thought of going to Dingwall for news. She even got as far as throwing a few things in her trunk before the reality hit her. She could not take the children on an unnecessary journey through country containing several armies on the rampage. And besides, she had promised that at the first hint of danger she would take them the few miles along the road to sanctuary at Tain. And she could not leave them there. She could not risk being used against Ferchar.

The next day came wild rumors that the islesmen had been sighted, hordes of them rampaging toward Carron. But the scouts saw no such sight and the countryside remained quiet. Hard on the heels of that, a pilgrim heading for Tain told them a great battle had been fought and lost in the south of Ross and the MacWilliams were marching into Moray. He knew nothing of Ferchar.

It turned out he knew nothing of anything, because only hours later one of Ferchar's own men brought the news of victory. Donald Ban was dead, the Islesmen and Irishmen driven off with great slaughter.

The man was dead on his feet, but Affrica couldn't release him yet. "And Ferchar? My husband?"

"Well, lady," the man said with the ghost of a smile. "Gone to the king with his gifts, but he doesn't expect to be long."

Affrica sat down with a bump, her arm across her stomach comforting herself as much as her unborn baby. "Thank God," she whispered, pushing the ale jug sightlessly across the table. "Sit. Drink. The servants will bring you food directly..." She frowned. "Gifts? What gifts."

The man looked suddenly wary and buried his face in his cup. She kept staring. "Enemy heads," he said apologetically.

*Oh, no. Please not that.* "Donald MacWilliam?"

"Aye," the man said with such relief that she knew.

"And the earl's?" Her voice seemed to come from a great distance, but she saw the man's unhappy nod.

At least she made it to the bedroom before she was thoroughly, violently sick.

⇒⇒⇒⇐⇐⇐

"ARE YOU A *ruthless soldier?*" she had asked him once.

"*When I have to be.*"

If that were true, his idea of necessity and hers obviously differed. She had known in her heart that for this last betrayal, Kenneth would die. If Ferchar didn't see to it, the king would. But to desecrate the body of her cousin, his old friend, to take it to the king like some boastful trophy...

Dear God, that was not the man she thought she knew, the man she had loved beyond everything. That was the act of some barbarous stranger, one she didn't know she could ever come terms with.

She drifted through the next couple of days in a sort of anguished daze. Until, at last, another messenger came from Ferchar—Hairy Harry himself.

His words were few, and no less difficult to bear. In fact, they shattered what was left of her world.

*"You are the Lady of Ross."*

---

IT WAS AN hour before she could bring herself to speak to Harry. She found him in the hall, seated at one of the trestle tables put up especially for him and his solitary meal. That is, he was the only one who ate, though he was surrounded by indoor and outdoor servants and the few guards Ferchar had left behind. Desperate for news instead of fearful of it, as she was, they hung on Harry's every word.

But seeing her, he closed his mouth and a few of the servants scuttled off. Affrica waved one hand and the rest left, too, however reluctantly.

Affrica sat on the bench opposite him. "How am I the Lady of Ross?"

"The king knighted Ferchar for his service, asked him to be Guardian of Ross. Which Ferchar accepted, on condition it was through you as Lady. The king—cocky young lad, if you ask me—said Ferchar would have to prove himself before he invested him formally as earl, but that's what he is, as your husband."

"But I am not the heir of Ross. There is Ranald—"

"Ranald is dead," Harry interrupted. "Died with the

MacWilliams."

"Did the king get his head, too?" she asked bitterly.

Harry's eyes slid away. "No. But he's dead all the same."

"Then Nechtan and Colin..."

"Nechtan and Colin won't touch it. They've both acknowledged Ferchar."

She stared at him. "Nechtan? Nechtan was closer to Kenneth than any of us! Nechtan has acknowledged Ferchar as Earl of Ross?"

"He had no choice, lady."

"Ferchar threatened him?" she demanded in fresh fury.

Harry looked confused. "Not Nechtan. *Ferchar* had no choice. Frankly, the earl had to die to stop the incessant uprisings. We all know that, and he made damned sure it was Ferchar who did it. The head? Well, Kenneth didn't need it anymore, did he? More than proof, it was a symbol, a necessary symbol from Ferchar to the king."

"Did he tell you that?"

Harry met her gaze. "No, I worked it out for myself. I'm not stupid if I keep off the ale, and neither are you."

Her fingers twisted violently together, but she had to know this, too. "Did he cut off my cousin's head himself?"

"No. He killed him in battle, and once the MacWilliams were defeated, he sent for the earl's head."

"And now he is knight and earl with the army of Ross under his command." Just as Kenneth had warned her.

"Be grateful," Harry said bluntly. "We are. For years you have been our lady in fact. I've lost count of the people who told me that over the years that you would have made a better earl."

And therein, perhaps, lay Kenneth's problem. And Ross's. But she could make no sense of this, not yet. She'd had so little sleep since Ferchar left, perhaps that was what she needed...

She rose stiffly. "Does he expect me to go to Dingwall?"

"No," Harry said in surprise. "Not yet at any rate. He's on his way here. Sent me ahead to warn you. He'll leave some of the men at Dingwall, disperse the rest on the way, and come home. He needs to see you."

She managed to nod as she crossed the hall to her own room. But in truth she could not bear to see Ferchar. Not yet. Perhaps not ever.

※※※

SHE SEEMED TO have only just fallen asleep when Sinead's familiar voice repeating her name over and over, dragged her back into the world where she had to think and remember and *feel*.

"What? What is it?" she mumbled, hauling herself to a half-sitting position as she shaded her eyes from the blinding lamp in Sinead's hands. "Is one of the children ill?"

"No, nothing like that," Sinead said hastily. "But we thought you had to hear this. Father Stephen sent someone over from Tain to tell Ferchar."

She frowned. "Tell Ferchar what? He isn't here yet. Is he?" she added in sudden dread.

"No, but it's what Father Stephen came to say that worries me. You remember one Liam O'Neill?"

Affrica dropped her hand and sat up straight. "Of course, I do. He burned Carron."

"Father Stephen saw him at Tain, remember? When we went into sanctuary."

"And?"

"And he saw him again, skulking around the girth this evening, talking to the guards, asking about Ferchar."

Affrica threw back the covers. "We need to double the watch-men."

"Already done, lady. No one will get near."

With that matter taken care of, she turned to the rest of what

Sinead had said. "Asking about Ferchar? Why? Did he think to assassinate him at Tai..." She broke off and stared at Sinead. "He's on his way here. Probably alone. Liam must have wind of that. Do we know where Ferchar is? I need to speak to Harry!"

She was already on her feet, pulling on the first clothing she could find, shoving her bare feet into boots.

"He's waiting in the hall," Sinead told her.

Affrica clumped out with her boots only half-fastened. "Where is Ferchar?" she demanded, plopping onto the nearest bench to fasten her boots.

Harry, who was speaking to one of the other men turned to her at once. "Approaching the wood. Colban saw him from the hill."

"With the men?" she asked quickly.

He shook his head. "No men."

"And Liam O'Neill?"

"No sign," Harry said grimly. "But he's not gone south, or very far west. He's disappeared somewhere between Tain and here."

Somewhere such as Carron woods. She rubbed her fingers hard into her temples. She had to leave most of the men here to guard the children, just in case Liam decided to welcome Ferchar home by burning his hall again. On the other hand, even a lone assassin in the woods waiting for an unsuspecting man...

"Harry, are there enough men for a doubled watch if you come with me?"

"Aye, but—"

"Then come with me," she said.

"Lady, no!" Sinead objected, reaching for her arm to keep her in place, but Affrica had always been quicker, and in any case. Sinead's word was no longer law. She hurried out into the night with Harry.

>>>«<<

FERCHAR HAD A great deal on his mind as he approached home. So much that he thought of going to Tain for the night in order to face Affrica in the morning when he was rested. But some need was stronger than sudden marital cowardice. The need just to see her, hear her voice, hold her if she would let him, drove him through the woods toward home. Affrica, and the solace of peace…

His distraction meant he was some distance into the wood before he realized he was not alone. The faint crackles and rustles that shadowed his own were not made by any animal. It was a two footed creature, and it was veering gradually toward him.

Ferchar knew these woods like his own hall. He had played here as a boy and followed every track as a man. He had hunted here and walked with his daughters. He had even dallied with Affrica although this was no time to distract himself with such delicious memories.

His shadow knew the woods, too, well enough to risk them at night, although not well enough to avoid the occasional blunder down sudden dips and hollows, or into the thickest of the bramble bushes and their trailing tentacles of thorns. Could it be one of his own men, unsure who Ferchar was in the dark? Some thief or cutthroat who had escaped the battle? And hunted in the darkness. Very little light, even on a midsummer night, penetrated the canopy of the trees. In the open, they would both see better, but that would take some time.

Ferchar held the reins in one hand, and as stealthily as he could, drew his dagger, listening while his horse walked on. It seemed to him that his shadow had moved ahead of him toward the hall. He wondered if the man had abandoned him, gone home. In fact, surely that was a light ahead? Moving along the path toward him, it bobbed like a lantern carried by someone in a hurry. Someone looking for him? Or for his shadow?

He focused upon the light, every sense on alert, for it would be incredibly stupid to die now after winning two battles and the king's favor, just because he was so desperate to see his wife that he grew careless. The pale lantern glow began to show him ghostly tree limbs, a human figure...or was it two?

More rustling, much closer than the light. Not abandoned by his shadow, then, although the direction had altered subtly as though it came not from beside but... *Above.*

He barely had a moment to realize it before a sudden light blinded him and a heavy weight landed on his shoulders, knocking him off the horse and onto his back on the ground, winded and paralyzed with his attacker on top of him.

The light showed him the unmistakable features of Liam O'Neill. And the gleaming dagger plunging for his throat.

※

A LIGHT SUDDENLY blazed ahead of them, like a shielded lantern suddenly uncovered. From instinct, Affrica began to run toward it, and Harry swore as he loped past her, dagger drawn. They were following the most used path through the woods, but it was still uneven and difficult, with exposed tree roots to trip the unwary and trailing branches to smack into. Affrica was aware of neither, only the light ahead, which was surely too high to be carried by a man. Even so, it shone clearly on the horseman approaching along the path and on the figure that launched itself from the tree branch above him.

A cry broke from Affrica, for the rider's familiar shape she knew to be Ferchar. And in that moment if she had had a means of annihilating his attacker she would have done so without hesitation. She would have clubbed him, stabbed him, filled him full of arrows, anything to save Ferchar's precious life. But Harry had the weapons, and the strength and the longer legs.

The men rolled on the ground, like some monstrous beast whose body parts were blurred. Then one of them sprang up—just as Harry raised his boot to separate them—and spun to face Harry with his dagger dripping darkly.

"Ferchar!" Affrica sobbed and, dropping her horn lantern, she hurled herself into her husband's arms. The dagger, fortunately, fell to the ground between them. She seized his stunned face between her hands, driving her fingers fiercely into his hair as she clutched him to her, convulsively pressing her cheek to his.

His arms tightened. He moved his head just enough, and she fastened her mouth to his.

This, *this* was what mattered. The body parts of a man already dead, taken to another powerful man as a symbol of peace, was a barbaric male ritual that had nothing to do with her unalterable love for this one visionary, clever, ambitious man. The very threat of him being taken from her had washed all other chaotic emotions aside, like debris on the tide.

She poured all her agony, all her love into that kiss, and he gave her it back, fiercely.

"I thought you would be angry," he muttered against her lips, his fingers tangling in her hair. "I thought you would hate me."

"I was," she whispered as the tears flowed helplessly. "I did. Until the thought that *he* might—"

She broke off and they both glanced at the still figure barely a foot away. Harry crouched by his side, going through his clothes. He had already piled up his weapons.

"Is it Liam?" Affrica asked.

"It was," Ferchar said. "I looked for him in the battle, but never found him. I heard he'd slipped away when he realized the day was lost. I even had men looking for him in the west. It never entered my head he would risk coming back here."

"You kept destroying his plans," Affrica observed, holding tight to his hand although his arms had released her. "In Paris, when they wanted to use me to force my father's cooperation. Then in Dingwall, when I'm sure he would have abducted me if he could. And in Tain, you spoiled his last chance of achieving something out of the last invasion."

"You again," Ferchar said. "And then I married you."

"And defeated him and Donald Ban before the king even knew they were there. I expect his losses had become your fault rather than his. It happens with entitled people."

*Like Kenneth.* Neither of them said it.

"I take it he *is* dead?" Ferchar said to Harry.

"Very."

"My thanks for the intervention, but what the devil were you about bringing my wife out here in the middle of the night?"

"I thought you'd prefer it to her coming alone," Harry said sardonically, rising and lifting the pile of weapons in his arms. Above him, Liam's lantern, hanging from a tree branch, went out.

"Then you knew he was in the area?"

"Father Stephen recognized him at Tain," Affrica said. "He was clearly searching for you, and we knew you were on your way alone."

Ferchar moved to pick up the light Affrica had carried from the hall, and his arm settled around her waist. "Shall we go home?"

"Yes," she said emphatically. "We shall."

<hr />

SOME HOURS LATER, after a hectic, almost desperate loving, she lay in Ferchar's arms, a tangle of limbs and sheets and sleepy contentment.

"Will we have to move to Dingwall, now that you are earl?" she wondered.

"You are the Lady of Ross. You may live where you like. But I will have to be at the castle some of the time."

She kissed his shoulder. "Carron can be our hideaway. Like Malcolm and Halla had Brecka."

He turned his head on the pillow to look into her face. "Then you accept the earldom? I had it in my mind you might regard it as betrayal—of Kenneth, of your brothers…"

"It crossed my mind, too," she admitted. "But more…more because it was what Kenneth always said you would do if I married you. I was afraid."

He moved, looming over her. "Afraid I had married you for the earldom after all? That all this—" he broke off to kiss her, open-mouthed, while his hand swept downward over her breast to her thigh, "…had been a lie?"

"Yes," she said. "But tonight, when I was afraid Liam would kill you, I realized I didn't care about such a lie or betrayal or severed heads. All I wanted was you to *live*. With me and our children. Because I love you so much. And because *this*—" she flung her arms around his neck, "…could never be lies. I have lived with you, in love, for nearly three years, and I *know* you." She smiled, a little crookedly. "At least, I know you *enough*. Perhaps I always did."

He kissed her softly. "Do you know, I was afraid, sometimes, that you married me because of some vision, some dream of yours or of Adam mac Malcolm's? He seemed to recognize me."

"I think he did. But he never told me. Ferchar?"

"Yes?"

"Is this enough? Do you still want more?"

He smiled wryly. "The kingdom, perhaps? No. My place is in Ross, with you, keeping the king's peace and seeing to the prosperity of our people. I still have to win the earldom in legality. And one day, when things are settled here, I would like to take you to Rome, to Constantinople, to see your uncles."

"I would like those things, too. I want *all* the adventures. With you."

"Good," said the son of the priest who was now her husband, the Earl of Ross. He flopped down beside her, holding her close against him until, in shared peace and happiness and bright hopes for the future, she drifted into pleasant dreams.

# Epilogue

*Buchan, spring 1235*

THE LADY OF ROSS dreamed seldom as she grew older. Until the day her son Will married Joanna Comyn, daughter of the Earl of Buchan.

Perhaps she was particularly sensitive to weddings—after all she had dreamed at her own, as apparently her grandfather had dreamed at his. Or perhaps this wedding was special because it had been foretold by her grandfather, and yet had happened against all likelihood.

Recalling her grandfather's words, she looked beyond Will and Joanna, her proud gaze gliding over her stepdaughters and their important husbands, her own lively daughters, and Malcolm, her brave younger son. She stared into the torchlight brightening the darkness of the chapel's interior, and with a spark of yearning, glimpsed her grandfather.

She knew him only from his strange, swirling eyes, for this Adam was young and vigorous and clearly dreaming, while a beautiful lady all but held him up. The young woman's face was half-covered in a mask, as was her grandmother's practice. Somehow, a blaze of happiness reached Affrica from that distant past, joining her in spirit with her grandfather for one joyous instant. And through him to all their family, past and future.

She reached blindly for her husband's hand and found it. Ferchar's fingers curled strongly around hers, solid and comforting as always. She was not the last MacHeth as people still whispered. She was not the last anything, whatever surname her children bore. Her brothers might be childless, her uncles without legitimate heirs. But her family still spread its tentacles, connecting with others here in Scotland and all over the world, as it always had and always would. There was no end in death, just new beginnings, new connections throughout eternity. One did not need Adam's sight to understand that. Just love.

She rested her head on her husband's broad shoulder and smiled in gratitude.

# Author's Note

Ferchar "Maccintsacairt" (sometimes Anglified as Farquar MacTaggart), who became Earl of Ross some time before 1230, is one of the most fascinating and infuriating characters ever to flicker across the pages of Scottish history.

Fascinating because, surnamed merely "son of the priest," he would appear to have been a local man with no kin, certainly no great kin, and yet, somehow, he rose from this relative obscurity to command a local force that decisively defeated an army led by a MacHeth and a MacWilliam, fearsome names long associated with Ross, royalty and rebellion. His meteoric rise to be Earl of Ross is all the more unusual because he was a native Gael at a time when the rising families tended to be the incomers of Anglo-Norman descent (like Sir William Comyn, who became Earl of Buchan), often planted in turbulent regions to promote loyalty and obedience to the King of Scots.

Infuriating because we know so little about him. Learning what happened in Scotland during this period is largely a matter of patching together tiny pieces of information mentioned in chronicles with the names and titles of witnesses from surviving contemporary charters. We do know that when Donald Ban MacWilliam, led a rebellion in 1215, in alliance with Kenneth MacHeth and a prince of Ireland, Ferchar defeated Donald and Kenneth in battle, after which he sent their heads to the King of Scots. He was knighted for his pains and in time given the earldom.

His surname, "son of the priest," is equally tantalizing. (In the Celtic church there was no ban on marriage, but even in the more rural areas of Scotland, Roman standards were being enforced by this period). Ferchar has sometimes been associated with Applecross in Wester Ross, but historians now think it likelier that his father was the keeper (or coarb) of St. Duthac's shrine and holy sanctuary at Tain in the northeast, and that Ferchar inherited the temporal duties from him. This would have been unusual but would explain a later unsavoury incident during the Wars of Independence, when Ferchar's descendant, the Earl of Ross, was able to deny sanctuary at Tain to Robert the Bruce's wife and daughter.

As to the MacHeths, we don't even know that Kenneth was ever Earl of Ross, or if he was fighting, perhaps, to become so. The precise position of the family after Malcolm MacHeth's death in 1268 is not known, but in the absence of any other named Earl of Ross, I think it likely the earldom passed at least informally through the family to Kenneth, despite a tangle of war and rebellion in the 1180s in which the family may or may not have been involved. The other "live" MacHeths in my story, including Affrica, are invented by me (apart from Adam, although his name and his death are unrecorded).

Also, for the record, we don't know that Donald Ban was part of his brother's earlier invasion in 1211. The Ulster prince, Liam O'Neill, is a partial invention, because the chronicles tell us that Donald Ban and Kenneth MacHeth were joined in their rising of 1215 by an Irish prince, annoyingly unnamed.

Between being knighted for defeating the rebellion of 1215 and being formally invested as Earl of Ross, it seems likely that Ferchar ruled the earldom for the king, who probably confirmed his position when Ferchar had proved his loyalty for long enough.

We do hear of Ferchar later, marching into Galloway in the summer of 1235 and dramatically saving the King of Scots from defeat there. He was obviously a military man, although no records exist of him crusading as in my story. Or of his studying in Paris or anywhere else, so I could not give him a degree! But since he seems to have been a man of intelligence, ability, and breadth of vision, it's quite possible he did travel beyond Scotland and learn a good deal, whether formally or not.

The name of Ferchar's wife is not recorded either. I have given him a MacHeth lady who might just have been the reason he was able to gather enough of an army to defeat another MacHeth and be acceptable to the local thanes. We know he had two daughters (I have made them stepdaughters in my story, which is not impossible)—Christina and Euphemia—who made powerful marriages in the 1220s to the King of Man and the Lord of Duffus respectively. He also had at least two sons, William and Malcolm. William, who succeeded Ferchar as earl, married a daughter of William Comyn, the Earl of Buchan.

After 1215, no more is heard of the MacHeths. They may have died out, or perhaps, as I have imagined, whoever was left became assimilated into Ferchar's family. At any rate, this novel brings to an end my fictionalized story of who and what the MacHeths might have been. And if they and Ferchar didn't really do some of these things—well, they might have! There is nothing to say they did not.

*Mary Lancaster, 2022*

## About Mary Lancaster

Mary Lancaster lives in Scotland with her husband, three mostly grown-up kids and a small, crazy dog.

Her first literary love was historical fiction, a genre which she relishes mixing up with romance and adventure in her own writing. Her most recent books are light, fun Regency romances written for Dragonblade Publishing: *The Imperial Season* series set at the Congress of Vienna; and the popular *Blackhaven Brides* series, which is set in a fashionable English spa town frequented by the great and the bad of Regency society.

Connect with Mary on-line – she loves to hear from readers:

Email Mary:
Mary@MaryLancaster.com

Website:
www.MaryLancaster.com

Newsletter sign-up:
http://eepurl.com/b4Xoif

Facebook:
facebook.com/mary.lancaster.1656

Facebook Author Page:
facebook.com/MaryLancasterNovelist

Twitter:
@MaryLancNovels

Amazon Author Page:
amazon.com/Mary-Lancaster/e/B00DJ5IACI

Bookbub:
bookbub.com/profile/mary-lancaster

Made in the USA
Middletown, DE
10 March 2023